For the Sake of Her Family

Diane Allen was born in Leeds, but raised at her family's farm deep in the Yorkshire Dales. After working as a glass engraver, raising a family and looking after an ill father, she found her true niche in life, joining a large-print publishing firm in 1990. Having risen through the firm, she is now the general manager and has recently been made honorary vice president of the Romantic Novelists' Association.

Diane lives with her husband Ronnie in Long Preston, in the Yorkshire Dales, and has two children and four beautiful grandchildren.

DIANE ALLEN

For the Sake of Her Family

PAN BOOKS

First published 2012 by Pan Books
an imprint of Pan Macmillan
20 New Wharf Road, London N1 9RR
Associated companies throughout the world
www.panmacmillan.com

ISBN 978-1-5098-9551-9

A CIP catalogue record for this book is available from
the British Library.

Typeset by SetSystems Ltd, Saffon Walden, Essex
Printed and bound by CPI Group (UK) Ltd, Croydon, CR0 4YY

Visit **www.panmacmillan.com** to read more about all our books
and to buy them. You will also find features, author interviews and
news of any author events, and you can sign up for e-newsletters
so that you're always first to hear about our new releases.

This book is dedicated to my family, especially my husband Ronnie, who is always there, no matter what life throws at us. My daughter Lucy, her husband Steven, Amy our little princess, Ben the newest member of our family, also my son Scott and his wife Zoe and their children, the beautiful Amelia and Ollie, our little soldier.

I'd like to thank good friends Helen Bibby and Hilda Stronach for their encouragement and help. Also Judith Murdoch and Wayne Brookes, to whom along with my readers I owe everything.

For the Sake of Her Family

1

Yorkshire Dales, 1912

The screams carried up into the high pasture – agonizing, soul-stripping screams. Alice sat, hands covering her ears; she just couldn't bear it any longer. When was it going to end? Surely the doctor could make it stop? In defiance of the screams she kicked her boot into the hard, frost-filled ground, not bothering that the solid earth hurt her foot.

Bess Bentham's husband and children had watched helplessly as her condition deteriorated, turning her from a beautiful buxom woman to a frail, skeletal form. For months she had struggled to perform chores around the farm or look after her family. The aged country doctor's fees were something they could ill afford, so Bob Bentham had delayed as long as possible before sending for him. With hindsight, the family wished he had acted sooner.

Alice, the younger of the two Bentham children, sat behind the tall pasture wall that backed onto the great high-reaching peak of Whernside. She was a stubborn child, a true Bentham, Dales bred, proud and too feisty for her own good – just like her father, or so her mother had often told her. When she was in one of her moods, she'd a face on her that could turn milk sour. Now, as her mother lay dying, she was angry at the whole world and knew no other way than to take it out on the frozen earth that her mother would soon be buried under.

Shivering, Alice got to her feet, pulling her jerkin around her; the bottom of her skirt was stiff where she had got it wet going through the farmyard. It was November and bitterly cold; already the highest points of Whernside were capped with a covering of snow. Shoving her fingerless-mittened hands into her pockets, she looked towards the farm and thought about her mother lying on her deathbed. Much as she wanted to be by her mother's side, Alice couldn't have endured another minute in the low-beamed house. For days, the smell of death had filled every nook and cranny, making it unbearable. When the doctor had finally been summoned to concoct potions to ease the pain, Alice had taken her chance to flee. She sighed and shook her head, remembering the look on her father's face as he told her to come back indoors. Instead she had slammed the kitchen door and run as fast as her legs would carry her. Didn't he realize she had to get away, if only for a minute or two? All she wanted was to escape the sorrow and to breathe the clear, fresh air on the fellside.

The screaming stopped suddenly and was replaced with a deathly silence. Alice could hear her heart beating; the pounding was so strong, it felt as if it was escaping through her chest wall. The breath from her mouth came out in pure white clouds as she waited for further sounds from home. But the farm was silent now, so terribly silent. A snowflake fluttered to earth and Alice was listening so intently she could have sworn she heard it land. Gathering her skirts around her, she got up and ran, slipping and almost tumbling as she raced along the cobbled droving road. By the time she reached the farmyard she was fighting for breath, her face flushed from the cold air biting at her cheeks and her haste to reach her dying mother.

'Miss Alice . . .' Dr Bailey bowed his head. It pained him, having to break the news to this young lass, knowing how the words he was about to say would change her life. 'I'm afraid your mother died a few minutes ago. You have my condolences. Now, go and join your father and brother. I'm sure you will find comfort in one another's grief.'

His face was grey and sombre as he mounted the gig, pulling a wool blanket over his knees to guard against the bitter wind before lifting the whip to stir the two patient bays into motion. He paused for a moment, as if uncertain whether to offer guidance, then said, 'Your mother loved you. She'd have wanted you to show the same love to your father and brother, so you must be strong now for her sake. I'll stop by and tell Mrs Batty of your loss – you'll need her help to lay your mother out.' And with that he tipped his hat and whipped the team into motion, the gig swaying from side to side as it descended the rocky path towards the village of Dent.

Alice watched the gig until it turned out of the yard. Tears filled her eyes, and no matter how she tried she couldn't keep them from rolling down her cheeks. She hadn't meant to leave her mum; all she'd wanted was a moment's peace – surely Mum would have known that? Her hand trembled as she lowered the catch on the oak door into the kitchen. If she could have turned and run away, she would have, but she had to be brave. Wiping her nose with the back of her mitten, she stuck out her chin, swiped away the tears that would not stop falling, and entered the kitchen of Dale End Farm.

'So, you've decided to show your face, then? Your mother asked for you with her dying breath, and where were you? I'll tell you where you were – up that bloody fell, like a raggle-taggle gypsy child.' Bob Bentham was angry with his daughter, but secretly he was even angrier with himself for not getting the doctor to his wife sooner. He turned away from Alice and spat a mouthful of saliva mixed with black chewing tobacco into the fire, making it hiss. Then he reached for his pipe and tobacco tin from above the mantel. 'You'd better go and say your goodbyes now, before old Ma Batty gets here.'

Alice stayed where she was, trembling and snivelling, head bowed, not wanting to go up the darkening stairs.

'Now then, our Alice, come on. I'll go up with you.' Will, her big brother, put his arm around her in sympathy. Hard as it was for him, he knew that for a sixteen-year-old it must be even worse. Bowing his head, his lanky body too tall for the low roof of the homely kitchen, he led her towards the stairs.

'I'm frightened, our Will. I've never seen a dead person before.' Alice's body shook as Will squeezed her tight.

'It's not the dead 'uns that hurt you, lass, it's the buggers that are wick that does that,' Bob said sharply, his eyes never leaving the fire.

Will held Alice's hand as they climbed the creaking wood stairs to their parents' room. Downstairs, she could hear her father muttering to himself and riddling the fire embers; he was cross with her and it'd take him time to come round.

The oil lamp next to the bed was burning and, with the coming of the night and the dark snowy skies closing in, shadows from the flames were leaping on the dim walls, creating sprites that danced on the whitewashed stone. Alice turned her remorseful gaze to her mother's corpse. Bess seemed at peace, her long hair loose around her alabaster skin.

'Do you think our mum's in heaven now?' Alice asked, wondering if her mother could still see her and hear her.

'I'm sure she is. She's probably looking down on us

and blowing kisses.' Will gave her arm a reassuring squeeze. 'Time to say your goodbyes, our Ali. Give her a kiss – she'd like that.'

'If Mum is in heaven, she knows I should have been with her instead of sitting up the fell. She won't love me any more.' Tears began to fall from Alice's eyes and she started sobbing, grief taking over her small, crumpled body.

'Yes, she'll know you were up the fell, but she wouldn't have wanted it any other way. You always were headstrong, Mum knew that. That's why it's our job to look after Father. She asked that of us with her dying breath. So, don't you worry, she loved you for the spirited person that you are – she told me so.'

Alice controlled her sobbing for a brief moment and bent to kiss her mother's brow. Already the skin was cold and bluish white. The brief contact made her feel sick and her legs turned to jelly. What was she going to do without her mother? She almost dissolved into sobs again, but by holding her breath and blowing her nose she managed to bring her emotions under control.

'There, our lass, she knows you loved her. Go and brush your hair, then come downstairs and make some supper before Mrs Batty gets here. She'll want to lay Mum out in the parlour while her husband brings the coffin. Reckon it'll be down to us to get everything ready – Father doesn't seem up to it. I'll see to the parlour while you do us all some bacon and eggs.

6

We've not eaten all day, and you know Mother – she wouldn't have wanted that, now, would she?'

'I did love her, our Will.' Resolving to pull herself together and stop sniffling, Alice placed her hands on her hips and announced: 'Don't worry, I will look after everybody as Mother would have wanted. I'll not let Father down again.' With that, she went off to her bedroom to tidy herself.

Will ran his hand along the banister, ducking his head to avoid the low ceiling above the stairs.

'Is she all right – our lass?' Bob asked his son. 'I was a bit hard on her when she came waltzing in. I was angry, what with her mother having asked for her, and Alice not there.' Bob knew his own faults, one of which was a tendency to be too hasty with his words. A fault that he could also see in Alice; it even made him smile sometimes, the fact that she was so like him.

'She's all right, Father. Alice was with Mum in her own way; she was just upset. You know how she always goes and hides up behind that top wall in the high pasture when things get too much for her.' Seeing the pain on his father's face, Will briskly changed the subject: 'Now then, I'm going to make the parlour ready while Alice fixes some supper for us all. Why don't you have a rest; it's been a difficult day for you. I know you're going to miss Mother, but we'll always be here to see to things.'

'Aye, I don't know what I'll do without her, our

lad. My Bess was everything to me, and I let her down. I should have got the doctor. Brass isn't worth anything compared to them you love.' Bob sighed and put his head in his hands.

'We'll be all right, Father,' said Will, patting his father on the shoulder. 'Our Alice is nearly a woman and a good hand about the place, and with my job at the big house, we'll get by. The last thing Mother would have wanted is for you to be upset.' Hearing Alice come down the stairs, Will turned. 'Are you all right, our Ali?'

'I'm fine. I'll go and make us something to eat.' Alice felt shaky and she knew she was white as a sheet, but she had to be grown-up and handle the situation like a woman. The family needed her.

'That'll be grand, Alice.' Her father tried to force a smile. 'You're not a bad lass. I'm sorry I shouted at you – it was the shock of losing your mother. Do you want me to cut you some bacon off the flitch in the dairy? I'll do that while you go out and see if the hens have laid us some fresh eggs. If you can feed them at the same time, that would be a grand help.'

'I'll do that, Father, you don't have to ask. I'll feed Jip, too – poor old dog will be wondering what's happened. He got overlooked this morning.'

Taking her shawl from behind the door, Alice wrapped it around her. Then, determined to show her dad that she was not going to let him down, she drew herself to her full height, opened the back door and stepped out into the bitter evening air.

Outside, it was still trying to snow and the sky was heavy and threatening. Having made sure the dog was fed, Alice moved on to the hen hut to check for eggs and to feed the clucking brown birds. The smell of poultry and the warmth of the tarred hut made her remember how, as a child, she used to collect eggs with her mother. The memory conjured an image of Mum laughing as Alice hid behind her skirts because she was frightened of the one hen that always was too curious for its own good. Forcing herself to focus on the present, Alice checked the nesting boxes for eggs: only half a dozen, but that would do for supper. She'd heard Dad say that they hadn't been laying so well because of the cold weather. Making a pocket in her shawl to put them in, she closed the hut door behind her.

She was turning to make her way back to the house when Mr and Mrs Battys' cart arrived, with her mother's cheap, rough-made coffin strapped on the back. Alice looked at it, hoped it was strong enough to protect her mother from the cold, dark earth. It was a pauper's coffin, probably not even the right size for her mother's frail body. Tears came to her eyes and a feeling of bitterness filled her stomach. One day, she vowed, she would have money. No one she loved would ever again be given a pauper's funeral. And no one she loved would die for want of cash to pay a doctor. She would make certain of that.

The light from the kitchen spilled out onto the dour couple as they carried the shabby coffin into the house. Alice lingered in the yard, watching as Will pulled the

9

curtains in the parlour – when she caught herself referring to the shabby living room as a parlour, Alice smiled; her mother had always called it 'her parlour', furnishing it as posh as money would allow. It might not have chandeliers and sparkling crystal ornaments like the manor, but Mum had kept it spotless and loved. It was only right that she would be laid to rest in there for folk to pay their respects.

Alice delayed a while longer, sheltering inside the barn, giving old Mrs Batty time to make her mother respectable and for the coffin to be carried into the parlour. She'd have stayed there until the sickeningly pious Battys had gone, but eventually the cold drove her into the kitchen to face them.

'Ah, Alice – we were wondering where you'd got to.' Bob looked at her with concern.

'I was just making sure all was fed, Father. And I closed the barn doors before the snow comes.' Having placed the eggs in a dish and hung her shawl up, she turned to look at the couple who dealt in death. 'Mr and Mrs Batty, thank you for seeing to our needs and being so quick bringing the coffin.' It cost her an effort to be polite; she felt more like spitting the words at them. In her mind's eye she pictured the Battys' yard with its ugly pile of coffins, hastily thrown together and left out there in all weathers, until some poor soul like her mother needed burying. These coffins were meant for the poor. The lovingly polished oak coffins intended for the posh folk of the dale could only be seen if you peered through the door leading to the workshop.

10

'Aye, you've got a grand lass here, Bob.' Ernie Batty smacked his hands together, his ample body slumping into a kitchen chair. 'A right polite bit of a lass.'

'We were sorry to hear of your mother's death, Alice.' Hilda Batty put her arm around Alice. 'She's at peace now, my dear. I've made her look so pretty, at rest in her coffin.'

Cringing at the old woman's hand of death resting on her skin, Alice moved away on the pretext of getting supper ready.

'Right then, Bob, we'll be on our way.' Ernie Batty heaved himself to his feet. 'Now, you know I don't want to ask this,' he said, his face turning sombre, 'but I need paying for the coffin, and my old lass here will expect a bit of something for laying your good lady out.'

'Tha'll get the money. You can take this for your bother now and I'll give you the rest at the end of the month when our Will gets paid.' Scowling, Bob reached up to the tin cashbox kept above the fireplace. Opening it up, he threw what coins he had onto the table. 'I've always been a man of my word, tha knows that.' The cheek of the man! Asking for his money before his wife was even cold, let alone buried. 'Alice, open that door and see Mr and Mrs Batty out.' The sooner they were gone, the faster he and his family could grieve in peace.

'With pleasure, Father.' Alice darted to the door, eager to get rid of the predatory couple.

'Our condolences once again.' Ernie bowed his head

11

as he left the building, his wife shoving him out of the door as he tried to count the handful of coins.

The snow was falling steadily now. There was a good covering on the ground already, the wind whipping it up into white blankets over the walls. As their horse and cart set off down the lane, the sound of Mrs Batty chastising her husband for having no tact could be heard above the howling of the wind.

Alice put her arm around her father. 'Never mind, Father. We'll manage. We will get the money some end up.'

'I know, lass. Grovelling old devil – fancy asking for his brass straight away. Now, I'm going to have five minutes with your mother. I need to talk to her.'

Patting Alice on the shoulder, Bob turned and wearily made his way into the parlour and his beloved Bess.

Alice went to join Will, who had been sitting quietly next to the fire since letting in the Battys. 'One day I'm going to have so much money that people like the Battys will have to grovel to me, same way they expected our father to grovel to them tonight. You'll see, Will: my parlour will be a proper parlour with maids and servants, and I'll be a lady.'

Will looked up. 'Alice, does that really matter? We've just lost our mother, Father's in mourning, and at the moment we haven't a penny – so stop thinking of your bloody self for once.'

Alice flicked her long blonde hair from out of her face and got up to start supper. Why did people always get her wrong? She wasn't thinking only of herself; she was thinking of all of them and the parlour they were going to share.

It was five long days before they could bury poor Bess. The snow had fallen for forty-eight hours, covering the dale with a white blanket so thick that it made travel impossible, and digging a grave was out of the question. When the mourning family did finally manage the journey down the rough stony track into the little churchyard of Dent village, it was raining. The rain added to the greyness of the day, bringing with it encircling mists.

Walking behind the coffin in the shadow of the four bearers, Alice shed tears for her dead mother. In church, she silently took her seat in the pew, smiling bravely as her big brother squeezed her hand in sympathy. As she gazed through brimming eyes at the rough wooden coffin, a steady stream of raindrops splashed down on it from a hole in the church roof. The light from the candles fragmented and shone like a miniature rainbow in the drips. Anger swelled up into her throat as the congregation sang 'Abide with Me'. She cursed the world as she looked out of the church window, the trees outside waving their branches wildly in the wind, raging with the same anger as Alice.

Some day, she told herself, things would be right; they'd have money and a fine house. She didn't know how, but as long as she had breath in her small body she would fight for her family and never would they have to beg for help again.

2

There, that was the parlour dusted; another job done for the day. The sun shone through the small-paned windows only weakly yet, but it gave hope that spring was on its way. During the four months since her mother's death Alice had been keeping house, cleaning, cooking and helping out around the farm. She didn't want to admit it, but having more responsibility had turned her from a girl into a young woman.

Alerted by a random sunbeam to a streak of coal dust that had managed to survive the attention of the duster, she turned to give the edge of the dresser one last going over. It was then that the gap caught her eye . . .

Not the clock, please not the clock! Alice gazed unbelieving at the space where the little brass carriage clock had stood. Crestfallen and exhausted, she slumped into the one comfy chair that the Bentham family owned. In the absence of the clock, the green chenille mantelpiece cover looked bare, its tassels hanging limp over the unlit fire, held in place only by the two grinning Staffordshire pot spaniels. Her mother had been so proud of that clock, which had been presented to her when she left service at Ingelborough Hall to get married.

It wasn't the fact that the clock was missing that made her put her head in her hands and sob; it was the fact that she knew all too well what had happened to it. How could he!

Anger spurring her on, she surveyed the room for other missing items. What else had he pilfered? At least the paintings were still hanging, the highland cattle serene as ever in the face of her distress. The mock-silver teapot was still on the table, but then it would be – mock silver wasn't worth much. Hands on hips, mind racing, she forced herself to take a deep breath. If only her worries could be expelled as easily as a lungful of air. Never mind, it was done now. Too late to get the clock back, even though she had a good idea where it was. Besides, the loss of the clock paled into insignificance alongside the real problem: how the hell was she going to cope if things carried on like this? She might be only sixteen, but the seriousness of their situation was not lost on her.

'Ali, get the pot on – we'll not go hungry tonight!' Will's voice rang out, followed by the sound of the kitchen door closing. 'Would you look at these two!' He appeared in the parlour doorway, stooping because of the lack of headroom, his gun resting on one shoulder and two very dead rabbits in his other hand, dripping blood onto the clean floor. 'What's up, our lass? What's to do – you've not been worrying over supper, have you?'

Alice turned from the window and smiled. 'Why should I worry about supper when we have the finest shot this side of Leeds living under our roof? Now get yourself out of this parlour, Will Bentham, before you get blood everywhere.' She pushed him lovingly out of the doorway. 'Them rabbits are a grand size, all right. Just you be careful that Lord Frankland doesn't catch you – he'd have you up in front of the magistrates before you had time to blink.'

'They're from our high pasture, Ali, honest. Besides, even if they were that bastard Frankland's, he wouldn't miss 'em – too busy carrying on with his floozies, from what I hear.' Will lumbered out into the farmyard, tugging his knife out of his pocket ready to skin and gut his kill.

'You listen to too much gossip, our Will. His lord-ship's a gentleman, and he's always polite to me.'

'That's 'cos he has an eye for the ladies – I'd watch him, if I was you. And I don't need to listen to gossip. I know exactly what he's like because I see him every day, working his charms at the big house. When it comes to what goes on at the manor, what I don't know isn't worth knowing, our lass.'

'You talk rubbish, our Will, but I'm glad you caught those rabbits. I don't know what we'd have had for supper otherwise. Get a move on and skin 'em, then I can stick them in the pot and have everything ready by the time Father returns.'

16

Alice busied herself filling the big stockpot and placed it to boil on the Yorkshire range. She'd decided not to tell Will about the missing clock; no need to worry his head when he had enough on already, looking after the farm and working three days a week for the Franklands.

Besides, she knew who had taken it, and why – and there was nothing she or Will could do about it.

Uriah Woodhead wiped the pint tankards with a cloth that had seen better days, spitting on the stubborn marks and rubbing them vigorously, before hanging them back on the hooks around the bar of the Moon Inn. At this time of day, the pub was quiet; in fact, he had only one customer. Over the last few months, the man had become his best customer, but it was high time he went home. Soon the place would start to fill with evening drinkers and the last thing Uriah wanted was a non-paying guest sleeping in his snug. Stepping out from behind the bar, he gave the wretched body of Bob Bentham a rousing shake.

'Aye, I'll have another pint with you,' Bob slurred, dribble running down the front of his already filthy jerkin as he stumbled to his feet.

'Nay, I don't think you will. Come on, Bob, you know you've had enough. Besides, your credit's run out – that little clock's not worth what you've already drunk. Only reason I took it off you was because I knew you had no brass; it's not as if it's much use to me.' Seeing that his words were having no effect and the man was about to settle back into his seat in the snug, Uriah grabbed him by the arm and began steering him towards the door. 'Time you got yourself home, Bob. Your lass will be wondering where you're at. She's having it hard, from what I hear.'

'You bastard!' protested Bob, swinging his fists in an effort to resist the strong arms hauling him over the threshold. 'You've robbed me, you thieving bugger!'

Dodging the drunken punches with ease, the landlord ejected Bentham from the premises with a final push that sent him sprawling onto the narrow cobbled street.

'Get yourself home and square yourself up, Bob. You've a family that needs you.' With a shake of his head, Uriah closed the door on him. It was sad to see a man go downhill so fast. Sometimes his trade was not the best to be in.

Bob lifted himself up and, head swimming, stumbled along using the walls of the cottages lining the street to steady himself. His erratic gait and frequent falls soon began to draw taunts from the local children, who abandoned their games to enjoy the spectacle of him sprawling on the cobbles. Their laughter ringing in his ears, he dragged himself out of the village and along the road home. At least it was a mild spring evening; during the winter there had been times when Bob had felt like giving up and crawling into a hedge, drifting off to sleep while the warmth of the alcohol still filled him with a fake sense of well-being, hoping that the bitter cold would do its work and end his suffering, and he would wake up in the arms of his Bess . . . How he missed his Bess. Without her, he was lost.

He paused to rest his weary body on a seat at the side of the road. From this vantage point he had a wonderful view over the dale. Looking around him, he noticed the first flowers of spring in the roadside bank: delicate wood sorrel and the pale yellow hues of the first primroses. His Bess would have been picking them and bringing them into the house. Bending to take in the sweet smell of the flowers, he lost his balance and toppled into the road, landing on his back. Not knowing whether to laugh or cry, he lay there for a while, until he became aware of the sound of hooves tripping along the road. A few minutes later, a horse and trap came to a halt inches from his head.

'What are you doing, man? I could have killed you, rolling about in the road in this bad light!' Dismounting, Gerald Frankland leaned over the dishevelled pile of rags, only to recoil immediately. 'Good God, you stink! How much have you had to drink? You're a disgrace, man!'

Raising himself up and squatting on his heels, cap in hand, Bob dared not look Lord Frankland in the eye. Of all the people to come down the lane, why did it have to be him! He felt a hand pulling him to his feet. Dizzy with drink and stomach churning, he tried to draw himself to his full height. 'Beg pardon, sir. Didn't mean to be in the way,' Bob mumbled, doing his best not to slur his words.

'For goodness' sake, Bentham, pull yourself together.

I can't have my tenants carrying on like this.' Gerald Frankland studied the swaying figure with a look of disgust. He had heard that Bentham had taken the death of his wife badly, but he hadn't realized things had come to this. 'Well, I suppose I can't leave you here in that state. God knows how you'd get home. Climb in the gig and let's get you back where you belong.'

Shoving the malodorous body into the trap, Frankland turned towards Dale End Farm, whipping the horse into a trot. He was going to have stern words with Bentham's son once he got his drunken father home. Young Will was a fine lad – couldn't do without him. He'd shown an uncanny knack with horses and was a bloody good shot with that two-bore rifle of his. After last autumn's pheasant shoot, a number of his friends who'd travelled up from London for the event had told him how impressed they were with the lanky lad who'd made such a good job of running the show. Damn shame about the father, though. If this sort of behaviour continued, he'd have to strip them of the tenancy. Bloody locals, you gave them a roof over their heads and this was how they repaid you!

Alice stood in the doorway, peering down the lane for any sign of her father. She was both anxious and yet at the same time dreading his return. These days there was no way of knowing what state he would be in, or what his mood would be. It could be anything from sentimental and loving, cheerfully serenading her with music-hall songs, or argumentative and lashing out at Will with his fists. What her poor mother would have made of it, she didn't know. As dusk descended on the farmyard and the missel thrush trilled its last song of the evening, Alice wished she could be like that little bird: free to sing and to spread her wings and fly away as far as possible.

'Come in, our lass. It might be spring, but it soon gets chilly. He'll be home in his own time.' Will had started lighting the oil lamps for evening. The flame flickered as he beckoned for her to come away from the door. 'The devil looks after his own, you know – and the way Father's been acting lately, it wouldn't surprise me if he's possessed.'

'Don't say stuff like that, our Will, it'll bring us bad luck.' Alice closed the door behind her. 'I can't help feeling he's been getting worse lately.'

'I wish I knew where he's been getting his brass from. Can't see old Woodhead letting him sup for nothing. Happen he's doing odd jobs for his beer money. Doesn't seem likely, though – there's plenty jobs around here wanting doing, and he can't be bothered to lift a finger.'

Alice kept silent. Much as she wanted to tell Will about Mother's treasured possessions disappearing, she didn't want to cause trouble between father and son, especially as her father might return in a fighting mood.

They both stood frozen in place for a moment at a sound from outside: hoofbeats, coming into the yard. Racing to open the door, they were aghast to find

Gerald Frankland struggling to get their father down from his trap.

'Don't just stand there – help me with him, lad!' Lord Frankland bellowed at Will. 'I can't stand smelling him for another minute. Get him washed and tidied up – the man's a disgrace.'

Will rushed quickly to the aid of his employer, propping his father up and carrying him into the warm kitchen. His lordship followed, removing his gloves and hat before seating himself next to the fire. Alice busied herself putting the kettle on the range to boil, not knowing what to say and do in the presence of the landlord. Will seemed equally at a loss; having deposited his father in a kitchen chair, he stood over him looking as if he wished the ground would swallow him up.

Scowling, Frankland leaned back in the Windsor chair and crossed his long legs. With his dark hair and sharp cheekbones, he looked every inch the refined country gent. 'You're lucky he's alive, the drunken fool. I nearly ran him over, lying there in the middle of the road. How long has he been like this? If he wants to stop in one of my farms, he's going to have to straighten himself up.'

Will, tongue-tied, offered no reply. Seemingly unperturbed by this, Lord Frankland surveyed the kitchen; it was tidy and spotless, but a little sparse. His gaze came to rest on the stockpot, its bubbling contents filling the room with a herby aroma. 'I suppose whatever's cooking in there has been poached from me.'

Inwardly, this amused him. He'd known for a while that the rabbit population was being held in place by Will, but had not said anything; after all, in feeding his family Will was reducing the estate's vermin population.

'Now see here,' Frankland continued, 'either your father straightens himself up or I'll have to consider renting this farm to another tenant. Take this as a warning.' He rose from his seat and gathered up his gloves and hat as if to leave, but on reaching the door he turned and faced Alice. 'How old are you, girl? And what's your name?'

Alice blushed. 'I'm Alice, sir. I'll be seventeen in June.' She could feel her pulse and heart pounding as she dared to look at the dark-haired lord.

'So, old enough to come and work at the manor. My sister wants someone to attend to her needs. You look presentable enough, and I think you might be suitable. Come and see Mrs Dowbiggin next week. I'll arrange for her to show you what will be expected of you.'

'But I don't want a job,' Alice protested. 'I've enough to do here.'

'She'll be with you, sir – I'll bring her myself.' Will stepped forward, desperate to rectify his sister's mistake. 'Our Alice doesn't think what she says sometimes, sir. We are most grateful, thank you; that'll be a grand help to us. Say thank you, our Alice.'

Alice glared at her forelock-tugging brother. She didn't want to work at the manor and there was no way that she was going to kowtow to the likes of the Franklands. Nevertheless she curtsied, knowing that was expected of her, and then thanked him in a cool tone of voice.

'A girl with spirit, eh! That's what I like. Right, I'll see you both next week.' He waved a glove at the snoring body of Bob. 'And get him sober. I bid you goodnight.'

Nothing was said until the sound of the horse and trap faded down the lane. Then Will turned on his sister: 'How many times have I told you, our Ali – always be right with them at the manor, especially himself. We need this farm.' Will kicked his father's foot as he snored, oblivious in his drunken sleep. 'I was right: the old fool fetched the devil into this house tonight. I never wanted you to work at the manor, but we've no option now. You'll have to watch yourself, lass, and as for Father, he can just bloody well straighten himself up.'

'Don't be hard on him, Will – he's missing Mother. And I'll be fine; I can look after myself. But you want to decide which tune you're dancing to: either Lord Frankland's the devil or he's a saint in our hour of need.'

Will fell silent. He hated Gerald Frankland. He hated the way he looked down his nose at those who worked for him. The way he leered at the young women from the village – and the fact that, for all his breeding, he was no gentleman.

'Just you remember this, Ali: no matter what happens, keep your thoughts to yourself and never let them know you're scared,' Will retorted.

'What do you mean, our Will? I don't understand.'

'You'll find out soon enough. I've heard some tales about him – and his sister. Take it as a warning.'

Alice had never seen this side of Will, and it worried her. Why did he hate Lord Frankland so much? Could things really be that bad at the manor?

Alice stood gazing up at the austere grey facade. Whernside Manor was a huge square Georgian building with ramparts running around the bottom of the roof, giving it the appearance of a Gothic castle. The notorious Sill family had built it, using their ill-gotten gains from slave trading in Jamaica. Local legend had it that the house was haunted by a young slave boy who had been beaten to death by the only son of the Sill family. With his dying breath he had cursed his master and the master's family, proclaiming that none of them would bear offspring and they would all die in poverty. Sure enough, his curse came true: one by one the Sill men died in suspicious circumstances and both daughters died old maids with not a penny to their names.

It was also rumoured that an underground passage ran between the manor and one of the houses that the Sill family used to own. It had been used for secretive transfer of their serving slaves. Alice shuddered at the thought. Dark days, indeed; she was not proud of the slaving history that tainted her beloved Dales.

The gravel crunched under her feet as she nervously made her way to the front door of the manor. She hesitated before plucking up the courage to climb the spotless granite steps and rap the polished brass door knocker. Adjusting her hat and smoothing her skirts, her heart beating wildly, Alice waited for someone to answer.

'Yes, what do you want? We don't encourage beggars here!' The tall, sombre-faced butler peered down at her, his hand resting on the huge oak door's handle as if preparing to close it in her face.

Alice had never been so insulted. 'I'm not a beggar,' she retorted. She'd have liked to tell him exactly what she thought of his arrogant tone, but instead she bit her tongue, paused for a moment to consider how to phrase her response, and then announced: 'I'm here to see Miss Frankland. My name's Alice Bentham, and I'm to help her with her needs.'

'Well, Alice Bentham, your first lesson at the manor is that servants always use the back door. You are never to climb these steps and knock on this door again. Typical farm girl – no manners,' he sneered. 'Now, go around the back and ask for Mrs Dowbiggin. She'll take you to Miss Frankland, who I'm sure awaits you.' And with that he closed the door, leaving Alice feeling worthless on the steps.

She stood for a minute in shock, humiliated and at the same time furious with the pompous butler. How dare he take her for a beggar! And how dare he say she had no manners. It was him who had no manners, snooty old sod. She didn't want this bloody job anyway.

Defiantly she turned on her heel, marched back down the steps and set off up the drive. Blow it, she wasn't going to work for this hoity-toity lot; she was a Bentham and they were nothing but off-comed-uns. No doubt Will would have something to say when she got home, but she didn't care.

'Leaving us so early, Miss Bentham?' a voice shouted after her. Alice stopped in her tracks and slowly turned round to see Lord Frankland walking round the side of the manor, riding crop in hand. 'Are we not to your liking, Alice? Have you fallen out with my dear sister Nancy so soon? Surely she's not that wearing?'

Alice could detect a hint of mockery in his voice and noticed a slight smile on his face. She was doing her best not to stare, but his elegant dress and good looks had her enthralled.

'No, sir, not at all. Indeed, I did not get to see your sister, sir – as a matter of fact I've not even been invited across the threshold.' She couldn't stop herself; she had always been brought up to tell it as it was, so why should she stop now?

'I bet it was Faulks, my butler. Better than any guard dog, but a bit too much bite sometimes. Come, Alice, let me invite you into my home.'

He waited for her to retrace her steps to the main entrance and opened the front door for her. Hesitantly, Alice stepped into the great hall with her new employer behind her. At his bidding, she followed his example and took off her hat and coat, which he then thrust into the arms of Faulks, who had appeared like lightning at the sound of his master's voice.

'Faulks, this is Miss Alice Bentham. She is to assist my sister – whatever she needs, you will see that she gets it.'

'Yes, sir.' The butler bowed, giving Alice a questioning sideways glance before scurrying away with the clothing.

'Well, that's told him,' said Lord Frankland, casually leading the way across the marble-tiled hallway. 'Come, Alice, let me introduce you to my sister. I'm sure she'll find you a tonic – it will be good for her to have someone her own age to talk to: she's always complaining about the staff all being too old. That's why I've taken you on, along with the fact that you seem to have a few more skills than some of the local girls.'

Transfixed by the grandeur of the hallway, Alice was still standing just inside the front door, taking it all in. How her mother would have loved the huge chandelier, the delicate ornaments, the smell of fresh polish and the huge sweeping staircase. The beauty of it all took her breath away; it was like a dream.

Lord Frankland, who had started up the stairs only to realize that Alice wasn't at his side, gestured impatiently for her to follow. 'Come, Alice, I haven't all day, and Nancy is waiting. If there's one thing she doesn't possess, it's patience, as I am sure you will shortly find out.'

With bygone generations of the Frankland family gazing down at her from the portraits lining the walls, the awestruck young girl gathered her skirts and hurriedly followed him up the luxuriously carpeted stairs.

The room was dark, the curtains still drawn, preventing the sharp spring light from entering.

'Nancy, I bring you a companion, someone to entertain you, to help you with your toilet and hopefully temper your moods, dear sister. This is Alice Bentham; her father is a tenant of mine and her brother Will is one of my best men.' He strode across to the window and tugged the curtains open, flooding the room with light. 'How can you live in such darkness, girl? It's a beautiful day – come on, get out of bed and say hello to your latest companion and help.'

Once Alice's eyes were accustomed to the light, she was able to make out the shape of a body on the lavish four-poster bed. It stirred and moaned and then, much to Alice's surprise, an arm snaked from under the covers, seized a candlestick from the bedside table and hurled it at Lord Frankland.

Ducking out of the missile's range, he remonstrated with his sister. 'Now, Nancy, be reasonable – you'll frighten poor Alice. She's not used to your ways. Heaven knows who is.' Clearly exasperated, he shook his head and made for the door. 'Enough! Get out of bed and show a few manners. I'm going to leave you to get acquainted, so stir yourself.' And then he was gone.

Bemused, Alice stood wondering what to do next. Should she speak, should she go, should she tidy the curtains that had been flung back and left any old how? The words of her brother echoed through her mind – was there a monster lurking under those covers? She caught sight of her reflection in the wardrobe mirror: a shabby little farm girl, out of place in these grand surroundings. What on earth was she doing here?

'Do you not speak?' Alice was shocked to hear a voice from deep under the bedcovers. 'Has my brother brought me a mute? That would be useful. At least you wouldn't be able to talk about me.'

'I can speak, miss,' Alice retorted sharply. Then, remembering where she was, she fell silent again, awaiting instructions.

'Well, Alice, contrary to what my brother may have led you to believe, I do not require a companion. In fact, I like to keep my own company. I'm tired of his mealy-mouthed "companions". I don't know why he's brought me another one. Now get out of my room and go home.' This speech ended in a huge sigh, as if the effort had left the speaker completely drained.

No one had ever accused Alice of being mealy-mouthed, and she wasn't accustomed to being spoken to as if she were worthless. It was all she could do to stop herself from giving the little madam a piece of her mind. Instead, having carefully edited her thoughts, she said in a quiet, even tone: 'Miss Frankland, your brother asked me to help you and that's what I'm here to do. Let me assure you, I am not mealy-mouthed. In fact, I was always told to speak my mind, as long as it didn't cause offence.'

Suddenly the bedcovers moved, thrown dramatically from the bed to reveal the slight body of Nancy Frankland. At the sight of her, Alice let out an involuntary gasp. Framed by a shock of jet-black hair, dark eyes blazed at her from a face that had once been beautiful but was now a grotesque mask, the skin on the left side so scarred and twisted that the eye was almost obscured by angry red flesh.

'I see my brother didn't tell you about me. But then again, why would he? After all, he is quite desperate to find someone to amuse me. See, Alice, how could you befriend such a monster as I? Am I not truly ugly? A poor little rich girl who can never be seen in public. Now, perhaps you'd like to tell me what you think, without offending me?'

Regaining her composure, Alice plucked up the courage to reply: 'My mother always told me beauty was skin-deep, it's the person inside that matters.' She hesitated, not knowing if she had overstepped the mark, unsure whether to carry on. 'I've always been known as a plain Jane. My chin's too long and my hair's lank, but my family still love me – as I'm sure your family love you.'

'I must give you your due, Alice. You've not screamed, you've not given me a sugar-sweet reply and curtsied or smiled at me before fleeing the room in revulsion; perhaps you are made of sterner stuff.'

Moving to the edge of the bed, Nancy picked up a robe and put it on over her high-necked nightdress. Then she went to her dressing table, sat stiffly in the chair and looked into the mirror. 'How can anyone love this face, Alice? Look at me – how am I ever to live a life? I'm so ugly, I never want to be seen outside these four walls.'

Alice was overcome by a wave of pity; plain she might be, but at least she could always pretty herself up with a new hat and a bit of rouge. Putting on a brisk air, she approached the dressing table. 'Now, Miss Nancy, feeling sorry for yourself never did any good for anyone. Here, let me brush your hair, that'll make you feel better. I've never seen such a beautiful comb as that one.' She gestured to a dragonfly-shaped comb that glittered and glistened in the sharp morning light.

'What good are beautiful things on such an ugly face?' Nancy picked up the filigree dragonfly and toyed with it. 'A useless reminder of the past.'

Alice reached for a mirror-backed brush and went to work on the thick, dark hair; it was silky and smooth and smelled of perfume. Smiling at Nancy's reflection in the mirror, she started to pile the hair on top of her head.

'Stop it! Stop it at once! You can see even more of my face when you do that. You stupid bitch, are you doing it on purpose? Have you come to mock me?'

Spinning round, Nancy grabbed Alice's hand, making her drop the brush. As it hit the floor, the glass shattered into pieces. 'Get out! Get out of my room now!'

Without a word, Alice stooped to pick up the shards of glass, cutting her fingers in the process. Then she stood and looked at her accuser, blood dripping down her fingers.

'What I see before me is not an ugly rich girl but a spoilt, self-pitying rich girl. I was only looking at the shape of your face so that I could decide what to do with your hair, miss. But I can see I'm not wanted here. As for being a bitch – why, even our old dog has more manners than you do. Good day, Miss Nancy. I'll see myself out.'

She could feel her legs and her hands shaking as she descended the grand staircase. Faulks and a woman who she supposed must be Mrs Dowbiggin were standing in the hallway, heads together, obviously discussing what they had overheard of the goings-on upstairs.

'Will you be leaving us so soon, Miss Bentham?' The sneer that Alice had seen from Faulks on the doorstop was even more prominent.

'I am, and what's more I'll not stop another minute where I'm not wanted.' Alice set the remains of the brush on the hall table and wiped her bleeding fingers on the edge of her skirt.

'I'll get your things.' Faulks disappeared through a door and returned a moment later with Alice's well-worn coat and hat. 'I presume you'll be leaving by the back door,' he said, and immediately began ushering her through the hallway, until they were both stopped in their tracks by a voice from the top of the stairs.

'Stop! I will not let you go! Come here this minute. How dare you talk back to me! I am Miss Nancy Frankland.' Nancy was hanging over the banister, her long, dark hair cascading down and her robe floating around her, lending her the appearance of a ghostly apparition.

'I will return once you have calmed down – if your brother wants me to.' Alice turned from the screaming banshee to face the butler. 'And no, Faulks – I will leave by the front door. I may not know my place, but I do know one thing: I have more manners than the lot of you put together.'

Turning on her heel, head held high, Alice marched across the hallway, opened the huge front door and descended the steps. Her anger and indignation carried her homeward with such speed, before she knew it she was back in the farmyard.

'Flippin 'eck, our lass, you slammed that door hard. What's up with you?' Turning in his chair, Bob Bentham registered the red cheeks, firm chin and hands on hips, and knew immediately that something was amiss.

'Never have I been treated so badly, Father,' Alice huffed, hanging her coat on the hook. Rolling up her sleeves, she made straight for the stove, took the boiling kettle from the hob and poured scalding water over the dirty pots that filled the sink. 'And I'll not be going back. No one speaks to me like that.' She added an equal measure of cold water from the pitcher by the kitchen door and set about doing the washing-up.

'Calm down, lass, things can't be that bad. Our Will says they're a strange lot, but that's the higher classes for you: inbred and flighty. You'll have to get used to them.' He knocked his pipe, emptying its contents into the embers of the fire before refilling and lighting it. 'Mind you, they say that sister of his is strange. Nobody ever sees her. He brought her to the house in the middle of the night and she's not been seen since.'

'Now you tell me! I bet our Will knows more than he's letting on. Why won't he tell me?' Alice could feel her face going redder than ever.

'Some folk reckon she's a witch – eyes that burn into your soul.' Bob gazed into the fire, brow furrowed in concentration as he tried to recall the gossip. 'Others say she's mad. 'Course, nobody really knows, because only her brother and that miserable couple of house servants ever see her.' He looked up from the fire. 'Did you see her? What does she look like? Is it right, is she a witch?' Bob was on the very edge of his chair, eager to hear his daughter's account.

'Well, I'm sorry to disappoint you, but all I saw was a spoilt brat with a temper – she called me a bitch! As for that butler – who does he think he is!' The pots and dishes in the sink were getting rough treatment as Alice vented her anger. But then she paused and turned to her father. 'I can understand her feeling sorry for herself, though. Her face is all marked and twisted.

What happened to her? Must have been something terrible – and she doesn't look much older than me.'

'Nay, lass, I don't know. 'Appen our Will'll tell you; him and that Jack earwig all sorts. Ask him when he comes home. Only thing I know is that her brother has some strange-looking friends that come and go at all hours. Nevertheless, he's always done right by us. We could have a worse landlord, a lot worse. And Will reckons he's not a bad boss either; him and Jack have done well for themselves, working at the manor. It's just the company he keeps – rum lot.'

'If you ask me, Father, his lordship's all right. But his sister definitely needs a lesson in manners. I'll not be rushing back, no matter what you and our Will might think.'

'You'll do what Lord Frankland wants you to do, our lass. We need to keep a roof over our head, remember. So don't go getting on your high horse. Right then . . .' He got to his feet and stretched himself. 'I'm off for a stroll into Dent. I'll be back for my supper, so don't start pulling that long face. I'm only going to have a bit of banter with some of my cronies, stretch my legs on this grand spring evening.'

Bob put his top coat on and fingered the few pence that he had in his pocket. Might just be enough for a pint or two. He looked up and caught Alice watching him as she wiped the pots and put them away. She knew him all too well, and she'd a sullen face on her if you didn't do what she wanted. He'd get round to that stonewalling in the bottom meadow tomorrow; that should keep her off his back for a bit.

'Fire needs stoking, our Alice. And the dog could do with something to eat – it's been moping about all day.' With a parting wave, he was off down the track, heading for the Moon Inn in search of a cold pint and a bit of gossip from anyone who would talk to him.

Alice followed him out into the yard. By the time she'd finished pumping water from the well, his cheery whistle had faded into the distance. She knew damn well that would be the last she'd see of him until throwing-out time at the Moon. Drying her hands on her apron, she went over to the old dog. It was lying with its head resting on its paws, soulful eyes looking up at her. 'I know, old lad, you're hungry. He doesn't care about you any more, does he? He doesn't care about anyone any more.' She gave a sigh and went into the house in search of some food for the poor animal, emerging with a bowl of stale bread soaked in milk. The old dog gulped it down, thankful that its stomach at last felt a little fuller.

She stayed with the dog until it had finished eating its meal, then urged it to join her on a walk. Wrapping her shawl around her, Alice wandered up the rough lane to the top pasture, the dog trotting in front of her, occasionally stopping when it caught the scent of a rabbit, sniffing the air and looking around in the hope that the meal of bread would soon be followed by some fresh meat. A distant sheep bleated, reminding Alice that it would soon be lambing time, the busiest part of the year on the farm. How would they manage this spring? If only her father would come to his senses . . .

As she walked on, inevitably her thoughts returned to Whernside Manor. She wondered what had happened to Nancy Frankland to make her behave so. Alice was conscious that her parting words had been a bit harsh, but she had her pride and it wouldn't stand for anyone calling her names or sneering at her the way that butler had done.

On reaching the wall at the bottom of Whernside, Alice sat herself down and gazed out upon the dale where she had been born. The sun was about to set and its dying rays were turning the sky to a gorgeous pink that slowly filtered into hues of gold before changing again to a deep blue. The whole dale seemed to shine, bathed in a clear frosty veil, which took Alice's breath away with its tranquil beauty. She leaned against the wall and listened to the cry of a curlew. The return of the curlews from their winter holiday on the coast had always been one of the harbingers of spring in the Dales, but this year all the months since her mother's death had somehow blended into one another. Alice couldn't even remember Christmas; it was as if it had never happened.

Only when the sun finally gave up the battle and disappeared behind the great rocky outcrop of Combe Scar did she stir herself, suddenly feeling the cold, the temperature having fallen with the sun. Shivering, she wrapped her shawl around her, whistled the faithful

Jip to her side and set off for Dale End. Will would be home soon and no doubt he would have heard about her visit to the manor. She knew he wouldn't be best pleased with her. Only that morning he had cautioned her to 'keep 'em sweet'. Sweet! She had been anything but sweet. Why did she have to have such an attitude? She only hoped her outburst wouldn't make things difficult for Will.

As soon as she arrived home, Alice busied herself getting the fire going and preparing supper for Will. She was busy laying the table when he opened the door. Knowing that a lecture was imminent, she didn't dare look round, not wanting to see his scowling face.

'Well, bugger me, our lass, what you been up to today? You're the talk of the manor, woman!'

'I couldn't help myself, our Will. She provoked me.'

'What do you mean, she provoked you? Whatever it is you think you've done, it can't be that bad – Miss Nancy wants you there tomorrow. First time she's ever asked someone back.' Will sat down to take his boots off, undoing the laces slowly and not looking up to see his sister's face. 'Jack's to pick you up in the trap, first thing in the morning; I had to tell him before I left tonight. Cost me a penny, you did – I had a bet on with Jack that you'd not last more than a day.'

'She asked for me? I don't believe you. Why would she want me back, after what I said?'

'Have you been telling it how it is, then, our lass? Old Frankland said you were like a breath of fresh air, just what his sister needed.'

'But . . . I don't know if I want to go back. They . . . She doesn't have any manners, and she swears, and them servants treated me like a lump of dirt.'

'She's spoilt, our lass. Treat her straight and you'll be fine. I've never set eyes on her, but I've heard her often enough. Her tantrums are that loud, you can hear them from the stables. Everyone's frightened of her, so she gets her own way. As for that stuffed-shirt Faulks and old Mrs Dowbiggin, they're both used to having their own way too. I wouldn't let 'em bother you.'

Alice was stunned. For a moment she stood there, watching Will kick his boots off, trying to fathom it out. Then she came to her senses: 'You can put those boots back on, our Will. Father's gone to Dent; no doubt he's in the Moon, spending what money we have left. He'll not be home in time to milk the cow, and the sheep could do with being looked at in case we have an early lambing. So don't get the idea you've finished for the day.'

'See? Keep saying it as it is and you'll be all right, our lass – you boss us around enough!' With a heavy sigh, Will reached for his boots and wearily began lacing them up again. 'I know he's my father and I should respect him, but I'm getting a bit fed up of doing his jobs as well as my own. I tell you what, our lass, Jack and I have been talking about leaving and finding something else. Now's the time to make our fortune, while we're still young.' He got to his feet and grabbed his coat and hat. 'I don't want to stay here and end up like Father, that's for sure. Anything's better than working for nothing, still forelock-tugging when you're nearly in your grave.'

'You can't leave me, Will. I couldn't manage on my own, not with Father in this state!'

'I know, but we can't carry on as we are. If he doesn't straighten up soon . . .' With a despairing shake of the head, he walked out, slamming the kitchen door shut behind him.

Alice was left feeling utterly wretched. As if it wasn't bad enough that she had to return to the manor in the morning, now she had the worry of Will and his itchy feet. She prayed that he would not leave – not yet, anyway. Please God, not yet. She couldn't face life on her own with a drunk of a father.

3

'It's no use you tutting, Jack Alderson – you'll just have to wait! I can't do things any faster . . . It isn't as if I want to go, mind . . . I don't know why you were sent for me in the first place.'

Both Jack and the horse found their patience stretched to the limit as they waited for their unwilling passenger to finish running around the farmyard in an effort to get all the jobs done before departing for the manor. Having finally climbed aboard, she sat panting for breath and fidgeting, making constant adjustments to her shawl and hat, obviously nervous about her imminent re-entry into the unfamiliar world of the manor.

'Are we right now?' Jack cast a quick glance in her direction, not daring to look into the ice-blue eyes of his best friend's sister. He was afraid that, if their eyes met, Alice would read his thoughts. Thoughts that he had harboured for the past year but didn't dare do anything about. How come that scraggy bit of a girl had turned into such a beautiful woman? And what would Will make of him fancying his sister? Jack made a conscious effort to put aside all such thoughts for the moment and go back to treating her as the lass he had grown up with.

'Well, what are you waiting for? Let's get going!' Clearly Alice was in one of her assertive moods. 'You'll probably be bringing me back again as soon as we get there.'

The morning had not started well at Dale End Farm. Alice had woken to discover that her father had not returned – no doubt he was in a hedge somewhere, sleeping off his hangover. In addition to making herself presentable for the sneering folk at the manor, she'd had to milk the cow, feed Will and send him on his way, as well as attending to all the other jobs that needed doing – and everything had had to be done at twice the speed that it should have been. She was going to have stern words with her father tonight, even if it wasn't her place to do so.

With a rueful shake of his head, Jack whipped the horse into motion. God, she was a feisty one, but she looked so pretty when she was angry that he couldn't help smiling.

'What are you smiling at, Jack Alderson? I can't see anything to grin about. My father's gone missing, I'm entering into a job that I don't want, stuck all day with a spoilt brat when there's chores waiting to be done at the farm, and all the while you're leading my brother on, trying to get him to leave the dale. I don't see how things could get much worse.'

'Don't you blame me for Will's wandering feet – that's down to your father's antics and Lord Frankland putting ideas in Will's head, telling him what a good worker he is.' He turned to face her, his voice softening. 'It'll be good to see you working at the manor, Alice. You can tell me what Miss Nancy looks like – I've never seen her. Nobody has. And I'll show you around the place, when you have some spare time . . . if you want me to.' Will blushed and stumbled over this last sentence, his confidence ebbing away under Alice's scrutiny. His eyes returned to the road ahead, focusing intently, as if the bumpy old farm lane required his undivided attention.

Alice had never known Jack to blush, and she thought she knew the reason why: 'So you fancy your chances with Miss Nancy, do you, Jack? Look at you, all tongue-tied and blushing. Wait until I tell our Will!' she joked at the bashful Jack's expense. She could see his face glowing even redder with embarrassment, his dark hair complementing his rosy cheeks. 'I wouldn't be setting my sights on her, Jack. She's too posh for you, and a right madam, besides.'

'It's not like that, Ali, honestly it isn't. I know my place. So you needn't tell Will anything.'

Both fell silent as they entered the driveway of Whernside Manor. To Alice, the building looked even more daunting than it had the previous day, especially now she knew what the occupants were like. Jack slowed the carriage, but continued past the grand front entrance and pulled up at the back door.

'Good luck, Alice,' he said, as he helped her alight from the gig. 'I'll be in the stables if you need me.' Then he gave her a parting smile and turned away, leading the horse across the yard.

Alice sighed. There was a sick feeling in the pit of her stomach, and she really didn't want to enter that cold, unwelcoming building. She was hesitating on the doorstep when Mrs Dowbiggin came bustling out. In her long black dress with its pristine starched white collar and cuffs, she looked every inch the perfect housekeeper.

'Oh, hello, dear. So you've come back. I said to Reggie – Mr Faulks to you – that it took some courage to stand up to Miss Nancy. We've never dared, you know. She's got a temper, has that one; likes her own way. Anyway, she must have taken quite a fancy to you or you wouldn't be back. Either that or the master has. Wouldn't be the first time that some slip of a lass has taken his fancy.'

Before Alice could get a word in, Mrs Dowbiggin took her by the arm and began steering her across the yard.

'Seeing as you're here, you can come and help me bring the washing in from the orchard – I could do with another pair of hands to help me fold the sheets. It's Alice, isn't it, dear? Well, since you are going to be part of the team, Alice, let me inform you of the rules of the house, the main one being that the house servants do not consort with the outside staff. It's just not done.'

This remark was accompanied by a disapproving glance in Jack's direction. Still reciting rules, she bustled onward in the direction of the orchard, where white sheets were billowing in the wind. Alice fell in beside her, nodding and occasionally managing to fit in a word of assent. Mrs Dowbiggin certainly could talk. She'd not given Alice a second glance yesterday, but she was making up for lost time now. Though her sole topic of conversation thus far had been the many rules and regulations of the manor, at least she was talking to Alice as if she counted for something and not like some worthless beggar.

Together they retrieved the sheets from the washing line and folded them ready for ironing, then loaded them into a wicker linen basket and carried it between them back to the manor. When they entered the kitchen, the fresh smell of spring air clung to the sheets, its perfume filling the room.

'Well, here we are, dear. Would you like a drink of tea before you go up and see Miss Nancy? She'll be waiting for you. Master Gerald made her get up this morning and put on a dress in readiness for your arrival. She even ate some breakfast, which is highly unusual.' Mrs Dowbiggin shook her head and sighed as she bustled to the huge kitchen range and put the kettle on the glowing fire.

'Thank you,' said Alice, 'but I think I'd better go straight up and see Miss Nancy. After all, it is her I'm answerable to – her and Lord Frankland. I need to apologize to her for being a bit sharp yesterday. I know

I shouldn't have, but I'm not used to being talked to in such a manner.'

'My advice, Alice, is to start as you mean to go on – and you certainly did that, my girl. It'll have done her no harm. Why, I even got a thank you this morning! I could have dropped down dead on the spot – I haven't had a thank you from her in months. Now, do you know the way to her room or will you need Reggie to show you?'

'I'll be fine, thank you, Mrs Dowbiggin. It's best if I find my own way around.' In truth, Alice wanted to be by herself for a moment, to walk through the beautiful hallway and to sweep up that magnificent staircase at her own pace, taking in the glorious scene.

Leaving the warm kitchen with its copper pans, jelly moulds and drying herbs mounted on the walls, she climbed the few steps up to the level of the hallway. Almost on tiptoe, keenly aware of the echo of her footsteps in the great hall, she crossed to the stairs and gingerly mounted them. When she came to Miss Nancy's door, she hesitated for a moment to compose herself before knocking.

'Enter.' The voice that she'd last heard screaming abuse at her came from the other side.

Alice turned the doorknob, not knowing what to expect. All she knew was that she had to keep calm; these people owned her family home and no matter what she thought of them or how they behaved, she had to show them respect.

Nancy was sitting in the chair next to the dressing

table, wearing a dark blue satin dress with a sash. She was facing away from Alice, her dark hair cascading down her back and reaching almost to her waist.

'Miss Nancy.' Alice curtsied. 'May I apologize for my abrupt behaviour yesterday. I had no right to talk to you in such a manner.' It galled her to have to beg her ladyship's pardon, but the more she'd thought about the way she had acted, the more Alice regretted having been so forthright. What with worrying about her father and mulling over the previous day's events, she felt as though she hadn't had a moment's sleep.

Nancy turned. Though the girl appeared demure and contrite, Nancy could detect no fear in her eyes and she did not drop her gaze when confronted with that scarred face.

'I, too, should apologize. I was no lady – as my brother was quick to point out. I have bad days, I'm afraid, when my temper and memories get the better of me. Let us both start afresh today, Alice. I need someone to help me and become my companion, for I never go outside of these four walls. Though I should add that is my own choice.' She patted the seat next to her, summoning Alice to join her. 'Now, tell me a little about yourself. My brother informs me that you have recently lost your mother. You must miss her; I know I miss my parents deeply. If it wasn't for my brother, I fear I would go out of my mind with despair . . .' Her voice trailed and faltered, as if she was reliving the deaths of her parents. Pulling herself together, Nancy continued: 'He also tells me that your brother – Will, is that his name? – is his best shot and the star of his beloved shooting parties. How grown men can take pleasure in shooting innocent birds, I do not know.'

Alice sat in stunned silence, her hands clasped tight on her lap. She could hardly believe this was the same person she'd encountered yesterday. At the mention of her brother's name, she couldn't resist a little show of pride:

'Our Will is getting big-headed with the praise that he keeps getting – it'll be the undoing of him.' She gave a smile to show that she was joking. Looking into the face of her new employer, she continued: 'I do miss my mother, and I'm so sorry to hear that you have no parents. I didn't realize . . .' She would have liked to know what had happened to them, but didn't dare pry, especially when the conversation was going well.

Perhaps sensing her interest, Nancy immediately steered her companion away from the painful subject of her family: 'Tell me, Alice, what goes on in the world outside these four walls? All my brother talks about are his boring friends, who spend all their time drinking, shooting and playing cards. I know nothing of the locals, and I'm sure there must be plenty of tales to tell. But first, let us have some tea.'

She got up and rang a small bell by the side of her bed. Within minutes, Faulks arrived. Barely acknowledging his presence, Nancy commanded: 'Tell Mrs Dowbiggin we would like tea and some of her excellent biscuits. I'm sure Alice would like to sample them.' Then, dismissing him like an unwelcome intruder, she proceeded to interrogate Alice.

While enjoying the tea and biscuits that Faulks laid out before them, Alice tried to portray the inhabitants of the dale. She told Nancy about the shopkeepers in Dent, the comings and goings of merchants, the various characters who frequented the market, and how most of the farmers did their deals in the bar of the Moon Inn rather than through the local fairs. She mimicked some of the locals and passed on the latest gossip of the dale, the general chit-chat that made up everyday life. So engrossed was she in trying to convey the smells and sights of the dale, she quite forgot where she was. In fact, the time went so quickly she could hardly believe it when she realized it was lunchtime already.

'I'm sorry, I didn't mean to keep talking this long. You must be weary of my voice,' Alice apologized.

'Indeed I am not – I have enjoyed your company immensely,' protested Nancy. 'My brother was right: in you he has found someone to entertain me. However, you must forgive me, Alice, but I am getting a little tired. I usually have a midday nap. Would you mind leaving now, and I will see you in the morning. I shall look forward to carrying on our conversation tomorrow.'

Though things had gone better than she could have imagined, Alice nevertheless breathed a sigh of relief as she closed the bedroom door behind her.

'Would you like a bite of lunch, Miss Bentham?' Mrs Dowbiggin asked as Alice joined her and Faulks in the kitchen.

The butler, no doubt remembering how she had spoken to him the previous day, maintained a deadpan expression as he studied Alice in silence.

'There's just enough for a little one.' Mrs Dowbiggin's smile seemed genuine as she motioned to the near-empty stew pan.

'That's very kind, thank you,' said Alice. 'I am a little hungry. I missed breakfast this morning.' In truth, 'a little hungry' was an understatement. She was ravenous, having been too much on her best behaviour to do more than politely nibble at the biscuits served with tea earlier. The stew smelled so good, her mouth started salivating at the thought of it.

'You can sit there.' Mrs Dowbiggin ushered her to the chair at the end of the immaculately scrubbed pine table. 'Here you go – you will all the better be for having that in you. My, you're a little 'un. Isn't she a dot, Reggie? So slim.'

'It's not my place to say. If you'll excuse me, I'd better take Miss Nancy her lunch before she has her nap.' Faulks rose from his chair, donned his jacket and picked up the tray, which was all laid out in readiness, then strutted from the kitchen like a prize cock.

'Stuffy old devil,' muttered Mrs Dowbiggin. 'Thinks hisself God's gift! Still, his heart's in the right place, once you get to know him.' She ladled stew into a dish and added a huge chunk of freshly baked bread, then placed it in front of Alice. 'Here, you set to and eat that – it'll fill you for the day.' Looking on approvingly as Alice ate, she sank into the chair opposite and sipped her cup of tea. Obviously delighted to have someone to talk to, she leaned across the table, her ample bosom heaving as she quizzed the newcomer on the morning's events: 'She's behaved herself, then, Miss Nancy? She has good days and bad days, you know. I reckon it's the pain from her scars.'

'Forgive me if I'm talking out of turn, Mrs Dowbiggin,' said Alice, 'but do you know how Nancy got the scars? She must have been a great beauty; it's a pity her face is marked so.'

'Well, dear, it is a cruel story. It happened before Master Gerald and Miss Nancy came to Whernside, back in the days when the family lived in Russia. You know where I mean?'

'Yes, I've heard of Russia.'

'From what I hear, Nancy was very young at the time and Master Gerald was in his late teens. Their parents owned a mine near Moscow – in fact, Master Gerald still has involvement in it, but that's another matter.' Mrs Dowbiggin paused to draw breath. 'Anyway, the workers in Russia decided they'd had enough of toiling long hours for a pittance of pay and so they went on strike. Very soon the trouble spread all over the country and things began to turn nasty, with workers out to get their revenge on employers. Unfortunately, the Franklands being English, they came in for a lot of resentment and the troublemakers accused them of raking in a profit at the expense of poor Russians. One night a mob of them set the Franklands' mansion alight, burning it to the ground. Master Gerald was spared, being at school here in England at the time, but Miss Nancy was found the next day, wandering in the garden in a terrible state. Poor girl must have seen some frightful things. Both her parents died in the fire, nothing left of them but ashes. And Nancy's face and shoulders were so badly burned it took ages for the skin to heal.' She paused and took a long, deep drink of her tea. 'Terrible, terrible times. So it's understandable why she's the way she is.'

'Gossiping again, Hilda?' Faulks had sneaked in through the kitchen doorway unnoticed. 'Don't let Master Gerald hear you – he'll have you out of the house as fast as you can say "Eggs is eggs".' Giving both women a haughty glare, he resumed his seat.

'Oh, what's it to you, you old misery? The lass has to know how the land lies if she's to work here. It's only fair she knows what she's up against. Aye, and while I'm on the subject, you'd best steer clear of Master's gambling mates, Alice. Some of them are not to be trusted.'

'Hilda, that's enough! I will not have gossip in my kitchen.'

'Since when did the kitchen become yours? I'll have you know this is *my* kitchen and I will gossip all I like in it. In any case, it's not gossip; it's giving good advice to a young, vulnerable lass. Now go and get me the brasses from out of the parlour so I can give 'em a polish.'

With a baleful look, Faulks grudgingly left the room.

'Sometimes he gets ideas above his station, that one. Have you finished your dinner, dear? And is there anything else I can tell you?'

Giving Alice no time to answer, Mrs Dowbiggin whisked away the empty plate and began getting the brass cleaner out and spreading newspaper on the kitchen table, ready for the afternoon's polishing session.

'Would you like to give me a hand, dear? I hate this job and there are so many brasses to clean. If you've time, I'd appreciate the door knocker, bell and letter box being polished. That'd give me ten minutes' peace before I have to start preparing this evening's meal.'

'I'll do all the outside bits for you, Mrs Dowbiggin, but then I have to go home. I've to make dinner for our Will and my dad. Thank you for telling me about the family history.' Alice picked up the tin of Brasso and two orange cloths: 'Are these to be used for polishing?'

'That's it, lass. Much obliged, that'll help a lot.' Mrs Dowbiggin turned away and began taking the copper pans down from the shelf in readiness for their clean.

Resolving to do the front door first, Alice set off in that direction. The huge lion door knocker had caught her eye yesterday as she had nervously stood on the huge steps. Now here she was, part of the manor. How curious that twenty-four hours could alter things so quickly.

She had just finished smearing Brasso liquid on the features of the lion and was about to start polishing when she heard Will calling her name. He sounded agitated.

'Alice, Alice – for God's sake, leave that alone! It's Father – they've found Father!'

The yard of the Moon Inn was crammed with curious onlookers, all trying to peer into the dark orifice of the beer cellar.

'Back now, get yourselves back!' Arms out wide, Uriah Woodhead was frantically trying to steer the crowd away. 'Give the doctor some room now.'

Moments later, the doctor emerged into the light, his wiry old body struggling to climb the cellar steps. He was shaking his head.

'Well, Dr Bailey, is he . . . is he dead?' Uriah Woodhead pulled his handkerchief out of his pocket and wiped his brow. The sweat was pouring off him. Ever since he'd made the gruesome discovery, he'd felt as if he was having a heart attack.

'Aye, he's dead, all right. Looks like he tumbled down your cellar steps and dislodged one of the barrels. When it fell on top of him, it broke his neck clean in two.'

The crowd gave a gasp of horror. Poor old Bob Bentham: what an awful end to his life. What would become of his family?

His voice rising above the murmurs of sympathy and concern, Uriah was anxious to absolve himself of any blame: 'I told him to get hissel' home. Silly old bugger, I thought he'd gone. How was I to know he'd go creeping around in my yard?' For all his protests, Uriah was feeling guilty. He'd meant to close the cellar doors before the evening rush got underway, but in the event he never got round to it. By then it was too dark to see Bob lying at the foot of the steps. It had given Uriah a terrible shock when he went down at lunchtime and stumbled over his body.

'Don't you fret, man.' Dr Bailey patted him on the shoulder. 'You had no way of knowing that this was going to happen. He'd not been coping well since losing his wife last year. It's a shame for his family, but at least Bob's at peace with hisself now. I'll class it as death by misadventure, but I'll have to tell the local constable what's happened, to make it official. All right with you if I go into the Moon to make out the death certificate? I could do with a tot of brandy . . .' Seeing that his heavy hint had fallen on deaf ears, Dr Bailey added: 'Medicinal purposes only, of course.' Still no response from Uriah. Reluctantly admitting defeat, the doctor left Uriah and went into the bar.

No sooner had the doctor gone than the sound of running feet reached them from the cobbled street. The villagers fell silent when they recognized Will and, a hundred yards behind him, his sister Alice. Both were breathing heavily, their faces taut with anxiety, as the crowd parted to let them through. Uriah Woodhead immediately stepped forward to intercept Alice, drawing her away from the cellar entrance.

'You want nothing of looking down there, Alice. Come inside, lass. My Annie will take care of you.'

Will glanced sharply at Uriah, then descended the steps. A lantern illuminated his father's lifeless body, lying among the beer barrels. Falling to his knees, Will took his father's limp hand and clasped it to his chest. He wanted to rant and rave at the old fool for letting it come to this, but then grief overcame him and his shoulders heaved with dry sobs. He was still bending over the body when Ernie Batty arrived.

'Leave him to me now, lad.' The portly undertaker patted him gently on the back. 'Let's have him out of this dark place, eh? Mrs Batty and I will see to him, don't you worry.'

Wiping his nose on the sleeve of his corduroy jacket, his eyes full of tears and his nose running like a tap, Will climbed the cellar steps. He emerged to find the crowd had gone – dispersed by the local bobby, they'd all hurried off to their homes, the gossips among them eager to spread the word and discuss the Benthams' misfortune over a cup of tea.

A lone figure was waiting in the yard: Uriah. 'Now, lad, come into the pub. My missus is looking after Alice. I can't tell you how sorry we are for the both of you.' The landlord wasn't good with words at the best of times; knowing what to say under these circumstances was beyond him. Putting an arm around the boy, he led him into the snug. Alice was already there, hands shaking, eyes red with tears. Annie Woodhead sat by her side, doing her best to console her.

'Well, is it him? Tell me, our Will, is it him?' she pleaded. 'Happen this lot have got it wrong; happen it's some passing tramp that fell in, not knowing the hole was there.' Alice didn't want to believe that in the space of four months they had lost both parents.

'No, Ali, it's Father . . .' Will wished he could say something to ease his sister's grief, but in his state of shock, words failed him.

Numb with pain and looking for someone to blame, Alice jumped up from the bench, eyes blazing, and turned on Uriah. 'You killed him! It was you who killed him! You've even pinched my mother's clock – it's right there on the mantelpiece.' She motioned to the carriage clock that had been her late mother's most cherished possession, occupying pride of place in her parlour.

Uriah, his face flushed in a mixture of embarrassment and anger, felt compelled to defend himself against the accusation. 'Now wait a minute, Alice. I'm as shocked as you are about this. I thought your father had gone home. The only way I'm responsible is that I left the cellar door open overnight. As for the clock, well, he traded it for beer. I only took it because I felt sorry for him – that's my biggest sin; happen I did encourage him to drink. God knows, I wish I hadn't now, but a man's got to make a living.'

Alice, spent after her angry outburst, had collapsed in a sobbing heap. Wrapping his arms around her and stroking her hair, Will said in a low voice, 'Shh, our Ali, you're upset. Uriah's not to blame and you know it.'

'I've spoken to Ernie Batty. He'll put your father in the chapel of rest until you've arranged a date for the funeral. I've told him I'll pay.' Uriah considered himself an honourable man, at least in business, and the last thing he wanted was the death of one of his regulars on his conscience. Drawing up a stool, he sat down opposite the grieving youngsters. 'If there's anything that me and the missus can do for the pair of you, let us know. Your father was a good man; he just couldn't cope with life without your mother.' He reached out a hand and patted Alice's arm as she sobbed into the jacket of her brother.

'Thank you, Mr Woodhead, that's good of you. I don't know how me and my sister would have managed to pay for a funeral.' Will got to his feet, gently drawing his sister with him. 'We'd best be off home now. It's a lot to cope with, today's happenings. We need a bit of time to ourselves.'

With quiet dignity, Will helped Alice through the door and into the evening air. Jack was waiting in the lane with his horse and trap. The moment he saw them, he dropped the reins and reached out to Alice.

Thankful for the presence of a friend, she ran to him, burying her head in the warmth of his tweed jacket, clutching him tightly as if she were clinging to a rock, afraid of being swept away if she released her hold.

'Shh, I'm here. Don't cry, Alice,' he soothed, wrapping his arms around her. He wanted to squeeze her and tell her everything was all right, that he would always be there for her and that she would never need anyone else, but he was mindful of Will's presence and didn't want him to think he was taking advantage of the situation. While Will settled things with Ernie Batty and thanked Uriah Woodhead once more for agreeing to pay for the funeral, Jack held on to Alice, lovingly stroking her long blonde hair, which smelled like the wild thyme that grew on the fellside. Her blue eyes brimming with tears, she looked up at him.

'Take us home, Jack . . . although I no longer know where home is. What are we going to do? No parents and no money – whatever are we going to do?'

He helped her up into the trap, whipping the horse into action the moment Will climbed aboard. They rode in silence, broken only by the alarm call of a nesting blackbird, disturbed from her nest by the sound of the horse and trap. The piebald, familiar with the trail to Dale End, needed no words of guidance from Jack as it carried its grieving load homewards.

4

Kneeling by her father's grave, Alice removed the previous week's flowers and set a freshly picked posy of white dog daisies in their place. Rising from her knees, she looked around her. The graveyard was set on a gently sloping hillside, with views all the way up to the head of the dale. The scurrying clouds cast shadows on the flanks of Combe Scar, which was covered with the white balls of fluff of grazing sheep and their lambs. She took in a deep breath of the clear air with its smell of peat and sphagnum moss – how she loved that smell. Up here, surrounded by the graves of her kin, with the warm spring breeze on her face and the sounds of birdsong and the lamenting bleat of a distant lost lamb in her ears, she was reminded at every turn of her deep and abiding attachment to Dent and the surrounding dales. She wanted to carry on living here, until it was time for her to be laid to rest in this churchyard in the company of her parents and grandparents and generations of her kind; she only hoped that someone would love her enough to mourn over her.

'Paying your respects, Miss Bentham?'

Startled from her reverie, she turned to find Lord Frankland staring at her. He doffed his hat in acknowledgement.

'I'm sorry, I didn't hear you behind me. I was lost in my thoughts . . .' Alice hesitated, uneasy in his company as usual. She was never sure how to address him or whether she was supposed to curtsy. After the death of her father, Gerald Frankland had been nothing but caring and considerate, insisting that she need only attend the manor one day a week. That was bound to change, though, now that all the sheep had been lambed and normality had returned to Dale End.

'Nancy is missing you, Alice. Indeed, Nancy's not the only one who is missing you. I swear Mrs Dowbiggin is just about begging me to ask you to become a member of our live-in staff, and even Faulks asked after you the other day – now that surely is a miracle!' He smiled at her, then continued. 'What's more, it's time that a decision was made with regard to that farmstead of mine. The place isn't big enough to support the pair of you, and Will is too good a worker for me to let go. So, I shall come by this evening and speak to you both, if that's convenient?' Without waiting for Alice to reply, he turned and set off along the churchyard path towards the kissing-gate entrance.

Alice almost took to her heels in pursuit, but thought better of it; she had her pride, and she wasn't going to be seen begging the right to live in the farm. Will would sort it tonight. He'd tell Lord Frankland that, with her help, he could manage to do his job and still keep the farm on. Besides, now that she was finished at the graveyard she was off to see Uriah Woodhead, who'd promised her some work at the Moon Inn. In all their discussions on the subject of what was to be done, both Alice and Will were in agreement on one point: it was not good for the two of them to be dependent on the manor. Better not to have all your eggs in one basket, as her mother used to say. A day at the manor and a few days' work at the Moon would keep the wolf from the door. As for the tenancy, she was sure Will would sort something out.

True to his word, Lord Frankland arrived in the early evening. Things got off to a civil enough start, but for the last half-hour the sound of heated debate had filled the kitchen of Dale End as Gerald Frankland's voice was raised in disagreement with young Will Bentham.

'I tell you, Will, that's simply not possible. These are difficult times, and I must address my assets. This cottage will be sold and the land amalgamated into the manor's estate, and that's final. I've got to generate income from somewhere – the import of Italian marble is affecting my profits; the stuff we produce at the marble works is practically worthless nowadays. I think you'll find my terms are more than generous. I'm offering accommodation and full-time employment for both you and your sister . . .'

Will, red in the face and befuddled by talk of addressing assets and amalgamating land, stared dumbly at Lord Frankland. The last thing he wanted was for his sister and him to be beholden to the manor, twenty-four hours a day. 'Never be a bought man': the words of Uncle Will – his namesake who returned a hero from fighting in the Crimean War – kept running through Will's mind.

'. . . what's more, I'll guarantee you a good price for your stock. So there you have it: we can either do this the gentlemanly way, or I can evict you. Let's face it, what would the pair of you both do without a job or home? And how much do you think you'll get for your stock with the market the way it is? See sense, man!' Gerald Frankland hadn't come to Dale End with the intention of making threats, but he was fast running out of patience with the stubborn young whipper-snapper.

Will rubbed his head. He knew that he was in no position to haggle a bargain for himself, but at least he could make life easier for Alice.

'All right, you can have our farm back and we'll sell you the stock. I will even come and live at the manor, in the room above the stables. But not our Alice – she's not moving into the manor. Uriah Woodhead has offered her work and accommodation at the Moon. She can still come and befriend Miss Nancy one day a week, but she'll spend the rest of her time working for Uriah.' As he spoke, Will studied his employer's reaction: was it the farm he wanted, or was it his little sister? So far as Will was concerned, the look on Frankland's face told the real tale.

Having been warned by Will to keep out of the way while he and Lord Frankland conducted their business, Alice was sitting on the stairs, eavesdropping on the conversation. Tears filled her eyes as Will finally submitted to Lord Frankland's demands. Her beloved home! She loved living halfway up Whernside, away from everyone, with a view from her bedroom window that extended right down the dale. Her new home would be the attic bedroom of the Moon; all she would be able to see from there would be the rooftops of the village houses. Perhaps a room at the manor would have been better, but Will had been adamant that she should not live under the Franklands' roof and be forever at their beck and call.

'Good! I'll get someone to value the stock, and let's say a month's notice on the house.' Lord Frankland's voice took on a less satisfied tone as he continued: 'I don't think you are being fair to your sister. She's worthy of something better than being a serving girl in a hostelry. I could offer her comfort and security in my employment.' Lord Frankland tapped his walking stick sharply on the ground and stared intently into young Will's face.

'I'm sorry, sir, but I reckon she will be best suited to living in the village. She can come and visit Miss Nancy anytime she pleases, in addition to the day we have agreed to. You have my word on that. But she'll be staying at the Moon Inn.' Will may not have been able to save the farm, but he would continue to look after his little sister's best interests; he owed her that.

'Very well. We'll leave it that way for now. Perhaps you'll change your mind in time.' Setting his hat hard upon his head, he turned towards the door. 'As for your own future – I have great plans for you. Once this business with the farm is sorted out, I'll be taking you up to Stone House. I have a little job for you at the marble works.' Without so much as a backward glance at the worried look on Will's face, he was gone.

Hearing the door close, followed by the clatter of hooves, Alice hurried downstairs to find Will. He was sitting in what used to be their father's chair, head in hands. At the sound of the bottom stair creaking with Alice's weight, he looked up.

'I'm sorry, Ali. I'm so sorry. I tried, but you can't argue with the man who holds all the cards. And now the bastard is going to make me work at Stone House. I don't want to go up there. The men there are a bunch of foul-mouthed old navvies, left over from building the railway, and the foreman is the worst of the lot – drunk nine times out of ten and doesn't give a damn about anyone's safety. There's an accident at the marble works nearly every week. What am I to do?'

Alice sat on the edge of the chair and put an arm around her brother. She'd never seen him in such a state; no matter what they'd had to face, he'd always remained strong and cheerful.

'It isn't your fault, Will. You did your best for us. We may not have the farm, but as long as we've got work and one another, we'll survive. Just promise me you'll not leave me. I've no one else in the world but you. Promise me, Will – promise me!' Her face was set; she wanted her brother to know that she was in deadly earnest and this was not a promise to take lightly.

Will lifted his head, eyes red with tears. For all that he was a grown man of nineteen, it was hard fighting battles that he could not win, leading a life that he had no control of. Meeting his sister's gaze, he felt his resolve strengthen. 'I promise, Ali. I'll always be here for you.' He gave her a shaky smile. 'Besides, who ever gets the better of Jack and me? As long as you are safe at the Moon with old Uriah and his wife, we will be all right.'

'That's better, Will. We Benthams never give in. Why, before you know it you'll be running that marble works. And I'll meet a rich gentleman who'll keep me in a manner befitting my breeding.' She smiled and dropped a mock curtsy. 'And then we can both tell old Frankland where to shove his job!'

In her heart of hearts, Alice was deeply troubled. It had been hard enough losing their parents, but now they had lost their home, the one thing that had kept them together. From now on it was going to be a battle to survive. But she had no doubt whatsoever that she would survive, come hell or high water, because she was a Bentham and a Bentham never gave in – not as long as she had breath in her body, anyway.

Will Bentham wiped the sweat from his brow. It was almost time to go; just one more job remained to be done, and then he would have to turn his back on his family home. His heart was heavy: the last job was the one he was going to hate the most.

He looked down into the trusting eyes of old Jip; he'd been a good dog, long in the tooth but faithful to the end. He threaded the string that was to hold Jip to the wood stock tight, so that he couldn't move his head. Then he patted him and whispered, 'I'm sorry, old mate.' Tears filled Will's eyes as he raised his gun and fired at the farm's most-loved animal. The dog slumped to the ground and Will untied him, making sure he was dead, and then lovingly carried him up the path to a place where he had seen him sitting in the past, surveying his kingdom. There he had dug a hole just big enough to hold Jip's body. Laying the dog tenderly down, he slowly filled in the hole, fresh earth and salty tears falling upon the black and white fur until the body was covered.

'I'm sorry, old lad, but you'd not have worked for anyone else – you were too old for anyone to want.' He stood tall and looked out over the valley. 'I hate that bastard Frankland. I've lost everything, even my bloody dog.' He wiped his nose and spat, then lifted the spade onto his shoulder and set off down the hill, the dusk closing in around him.

5

The attic bedroom of the Moon Inn was squat, to say the least; the only source of light was the skylight and that was overshadowed by the pub's tall chimneys, which spent nine months of the year belching smoke. The few possessions that Alice had brought with her from Dale End looked strangely out of place in her new home. And was it her imagination or had the Staffordshire pot dogs' smiles developed a downward tilt? Now ensconced on the small chest of drawers in the corner, they certainly looked much sadder than they had on the mantelpiece in her mother's parlour. Still, the woollen blanket that her mother had knitted brought a splash of colour, as did the posy of meadow flowers she had picked that morning before leaving home. They brightened up the black iron fireplace where she had placed them, nestled in a vase that had belonged to her grandmother.

'There, Alice, I've brought you a jug of water for your morning's ablutions. I thought you might like this too.' Mrs Woodhead handed Alice her mother's carriage clock. 'It'll only get broken down in the bar, so let's have it back where it belongs. Your mother would have wanted that.'

'Thank you, Mrs Woodhead, that is very thoughtful of you.' Alice was too choked at this act of kindness to say more. Her hands held the clock lovingly, fingers tracing the outline of its face. Seeing it brought back sweet memories, but also reminded her of everything that had been lost.

'Nay, lass – it's got a double purpose. You'll need to know the time if you're working for us. I want you up bright and early, lighting fires and making breakfasts for Mr Woodhead and any guests that's staying with us. No use having a dog and barking yourself, is there?' This was accompanied by a laugh that sounded to Alice very much like a bark. 'So let's have you down in the kitchen at five in the morning. Oh, and one other thing: when we are alone, you may call me Annie, but in front of residents and Mr Woodhead, I think we had better be more formal.' Briskly adjusting her mob cap, which was struggling as usual to confine the abundance of auburn curls, a legacy of her Scottish ancestors, Mrs Woodhead bustled from the room.

Five o'clock! The only time Alice was ever up that early was when the sun beamed through her window in midsummer, and the combination of clear blue skies and the twitter of swifts compelled her to venture out of doors and up the fellside before anyone else was awake. Now she going to have to do that every morning – not in order to breathe in pure mountain air, but to lay coal fires and prepare other people's meals, without so much as a glimpse of the outside world.

As she placed the clock in its new place next to her bed, Alice realized that she would never again see it as a reminder of her old life at the farm. From here on the clock would be her master. She'd be counting off the hours to Sunday lunchtime, her one afternoon of rest; maybe even counting to the day she went to the manor.

Oh, why had she sat listening on the stairs that terrible evening instead of marching in there and fighting for her birthplace, for her right to remain at Dale End? Alice tightened her fists in frustration, fingers going white and numb with anger. Perhaps working at the Moon hadn't been the right decision, but for the time being she had no alternative but to put her head down and make the best of it. It would do for now, but she had no intention of remaining in this attic bedroom a moment longer than she had to. When and if an opportunity arose to better herself, she would be ready to grab it with both hands – and damn the consequences.

'Put your back into it, you lazy bugger! No wonder they fecking well call you Glassback Murphy.' Sean O'Hara wiped his brow with his sleeve; sweat was dripping off him as he oversaw the loading of the marble slab. That Murphy was going to have to go: he was bloody useless. The rest of them weren't much better. 'Come on, men – what are you waiting for? Open the sluice gate, damn you. Let's get this wheel turning. Bloody stuff won't cut itself!'

As the crew rushed to obey his commands, the great waterwheel powered the saw into action. About fecking time, thought O'Hara. Sure, hadn't he been up since the crack o' dawn getting that chunk o' stone in place – and what the feck for? All so some rich man in London could have a new fireplace in his dining room, and lean against it hobnobbing with his well-to-do friends. Those types had more money than sense. Sure, what was wrong with an open fire, so long as you'd a tot of whisky in hand?

There, that was the trickiest part of the job done. He could leave the buggers to it for a while. Boss wouldn't show up for a few hours yet, so he might as well nip home for a quick nap.

He was almost at the cottage door when he heard horses' hooves striking the cobbles of the works yard. Hurrying in the direction of the sound, he found Lord Frankland dismounting from his trap, accompanied by two young men who seemed vaguely familiar, though the Irishman couldn't remember where he knew them from.

'Ah, O'Hara – just the man.' He turned to indicate his companions: 'The tall fellow is Will Bentham; the other is Jack Alderson. I want you to show them around the quarry and mill, and explain to them what it is we do here. Think you can manage that, O'Hara?'

'To be sure, sir.' Sean eyed the two young men,

trying to fathom why they would be wanting a tour around the quarry and works. They didn't look like management; judging by their clothes, they were a couple of farm lads. Their faces gave nothing away. If anything, they appeared every bit as bemused as he was. 'Are they to be working for me, sir? Only, I've all the men I need, and I—'

'For the time being, I just want them to observe and report back to me. Since taking the place over after the death of my parents, I've been too busy with other commitments to give the marble works much attention. It strikes me that a couple of pairs of fresh eyes are needed to judge how efficiently the place operates. I myself will be out of the country for the next few weeks – my business in Russia requires my attention. In the meantime, I expect you to take care of them, O'Hara, and show them everything. And I do mean everything.' Gerald Frankland tapped the Irishman lightly on the shoulder with the tip of his stick, as if pressing home the message.

'I will, sir. Don't you worry, sir, I'll show them how well run Stone House is. I'm sure they'll be impressed, indeed they will, sir.' Despite his jovial tone, O'Hara was inwardly seething. The last thing he needed was two wet-behind-the-ears farm boys sticking their noses in and running back to his lordship telling tales. Pair of spies, that's what they were. So far as O'Hara was concerned, the marble works was running very nicely, thank you; he'd spent the last few years arranging things to his satisfaction. And if these two thought they

were going to interfere . . . His thoughts were interrupted by another tap of Frankland's stick on his
shoulder.

'One more thing – these fellows are locals, but
they'll need transport to get to and from their living
quarters. See to it that the horse and buggy is at their
disposal for the duration of their stay.'

'But, sir, I might need it myself.' So far as O'Hara
was concerned, this was the final insult. His face
betrayed his indignation, and the mutinous look in his
eye prompted a steely response from Lord Frankland.

'I've seen you with that gelding I got you, O'Hara.
Good horse, but it doesn't appear to enjoy being
mastered by you. Now, Jack here is my top man when
it comes to horses – he might just bring it under control
for you.' He laid a hand on Jack's shoulder and nudged
him slightly to the fore of the group.

Jack was at a loss what to say. Smiling nervously,
his blush getting the better of him, he reached out to
shake O'Hara's hand.

'If you can make anything of that beast, you might
as well have him, the flighty bastard!' O'Hara ignored
the outstretched hand. 'Only thing he understands is
the touch of the whip. Ah! You're welcome to him –
go on, take him, fecking useless brute.' As if to empha-
size his contempt for Lord Frankland, his horse and
the two cuckoos about to occupy the marble works
nest, O'Hara spat on the path, then stormed off in the
direction of his cottage.

'Well, boys, you heard what I said.' Gerald Frankland, unfazed by the Irishman's wrath, slapped them both on the back. 'Your silence on the way up here and the look on your faces told me everything I needed to know – the gossip I've been hearing about Stone House is true. When I return in a fortnight, I shall expect you to report to me and tell me exactly what is going on here. Don't let O'Hara bully you – he's a brute of a man, but he'll not dare hurt you while he knows you've got my support.'

'I'm not happy with this, sir.' Will looked Gerald Frankland in the eye. Why had he picked him and Jack? They knew nothing of marble works.

'Nonsense, lad, it'll be the making of you. Right, I'll be off. I suggest you spend the first couple of days watching and listening, and then start asking questions. Get to know the workers, see what they have to say. By the end of the fortnight, I expect you to be able to tell me everything there is to know about Stone House.' He mounted the trap and turned his horses in the direction of home. 'And, Jack, take a good look at that gelding – it was in a bad way last time I saw it.' With that he whipped the horses into action, and the trap was soon lost in a cloud of dust as it sped off towards the manor.

Will and Jack watched him depart, feeling like a pair of foundlings abandoned in a hard, dangerous world. Ever since Frankland had first mentioned his intention of sending them to Stone House, they'd been dreading this day. Both lads had assumed they were going to be joining the marble works crew; though neither of them had relished the prospect, it would have been preferable to this. Telling tales on the burly Irishman was risky enough – O'Hara was notorious for his violent temper – but Frankland had forewarned the man. He was going to be watching them like a hawk.

Will turned to his friend. 'What do you make of that, Jack? Talk about a carry on! I don't know if I'm right happy with what he expects us to do. I'm not one for snooping on folk.'

'Before we do anything else, let's go take a look at that gelding. I don't like to hear of any animal being bad done to.' Jack's soft nature was taking over. 'As for the rest, I reckon we'll be all right if we stay together and steer clear of O'Hara. At least we can go back to the manor of a night.'

'OK, we'll give it a go. But I still think he should do his own dirty work.' Will had never cared for Gerald Frankland – toffs weren't to be trusted, as far as he was concerned – and his recent eviction from Dale End Farm had only served to reinforce that view.

Together they set off up the rough, weed-filled yard in search of the stable. Guided by the reek of rotting manure, they followed their noses until they reached a tall wooden door. When they opened it, vile-smelling remains of what had once been bedding tumbled out onto the yard floor. Peering into the gloom of the stable, they saw what looked to be a decrepit old nag, its back and flanks covered with festering sores and its ribs showing through as if it had been starved for some time. It flinched in fear as Jack entered the stable. Speaking gently all the while, Jack gradually calmed the beast so that he could run his knowing hands over its body and judge its age by checking its teeth. His face was grim and his jaw taut with fury by the time he'd finished. Will couldn't remember the last time he'd seen his mild-natured friend so angry.

'We're stopping, Will, 'cos of this poor fellow. He looks at least twenty, but he's only a young 'un. If O'Hara can treat a horse like this, God knows what we're going to find at the works and quarry. By God, I'd like to do to him what he's done to this animal, the bastard.'

Will simply nodded. There was no point arguing: they were stuck with their new job as spies for the manor. Life was not going to be comfortable for the next fortnight. Then again, it was only fourteen days. What could happen in fourteen days?

6

'Now, sir, would we like another dish of porridge?'
Alice smiled sweetly at the toothless leer of Old Todd,
a travelling salesman who stopped at the Moon at least
once a month, making him the inn's most regular guest.
She swore if he slapped her bottom one more time, she
would accidently spill his porridge right down the front
of his throbbing breeches. That would cool his ardour
for a while, dirty old man!

She'd only been at the Moon a week when Old
Todd, whose lecherous eyes never missed a single move
she made, caught her putting some bits of bacon in her
apron pocket. Just a few offcuts she was planning to
give to Will so he wouldn't go hungry; they had more
food in that place than she'd ever seen in her life, and
when she found out they were in the habit of throwing
the offcuts away, she didn't think anyone would mind
if she helped herself. But Old Todd had accused her
of stealing, and then he'd threatened her, saying if she
didn't come to a 'little understanding' with him, he'd
tell Annie Woodhead and then she'd be kicked out on

the street and everyone in the dale would know she was a thief. Left with no choice, Alice had agreed to his 'little understanding' and gone to meet him in the churchyard, where she'd had to endure his fumbling hands on her and his stinking breath. It had been such a relief when he'd packed his bags and departed on his travels, but now he was back, leering at her every time she passed his table. How she hated the sight of him.

Working at the Moon had opened her eyes to a whole new world. But no matter what went on in the bar or under the Moon's roof, it stayed there; tittle-tattle was frowned upon. 'No matter what, keep your mouth closed and get on with your job,' Mrs Woodhead had told her. Alice had never worked so hard in her life, but still she was thankful for a roof over her head and a full stomach. Annie Woodhead was proving to be a good cook and a fair boss; she always made sure that Alice got her meals and had her privacy in the evening, when all the jobs were done.

Her only break was on a Sunday afternoon, when she could do as she pleased. Usually that meant spending time with Will, catching up on the week's events. Wednesdays were spent at the manor; though she'd never have believed it in the light of their stormy first meeting, Nancy Frankland had turned out to be Alice's saviour. Although she had a temper and sometimes did not get out of her bed, now that Alice understood the pain, both physical and mental, that tormented that petite body, she was prepared to make allowances. She was convinced that if she could only persuade Nancy to leave the manor occasionally and join her in visiting some of her favourite haunts it would do the poor girl the world of good. As it was, she would settle for enticing her out of her bedroom and down the stairs . . .

Her thoughts were interrupted by a hand grabbing at her skirts as she collected the empty dishes from Old Todd's table. Alice flinched, but much as she hated him, she knew she daren't upset him. She'd been naive enough to believe that if she submitted to his 'little understanding' it would only be the once. Now she knew better: he had a hold on her and he wasn't going to let her forget it.

'What about it, lass – fancy doing an old man a favour for an extra bob or two?' Drooling at the thought of sex with a young virgin, he wiped his toothless mouth on his sleeve, smearing saliva over his chin.

Feeling sick at the thought of the old lecher's hands on her, Alice retreated to the safety of the main bar.

'Is Mr Todd giving you bother, Alice? He's always been an old devil where the lasses are concerned. I wouldn't mind, but his daughters are about your age. If only his wife knew. I bet he's up to his tricks in every pub in the district.' Annie Woodhead gave the culprit a discreet glance, watching him check his pocket watch while he finished his breakfast tea. 'I'll have words, if you want?' she whispered.

'You'll do no such thing, Annie Woodhead!' snapped Uriah, whose hearing was sharp enough when it suited him. 'That's what keeps the randy old devil coming back to us – he still thinks he's a young stallion. Besides, Alice can handle him, can't you, girl?' He winked at her and smiled.

'I can handle Mr Todd. I just wish he'd realize how daft he makes himself look. Has he no respect for his wife and family?'

'While the cat's away, the mice will play – surely you should know that?' Uriah winked at her again and nodded at Mr Todd's empty teapot.

Annie gasped. 'Uriah Woodhead! Is that what you think? Well, let me tell you, there will be no playing around when I'm here – or away – so you can think on.' Annie slammed her tea towel on the counter. 'You go and fill his teapot, Uriah – I bet he won't feel your bottom, dirty old devil!'

Still fuming, she watched as her husband went to ask the offending customer if he needed more tea. 'That'll teach him to make light of men's advances. You can't trust any man, lass, no matter how honourable they might seem. I feel I owe you that advice, seeing your mother's not alive, bless her soul.'

'Don't worry, Mrs Woodhead. Old Todd's 'armless enough. I reckon he just fancies his chances, but he's playing the wrong game with me – I'm waiting for Mr Right. He must be tall, good-looking and, above all, wealthy, because I never want to be poor again.'

'Aye, lass, we have all wanted one of them in our time. Trouble is, you get what you're given or what your heart determines. Take me and Uriah – his mother and mine fixed us two up. They knew that I could cook and that he'd inherit the Moon one day, so we were lined up for one another as soon as we left school. Never mind love and looks; they didn't enter into it. But after a while you come to feel a bit of something about one another.' Seeing her young helper gazing out into the yard as she wiped the pots, obviously lost in daydreams about Mr Right, Annie laughed. 'Have you been out with a lad yet, Alice?'

Alice shook her head.

'That young Jack Alderson always looks so sweet on you – I'm surprised he hasn't asked you out.'

'Jack? Jack Alderson? Oh! The thought of it!' Alice turned her nose up in disgust. 'Him and our Will are best friends – they'd talk about me. Besides, he hasn't any money.'

'Money isn't everything, miss, just remember that. And don't you be so haughty about Jack. He's a grand lad, and his father has a good farm at the top of the dale. It's their own, too, so they'll not be short of a bob or two. Aye, think on, young lady. All too often them that flash the cash are the ones with nothing in their bank balance – take it from one who knows.'

Hands on hips, Annie Woodhead glared at her young employee. She hadn't realized that the girl was so shallow. Who did she think she was? With no family to speak of and no real roof over her head, Alice Bentham could do a lot worse than young Jack. It was high time she realized that beggars can't be choosers.

The more Annie thought about it, the more riled she got. She was even beginning to wonder whether taking the young orphan in had been such a good idea.

Sensing Annie's outrage, Alice kept her head down and focused on cleaning the pumps and wiping the bar down. She hadn't meant to cause offence, but when the woman started trying to pair her off with Jack . . . well, it just didn't bear thinking about. No, her sights were set on something better than a common farm lad. Mind you, she hadn't realized that Jack's dad owned his own farm; she'd always thought it was rented, like theirs had been. Perhaps it wouldn't hurt to be nicer to Jack – after all, he did blush every time he talked to her, and it was true that he never seemed short of a bob or two. She'd ask after him on Sunday when she met Will. Right now, though, she needed to come up with a quick excuse to leave the bar for a few minutes – and it would only be a few minutes, she thought grimly, rubbing the brass foot rest with vigour.

'Just going to pick up the bread from Mason's, Mrs Woodhead. Shan't be long.' Without waiting for a reply, she grabbed her shawl and basket and darted out of the bar. Sooner she got there, the sooner it would be over.

As she hurried to the secret rendezvous place, Alice's stomach heaved with revulsion at what was to come. Still, if that was the price of his silence, what choice did she have? The prospect of being branded a thief and the whole village getting to hear about it was far more terrifying than the thought of the old man pawing at her.

Her footsteps echoing on the cobbles, she turned into the deserted churchyard. What kind of man chose a church for such a disgusting purpose as these 'little understandings'?

'So, you've made it, bonny lass,' came a voice from the side entrance of the church. 'I knew tha would.'

Alice looked at the disgusting old man, the bulge in his trousers fighting to be released. He must have been fumbling with himself while he waited for her. When he reached out to stroke the side of her face, she couldn't help but cringe.

'Now, lass, remember our arrangement: if you keep quiet, I'll keep quiet. And don't forget, there's a florin in it for you . . .'

He pushed her back against the granite church wall, fumbling with the buttons on his breeches, his breathing heavy with excitement. Thoughts rushed through Alice's head, cutting out reality as he pulled her skirts up and tugged her bloomers down. His fingers caressed her intimate parts, making her quiver and causing him to lose control. He tried to thrust his tired manhood into her, but in a repeat of last month's performance, he was too late. Anticipation had got the better of him. His moment had come and gone, leaving him weak and embarrassed.

To Alice's relief, he hurriedly buttoned his breeches, hiding the offending organ, and then reached into his waistcoat pocket. His face was ruddy and his breath was short as he pressed the florin into Alice's palm.

'Remember, lass – you say nothing, I say nothing. I'm back next month, so you can earn yourself another bob or two.'

With that he slipped away, leaving Alice feeling sick and disgusted with herself. She pulled up her bloomers and adjusted her skirts, then leaned against the church wall, her body shaking, the florin clutched in her hand. No matter how she tried to justify her actions, a niggling voice kept telling her that she was no better than a common whore, taking the old man's money. She knew her parents would be ashamed of her, firstly for stealing, but more so for letting a dirty old man touch her. A tear trickled down her cheek and she rubbed it away with the back of her hand.

Sticking her head out of the doorway to make sure he was gone, she did her best to compose herself before heading to the baker's to pick up the bread. The shiny florin was still clutched in her hand. She'd been certain that everything would go the same as it had the previous month: all over in no time and him incapable of anything more than a bit of fumbling. But even so, was it really worth a florin and his silence? If she told the Woodheads about the bacon, and explained that she hadn't meant to steal from them, that she'd only been trying to look after Will, perhaps they would understand. The way she saw it, it was Old Todd who was in the wrong, taking advantage of a young girl who was down on her luck.

If he tried to blackmail her again, she promised herself that she would tell Annie. Surely she would understand?

It was a beautiful summer's day. The sun shone, dragonflies skimmed and darted over the glittering river – and best of all it was a Sunday, so Alice could lie back in the long meadow grass amid the smell of new-mown hay instead of being cooped up in the Moon.

'Yes! Yes! Our Ali, did you see that?' Will's voice rang out from the direction of the river, where he was playing 'ducks and drakes'. 'Seven leaps with one stone, right across to the other side of the Dee. Bet you can't do that!'

'When are you going to grow up, Will? Skimming stones is for kids.' Alice was in no mood for her brother. She was having a hard time driving horrible thoughts of Old Todd from her head, and here was Will, so full of himself after his week with Jack at Stone House marble works that he hadn't even noticed how unhappy she was.

'Pardon me for breathing! What's up with you, my lady? You used to enjoy playing in the river. Besides, it's Sunday – we've got the whole afternoon to ourselves, nobody breathing down our bloody necks.' He picked a buttercup and tickled his growling sister under the chin with it. Furious, she snatched the flower out of his hand.

'I'm fed up with having no home, no money and no say in where my life is going. I don't want to be a serving girl in a pub with part-time work at the manor. I want to be looked after, have fine clothes, maids and servants and a gentleman husband.' Alice crossed her legs and pulled her skirt over them, then lay on her back, the sun's rays filtering through her eyelashes, dreaming of the things she could do if she only had money.

'Well, hard luck, our lass – you're stuck here with me.' Alice was forever harping on about wanting fine this and fancy that. Sometimes it seemed to Will that all his little sister thought about was brass. 'If I'd known my company was going to be such a disappointment, I'd not have bothered coming. I should have gone shooting with Jack instead.'

Alice sat up quickly, bushing the buttercup debris from her bodice. 'How is Jack? He wasn't at the manor when I called on Miss Nancy.'

'He's all right. Why the sudden interest? Usually you don't look the side he's on.'

'I've missed his friendly face, that's all. And I was thinking, since he has such a kind disposition, perhaps I could entice Nancy downstairs next week so that she could meet him – I'm sure she gets fed up of my face. Of course, I'd have to get Lord Frankland's permission first.'

'Hark at you: "a kind disposition"! You mean he's soft.' Will was taken aback as much by his sister's change in attitude as her newly acquired vocabulary. Alice never had a good word for his best mate. It was the opposite with Jack; he was always asking for news of Alice. 'Any road, you'll not be seeing Jack or his lordship next week. Jack'll be at the marble works with me, and his lordship's away in Russia until the end of the week. And when he does return, first thing he'll want to do is see us.' Seeing the effect his words were having on Alice, Will decided to antagonize her further by playing up his newfound importance: 'Me and Jack are his lordship's right-hand men at the moment. We have a lot to report. He'll not have time for you.'

'You two – his lordship's right-hand men? Since when!' Alice sat up.

'As I've been telling you for the last hour, since he's had us up at Stone House watching what goes on there. And by God, is he going to be altering things when we tell him what's happening up there. Do you ever listen to a word I tell you?'

'Not if I don't have to. It's always "Me and Jack this . . . Me and Jack that . . ." I just shut it all out.'

Alice primly smoothed down her hair and then put her hat on as if she were preparing to depart. Ever since she was a baby, Will had been able to gauge her mood by the set of her chin; when it was set firm – as it was now – there was no reasoning with her. He took out his pocket watch and glanced at the time.

'I can see I'm wasting my breath here.' Slipping the watch back into his waistcoat, he picked up his cap and set it on his head. 'The trouble with you, our Alice, is you think of nothing but yourself. If you'd bothered to listen, you'd know the work I've been doing at Stone House could very well lead to something better. By the end of the week, when his lordship comes back, I know for certain there'll be one out of work up there. And he's in a cottage that might just do us two – that is, if you can be bothered to live in a two-up two-down.'

Alice said nothing, just sat and watched him as he turned away from her, thumbs in waistcoat pockets and his cap at a jaunty angle, and set off along the riverbank. When he got to the bridge, he raised his hand in a wave. She didn't bother to wave back. Let him stew. Always going on about his life, couldn't be bothered to ask about her. She tore off tufts of grass and threw them in the river, watching as they were carried by the current, veering round stones and whirling in giddy circles. All the while, Will's words echoed in her ears, bringing back memories of another occasion when she'd been told that she thought only of herself: the day her mother died, the day her father had shouted at her for hiding up the fell while her mother lay dying. Was she so selfish? She didn't think so. She was trying to make the best of her life, that's all.

Tears welling in her eyes, Alice pulled her feet together and wrapped her arms around her knees, slowly rocking her body back and forth. She felt so lonely: nobody in the world to look after her, and now she'd upset Will on their afternoon off. Her and her big mouth and sulky moods!

There had been times when the only thing that kept Will and Jack at Stone House was the knowledge that on Lord Frankland's return O'Hara would be brought to account for his brutal, tyrannical behaviour. Finally the two weeks had come to an end and they could stop counting the days: this morning they would make their report.

They had decided to talk to his lordship at the manor rather than risk being overheard at the marble works. As they sat on the kitchen-garden wall awaiting his summons, Will could see that Jack was nervous. He was nervous himself; from the moment Lord Frankland had given them their orders, they'd known that a difficult choice lay ahead. Spying for their employer didn't sit easy with them; it went against the grain to run to the boss telling tales. What's more, though he hadn't dared lay a hand on them over the past fortnight, O'Hara had watched them like a hawk, his menacing presence and reputation for violence sufficient to remind them that they would suffer if they didn't keep quiet.

'I say we tell him exactly how it is, every last detail.' Jack couldn't hide how he felt about the foul-mouthed foreman. After devoting much of the fortnight to tending the horse and trying to nurse it back to health, he hated its abuser with a vengeance.

'If you don't, I'm certainly going to. Once his lordship hears about all those illegal money-making schemes, I bet you anything he'll have O'Hara gone by the end of the day. It's small wonder that Stone House isn't making any profit.'

'Aye, he'll lose his job, all right. And then the

bastard will come after us. He'll break our necks for telling on him.'

Knowing the truth of this, they both fell silent. They remained that way for some time, until Will decided to break the gloom by introducing a lighter topic of conversation.

'I don't know what got into our Ali last Sunday. One minute she was in the mood from hell, and the next – you'll not believe this, Jack – she actually asked after you! She can be a funny bugger sometimes, our lass.' Will kicked his heels against the kitchen-garden wall.

'What did she say? Is she missing seeing me at the manor?' Will blushed from head to toe.

'Aye, she did say she missed you. She was thinking of introducing you to Miss Nancy – rather you than me! Two crazy women together? Good luck with that, mate.' Will grinned and slapped him on the back.

'Will, I've been thinking about this for a while now . . . Would you mind if I asked your sister to take a walk with me one evening, or perhaps on Sunday when she has more time?' Jack stared at his feet and shuffled the gravel underneath them, not daring to look his best friend in the face.

'You what? Our lass? Get away! God, you must be a glutton for punishment, either that or you're light in the head, man! Do you honestly mean it? Because if you do, I suppose I'd better say you can. Not that it's up to me – she's her own woman, our Ali. I daren't tell her anything. You'll soon find that out yourself.'

'Cheers, Will. I've kept looking at her and thinking how bonny she is.' Jack beamed.

'Man, I don't want to know! She's my sister – just you remember that.' Will grinned.

He was still smirking at the thought of Jack walking out with Alice when the kitchen door opened and Lord Frankland appeared.

'Gentlemen, would you care to join me?'

Jack and Will followed him in, stopping just inside the door. They felt awkward in the unfamiliar surroundings, and both were aware of Mrs Dowbiggin casting sideways glances at them as she scuttled around the kitchen.

'Sit down.' Lord Frankland nodded at the kitchen chairs around the large pine table in the centre of the room. He turned to the housekeeper: 'That'll be all, Mrs Dowbiggin. Can you make yourself scarce for an hour – I need to talk to these two young men.'

'Yes, sir.' She curtsied. 'But I hope you don't mind when lunch is late.'

It was unheard of for the master to bring outside staff into the manor. And what was so important that he wanted to deprive her of her beloved kitchen for a whole hour? Unable to contain her curiosity, Mrs Dowbiggin loitered at the kitchen door after closing it, hoping to eavesdrop on their conversation.

Gerald Frankland smiled at both young men and raised his finger to his mouth, warning them not to say a word. Then he swung open the door that Mrs Dowbiggin had just departed through.

'Hello, Hilda – was there something you'd forgotten?' He'd learned from experience that in the manor, walls had ears in the shape of Mrs Dowbiggin. This was something he did not want her to know about. Red-faced and stuttering, the housekeeper took off along the corridor.

Lord Frankland closed the door behind her. Pulling up a chair, he sat opposite them and leaned across the table.

'Right, men – tell me how it is. I want the truth, mind. No half-cocked stories or unfounded gossip, and no keeping things back out of loyalty to any of the men up there. The whole truth and nothing but the truth – and if I get it, you shall both reap the benefits of my gratitude.' He fixed them with his gaze, reading their faces as if trying to judge whether his instincts about them had been correct. 'I know I left you in an awkward situation, but since you've both survived to tell the tale, I obviously made the right decision.'

Will and Jack looked at one another. It was time to tell him all, but where to start?

'Most of the men at Stone House are good workers – rough around the edges, but they work.' Will was the first to speak. 'Your main trouble is O'Hara. Jack here will back me up when I say you can't trust him as far as you can throw him.' Jack nodded in agreement. 'He never pulls his weight; he's always drunk; he has numerous little deals on the side, where he gets a part payment from a customer in return for not telling you what he's supplying them with.'

Frankland's face darkened and Will paused, expecting to be interrupted, but his lordship merely nodded for him to carry on.

'O'Hara lends money to the workers up there and charges them a high rate of interest, threatening them with losing their jobs if he doesn't get his money. We haven't seen the books that his wife keeps, but one of the workers told me that there's one lot with the true figures and then the one that she gives you.'

Will stopped. Beside him, Jack had remained quiet, watching anxiously as their employer's expression went from stern to thunderous. By the time Will had finished, Lord Frankland looked as if he was going to explode.

The chair legs scraped across the polished floor tiles as he sprang to his feet and began pacing back and forth between the window and the table, pounding his fist into his hand.

'Damn the man! I knew he was up to something. Damn him to hell, he's taken advantage long enough. And you say his wife keeps two sets of records? My God, I'll make him pay. I'll have him off my property before this day's out.' Suddenly he paused in his rant, a look of concern on his face. 'Has he done anything to disrupt your activities while you were there, or made threats? I dare say he'll want to get even with the pair of you when he realizes his days of easy money have come to an end.'

'Mostly he's kept his distance from us,' said Jack. 'Apart from a couple of times when he cursed me for looking after the horse and not letting him take it out. Bloody criminal, the way he treated the poor creature.' Jack wanted the abuse O'Hara had inflicted on the horse to be taken into account.

Their conversation was halted when the kitchen door was abruptly flung open and one of the workers from Stone House rushed in. He pulled up when he saw them, and for a moment just stood there, struggling to breathe after his long run, while they looked on dumbstruck. Then he drew in a great lungful of air and, twisting his cap in his hand, turned to Lord Frankland.

'Begging your pardon, sir, but come quick, sir, please, come quick. It's O'Hara – he's threatening to kill some of the men and he's set his cottage on fire. He's gone mad, sir – he's gone mad!'

With Jack and Will at his heels, Gerald ran to the stables. The three of them rode as fast as they could, but by the time they reached the top of the dale it was clear the fire had taken hold. Smoke from the burning cottage could be seen billowing and clinging to the treetops all the way down the valley. The heat and smell of the fire striking fear into their souls, they tethered their horses a safe distance away and made for the cottage. Before them was a scene of absolute chaos. Men were dashing backwards and forwards from the nearby stream with buckets of water in an effort to put out the blaze, but it looked as if their efforts would be in vain. The flames were leaping into the air, licking at the upper bedroom windows. Choking thick black smoke made it difficult to see, but they could hear the horse in the stable across the yard frantically trying to kick down the door in an effort to escape.

Dodging the bucket-laden workers, Jack ran to the stable. Shrugging off his jacket, he opened the door. The horse's eyes were wild, its nostrils flaring in fright. Jack used his jacket to cover the horse's head so that he could lead it away to safety.

In the meantime Gerald Frankland had swiftly taken command, ordering his workers to form a human chain passing buckets of water to combat the fire. Suddenly a shout went up: one of the men thought he caught a glimpse of Mrs O'Hara at an upstairs window. Flames were climbing the curtains and the windowpane exploded with the intensity of the heat. This was immediately followed by a series of booms and an almighty rumble as the timber rafters collapsed and the roof came crashing down with a great cloud of smoke. If O'Hara's wife had been in there, it was too late to save her.

'Stand back, men, stand back!' Stripped to his shirt, sweat pouring off his brow, Gerald Frankland ordered his men clear. When the smoke subsided, all that remained of the cottage was a smouldering shell. 'Don't bother with the cottage, men – it's gone. Keep the outbuildings wet; at least we can save them!'

As he set about reorganizing the human chain, a voice rang out, making itself heard above the raging fire and the frenzied efforts to put it out. 'You, ya bastard! I'm going to kill you!'

All eyes turned to the stocky figure of O'Hara, standing with a shotgun aimed at Frankland's head.

Gerald stood, frozen with fear. Trying hard to control the tremor in his voice, he attempted to reason with the man. 'Don't do it, man. There's nothing to be gained by shooting me. You're in enough trouble already – you've killed your wife and burned my cottage down. If you put the gun down—'

'I've nothing to lose, then, have I? No home, no wife – I'm left with bloody nothing all because you had to send your spies in and get 'em to tell tales about me – snivelling bastards!'

Raising the shotgun level with his eye, he took aim at Gerald Frankland's forehead and pressed his finger on the trigger.

Helpless, Frankland closed his eyes, waiting for the bullet that would end his life. A shot rang out, breaking the silence, and the whole scene stopped still. It was a few seconds before Frankland dared to open his eyes. Only then did he realize that the shot had not been fired by O'Hara and the bullet had not been for him.

His shotgun half cocked and still smoking, Will was standing over the writhing body of O'Hara. 'Thought I'd better fetch my gun, sir. I knew that there'd be trouble.'

Will looked on in disgust as O'Hara, now screaming abuse and yelling in pain from the shot to his leg, was bundled into the works buggy by the men he'd tormented for so long. Frankland gave orders that he be taken to Dent police station; the doctor could attend to him there.

'I hope I'll not be charged, sir. It was either his leg or your head.'

'You'll not be charged, Will, I'll see to that. I owe you my life, and I'll not forget it. I owe you dearly.' Gerald Frankland grasped Will's hand and shook it. He was indeed grateful to the lad whom he had so recently made homeless.

Turning from Will, he surveyed the smouldering buildings and the blackened faces of the workers looking to him for orders. What to do now? Would the place ever be the same again? He couldn't help wondering whether he had brought all this on himself by not doing his own dirty work. Perhaps if he hadn't gone to Russia, things would have gone differently. But when the lovely Tatiana sent for him, he was powerless to resist. Even in the midst of all this devastation, the memory of her smile, the feeling of her hand touching his skin and those dark eyes gazing into his as she implored him to stay had the power to drive all else from his mind.

The crash of an outbuilding collapsing jolted him back to reality. Seeing his property reduced to charred piles of rubble brought back other, less pleasant memories of Russia. He had been on his way back from England when his parents' house was burned down, but the embers were still smouldering next day when he arrived, and he was present when their remains were found in the ashes. That fire, too, had been started as an act of revenge by Frankland employees. Was history repeating itself?

He feared what would happen were Nancy to hear of today's events. She would surely lose her mind completely if she learned of the fire, let alone how close her brother had come to being killed. The poor girl had been making such good progress since becoming friends with young Alice Bentham. He smiled at the thought of the feisty young farm girl. From the very first time he'd spoken to her in the small kitchen of Dale End, he'd felt drawn to her. Not that she was particularly pretty – if anything, she was rather plain, and she had none of the allure or refinement of his Tatiana – yet something about her brought a smile to his lips.

Again it took a sudden noise in the yard to break his reverie. His mind seemed to be all over the place – perhaps it was an after-effect of the shock. Those moments he'd spent staring into the barrel of O'Hara's gun had been the most unnerving of his life.

Summoning Will and Jack to his side, he told them: 'Go home, the pair of you – you've been through enough today. I'll see you both in the morning.'

'But what about the police?' said Will. 'Shouldn't I wait for them to get here?'

'I'll speak to them. No doubt they will need to talk to you, but it doesn't have to be right away. When you do speak to them, I want you to say exactly what

99

happened – we have nothing to hide. Go on, now – get yourselves home.'

Frankland waited until Will and Jack were out of sight before gathering his remaining workers together. Those two lads had seen enough already; he didn't want them to be on hand for the unpleasant task that lay ahead.

'Right, men, I'm afraid we have a grim job in store. We need to go through what's left of the cottage until we find the remains of Mrs O'Hara.' He gazed around him at the smoke rising from the rubble, and the weary, ashen faces of his workers. Under his breath, he added: 'Poor woman – she might have been crooked, but she didn't deserve this.'

Will and Jack were only too relieved to leave the smoke and misery behind. Never in their wildest dreams had they imagined that their activities of the last two weeks would end in such destruction and heartbreak. O'Hara had obviously cracked at the prospect of his world falling apart, but for him to set the cottage alight with his wife in it was unthinkable.

Having ridden to the manor in stunned silence, they unsaddled their horses and then took their leave of each other, for both were in need of some time alone.

Will retreated to his bunk bed above the stable. He'd never shot a man before – still couldn't believe what he'd done. Though he knew he'd done the only thing he could do in the circumstances, he couldn't stop wondering what would have happened if his aim

100

hadn't been sure. What if he'd killed O'Hara? Would he be up on a charge of murder? He tossed and turned, replaying the scene in his head, worrying about what would happen when the police came, until finally sleep overtook him. The next thing he knew, it was night. He got out of bed, shivering from the cold, and looked out of the window. The lamps were lit at the manor, so he made his way to the kitchen door, hoping that Mrs Dowbiggin might be persuaded to give him something to eat – it had been a long time since breakfast.

When she opened the door, her face told him what he must look like.

'Come in, lad, come in! Master told me what you've done for him today. Get yourself over there and sit down – I've saved you some cold mutton, and there's pickle and fresh bread to go with it.' Hilda Dowbiggin scurried around, fetching things from the larder and fussing over him. 'And when you've eaten, let's get you out of those clothes – they reek of smoke. I'm sure Master won't mind if I run you a bath upstairs and find you some of his old clothes. I'm sure we can find something that'll fit you and he said I was to get you anything you needed.'

Will sat at the end of the table chewing the mutton, enjoying the warmth of the kitchen. He felt much better with a full stomach. What he didn't feel comfortable with was having a bath upstairs in the manor's new bathroom. He was used to having a wash in the tin bath once every six months – if that. Apart from the folk at the manor, he didn't know anyone who had a room just for taking baths in. The only reason he knew there were such things was because of Alice; she'd explained all about it and told him that she expected she'd have one in her house one day. That girl was forever going on about her wants and needs. Why couldn't she be content with her lot? With a rueful shake of his head, Will leaned back into the chair and was just stretching his legs and making himself comfortable when Mrs Dowbiggin came bustling in.

'Come on, then, stir your shanks – the bath's run. I've put some of Master's old clothes out ready for you, and there's some soap in the dish that'll sweeten you up.'

She ushered him through the hallway and upstairs. Never had Will been in such a room. Through the steam he could see gleaming tiles on the walls and floor, a big bath with gold taps, and all the amenities that went with a modern bathroom. He ran his hand in the foaming water of the bath and sniffed the newly laundered towels.

'Well, get your clothes off and then I can wash them.' Mrs Dowbiggin stood at the doorway, waiting for him to strip. 'You haven't got anything I haven't seen before, young man, so there's nothing there that'll surprise me.'

Will stood there blushing. He had no intention of undressing in front of the housekeeper. For one thing, she'd a reputation for gossip and he didn't want the entire dale to know about his privates.

'Shy, are we? All right, I'll wait outside and you can

pass them to me.' Sniggering to herself, she stepped out of the room leaving the door ajar. Will stripped off quickly, wrinkling his nose at the stink of smoke that clung to his garments, then bundled everything up and stuck his hand through the gap in the door. As soon as he felt her take the bundle from him, he quickly closed the door and listened until he heard her depart, chuckling to herself as she went.

Gingerly, Will dipped his toes into the foaming bath, followed by the rest of his body. It was bliss; the warm waters floated around his body, making all his aches and pains disappear. This was a far cry from the old tin bath in front of the fire. For once, he could understand Alice's longing for the life of a toff.

What a day! If someone had told him as he sat on the kitchen-garden wall that morning that by the day's end he'd have shot a man, soaked his weary bones in the manor's bathroom and would shortly be wearing his lordship's clothes, he'd have laughed in their face. His mind lulled into relaxation by the warm and fragrant waters, he was just beginning to lose himself in dreams when he heard the bathroom doorknob turn. He quickly grabbed one of the white Christy towels from the edge of the bath.

'Oh, I beg your pardon. I didn't realize my brother had guests and that someone was using the bathroom. It is customary to lock the door.' Averting her eyes, the intruder quickly withdrew.

So that was Nancy. Though he'd heard a few of her tantrums, Will had never actually seen her. From the fleeting glimpse he'd caught of her, she was beautiful, nothing like the witch he'd imagined. And she didn't sound mad either. Perhaps Alice was right for once and Nancy was just lonely and grieving. It had certainly been a day full of surprises.

Feeling naked and vulnerable, he hastily climbed out of the bath and arranged the towel around him while he put on his lordship's cast-offs. They were in better condition than the clothes Will had given Mrs Dowbiggin to wash, and not a bad fit either. He admired himself in the mirror: in this get-up, he could pass for gentry. Wait until he saw Jack in the morning!

Hoping not to encounter anyone else in the meantime, Will quietly opened the bathroom door and crept downstairs to the safe haven of the kitchen.

'Well, you scrub up decent, young Will Bentham.' Mrs Dowbiggin put her hands on her hips and looked him up and down. 'If I was twenty-one again, I'd be trying to catch your eye! Now go on out of my kitchen, 'cos this old bird's off to bed. It's been a long day and unlike you young 'uns, I know when I'm tired.'

As he stepped out of the kitchen door into the night air, his hair still damp from the bath with the sweet smell of the soap clinging to his skin, Will was wondering whether his new appearance would result in girls trying to catch his eye. With Jack intending to start courting Alice, perhaps it was time he found a nice young lady for himself.

In the stable yard, bats were emerging from their hiding places, screeching as they caught insects on the wing. Will paused to watch them. Tomorrow he knew he'd have to answer to the police, and no doubt Gerald Frankland would want to talk to him again. Yet the prospect of these encounters no longer troubled him. For tonight, he was going to bed clean, well fed and thinking of that fleeting glance of Nancy.

7

Alice sat on the rough granite trough at the base of the drinking fountain, her hand idly playing with the water as it trickled cold and clear into the sparkling pool. The church clock was striking one o'clock, its huge bell announcing the hour to the people of Dent as it had done for centuries. Where was he? There she was, all dressed up in her Sunday best, and he was keeping her waiting. Jack always had been one for doing things in his own time. She kicked her heels against the fountain and adjusted her hat for the fifth or sixth time, fidgeting with her cotton gloves as she sighed and gazed up the road in the direction of Jack's home.

'Have you been forgotten, Alice, or has he thought better of it?' Uriah Woodhead shouted across at his young employee as he stood on the Moon's step, wiping his hands on his apron.

'Looks that way, Mr Woodhead.' Alice sighed and crossed her arms on her lap. 'It's typical of Jack. Him and my brother would forget their heads if they weren't screwed on.'

'He'll turn up soon, lass. He'll have forgotten the time, if I have to bet on it.' Uriah smiled and disappeared into the dark interior of the pub where there were customers waiting to be served.

Alice still wasn't sure why she was spending her precious afternoon off sitting on the fountain's edge waiting for her brother's best friend. She cast her mind back to the previous Friday when Jack had come into the Moon with her brother. The pair of them often came in for a pint or two on a Friday night, so it hadn't struck her as anything out of the ordinary. But on this occasion Jack had downed several pints, and then – in front of her jeering brother and all the Moon's regulars – he had turned to her, stuttering and blushing, and asked her to join him for a stroll the following Sunday. There was no way she could have said no, not in front of all those people. How could he have put her in such an embarrassing position? Why couldn't he have asked discreetly? As for Will, she could have hit him for six when he offered to be chaperone – the whole pub had laughed at that. She tugged her hat down around her head, brushing her burning red cheeks in an effort to get rid of her blushing. And after all that, here she was, sitting outside the church like a stood-up wallflower. Knowing Jack Alderson, the whole thing was probably a joke at her expense. More than likely Will had put him up to it. She wished she hadn't kept asking after Jack every Sunday, but since the fire up at Stone House she'd been worried about them both.

Having decided she'd waited long enough and might

as well go on a walk by herself, Alice was about to set off along the churchyard path when Jack came racing up in his horse and trap, the wheels nearly sparking on the cobbles in his haste not to be too late.

'Whoa there, whoa, Patsy.' Jack jumped out of the trap and ran towards her, his jacket flapping and his cap falling to the ground. Pausing to scoop up his cap, he rushed to where Alice stood.

'I'm sorry, Alice. I'm sorry I'm late. I was grooming Patsy, and before I knew it, it was one o'clock already.' Walking back to the horse, he patted it lovingly on its withers, then smiled apologetically at a glowering Alice.

'That's just typical, Jack Alderson – a horse taking the place of me. I've a good mind not to bother walking out with you.' She stuck her chin out and turned to pretend to show interest in the red roses that were growing on the churchyard wall.

'By 'eck, you are bonny when you're in a mood.' Jack couldn't stop himself, though he immediately regretted even thinking it let alone saying it out loud.

Alice turned sharply. 'Jack Alderson, you stand me up and then you accuse me of being in a mood. What sort of a date is this?' She started walking over the cobbles pretending to be heading back into the Moon. 'You can think again if you think I'm walking with you.'

'But, Alice, I've made us a picnic. I thought we could go in the trap up along the high road and picnic by Nellie's Bridge, and then perhaps call off at the

108

manor to see Will.' Jack held tight to the reins of the impatient horse while beckoning Alice to join him.

Alice stopped in her tracks; she loved going along the high road. It was the old drover road where two dales met, and the views up there were magnificent: on a good clear day you could even see the Irish Sea. She turned round and looked at the fretting face of Jack.

'Well, if you've gone to all that trouble, I suppose it wouldn't hurt to come with you. It's only this once, mind.' She pulled up her skirts, giving Jack a glimpse of her ankle while he held her hand as she mounted the trap. She could see him hide his blushes as he got Patsy underway with a quick swish of the whip in the air. Alice held on tight to the wooden seat as it rattled out of the cobbled streets of Dent and joined the narrow track that led up to the fellside. They were silent on the way up the winding track, the horse taking its time and Jack watching Alice's face as she took in the spectacular views unfolding with every turn of the trap's wheel.

'I thought you'd like it up here,' said Jack. 'You can see for miles and it's so quiet apart from sheep and skylarks.'

Alice sat gazing around her, holding on to her hat as the mountain breezes played with it, until finally she gave up and untied it, placing it on her lap, letting her blonde hair blow free across her face.

'I love it up here, Jack – it's so wild and free, and look, you can see the sea.' She pointed at a distant glitter of shining blue between the rolling dales. 'How I wish I could go to the sea. I've never been. My father always promised to take me, but we never got to go.' Her voice trailed off, remembering happier times.

'I love the smell of the peat,' said Jack. 'And the way when you breathe in the fresh air, it makes you feel good. I often come up here if I've something on my mind. It helps me to settle.'

He stopped the horse and trap and the young couple sat for a while, the warmth of the summer's sun on their faces, gazing out at the beautiful sprawling countryside that was their home. Above them the skylarks hovered and sang as they rode the moorland breezes. Below them in the valley, fields of mown grass lay drying in the sunshine, making hay for the winter months ahead. The tranquillity and the warm, pleasant breeze made them feel at ease, content in their own company. The horse chomped on its bit, impatient and wondering why its journey had been interrupted for no apparent reason.

'Do you know, Jack, it's my birthday. I'm seventeen today, but you're the only one who knows, 'cos our Will has forgotten and I've not told anybody else. Last year's birthday seems a million years ago. So much has changed. I miss my mum and dad, and sometimes I feel so alone.' Alice sniffed into her handkerchief and stifled the tears that she could feel welling up. 'There now, I'm even spoiling this beautiful day out with you because I'm feeling sorry for myself.' She sniffed again and swallowed hard, regaining her dignity and pretending not to care.

'Now, Alice, you know we are all fond of you.

110

You've been through the worst twelve months that anyone could have gone through. And as for your birthday, Will hasn't forgotten that it's today. That's why I've picked you up in the horse and trap – we have a surprise waiting for you. Nay, now I've said too much. I promised Will I wouldn't let the cat out of the bag, so stop snivelling and let's be off. Besides, Patsy's had enough of this standing around. She's a bit like thee: no patience. Why I want to spend my time with the pair of you, I don't know!'

'Jack Alderson, are you likening me to a horse? And what's this surprise? Oh, go on, Jack, tell me, please tell me. I thought you had all forgotten!' Alice was bouncing in her seat with excitement. She had thought that it was going to be just another day. Lately they had all seemed to run into one another, and even she had been taken by surprise when she realized that it was Midsummer Day and her birthday.

'I'm not saying another word; you'll just have to wait. But I can say it's something I've never seen either, so we're both in for a surprise today.' Jack flicked the reins and the horse began making its way along the fellside and down the green pathway to the local beauty spot of Nellie's Bridge. In the face of Alice's constant quizzing, he urged the horse to make speed, worried that he might not be able to hold on to the secret until they reached their destination.

Soon they came to the green leafy glades of the riverside, the smell of drying hay drifting in the breeze and the drone of summer bumblebees filling the air as they went about their business of collecting pollen for honey. The meadowsweet, red campion and other hedgerow flowers swayed in the gentle valley breeze and Alice sat back and enjoyed the steady pace of the faithful horse and its driver. She felt content for a change, and she'd made up her mind not to let anything spoil her perfect day. The anger she'd felt towards Jack for being late had given way to anticipation and excitement about what lay in store.

She held on tight as the trap swayed over the rough cobbles of the path that led to the old wooden bridge and the picturesque waterfall that cascaded above it. She could make out the shape of her brother, waving frantically at them as they approached the bridge, but who was the person that stood behind him? Could it be . . . ? Surely not? There was no way that it could be Nancy! How could she be there? She never left the house.

'Well, what do you think of that, then? What's your brother like – he's kept that quiet, hasn't he, the old dog?' Jack blushed and smiled at Alice. 'I've never seen her, but seemingly he met her when he was in the bath with nothing on.'

Alice gasped. 'What was he doing? She's met hardly anyone, let alone our Will in the nude. By, the poor lass – it's not a pleasant sight. I should know, I've filled his tin bath at home often enough.' She covered her mouth, realizing how familiar she had been with Jack.

'Yes, well, it was in a bath he met her . . . But shush now, they'll hear us.' Jack felt awkward. He was the only one who didn't know Nancy and yet he had heard so much about her. He made a conscious effort not to stare at her when he stopped the trap and helped Alice alight to the daisy-covered field.

'I bet this takes you by surprise, eh, Sis?' Will bounded over and hugged his astonished sister.

'Oh, never mind about you giving me a hug,' said Alice, breaking free so she could run to Nancy, who was standing half hidden under a parasol at the edge of the bridge. 'I can't believe you are here!' Forgetting that the Frankland family were her employers, she reached for Nancy's free hand as she would an old friend.

'I took a lot of persuading, Alice. I'm still very nervous – this is my first time outside in company for years. I had forgotten how wonderful fresh air smells, and how much I enjoy good company like your brother's.' Nancy twirled her parasol coyly and lowered her face so as not to look at the smiling Will.

'Our Will – good company? It must be the sunshine gone to your head. He's a big galoot! But still, it's good to see you outside and enjoying the sun. What I want to know is, how did he manage it? I've been trying to tempt you out for weeks and then he flutters his baby-blue eyes and here you are.' Alice smiled, putting one hand on her hip and hitting her brother's shoulder playfully with the other. 'And look at him, all dressed up like a dog's dinner! Where did he buy that suit? I think it's 'cos of him being around the manor so much; he has ideas above his station!'

113

'Never you mind, our lass. What you don't know won't hurt you.' Will smiled and called over to Jack. 'Well, lad, did you manage to keep it to yourself, or did my devious little sister wheedle the secret out of you? And what are you doing back there, hanging about like a bad smell? Come and meet Nancy – you know you want to!'

Will was deliberately playing on his friend's shyness in order to escape telling his sister that he had been keeping Nancy company since the day he had seen her fleetingly in the bathroom. Much to the disgust of the manor's servants – but he really didn't care what they thought or said.

'Pleasure to meet you, Miss Frankland.' Jack reached out his hand in greeting, moving slowly, trying not to look directly at the face of Nancy.

'Please, Jack, call me Nancy. "Miss Frankland" sounds so stuffy, and as we are to picnic together I don't want you to feel on edge with me.' She smiled and shook Jack's hand, looking him straight in the eye, not hiding the fact that her face was scarred.

Alice could not help noticing the change in Nancy. Today she seemed much less embarrassed by her scars; perhaps it was Will's doing. Having him there seemed to be boosting her confidence and making her life a little more worthwhile. She smiled quietly to herself as Will took Nancy's arm and led her to the tablecloth that had been spread out on the meadow floor with a delicious picnic upon it.

'May I, Miss Bentham?' Jack held out his arm for

Alice and grinned, pretending that he, too, was the perfect gentleman.

'I don't mind if I do, Mr Alderson.' Alice took his arm and sat next to Nancy, who was still holding the parasol, both for shade and to shield her scars from prying eyes.

'Isn't it a beautiful day.' Alice leaned back after eating her way through the manor's best pork pie and salmon sandwiches, washed down with home-made lemonade from Jack's mother. 'I wish every day could be like this.'

'Oh, before I forget, I've got a little something for you.' Nancy untied her beautifully embroidered Dorothy bag and took out a small package. 'You admired this so much on the first day we met, the day when I was such a beast . . .' She handed it carefully to Alice. 'It's just a thank you on your birthday for helping me get my life back. Without you I'd still have been dwelling in the past instead of rediscovering the good things in life.'

Alice looked at the gift that Nancy offered her, so delicately wrapped in purple tissue paper, the perfumed smell of sweet violets rising from the wrapping. 'Oh, no, I couldn't, I really couldn't accept this.' Her eyes filled with tears as she unwrapped the gift, the sun shining on the beautiful glittering jewelled wings of the dragonfly comb that she had so admired on her first meeting with Nancy. 'It's too precious, and it's from your Russian past.'

'Exactly, Alice. Time to put the past and Russia

behind me. Besides, it will look so beautiful in that long blonde hair of yours. Won't it, Jack?' Nancy turned and smiled at Jack, turning the scarred side of her face for him to see.

'Yes, yes, it would, it would look good in your hair, Ali.' Jack faltered over his words having finally realizing how badly scarred Nancy was. 'It will suit you down to the ground.'

'Well, if you insist. But really, I shouldn't. It's too fine for a farm girl like me.'

'Nonsense! If you were nothing more than a simple farm girl, my brother would not have asked you to be my companion – believe me, he knows quality when he sees it. Especially now that your brother has asked for me to walk out with him. Gerald is thinking about giving him more responsibility at Stone House marble works – he needs a new foreman and is going to give Will a trial run. Your Will has been an inspiration these last few weeks and I'm sorry I've not mentioned him visiting me on the days I have been with you, but we wanted to keep it a secret.' Nancy patted Alice's hand in apology, but Alice withdrew it sharply.

'You're what, our Will? Going to be foreman at Stone House? When were you going to tell me? I'm stuck working my fingers to the bone at the Moon, and you're planning a life without me. I thought we were going to stick together. And you walking out with Nancy – when were you going to tell me that?' Alice tried to keep calm but she was angry with her brother: he should have been the one to tell her, not Nancy.

'Quiet, our lass. If you've anything to say, tell me tonight when I pop into the Moon after seeing Nancy home. I'll tell you all then, not now in front of Jack and Nancy – you're embarrassing them both.' Will stood up, shook the crumbs from his lap and brushed the grass from the back of his breeches. 'Nancy, would you care for a stroll along the riverbank?' He offered her his arm and Nancy quickly accepted, wanting to be free of the situation she had caused.

Jack and Alice watched the couple walking by the side of the river. Nancy's long white dress seemed to have a mellow haze around it, the buttercups giving it a golden sheen. Dressed in his best bib and tucker, Will was the epitome of the aspiring young gent. They made a perfect couple. You would never guess, just by looking at Will, that he was from working-class stock.

'I can't believe it! What's he playing at, going out with Lord Frankland's sister? Has he lost his senses? My father will be turning in his grave!' Alice removed one of her shoes and started banging the heel on the ground in an effort to let out her pent-up aggression.

'If you're not careful, you'll break that heel, and then you will be in a bad mood.' Jack put his hand on hers to spare the shoe from getting any more anger taken out on it. 'Wait and see what he has to say to you tonight. I'm sure he will tell you all.'

'But he's spoilt the day.' Alice pouted and pushed her foot into the abused shoe.

'No, he hasn't. You should be glad for the pair of

them. Come on, sulky – I'll beat you to the waterfall.' Jack offered Alice his hand and smiled at her surly face as she stood up. He gave her a little shove. 'Race you, sulky.' And then he took off, running to the waterfall.

'Just you wait, Jack Alderson! I'll catch you – that was cheating.'

'I know, but it's stopped you sulking,' he shouted.

Alice caught up with him, panting, her cheeks flushed. Jack took hold of her hand and they both walked onto the ancient wooden bridge. As they leaned over the railings, looking at the sparkling waterfall and dark frothy waters below, their heads were inches apart. They turned to each other and laughed. Suddenly Jack plucked up courage and gently kissed Alice on her lips, whispering, 'Happy birthday, Alice.'

'Jack Alderson, you can just stop that!' Alice cried. 'What do you take me for? This is our first date!' Then she blushed and turned away, but she was blushing with pride and happiness.

Jack grinned at her. He wouldn't have had her say anything else, but he hadn't noticed her struggling when he'd kissed her. By, she was a grand lass.

'Look here, our Ali, I'm doing it for both of us. Would you have turned down the chance to potentially become foreman if you'd been offered it?' Will was finding it hard to persuade Alice that the job at Stone House was going to be good for them both. 'There'll be a house, once it's been repaired, and I'll get decent brass if I'm officially put in charge. I've even got my own horse. I've decided I want to make something of myself. It's like you've always said: put your mind to it and you can do better.' He strutted back and forth underneath the little attic window of Alice's bedroom. 'I thought you'd be pleased that Nancy and me are walking out together. What's wrong with that?'

'What's wrong with that? We're farmers, Will – she's gentry, she has different ways to us, and you'll be the talk of the dale. It was you who kept me away from the manor when I wanted to work there. Now you're going out with Lord Frankland's sister and being bought by him. Wasn't it you who told me he wasn't to be trusted? I thought I knew you better, Will. You've changed this last week or two.'

'You're only jealous. You always wanted money and posh things. Well, I've found out so do I. From the moment I soaked in that bath and put on clean clothes I realized what we had been missing. And by God, even if I have to marry a scarred banshee, I'm going to get it.' Will's temper was getting the better of him.

'You mean you've no feelings for her at all? You're just after her money?' Alice gasped. 'But she's been hurt enough – don't you go hurting her more. If Gerald Frankland finds out, he'll kill you.'

'You bloody little hypocrite! Do you think I've not been hearing about you? The men up at Stone House don't have the manners of us locals; when I heard them talking of the young lass doing favours for Old Todd, I soon put two and two together.' Will's face was thunderous. 'There, I've bloody well said it! I vowed I

119

wouldn't even think it, let alone tell you I knew, but I won't have you lecturing me, our Ali. Not when you carry on like that. Just be thankful that Jack doesn't mix with anybody but farm lads and me, else he'd have heard about it too. Then you would be in bother.'

Alice started to cry. She lowered her head, unable to look her furious brother in the eye. 'Do you think I'm proud of what I've done? Well, I can tell you I'm not. I didn't do it for the money; I did it because he made me. Can you remember that bacon I gave you, right after I first started at the Moon? He saw me putting it in my pocket. He threatened to tell the Woodheads and said I'd lose my job when they found out. You think I wanted that filthy old man letting his hands wander over me? It's true the old lech gave me money afterwards, and I wish I'd flung it back at him, but I thought I might as well get something out of it. I dread him showing up at the Moon. I was going to tell Annie about the bacon myself – even if she threw me out it'd be better than putting up with that old lech. Please don't tell Jack. How could he love me if he found out what I'm like?'

'Oh, Ali, you stupid girl, what have you done? Now stop crying. With me going up in society, things are bound to get better. Just keep your legs together in future and ignore the randy old bugger. If he tells Annie about the bacon, she'll only laugh. She knows you're no thief.' His anger subsided as he put his arm around Ali's shoulders. 'What I'm doing, I'm doing for us both. Let me get that cottage up at Stone House and make sure that my job as foreman is secure, and then I'll let down Nancy gently. I must admit, it doesn't sit easy with me, using someone like that, but I've found out you've got to look after yourself in this world.'

'That's all I was trying to do, Will. But I couldn't have gone on being Old Todd's floozy. I'd got to the point where I wanted to hit him where it hurts, never mind anything else.' Alice wiped her nose on her sleeve end and grinned at Will in between the sobs.

'What are we like, me and you! Two orphans out in the world and taking it head-on. You stick with Jack and your jobs, and I'll try to make the money and home for us, all right, our Ali?'

Alice nodded, relieved that Will had learned her secret, shocking though it was. She felt as though a burden had been lifted now it was out in the open.

8

It had been a busy morning in the Moon. The drovers who'd taken lodgings for the night wanted an early breakfast before herding their cows and sheep to Hawes for the weekly cattle market. With bacon in high demand, Uriah was kept busy cutting thin strips from the newly cured flitch. It was a job he insisted on doing himself because he reckoned Annie and Alice cut it too thick. When Annie told him to hurry up, he swore under his breath and muttered that he had to make a profit and that meant cutting it wafer-thin. You should be able to feed at least six on half a pound of bacon – and damn them all for rushing him.

'Uriah Woodhead!' Annie yelled at her husband across the kitchen floor. 'If I hear you swear once more, I'll send Alice over with carbolic soap and a scrubbing brush to clean your mouth out. Good decent folk don't want to hear language like that first thing of a morning.' Wiping the sweat from her brow with a tea towel, she went back to frying the bacon over the Yorkshire range that she was so proud of.

'It's enough to make any good man swear – I'm rushed off my feet. Tuesday mornings in this place it's like feeding the four thousand. I've done a full day's job by the time the rest of Dent start to think about getting up.'

'And what do you think us two get up to every day of the week, eh, mister? Don't you think I'd like an hour longer in bed sometimes? Fires always lit and doors open for business before you've even put a toe out of your side of the bed. So just you watch what you're saying. Bugger it!' Annie swore as the bacon sizzling in the pan spat at her, the fat leaving a scald mark on one of her ample arms. 'Now look what you've made me do!'

'Language, dear, language! Else I'll have to send Alice across with the carbolic.'

Alice, catching Uriah's wink out of the side of her eye, gave no acknowledgement beyond a smile as she got on with scrubbing the huge pine table of the Moon's kitchen. She'd found that when her employers fell out, it was best to keep her head down and get on with her work.

'I tell you what's odd this morning: we haven't got Old Todd stopping with us. It's not like him to miss market day at Hawes.' Uriah stopped carving for a moment to think about his absent guest.

'He'll turn up, like a bad penny.' Annie plated up the fried bacon. 'The creeping old devil wouldn't miss going to Hawes on a Tuesday if it were the last thing he did – more's the pity. I can't stand his grubby ways,

123

myself. Have you seen the way he drools when Alice here serves him?' She handed Alice the plates so she could take them to the customers. 'You'll not miss him this morning, will you, Alice? Dirty old man.'

Once again, Alice's only reply was a smile as she lifted the plates loaded with greasy bacon, fried bread and eggs, and hurried into the bar with them. Too true she wouldn't miss Old Todd. After her conversation with Will, she'd made up her mind there'd be no more 'little understandings'. The thought of what the old lech would do when he found out filled her with dread.

The Moon was packed with drovers and farmers who believed in starting the day off with a full stomach and a pint. Many didn't even wait to get to market, preferring to come to agreement over breakfast. Two weathered-faced farmers sitting in the corner concluded their business as Alice arrived with the plates; she saw one of them spit into his palm, then reach out to shake the other farmer's hand, signalling that it was a done deal and that his word was good. He sent Alice to fetch them drinks to seal the deal. She quickly poured two pints of bitter and hurried back to their table. As she bent down to place the two pints in front of them, she caught a snatch of their conversation.

'. . . I knew he was a bugger for the lasses, but this 'un was seventeen! You'd think the old sod would know better.' Oblivious to Alice's presence, the old farmer rubbed his head and took his first sup of the pint.

Alice, eager to hear more, began slowly clearing

plates from the recently vacated table next to them so that she could listen in to the conversation.

'It's his wife and family I feel sorry for,' said the younger of the two farmers. 'Fancy being told that your husband's dropped dead in a young lass's bed – on the job, as it were!'

'It's a right rum do, all right. But who can blame him for going with a young 'un, as long as he could stand the pace?'

'Aye, but it looks as though Old Todd couldn't stand the pace, and look where it got 'im!'

The older farmer spluttered into his beer at this, and then both men burst out laughing.

Alice felt a shiver run down her spine. So that was why Old Todd wasn't here: he'd died bedding a seventeen-year-old girl. How many young girls had he been getting serviced by? Alice felt dirty and sick at the thought of him dribbling and licking his lips as she served him, leering at her cleavage . . .

Suddenly realizing that it could have been her at the centre of the gossip, for ever more the subject of pointing fingers and known throughout the Dales as the seventeen-year-old floozy who finished off Old Todd with her wanton ways, Alice weaved her way through the crowded bar and out into the open air. Faint and flushed, she hurried to the fountain and splashed some of the clear, cold water on her face. Then she sat on the edge of the trough, trying to compose herself.

A blackbird came creeping along the street, head bobbing up and down when it heard a noise. So intent

125

was her gaze that anyone seeing Alice would have assumed she was fascinated by the bird, with its sharp beady eyes and the orange bill that stood out in stark contrast to its glossy black plumage. In reality, she wasn't even aware of the creature; her mind was completely focused on the news she'd just heard.

'Alice, Alice! Where the hell are you, girl!' She heard Uriah shouting her name. 'Bloody hell, lass, I'm run off me feet.'

'Coming, Mr Woodhead, I'm coming.' She clutched her apron and leapt to her feet, running across the cobbles in the rush to slip unnoticed into the pub. As she entered the bar, she gave a sigh of relief: Old Todd wouldn't be staying in the Moon any more; her worries were over. Her terrible secret would be buried with him.

'There you are!' Uriah glared at Alice. 'What you been up to? I've been shouting my head off.'

'I felt a bit faint and needed some fresh air, Mr Woodhead.'

'Well, you looks all right now. Get them tables cleared. I'm run off my bloody feet in here.' Wiping his forehead, he turned to head back to the kitchen, pausing on the way to thank a departing farmer for his custom.

By eight o'clock the bar was empty. There was still washing-up to be done and floors to be swept ahead of the midday rush, but first they were all in need of a break.

'Time for us to grab something to eat.' Annie placed three plates of breakfast on the table. 'It's been a morning and a half. I'm fair jiggered.' She heaved a sigh and peered at the plate of bacon and egg in front of her. 'I don't know if I can eat this after cooking the stuff all morning. Besides, I heard something earlier that made me feel sick.' She leaned back in her chair and folded her hands on her lap.

'Oh? What was that?' Uriah looked at his wife, curious.

'You mean you haven't heard about Old Todd being found dead in bed with the young barmaid at the Crown? I always knew he was a dirty old devil. Alice, cover your ears – someone your age shouldn't listen to this.'

'Never!' exclaimed Uriah. 'Why, the old devil. Who'd've thought it? Daft old sod, and him with a respectable wife and family. Good job he didn't take a fancy to our Alice here.' He winked at Alice as he tucked into his bacon and egg.

'Uriah Woodhead, how could you even think that? Our Alice is a respectable young lady. Besides, she's walking out with Jack Alderson. She wouldn't be the least bit interested in that old pervert, would you, Alice?'

Alice blushed crimson, wishing the conversation would change. 'No, Mrs Woodhead. He was a nasty old man.'

Uriah quickly caught the escaping mouthful of fried

egg. ' 'Course, Mother. How could I think otherwise?' Smirking, he wiped his mouth with the back of his sleeve and gave Alice a long, knowing gaze.

It was the smirk that told Alice: he knew. Uriah had known all along about the 'little understanding'. Her head began to spin and she felt sick deep down in the pit of her stomach. Just when she thought that her secret was safe . . .

'Don't forget, the bread's to be in the oven and the steps scrubbed by six thirty. Uriah, don't go to bed till you've made sure there's coal in and that fire's been banked up for the morning.' Annie Woodhead was giving Uriah and Alice their orders before setting off to see her ailing mother in Kendal.

She lifted her skirts and heaved herself up into the trap next to the small body of the driver, still checking and checking again that she had left everything in place for the smooth running of the Moon.

'We've all in hand, Mother. You're back in two days – what can go wrong in that time? Now, bugger off and make sure that the old lass is all right.' Uriah stretched up to kiss her goodbye, then gave the horse a smack on its withers to stir it into action.

'And don't forget to feed the cat,' Annie shouted as the trap set off on its journey.

Uriah turned and went into the Moon. 'Good God, I thought she'd never go. You wouldn't think that I'd run this place on my own, would you? Now, Alice, how about a cup of tea before the lunchtime rush? I could do with a look at today's paper, and then I'll have forty winks.' Picking up his paper from the bar, he went and sat in his favourite seat by the fire while Alice went to make him his tea.

When she returned, the paper was lying scattered on the floor and Uriah was snoring his head off, arms lolling by his side. So this was how it was going to be. She remembered that expression he was so fond of: 'While the cat's away, the mice will play.' Alice had a feeling that this little mouse would not have time for anything – she'd be too busy doing three people's work.

By the end of the day, Alice was shattered. She sat on the edge of the bed in front of the mirror brushing her hair, her cami straps hanging loose from her shoulders. Wearily she poured cold water into the basin, pinned her hair out of the way and stripped down to her bloomers. The cool water felt refreshing as she washed her face and then her body. It was a warm September's night, so instead of scrambling into her nightdress she paused to study herself in the mirror, turning sideways and caressing her firm breasts, wondering at the young woman she had become. As the moonlight from the attic window high-lighted the blonde in her hair, she couldn't help but smile at the reflection that she saw in the mirror. What had happened to the ugly duckling? Even if she said so herself, she wasn't too bad to look at.

Hearing a creak of floorboards, which she swore

came from outside her bedroom door, she turned sharply. 'Who's there?' she shouted, grabbing her nightdress to cover her nude body. 'Is anyone there?'

There was no reply, just a flutter of bat wings from way up in the eaves of the Moon. Perhaps she had been dreaming. She was that exhausted, it was hardly any surprise she was hearing things. As she pulled the bed sheets back, she glanced at the carriage clock that had once been her mother's ticking methodically on the bedside table. One o'clock: another four hours and she'd have to be up and about, ready for the next day. She rubbed her eyes, blew the candle out and slid into bed. Sleep came quickly, giving her peace for a few hours.

The following day was wet. Rain battered at the Moon's thick glass windows, making the whole place feel damp and cold. Not many customers came in for breakfast or lunch, which was just as well because Uriah had not banked the fire up the night before and Alice had to light it from scratch. He'd spent the morning walking around the pub like a groaning spectre, suffering the effects of a hangover after one too many 'nightcaps' from the whisky bottle at bedtime. It wasn't hard to see who was really in charge of the Moon when Annie was away.

'You can get yourself to bed early tonight, if you want.' Uriah peered at Alice over the top of his glasses. 'Either that or find yourself something to do. I've a few friends coming round tonight for a card game and they'll not want a young lass hanging about, distracting them from their betting, so you'd better make yourself scarce. Think on you don't say anything to the missus when she comes home – she doesn't like some of my mates.' Uriah fixed his gaze on Alice, seeking assurance that she wouldn't tell of his exploits.

Alice gave Uriah a nod. She'd had enough of being on her own with him, so was thankful for the break. 'I'll be off now, then. All's done for the morning. You know where I am if you want anything.'

Sighing a weary sigh, she climbed the stairs, untying her apron as she approached her bedroom door. Too exhausted for anything else, she lay on her bed watching the raindrops race one another on the skylight. The roof was taking a pounding in the storm and a small trickle of water was gradually forming a pool in the corner of her bedroom. She was not looking forward to spending winter in this cold and lonely little bedroom.

The next thing she knew it was dark and she could hear voices. She must have fallen asleep and been woken by Uriah's friends as they left the Moon by the back door, laughing and calling their goodbyes. She reached out to light her bedside lamp, the golden glow allowing her to read the time on the clock as she sat gathering her senses on the edge of the bed. It was then she heard the creaking of floorboards outside her bedroom door.

'Hello, who's there?' She stood up, half asleep but determined to find out who was out there. Clutching the lamp in one hand, she opened the door quickly. In the lamp's glow she saw Uriah, his cheeks flushed, swaying unsteadily.

'Mr Woodhead, what are you doing here? Do you want some help?'

'Aye, you can help me.' His jovial expression turned into an ugly leer. 'I want a bit of what you gave Old Todd!'

Alice struggled to close her bedroom door on him, but he forced his way in, almost knocking the oil lamp out of her hand as he pinned her against the wall. 'You think nobody knows what went on in that churchyard, you slut? Once Old Todd had a drop or two of the golden stuff, he'd not stop talking about little Alice and how she can't get enough of it. That's why you go to the manor once a week, isn't it? To look after his lordship's needs.' His whisky breath was inches from Alice's face as he held her captive while fumbling to undo his belt buckle.

'It isn't like that! Let me go!' Alice desperately tried to break free of his grip on her.

'Aye, he told us you were a feisty one.' His face broke into a lascivious grin. 'Makes the sport even better.'

Tightening his hold on her wrist, he removed the lamp from her hand and set it down on the table. Then he threw her face down on the bed. With his ample body pinning her down, she was powerless to stop him as he pulled her skirts up and ripped off her bloomers. Alice tried to scream, but he buried her head in the mattress so that it was all she could do to breathe. The iron bedstead dug into her legs as the drunken landlord took his pleasure, grinding the bed into the wall with every thrust. And all the while he was hurling foul-mouthed insults at her, gaining as much pleasure from that as the sexual act itself.

Then suddenly it was over. She felt him withdraw from between her aching, sore legs and he lunged to his feet, releasing her. Kicking his trousers from around his ankles, he stepped out of them and staggered out of the room without a word. She heard him breathing heavily as he descended the stairs.

Alice lay retching and sobbing on the bed, her body aching from the injuries he'd inflicted on her. Pulling her clothing down to cover herself, she curled into a ball, trying to make herself small. How could he? How could he? She felt dirty, worthless and so lonely. What was she to do now? Tears streamed from her eyes as she eased her body off the bed.

Terrified that he might return for more, she wedged a chair beneath the door handle so that it could not be opened. Then she took off her clothes and poured clean water into her washbasin. Desperate to get his filth off her, she scrubbed herself raw, tearing at the bruised intimate parts of her body.

It was some time before she gave up and finally laid her aching body on the bed. Tomorrow, as soon as daylight dawned, she would leave. She didn't know where she would go, but there was no way she would stay another night under the same roof as Uriah Woodhead.

*

133

'So where's Alice? And why have you not opened up, you big useless lump?' Annie Woodhead had returned from her mother's earlier than expected to find the doors closed at the Moon, even though it was past midday. She clicked her tongue, looking around at the state of the place.

'You'll never believe it, Mother: I found her in bed with Jack Alderson, the little tart. As soon as your back was turned, she had a man in her room! What do you think of that? And I heard she'd been seeing Old Todd and charging for favours. Well, you can see the predicament I was in, on my own with a loose woman. So I threw her out. I couldn't do no other now, could I? And I couldn't run the pub on my own, so that's why we are in the state we are.' Uriah offered his wife a chair to sit in while he hurriedly made excuses for the disappearance of Alice.

Annie looked at her husband, weighing up his explanation. Alice had seemed such a grand lass and Jack was a nice quiet lad . . . On the other hand, she had watched her around Old Todd, making eyes at him, and she'd been forever nipping out of the inn for a few minutes when he was staying with them – the brazen hussy!

'Oh my God, Uriah! And I left her with you. I should have known! She was always a bit too forward for my liking, even though she acted like butter wouldn't melt in her mouth. After we've been so good to her, taking her in and letting her live under our roof! Mind you, look at her father – it had to come out somewhere! We're better off without her. She'd have given this place a terrible reputation, and we don't want people tarring us with the same brush. After all, we have high morals and high standards. No, you did right to throw her out, Uriah. I hope I never see her again.' Annie's teacup rattled with indignation as she lifted it to take a sip of her lovingly prepared tea.

Uriah, meanwhile, was also offering up a prayer that he would never see Alice again. He knew it was more than his life was worth.

9

The grass was long and wet, stinging and sticking to Alice's legs as she made her way along the riverbank, stumbling over tree roots and turning her ankles on boulders in her haste. She was short of breath and the hurts she'd suffered the previous night made her want to cry, but she gritted her teeth and kept moving, desperate to get clear of the village without anyone noticing her slip away.

Unable to sleep, she'd stared up at the skylight window above her bed, waiting for the first glimpse of dawn. Then she had made her escape, gathering up her few possessions and creeping out of the back door of the Moon before the villagers began to stir. Avoiding the cobbled street and the drovers' road, she took to the overgrown path that followed the river to the top of the dale and the marble works, where she hoped to seek refuge with her brother. Will had mentioned that the foreman's cottage renovations were coming along well and it now had a new roof; she was hoping to lie low there for a day or two while she tried to think what to do next.

Pausing to catch her breath, she looked back the way she'd come. The village showed signs of coming to life: she could make out the faint glimmer of candles in windows, and smoke was rising from the bakery in a grey plume that blended with the sullen clouds hanging over the fells. A horse-drawn wagon rolled noisily over the cobbles; soon the road would be full of farmers and tradesmen coming and going.

A spasm of pain made Alice bend over, clutching her stomach. Beads of sweat broke out on her forehead as she sank to her knees, waiting for the nausea to subside. As bad as the pain were the feelings of guilt and anxiety. What was she going to tell her brother? He was bound to ask what she was doing, showing up at Stone House on a work day, but she daren't tell him the truth. If he found out what had taken place, he'd kill Uriah. No, best tell him something else – anything to keep her shame quiet.

She picked herself up and got moving again. After a while, she reached the point where the path passed by the drive to Whernside Manor. Keeping low so that no one would see her, she peeked through the undergrowth and saw Jack leading his beloved horse across the yard. Dear, sweet Jack, he would never hurt anyone. But for all that he was a good and loyal friend to her brother, Alice doubted he would want anything to do with her if he found out what had happened. She wiped her nose and swept the tears away. It was no good feeling sorry for herself; what was done was done. Nothing she could do to change it.

She took a deep breath, pushed her chin out and set off again. As she walked, she began to rehearse the story she would tell Will and Jack. She'd never liked working at the Moon – both the lads knew that – so the best thing would be to tell them that she'd fallen out with Annie. The only person who'd know what had really happened was Uriah, and he wouldn't say, not if he'd any sense. Will had been promising her that if he secured the cottage, she could move in with him. And if Lord Frankland would let her do more than one day a week at the manor, she'd bring in a bit of money. Besides, the manor was more the kind of place where she belonged. She should never have taken the job in the pub. Perhaps there had been a reason for the horrible events of last night, showing her what Uriah Woodhead was really like. Come what may, there was no way she would ever cross the threshold of that godforsaken place again.

It was nearly noon when Alice heard the ring of hammers on stone and the chug of the waterwheel. Then she turned the last bend of the river path at the head of the dale and there in front of her was the marble works. She could see the cottage with its smoke-damaged front; there was obviously lots of work still to be done on it, but thanks to the new slate roof it was looking more like the pleasant home it had once been.

Though she'd been walking since dawn and was exhausted from lack of sleep, Alice's spirits rallied at the thought she would soon see her brother. There was no one in the main yard, so she made a beeline for the cottage, hoping to find Will there. A handful of hens were scratching about by the back door, a sure sign that he was making this his home. There was a strong smell of smoke even now; it probably came from the pile of burned timbers stacked against the cottage wall. Alice shuddered, reminded of the terrible day when Mrs O'Hara died.

'Will, Will, are you there?' she called softly, opening the cottage door and peering into the room. The smell of smoke was even stronger in here. The walls were only half plastered; there was no furniture and no curtains at the windows. With a sigh, Alice crept in and set her bundle of possessions on the floor. She was disappointed that her brother was not at home. The last thing she wanted was to walk up to the works in search of him. She dreaded the thought of the men looking at her; most of them were ex-navvies with no wives and no commitments, and Will had said what a rough lot they were. Feeling sick to her stomach, Alice remembered how Will had gone on to say that they were the ones who'd told him about her doing favours for Old Todd. No, even if it meant waiting all day, she would just have to remain here until Will came.

The stairs had yet to be repaired, so there was no way of getting to the bedrooms. She went through a doorway into the adjoining room. This was obviously where Will was sleeping: in the corner was an iron bedstead, and on it was her mother's patchwork quilt. Alice sat on the edge of the bed. It seemed a lifetime ago since she had said goodbye to her mother; she had been lying in her bed at Dale End Farm, covered with this very quilt.

She picked up a corner of the quilt and hugged it to her chest, tears in her eyes, gently rocking her body. 'Oh, Mum, if you only knew what I'd been through,' she whispered under her breath. 'I miss you so much.' Overcome with grief for all that she'd lost, she collapsed on the bed, her body shaking with violent sobs.

'No, no, get away, stop it, stop it!' Alice screamed at her aggressor, flailing at the hands that were trying to grab her.

'Ali, Ali, it's me. Shh, it's me, Will. What's all this about? Why the screaming?' Putting his arms around his drowsy sister, Will hugged her to him, stroking her hair and speaking softly in an effort to calm her down. 'That must have been some nightmare, our Ali – I thought you were going to knock me out!' Will smiled at his young sister, but his eyes were full of concern. He could see she was troubled about something, and he wondered what she was doing at Stone House.

'I'm sorry, I'm really sorry. Did I hit you?' Alice sat upright and rubbed her eyes. She must have been asleep for hours. It was dark outside, and the only light in the cottage came from a couple of flickering candles.

'No, you didn't hit me. But I wouldn't want to be the fellow you were taking on in your dream – he'd have no chance.' Will grinned, released his hold on Alice and sat at the side of the bed.

'Who said it was a man? Has someone been talking? I was only dreaming.'

'I was only joking, Ali. Don't get upset. Anyway, what you doing here?' Will got up off the bed and picked up an oil lamp. 'Have you fallen out with Uriah? No, that can't be it; from the way he talks, I get the impression he thinks the world of you.' Will was busy examining the lamp, which had run out of oil, so he didn't see the tears welling up in Alice's eyes.

She gulped hard, fighting back the tears and wiping away all traces with the sleeve of her blouse. 'Yeah, well, impressions can be deceiving. Sorry, Will, I'm still half asleep. I've had words with Annie and she's sacked me. She says I'm lazy and that I haven't been doing my job properly.' Alice sat at the edge of the bed, unable to look her brother in the eye. She hated lying to him. 'I'm not going back. You should have heard her, Will. She accused me of all sorts – and you know how hard I work.' She let the tears out, hoping he'd assume she was upset at the unjust accusations, when really it was sadness and despair at what she'd been through.

'Now then, our lass, don't take on so. It's only a job. That Annie does have a tongue on her. She can make grown men cry when she's a mind to. She'll soon be begging you to come back, once she's had a few days with twice the work to do.' Will came and sat by her side, bemused to see his feisty little sister inconsolable after a telling-off from Annie Woodhead.

'I'm not going back, and you can't make me . . . I'd rather starve than work there.' Alice pulled on Will's jacket, frantically pleading with her brother.

'All right, all right, don't fret. I'm not going to make you do anything. I know you never wanted to work there in the first place, and you've no need now, anyway. Matter of fact, I was going to come and tell you my news this Sunday, but I can tell you now instead.' Will got to his feet, looking proud and full of importance. 'Who do you think is the new boss at Stone House? Who's gone and talked Lord Frankland into putting him in charge?'

'Will, you're not! He can't have! You don't know the first thing about cutting marble – we're farmers.' Alice looked up at her brother's beaming face while she dried her eyes with his slightly dirty hanky.

'That I am, pet. The bugger's confirmed it, official like. I've even got this bloody cottage. And look at this . . .' He walked over to a lamp hanging on the wall and pointed at the gas wick under the glass mantel. 'He's even putting me in them fancy gas lamps like they have at the manor. How about that, our Ali – us with newfangled lights! And upstairs there's going to be a toilet and bath. Now then, how's that for posh, our lass? No more sitting on a cold outside lav for us on a frosty morning. What did I tell you? I've made it, our lass. Now all I've got to do is keep in with his sister and I'll soon own this spot and the works.' He sat on the edge of the bed and slapped his leg in anticipation of the good life he could see ahead.

'And where do I enter into your scheme of things, our Will?' Alice scrubbed the last tear off her face and tossed her hair away from her eyes. 'Am I to skivvy for you and stand by while my true friend is taken for every penny?' Shoving the grubby handkerchief into his hand, she stared at him long and hard. She didn't like what Will was beginning to turn into.

'She's not your friend; she's your employer. Nancy's a toff and she's using you, just as her brother's using me – or so he thinks. But I'm going to turn it round and play him at his own game. She fancies a bit of rough on account of she can't get anyone else, what with that face and her being so moody, nice as pie one minute and screaming like a banshee the next. So I fit the bill – and I intend to take what I can get out of it. And why shouldn't I? It's not like Frankland showed much sympathy for us when Father died, did he? And I've seen the way he looks at you, too. You want to take care, our Ali: I'm sure he'd like you to do more for him than keep Nancy company. I've watched him with them friends of his – right shady bunch of characters. All foreigners, so you can't understand a damn word they say, but it's obvious they're up to no good.

"Business associates", he calls 'em, from Russia. It wouldn't surprise me if the business turned out to be a brothel, judging by the way they carry on.'

'Give over! He's been nothing but a gentleman. And Nancy is a true friend and always will be, so you'd better not hurt her, Will Bentham, else you'll have me to answer to!'

'Well, you'll know all about gentlemen, won't you? After all, you've had dealings with them – take Old Todd, he was a real gentleman!' Will regretted the words as soon as he uttered them. Regretted them even more when Alice once again burst into tears. 'I'm sorry, Ali, I shouldn't have said that. I'd no right. We're both as bad as one another, both of us just trying to make a living by fair means or foul. What a bloody pair! What would our mum and dad think of us?'

'Not a lot, I don't think. At least, not of me. You're doing well for yourself, but I keep going from bad to worse. And now look at me: I'm worth nothing; I'd be better off dead. Father always thought I was a selfish one, and he was right.' Alice went and stood by the window. Turning her face away from her brother, she stared out into the dark night.

Seeing that she was shivering, Will picked up her shawl and placed it on her shoulders. 'Sorry, Ali – I'm a hot-headed idiot. We've both said things we shouldn't. It's that bloody Bentham temper. Let's not fight, eh? We only have one another.' He smiled and kissed her on her brow. 'Things will look different when you've had a good night's sleep. You put your head down in my bed and I'll make something up for myself in the other room. In the morning, we'll sort something out for you. I could do with someone to look after me. Can't you tell from the state of this house? It needs a woman's touch. Come on, our lass, I've said I'm sorry.'

'I forgive you, Will. Who am I to preach? And thanks for putting me up tonight; I'm grateful. I'll get myself sorted tomorrow, I promise.' Alice steadied her breathing and gave Will a kiss on his cheek before removing her shoes and crawling under the bedcovers. Tomorrow would be another day. Any decisions could wait till the morning, when she wasn't so tired and when the world made more sense.

Leaves twirled and twisted in the autumn wind, torn from trees that had been battered by the northern gales sweeping over the dale. There had been beautiful hues of orange, russet, yellow and brown as the first frosts nipped, but now the leaves were a nuisance, filling up the gutters and turning to mulch underfoot. It was that time of year when people felt depressed at the onset of winter, the thought of Christmas being the one bright spark, the time to be with loved ones and family.

It was almost two months since Alice's unexpected arrival at the cottage and for weeks there had been no let-up in the wind and rain. The cold, wet conditions were making life difficult at the marble works, with the men growing fractious and unsettled. O'Hara might have been a crook, but at least they could take it easy while he was sleeping off the previous night's hangover. The new boss made sure they kept on working even in the pouring rain. And what was he doing in charge of them in the first place? Barely old enough to grow whiskers and knowing nothing about marble and quarrying. There was only one thing him and his floozy of a sister were good at, and that was hobnobbing with the gentry.

To start with, they waited until Will's back was turned before giving vent to their resentment. But all that changed one particularly foul morning, with the rain lashing down so hard they could barely see the rock face and their tools slipping from their hands with the wet, and Will standing there yelling at them all the while, telling them to put their backs into it and earn their keep. They'd all been muttering under their breath, cursing him, but then one of them spoke loud enough so Will could hear it.

'What did you say?' snapped Will, glaring at the dark, thickset form. 'I'm talking to you, Middleton! Answer me!' The man was one of his best workers, but he was also a ringleader, and if Will let a remark like that go unchallenged, the others might follow suit.

'I said, it's a pity we can't all make our living by shagging the boss's sister.' Middleton rose to his full height. He was a big, burly man who would have no problem holding his own if it came to a fight. 'And I think I can speak for all of us when I say it's not fit weather to make a dog work, let alone us men.'

With that, he spat in his hands and bent to pick up his spade.

'How dare you talk to me like that!' Will stepped up and grabbed at the bending man's lapel, hauling on it to bring them face to face.

'Nay, I've said enough – I mean to keep my job. But if the cap fits . . . Think what you will, but I'm right about the bloody weather. We can do nothing on a day like this – and there'll be a lot of days like this 'un in winter.'

Shrugging off Will's hand on his lapel, Middleton made to carry on shovelling. Two of his fellow workers moved in, crowding Will and making him feel vulnerable and alone on the fellside.

'All right, men, finish for today – but I'm only paying you half a day's wages. And it'll be the same for every day wasted: no work, no pay.'

With that, Will turned and set off walking along the stony track that led to the cottage. He heard mutinous voices behind him muttering curses, and Middleton calling him a 'fucking bastard', but he kept on walking. These were not his sort of men. Most were decent enough, but there were a few who were still loyal to O'Hara. If he was to make a success of himself, he would need to win them over, and the best way to do that would be to prove he'd been given the job because he was worthy of it, not just because of his acquaintance with the boss's sister.

By the time he got home, he was drenched to the

skin. Middleton was right: this weather wasn't fit for working in, but he was desperate to get the works running at a profit again. Only then would his position be secure, regardless of his relationship with Nancy.

'By the gods, its bloody wet out there, our lass!' He stopped just inside the back door and threw off his cap and overcoat, leaving them in a wet heap on the floor. 'Fetch me a towel, wherever you are. I swear I'm going to lamp that Middleton one of these days. He's a right bloody troublemaker. I'm going to have to secure a few good orders to win him over. Alice, where the hell are you, woman? I'm drowning in here.'

Alice came rushing into the kitchen. 'Be quiet, our Will – we've company.' She handed him a warm towel from the airing rack above the fire. 'Miss Nancy and Jack are in the front room. Nancy got him to bring her up because she says she's missing you.'

Will towelled his dark hair dry, then ran his fingers through it to flatten and layer it thin to his skull, exaggerating his high cheekbones and sharp features.

'That's what I like to hear, lass,' he whispered conspiratorially. 'Treat 'em mean and keep 'em keen.' Taking the damp towel and aiming a swipe at Alice's bottom, he set off for the front room with a jaunty swagger.

'Nancy, my dear, what brings you here on this terrible wet day? It's a wonder you weren't washed away.' He leaned down and planted a gentle kiss on her cheek, then stood and turned to his friend. 'Jack, what were you thinking, bringing Miss Nancy out in this weather?'

'Don't blame Jack, my love. I needed to see you – it's been a whole week since you've been to the manor. Besides, I was sure that Alice would like to see Jack, now that she is hidden away up here at this terrible place. Did I hear right, my love? Are you looking for more orders? I'll ask Gerald to have a word with his contacts for you. I'm sure he can help.'

'Nay, I can manage. I've got to earn my own points with them men up there, else they'll never respect me.' Will turned to Jack, giving him a playful punch on the shoulder. 'I suppose it's my sister you've come to see, not me. That'll be why she's still lurking out there!' Raising his eyebrows and tilting his head in the direction of the kitchen, Will hoped his friend would take the hint and let him have some time alone with Nancy.

'Well, as it happens, there is something I want to ask her.' For a moment, Jack stood there looking sheepish and twisting his cap in his hands, awkward at being in the way of his friend's courtship. 'If it's all right with you, Miss Nancy, I'll go and see her. Let me know when you want to return to the manor.'

Alice was standing by the kitchen fire, hanging Will's wet clothes in front of the range to dry. She smiled at Jack when he entered. 'So you've had enough of playing gooseberry with the loving couple? Come and sit next to the fire and keep me company. It's not only Nancy who gets lonely, you know.' She plumped

149

up the newly made cushions and offered Jack the chair nearest the fire.

'Aye, well, there's something I want to ask you, and it's a bit awkward, but I've got to know because I'm not being tret right at the Moon. Uriah and his missus have all on to talk to me, let alone serve me. I've a feeling it's something to do with thee, but I can't weigh up what.'

'Don't be silly, Jack, you've done nothing wrong and I've never said anything about you to them. Besides, what is there to say? It's nothing but sour grapes over me leaving. They're taking it out on you because they know we're friends. That'll be all it is.' She reached across and took his hand and held it gently. 'You know I'd never do anything to hurt you. I think dearly of you.'

'Aye, and I think a lot of you, but they are acting strange and folk are talking. Everyone goes quiet when I walk into the pub for the odd pint that I can barely afford nowadays.'

'You're imagining it, Jack. Anyway, what's to do with you not affording to go for a pint? Things can't be that bad.' Alice tried to change the subject from the Woodheads.

'I'm not for saying, but you'll find out soon enough.' Jack's mood lightened and there was a definite twinkle in his eye as he added, 'Let's just say I'm counting the pennies at the moment.'

'Go on, Jack, tell me – what are you up to?' Alice's thoughts were racing. She'd come to realize that there was more to Jack than she'd given him credit for. He might be quiet, and his job at the manor didn't have the same prospects as Will's, but she'd found him to be a caring, sensible lad. What's more, he was good with money – something not to be overlooked.

'Nay, you'll have to wait; I'm not saying anything. But I've got to look after my money, so there will be no more fancy tea and scones in Mrs Handley's tea rooms on a Sunday. Sorry, Alice, but this is more important.' He gave Alice a stern look, frowning slightly as he calculated the saving that he would make by not giving her a Sunday treat.

'Oh, Jack, you mean thing! All you think about is money. You don't care about me one bit. I bet you're only saving up for a bloody horse or a new saddle – anything but looking after me.' Sunday was the only day of the week Alice got treated like a lady and she spent the rest of the week looking forward to it. 'I can't be bothered to talk to you, Jack Alderson. I'm off to join my brother in the other room – at least him and Nancy can think of better things to talk about.'

'Alice, it's only until spring and then you can have scones and tea every Sunday,' Jack pleaded, grabbing her by the arm. 'You'll soon see that it's worth going without for.'

Alice shook her arm free. 'Spring! That's nearly five months off. Things can all have changed by then. I'm not always going to be here – I aim to do something with my life, not spend it waiting for a servant lad.'

Her sharp words stung at Jack's heart and her blazing eyes burned his soul. So that was what she thought of him, a servant lad, nothing more, nothing less. Well, he was going to show her, and by God, she'd want him then, because he loved the fiery Miss Bentham and he was going to get her, no matter what it took.

'Suit yourself, Alice,' he said to her retreating back. 'But you'll still be here. I know you will.' Then he turned and sat by the kitchen fire, hoping that Nancy would not stay long. He wanted to get home and nurse his wounded pride.

The shadows had lengthened by the time Nancy came through into the kitchen. Jack, who'd been dozing in the comfortable padded chair, quickly roused himself after hearing the farewells exchanged.

'So that's sorted, then, Alice: you'll come to the manor three days a week. You can sleep in the maid's quarters. I'm sure my brother won't complain as the room's not being used. You'll be a great help for Mrs Dowbiggin: she's not getting any younger – but don't tell her I said so! And of course it means that Jack will get to see more of you.' Nancy turned and smiled at him. 'So, it works out well for all. Come, Jack, take me home – it will be night-time before we get there.'

There was an uncomfortable silence from Jack as he put his coat on and opened the kitchen door for Nancy. He remained silent throughout the journey home, and

Nancy said nothing, leaving him to his thoughts until they were back at the manor.

'Jack, are you all right?' she asked as he reached up to help her alight from the carriage. 'You seem a little upset.'

'I'm fine, Miss Nancy, thank you. Just in love with the wrong woman – and there's nothing I can do about it.'

10

It was a year since Bess Bentham died and the November day was not dissimilar to the one on which she passed away. A sharp wind blew from the north, whipping around the huge pillars of the Stone House viaduct, nearly blowing the railway workers who were busy repairing the track off the top of it. Alice watched them as she sat sheltered behind one of the limestone walls, alone with her thoughts, apart from the song of a solitary late skylark. She had walked along the rutted track, past the marble works and underneath the railway's towering arches to a secluded spot that had become her thinking place. Where she could sit surrounded by tufts of moorland grass and ling heather, the smell of which she was sure would make a fortune in the fine shops of London if you could only capture it in a bottle.

With a sigh, she gazed out at the view. In the distance she could see Combe Scar, tipped with snow, behind the little village of Dent and the vast slopes of Whernside rising up from the valley. She closed her eyes and covered them with her hands, quietly despairing at the situation she was in. Things had gone from bad to worse since her mother died, and now, to top it all, she had fallen out with Jack, all for the sake of a stupid cup of tea. Her and her sharp temper!

Still, maybe she could make it up with him once she started working more hours at the manor. Her mood lightened at the thought. She was looking forward to living in her own room at the manor two nights a week, knowing that she'd be warm and well fed if Mrs Dowbiggin had anything to do with it. Besides, she couldn't really call it work. Helping Nancy dress, keeping her company and lending a hand in the kitchen – that wasn't work, especially not compared to the Moon. She shuddered at the very thought of the place and horrid memories came flooding back to her. Alice hadn't dared show her face in the village since she left and hoped she wouldn't have to for a while longer yet.

The cold, biting wind finally got too much for her and, wrapping her shawl tightly around her, she set off down the track to the cottage that she had started to call home. To think that just over a year ago both her parents had been alive and she had been an innocent teenager. Life had certainly forced her to grow up since then, and she'd learned her lessons the hard way. But she hadn't let it beat her. Despite everything, she was still aiming her sights high: today the cottage, tomorrow the manor – and who knew where that would lead? She only hoped Mr Right would come along soon.

She stopped by the water trough at the back door of the cottage to take a sip of the icy-cold water. As she leaned over the pump, she was suddenly overcome by a wave of nausea. Her head felt so light and giddy that she had to support herself by hanging on to the pump until the feeling passed and she felt well enough to continue into the cottage.

'You're white as a sheet, our lass. Are you all right?' said Will, looking up from his seat at the kitchen table. 'I bet you've been up in your new hiding place on the fellside, haven't you? I've never understood why you have to go out in all weathers just to have a think. You must be frozen, you silly devil.'

With shaking hands, Alice took her shawl off and hung it behind the kitchen door. Beads of sweat formed on her brow. 'I feel sick, if you must know. Probably those duck eggs I had for breakfast this morning. I didn't know how old they were when I got them out of the pantry.'

'They weren't old – I only had them given to me the other day. Happen you're sickening for something. You'd better have a lie-down for an hour or two, because whatever you've got, I don't want it.' Will put his coat on and made for the door. 'I'm off out. Will you be all right?'

'I'll be fine. I told you, it's just something I've eaten.' Alice managed a wan smile for her brother, but as soon as he was gone she collapsed next to the fire and burst into tears. She knew all too well what was wrong with her, and it had nothing to do with anything she'd eaten. She'd begun to suspect when she missed two 'monthlies'. Now she knew she was pregnant; the nausea confirmed it. Why did she have to end up pregnant? Uriah and his wife had no children. How was it that he had managed with her something he'd been trying for years with his wife? The last thing she wanted was Uriah's bastard baby. What to do, though? She thumped her stomach hard, making her retch even more, trying to kill the unformed baby. If only she had someone to turn to, someone who would know what to do.

'Are you all right, dear?' Mrs Dowbiggin peered at her new help across the kitchen table of the manor. The last couple of mornings she'd come down from her room looking pale and had not even touched her breakfast.

'I'm fine, Mrs Dowbiggin. Thank you for asking.' Alice smiled, trying not to show how she felt. Since moving into her room at the manor, she had enjoyed being part of the little community and the last thing she wanted was to lose her new position. She especially liked the way Gerald Frankland bade her good morning personally every morning as she served him and Nancy breakfast. His dark eyes smiling and watching her as she waited on his every word and instructions for the day.

'Now, dear, I hope that you don't think me presumptuous, but I don't believe you. I've been around long enough to recognize a girl in trouble. You're being

157

sick every morning, my girl – I've heard you. So what are we going to do about this little secret?'

'I don't know what you mean. There's nothing wrong with me.' Alice put on her haughty look; there was no way she was going to tell Mrs Dowbiggin her troubles. She would be the gossip of the dale.

'Don't be stupid, girl – you're pregnant. Another few weeks and you'll not be able to hide it on that skinny frame of yours. And then what are you going to do?' Hilda Dowbiggin took a long sip from her teacup and studied the blushing Alice as she did so. She placed her teacup and saucer firmly down on the white linen tablecloth. 'If you don't want it, you need to get on and do something about it. How long gone are you? And who's the father?' Seeing Alice's reaction, she followed this with 'Will he stand by you?'

Alice hung her head and fiddled with her handkerchief, not wanting to look into Mrs Dowbiggin's prying eyes. 'I'm three months, but I don't want anyone to know. It's my secret and I'm not telling you who the father is.'

'Well, it's hardly going to stay a secret, now is it? If it's that Jack Alderson's, I'll give him a piece of my mind. He should have kept it in his pocket!' Hilda Dowbiggin stared long and hard at her. Then she smacked her lips and shook her head. 'You're not the first and you won't be the last, but I thought better of you, Alice. I thought you had more about you than some. There was me, trying to warn you about men, and all along you probably knew more than me.'

'It wasn't like that, Mrs Dowbiggin. I couldn't help it, and it's not Jack's, so please don't say anything to him, please, I beg of you. He would only be hurt.'

'Oh, hold your tears. It's no good crying over spilt milk. What are we going to do now? That's the question. I take it I'm the only one who knows? Else Miss Nancy wouldn't have got you working here three days a week. Let's hope his lordship doesn't find out, or we will be in for bother. Now, do you want to keep it?'

Alice sniffed and looked at Mrs Dowbiggin, bemused. 'What do you mean? I've no option but to keep it, have I?' A glimmer of hope was beginning to shine. Perhaps Hilda Dowbiggin was more worldly than Alice had thought, and perhaps she was going to be her saviour. Even if she didn't have a solution, it still felt better now that someone else was in on the secret and she could talk about her situation with another woman.

'There is a way out, if you want to get rid, but what I'm about to tell you, you keep to yourself, do you hear? And you don't mention me if anything goes wrong. I need my job and, besides, I've my reputation to think of. First, we'll try gin and a hot bath. And if that doesn't work, I'll have a word with Mrs Batty; she's good at her trade and discreet.'

Alice looked at Mrs Dowbiggin in astonishment. She was beginning to see this sweet, dumpy elderly woman in a different light. How did she know about such things? The thought of Mrs Batty performing an abortion on her – those hands of death working on her unborn baby – made her retch. Could she go through with it? She had to; there was no other way. If she wanted to make something of her life, she couldn't afford any bastard children clinging to her skirts. She cleared her throat and tried to draw on her inner strength. 'Does she charge for her services?'

'What do you think, lass? Freedom comes at a price, but I'm sure you'll find the brass if you are determined. Do you want me to have a word with her, then, just in case we can't get rid of it ourselves?'

Alice shook her head and bent it in sadness and horror at what she was about to do to herself. Mrs Batty, the horrible woman who had buried her mother, might soon be killing her baby.

'OK, my love, I'll make it right with her, but we'll try a bath first. Better that way than getting rid with Mrs Batty. You'll be all right, though; it won't be the first baby she's got rid of, I can tell you that.' Hilda Dowbiggin laid her hand on the trembling form of Alice and gently patted her. 'Discreet, she is. There's been one or two young ladies visited her from here – friends of the master, needing to get out of a fix. She does a good service, very professional.'

Alice's jaw dropped at the housekeeper's words. So her brother had been right in warning her against Lord Frankland; he *was* one for the ladies. From here on, she would keep him at a distance. All she wanted to do right now was get on with her life.

*

160

It was a dark winter's night with only a week to go till Christmas. A few snowflakes fluttered down as Alice stood shivering at the back door of the funeral parlour. Her stomach was churning in trepidation at what Mrs Batty was about to do. After all, it was nothing less than murder of her unborn baby. A baby that was not wanted, born out of rape, and would never be loved – or so Alice had convinced herself. A single quick action and it would be no more; that's what Mrs Dowbiggin had told her.

Losing her nerve, she felt like running, but it was too late. The door opened and, raising her finger to her mouth, Mrs Batty led her into the makeshift surgery she had set up in the mortuary. Alice needed no urging to keep silent; she was too numb to speak. Once inside Mrs Batty helped her out of her coat and then held out her hand for the blood money. Alice dropped the florins into her palm, remembering how she had come by them and the indignities of Old Todd's advances. She waved her to the mortuary table and gestured for her to lie upon it. Still not a word was uttered. Alice wondered whether the woman was frightened that her husband might hear her going about the deadly task. She gave Alice a stick to bite on to combat the pain. And then she finally spoke, whispering, 'You've had your pleasure, now you must pay for it.' And then she set about her cruel practice.

The pain was excruciating. Alice felt dizzy and wanted to yell out for the old crone to stop digging

161

and scraping and to leave her be and for the baby to live. Sweat poured off her and her head pounded with pain; then a deep, dark blackness stole over her as her body tried to block out the agony by numbing her senses. With the deadly deed done, she passed out.

The wooden cart rattled up the dale, the wheels and the trotting of the horses drowning out Alice's groans.

'Be quiet, will you – I don't want to end up with a noose round my neck.'

Mrs Batty was panicking. She'd had to load Alice into the funeral cart all by herself, and now she was taking her home: if she was going to die, it was better that she did it on her own doorstep.

Leaving the cart at the bottom of the lane, she pulled Alice's arm over her shoulder and began dragging her towards Stone House marble works. 'For a little frame, you weigh a lot,' she complained. To her relief, the girl was still breathing when they got to the cottage. She gently knocked on the door, fleeing into the darkness as soon as she heard movement from within.

'Alice? Alice, what the hell have you done!' Was that the voice of her brother? Her head was spinning. Her body ached and her clothes felt damp and she could feel snow falling on her face. 'Who's left you in this state? Who knocked on my door and left you like this? If this is anything to do with Gerald Frankland, I'll kill him. I'll bloody well kill him.' She felt Will's tears falling on her face as he gently carried her inside, swearing when he got her into the light and saw her blood-soaked clothes. 'Who's done this to you, our lass? What have you been up to? For God's sake talk to me, I don't want to lose you as well!' he cried, panicking at the sight of his young sister in such a state.

Alice muttered feebly, 'Sorry, Will, I had to do it. I'd no option. I can't be weighed down by a baby. I had to get rid of it.'

'You stubborn, selfish woman! Will you never learn, you bloody headstrong article? Why can't you be content with your lot for once instead of looking for trouble?'

But Will's words were wasted on Alice. Once again a cloak of darkness descended, easing her pain and torment. Tomorrow would be another day and, with the grace of God, she would make it through the night to continue with her search for a perfect life.

11

The snow had been relentless, with biting northern winds clawing at people's faces, making them red and weather-beaten. Snowdrifts were whipped into peaks along the wall tops, and sheep huddled underneath the walls in the belief that they would be safe from the weather, only to find themselves imprisoned in an icy snow grave, trapped until farmers came to free them, alerted by the frantic digging of their sheepdogs. The dale's human inhabitants huddled round their fireplaces, setting aside all thoughts of travel until such time as the blizzards should cease. The workers at Stone House sat in their quarters playing cards and dominoes, venturing out only to collect a few sprigs of holly for Christmas decorations and to curse the weather for stopping their work.

In the foreman's cottage, Will nursed his feverish sister, glad of the weather that covered her sin. Glad that no one suspected the terrible thing that his young sister had undergone, and that the weather would explain her absence from the manor. For four days she had drifted in and out of consciousness, mumbling incoherent phrases; the makeshift abortion had almost cost her her life. The morning of Christmas Eve found her coming out of her fever, able to sip some beef broth that Will gently fed her. After he'd finished spooning the salty, nourishing liquid into her, she laid her head down and dozed off again. Will sat by the bedroom fire, exhausted from worry and lack of sleep. For the first time since he was a small boy, he'd prayed. He prayed that his sister would be spared, that she wouldn't go to join the rest of the family and leave him all alone in the world. He prayed, too, for the soul of the baby whose life had been torn away before it had even begun. Then he sat watching the early grey glow of dawn filter slowly over the great hill of Whernside, and he wondered who the bairn's father was. Anger tearing at his insides, he swore that he would kill the bastard who'd got her in the family way and then paid her to get rid of it.

Alice stirred, gently calling his name: 'Will? Where are you? What day is it?' With her wet, matted hair and dark-rimmed eyes, she looked more dead than alive.

'Quiet now, our lass. You're all right. Mind, I thought I'd lost you for a while there.' He hugged her tight in his arms as she struggled to raise herself from the bed, face cringing with pain as she tried to prop herself up.

'I'm sorry, Will, I'm so sorry. I didn't want you to know. I'm so cold . . . I've been to a dark place in my dreams. I saw Mum and she told me to go back, that it was not my time yet. Will, I'm frightened. Did I die? If I did, I should be in the fires of hell for what I've done.' Alice grabbed her tearful brother's arm, pleading with him for answers. He stroked her damp hair and held her tight, helping her lie down again.

'Never you mind, Ali. What's done is done. Let's get you better, eh? Go to sleep now. Tomorrow's Christmas Day and we're together; that's all that matters.'

He pulled the covers over her and waited until she had dozed off before getting up to add another log to the fire. Then he crept downstairs to prepare the chicken he had killed for Christmas Day. He had hoped that he would be celebrating Christmas in style this year, his first in his new home. But that would have to wait. Family mattered more, and Alice needed him; there would always be other Christmases.

'I could have done with that Alice. Trust it to snow and block her off from her work.' It was lunchtime at the manor, there were sauces and stuffings to be prepared, not to mention the huge goose to cook, and Mrs Dowbiggin was on her own. 'Stop standing like a useless lummock and help me set the table.' She was getting in a flap and poor Faulks was catching it. Though she couldn't speak of it to anyone, she was also worrying whether Alice was alive. Mrs Batty had told her the operation had been hard on the girl. 'Oh!

166

Get out of the way. I can do better myself. Men – absolutely useless, no good for anything.'

Pushing the butler out of the way, she polished the cutlery on her apron, then arranged it to her satisfaction on the table. 'See, that's how you do it. There's no secret to it, is there?'

Faulks bit his tongue. It was no secret that Mrs Dowbiggin's husband had run off with a neighbour, but Faulks thought better of telling her he could understand why the man had done it. After all, it was Christmas.

The job done, Mrs Dowbiggin stepped back to admire her handiwork. 'I do love a well-set table.' She was never one to miss an opportunity to sing her own praises. 'Oh my Lord! Is that my soup?' She rushed out of the dining room as the smell of something burning assaulted her nose.

'Nice job, Faulks, very impressive.' Gerald Frankland strolled into the dining room and admired the Christmas table.

'Thank you, sir. It was nothing.' The butler smiled inwardly to himself at getting the praise that should have been Mrs Dowbiggin's. 'Would sir like an aperitif? And will Miss Nancy be joining you?'

'Damn, I think I will – just a small brandy. After all, it is Christmas. Nancy will be along shortly. Smells like Mrs Dowbiggin is going to surprise us with something exotic for lunch. Is Alice helping her today?'

'I believe not, sir. The snow has prevented her

getting to work.' Faulks poured a brandy from the sparkling cut-glass decanter and passed it to his master.

'Pretty girl, don't you think, Faulks? I believe Jack has his eye on her. I'd say she was a bit too spirited for him. What do you think, Faulks?'

'I'm sorry, sir, I don't think it's my place to say.' Faulks bowed, then asked, 'Will that be all, sir?' Gerald Frankland's remarks made him uncomfortable and he wanted to escape, even if it meant returning to the hostile kitchen.

'Tell Mrs Dowbiggin that we will be eating at one. And this evening I may have some friends joining us, weather permitting. I'm sure she will conjure something up to delight my guests, even though there is no Alice to help her.' Frankland smiled. Leaning against the huge fireplace, glass in hand, he watched as the mealy-mouthed butler departed for the kitchen.

'Have you been tormenting our butler? I couldn't help but overhear your conversation. You are wicked, Gerald. No wonder you have such a terrible reputation!' Nancy entered the room and beckoned for her brother to pour her wine. Her maroon satin dress rustled as she sat in a chair in the window alcove overlooking the garden. 'You do realize the locals think this is a brothel? Alice told me so; she was quite embarrassed when I asked her what the locals thought of us.' She stared at her brother, smiling at his surprised expression.

'Me? I'm nothing but a gentleman! Can I be blamed if Faulks and Mrs Dowbiggin believe every word I say?

I swear I laughed myself sick when Mrs Dowbiggin fell for my story about Mrs Batty – that old woman is the nearest thing to a witch that I've come across. I wouldn't take my dog to her, never mind a young woman in trouble. If they believe that, they'll believe anything.' He tilted his glass, savouring the last drop of brandy.

'One day, Gerald Frankland, you will get yourself in trouble with that sense of humour. You know all too well they believe every word you say and still you tell them tales.'

'My dear, let them believe what they will. No good comes to those who listen behind doors. Besides, they should know better.' He helped himself to another brandy and sat down next to his sister. Outside, a blanket of snow covered the grounds and turned the trees to sparkling white sculptures. 'A white wonderland on Christmas Day. Mind you, it's a bit of a hindrance. I don't think our friends will be joining us, so it will probably just be me and you tonight. There was some doubt as to whether they could make it even without the snow. The situation in Russia is taking a turn for the worse; Tatiana wrote to me the other day to say that the Tsar is not in touch with his people. Many are dying of hunger and there have been protests on the streets of Moscow.'

Gerald gazed out at the falling snow, remembering Moscow and his beautiful Tatiana. In his mind's eye he pictured the way she'd looked the first time he set eyes on her, when she was helping out in the hospital where Nancy had been treated. It was then he had fallen madly in love with his dark-eyed Russian, not knowing that she was a best friend to the daughters of the Tsar. Why couldn't he have loved a normal girl instead of one linked to the royal family of Russia?

'Gerald, you've given me an idea.' Nancy grabbed her brother's hand. 'You've got good contacts in Russia; Will's struggling up at Stone House. How about you sell one of your fireplaces to the Tsar? Now that would be something to talk about and it would get us noticed in this godforsaken place. Imagine the respect those loutish workers would give Will then!'

'Have you listened to a word I've said, Nancy, my dear? Your head is so full of Will Bentham, you've no thought for my worries. And may I point out his absence this Christmas Day? Snow or no snow, I'd have thought that he'd at least have made the effort to see his employer and his beloved sister today.' He finished his second glass of brandy, swilling the last few dregs round the bowl of the glass before pouring himself another.

'Look at the weather – would you go out in this? Let him have one day away from work, Gerald. Will's tried really hard this last six months. He is turning things around for you at Stone House, you know he is.' Nancy offered her glass for a refill and smiled at her brother.

'You are sweet on him, aren't you, my dear. He's only a country bumpkin, you know. Can you imagine what Mama and Papa would have said if they'd caught their special girl going with a farmer's son? Easy with the wine, old girl. We don't want you tiddly before lunch – what would Mrs Dowbiggin say?' He gave her a wink then half filled her glass and handed it back to her.

'No wonder women are demanding the vote, Gerald Frankland. Any more comments like that and I've a good mind to join the suffragette movement. I'll drink as much as I like. Getting back to Will, I am sweet on him, it's true. He's good company, he treats me kindly, and he's not bothered by these terrible scars on my face. We are close.' Nancy blushed and took a deep drink.

Gerald shot her a dark look. 'Oh, don't be so stupid! He's not in our class. A common labourer is not fit for the likes of you. Besides, he's the first man you have really known. However, I will see what I can do regarding the Tsar. That's a good idea of yours – it would be quite something to have the Romanov seal of approval on our marble. I'll suggest it to Tatiana. You never know, it might get us both what we want.' He raised his glass. 'Cheers, old girl. Here's to love and prosperity: long may we have both. But keep away from common menfolk, eh?'

Alice tenderly propped herself up on the edge of the bed. Her legs felt like jelly and she couldn't stop shivering as if someone had just walked over her grave.

'There, our lass, slip your arm in here.' Gently Will helped dress his sister and then gave her his arm to lean on, helping her to the warm fireside. 'Not so fast. You're not ready to run the Derby yet,' he cautioned, putting his arm around her thin waist to steady her. 'We're going to have to fatten you up, our lass. There's nothing on you!'

Having gently seated her in the fireside chair, he threw another log on the fire and wrapped their mother's quilt around her to make sure that she was warm enough, before putting the kettle on to boil.

'Well, this is a queer Christmas Day compared to the ones we used to have. With last year's and this one, I'm beginning to doubt it will ever be the same. Remember how Father used to get merry on Mother's sloe gin? By this time, she'd have been playing pop with him for hindering dinner and then, nine times out of ten, he'd hug her and give her a kiss and she'd pretend to be mad with him, but really she was loving every minute. Can you remember, our Alice?'

Alice nodded wearily, feeling sad about times past. 'I'm sorry, Will, you'd probably have been at the manor now, or up at Jack's having dinner with them. And instead you're stuck with me. If I was you, I'd disown me – I've been nothing more than a prostitute, and now I've killed an innocent baby.'

'Quiet, our lass. No doubt you had your reasons. I'm not going to ask who the father is, because I'd only want to go and bloody shoot him, so it's best I don't know. Just promise me it isn't Jack's – although I know he's too much the gentleman for that. He'd have married you if he'd have known you were in the family

172

way. Anyways, as long as you recover and we still have one another, that's all that matters. Because, by God, we've been through enough this year.' He picked up the singing kettle and filled the teapot, stirring it thoughtfully.

Alice wrapped the quilt tightly around her. 'It wasn't Jack's. And you're right: it's best you don't know whose it was, because it would only cause trouble. Don't worry, Will, I feel weak, but I've learned my lesson. Next year I intend to start fending for myself – 1914 is going to be our year, the year when we both prove to each other that we are strong.'

'That's right, Ali – come back fighting! Here, have a sup of your tea and I'll see to dinner. Mother must be laughing her head off up in heaven at my attempt to cook, but I'm determined to have a Christmas dinner of some kind. I've peeled the sprouts and tatties, and the chicken's in the side oven – it may be a bit late, but we'll eat sometime today.'

'You're doing grand. Thanks for taking care of me, Will; I'm so grateful. There's many would have turned their backs on me.' Alice hung her head, gripped by self-loathing.

'Give over, Sis. Now, get your tea drunk and stop feeling sorry for yourself. Listen, I think I can hear the men up at the quarry huts singing – it must be bloody Christmas after all!'

The faint sound of carols filtered into the little cottage, bringing hope and Christmas spirit to the exhausted pair. The roasting chicken and the warmth of the fire set Alice dozing while Will listened to the melodies of his workforce. He didn't know what the next year would bring, but surely it couldn't be as bad as the last one. He prayed for it not to be.

12

'So, Alice, you've made it back to us.' Gerald Frankland contemplated the gaunt, ashen young girl. 'You look ill, Alice. Are you feeling all right? Mrs Dowbiggin informs me that you have had the flu. I hope that you have recovered sufficiently?' He turned and gazed out of the library window.

'I'm recovering slowly, sir, but I'm fit for work. Besides, I wouldn't want to let Miss Nancy down, especially for tonight's New Year Ball.' Alice quickly finished tidying the hearth and turned to make her escape from his questioning eyes.

'Surely you are joining us tonight, Alice? Nancy has been insisting that you must. She would really enjoy your company and I'm sure she has a spare dress you could wear. God knows I've bought her enough dresses, so there's bound to be something suitable, not that I know much about these frivolous things. What do you say, eh? A few dance steps might put a bit of colour in those pale cheeks.'

'I don't think so, sir. I'd feel out of place.' Alice's

heart fluttered. She had long dreamed of the moment when she would be asked to the manor's New Year Ball, but she still felt a little unsteady and faint.

'Nonsense! Your Will's invited, so you can keep him company. I'll speak to my sister, see if she can find you something to fit. I'm sure you will enjoy yourself. It'll be nice to see some sparkle in those blue eyes again.'

Gerald Frankland turned from the window to watch as Alice left the room, her cheeks flushed from his last comment. She didn't seem at all well and he wanted to show his concern. Moreover he knew his sister would feel more relaxed with her protégé by her side.

Alice closed the door behind her and leaned against it, brush and pan full of swept embers in her hands. Could she really summon the strength to attend the ball? The mind was willing, but her body felt so weak ... Yes, she resolved. No matter how poorly she felt, it had to be done.

'Oh! Alice, you look absolutely beautiful! That shade of blue really suits you; it brings out the colour of your eyes. Here, let me tie the bow tighter to show your waist off.' Nancy studied her companion. 'A bit of rouge on those pale cheeks and then you'll be perfect.'

Alice peered at her reflection, gasping at the sight of herself. The long sky-blue satin dress made her appear tall and slender, while her blonde hair – pinned up with the dragonfly comb that had been her birthday gift – gave her extra height. She almost didn't recognize the woman in the mirror. A fortnight ago, she had been near death and now here she was, attending the dale's largest social event. She smoothed the dress over her thighs and turned sideways to admire the perfectly formed figure. Secretly she couldn't help but be astounded: what had happened to the ugly duckling that she had once been?

'Doesn't Alice look beautiful?' Nancy sighed as her brother entered the room. Alice turned to see Gerald Frankland admiring her, as Nancy clapped her hands in glee at the transformation she'd brought about.

'Now I've two beautiful ladies to accompany me tonight. Alice, you're simply stunning. Heads will certainly turn when you take to the dance floor. As they will when you do, Nancy, my dear.' Gerald kissed his sister tenderly on the cheek. 'Will certainly does not deserve two such lovely ladies. I hope you tell him so, Nancy.'

He smiled and made his way to the door. He'd known Alice was pretty, but this was a revelation. Never had he seen such a perfect creature. The blue dress reflected her eyes, and her hair shone with the Fabergé comb, delicately placed at an angle. If only she was better bred! He didn't mind his sister showing an interest in Will, provided that was all it was; the thought of the relationship getting any deeper was beyond belief. A working-class man and a lady, it didn't bear thinking about! However, with it being common knowledge among their tight circle that Nancy had inherited their mother's weaknesses, it was unlikely that anybody of their own class would take an

177

interest in his younger sister. And at least Will was making her happy. Gerald, on the other hand, could not form an attachment with someone just because she made him happy; it would have to be someone with class, someone to carry on the family name, not a common working-class girl.

'Ladies, I'll see you downstairs. Nancy, don't forget to circulate – we are the hosts, after all, and don't you spend all night with Will!'

'I won't. But some of the guests are so stuffy, Gerald. Do I really have to talk to everyone?'

'Everyone, Nancy. It's expected of us.' Gerald wagged his finger at his complaining sister as he left the room.

'Boring fuddy-duddy,' Nancy complained as she sat heavily on the edge of her bed.

Alice gave herself another glance in the mirror, still amazed at her reflection, then went to close the heavy curtains. When she got to the window, she stopped and urged Nancy to join her. The moon was rising, clear and glimmering white, its smiling face beaming down upon the manor. The sky was purple and pink with hues of the dying day foretelling of the hard frost that was going to cover the dale through the night. The snow twinkled in the moonlight, like scatterings of millions of diamonds, making the view magical.

'Isn't it beautiful? Like something out of a fairy tale. Let's hope that tonight we meet our princes; then it would truly be a wonderful night.' Nancy squeezed Alice's hand.

The two young women made their way down the stairs and into the hallway, their dresses rustling with the weight of material. Nancy's jewellery sparkled in the light as they reached the doorway. The strains of the Beresford Band could be heard throughout the manor, and holly, mistletoe and ivy adorned the hall and adjoining rooms, while log fires burned brightly in the hearths.

'Alice, go warm yourself by the fire and listen to the band while I welcome our guests.' Nancy patted Alice's hand and ushered her into the large ballroom, which had chairs all around the sides for guests who wanted a rest from dancing. The band was in the far corner of the hall, playing the latest refrains.

Leaning against the fireplace in his best suit and with his hair smoothed back was Jack. As Alice entered he looked up from warming his hands and for a moment or two stood gaping at her, lost for words, as she crossed the dance floor, smiling gently at him.

'By God, you scrub up real well, Alice Bentham.' Taken aback by her beauty, Jack had momentarily forgotten where he was.

'Thank you. You're not so bad yourself. No one told me you'd be here; it's a surprise to see you.' Alice bowed her head sheepishly: she hadn't forgotten that last time she had spoken to him, she had been sharp with her words, something that she'd been regretting ever since she said them.

'Aye, well, I came in my father's place. He's not so good – the rheumatics are playing up in this cold weather. By heck, I'm glad I did come, just to see you all dressed up like you are.' Jack grinned and then blushed.

'Jack, I'm really sorry. I was being selfish and self-centred when I lost my temper. I acted like a spoilt school girl. Can you ever forgive me?' She gazed bashfully at Jack. For once she was willing to admit that she'd been in the wrong; if Jack was saving up for something, it was none of her business.

'It's forgotten. Come on, let's help ourselves to a glass of the punch. I've had my eye on it ever since I came in, but didn't want to help myself.'

He held his arm out for Alice to take, which she did, smiling at easy-going Jack. How she'd missed him, if only as a friend. He was very special to her.

The room was full of Dales people enjoying celebrating New Year's Eve, wishing better fortunes to everyone for the coming year. The band played while everyone danced, drank or chatted, the ballroom alive with noise and laughter. At the stroke of midnight, everyone joined in a large circle, standing next to the one they loved, and sang 'Auld Lang Syne', their cheerful faces welcoming the new year in. Alice held Jack's hand as she rushed backwards and forwards with the crowds to the chorus, Jack admiring every move she made. Then, when the song ended, Jack held her tight around the waist and kissed her passionately, whispering, 'Happy New Year,' and telling her how much he loved her.

Burying her face in his shoulder, Alice tried to hide

the tears that were running down her cheeks, as she murmured her best wishes for the new year. But, try as she might, she could not bring herself to tell Jack that she loved him. She wasn't sure: her heart told her one thing and her head another. Jack was many a girl's dream, but he wasn't enough for her. She needed something more than to be a farmer's wife, she needed to see the world and have fun.

Jack lifted her chin and gave her a tender kiss, trying to get the response he needed to hear. She smiled fondly at him, trying not to hurt his feelings, knowing what he was expecting, but unable to say the words. Relief swept over her as Gerald Frankland saved her from the awkward situation by tapping Jack on the shoulder and requesting the next dance with Alice. Jack hesitantly released Alice into the hands of her employer, who immediately took command of the dance floor, sweeping her off her feet as they waltzed round the ballroom.

'Sorry, I thought you needed saving from Jack.' Gerald Frankland spoke quietly as they danced. 'He looked a bit intense and you appeared to be uncomfortable.' He smiled at Alice, who was feeling safe and secure in his arms, unaware of the interest people were showing in the couple as they glided round the room.

'I think he got carried away with the night, that's all.' Alice smiled, spotting Jack in the crowd watching the woman he loved dancing with the lord of the manor. He was taking a long sip from a glass of punch. Next time Alice turned to see him, he'd gone, making her anxious to know where he was but at the same time less nervous of dancing with her new partner.

The night flew by as the couple danced on, making all the locals gossip at the unlikely alliance of commoner and lord. By the time the clock struck two, the ballroom was beginning to empty and Alice was exhausted, nearly collapsing in his arms at the end of their last dance together.

'My poor girl, I've worn you out. You dance so perfectly and I've enjoyed your company so much, I forgot that you've been ill. Forgive me. Here, let me help you up the stairs.' Gerald Frankland unthinkingly offered to carry his dance partner to her room.

'Please, I think we have caused enough scandal tonight, without the lord of the manor carrying me to my room in front of his guests. I'll make my own way, thank you.'

Alice's cheeks were flushed with embarrassment and the excitement of the evening. She had loved every minute, but she didn't want to be the cause of further talk. Shakily she made her way up the stairs and into her bedroom. Heart racing, she lay down on the bed, thoughts of Jack and Lord Frankland racing through her mind. She whispered, 'Gerald,' under her breath, and then her conscience kicked in with thoughts of poor Jack and his confession of love for her. No, she must not think or even fantasize about her employer; she should be true to Jack ... Giggling quietly to herself, she kicked her shoes off and admired herself yet again in the mirror before stepping out of the borrowed dress and into her nightclothes. Best foot forward, she told herself. This was only the start of the year: 1914, a new year brimming with hope and the love of Jack and the longing glances of Gerald Frankland. Now, which one did she want?

'He did what? Over my dead body.' Gerald Frankland was fuming, raising his voice at the breakfast table.

'But, Gerald, I've said yes. I love him, truly I do, and he loves me.' Nancy Frankland pleaded with her brother.

'Will Bentham had no right to ask you to marry him, not without my permission. For God's sake, has the man no manners? You must tell him no, say that I have forbidden it. On second thoughts, never mind – I'll tell him myself. I'll go up to Stone House later this morning. He needs to know he can't simply propose like that – and to do it in our stable after trying to take advantage of my little sister!' Gerald Frankland sliced into his ham and eggs with the fervour of an outraged man.

'So it's all right for you to show yourself up, dancing all night with Alice, but it's not all right for me to accept a proposal from the man I love. No matter how lowly his roots, Gerald, I do love him.' Nancy stood her ground.

'Damn it, woman, it was a bit of fun with a servant, nothing more. I'm not like you, about to lose all status

183

for a bit of rough.' Gerald spat out the words. His head was throbbing from hitting the wine after his guests had departed.

All night his mind had been on the young woman who was sleeping under his roof, and he'd had to fight the impulse to go and knock on her bedroom door in the hope that she'd let him in. Then to top it all, Nancy had come to the breakfast table with news of her engagement to Will. He slammed his knife and fork down.

'Bloody hell, old girl, he's as common as muck. Still, if you love him, we'll have to do something about it. But believe me, Alice was just a bit of fun, someone to dance with in place of darling Tatiana – you know how much I miss her.'

Nancy rose from her seat, put her arm around Gerald and gently kissed his cheek. 'He makes me happy. Please accept that. I don't care if he's no money. And, Gerald, don't shout: Alice is only in the kitchen. You wouldn't want to upset your new sister-in-law now, would you? Love you, sweetie. You'll see, he will make me so happy.'

'Yes, we'll see. This last twelve-month does seem to have revolved round one or other of the Benthams. If you love him, we'll have to do something about it, I suppose. I can't go on ignoring this stupid fancy, but even though he did save my life, I don't agree with the match and never will. At least I know he's honourable, though. So I'll go and see him. And yes, to help him win respect, I'll conjure up an important order for him and that dratted marble works. Anything to make you happy. Now, leave me in peace with my breakfast. I've a thumping headache and I can't do with you sounding so happy around me.'

Gerald grunted and stirred his coffee as he watched his sister gaily running from the room. He wasn't happy, but he'd have to live with it.

'Well, I don't know what the world's coming to! A farm labourer marrying our Miss Nancy, it's just not right. He might be in charge of the marble works now, but that means nothing. Mr Gerald was only being right with him after that incident with the fire – and he even caused that.' Mrs Dowbiggin stirred the pan of soup, her back to Faulks, complaining about the proposal.

'Too true, Mrs Dowbiggin. I agree with your every word. Things are definitely not like what they used to be. And I'll tell you something else: his lordship is sweet on Alice. You know there was a time you expected your employer to take advantage of a good-looking servant discreetly, on the quiet. Not to dance with her in front of all and sundry. That's not on!' Faulks spat on the shoes he was polishing and brushed with vigour until he saw them shine.

'Quite so, Mr Faulks. Standards are slipping. I blame it on these suffragettes. A woman should know her place: in the kitchen, in the bedroom and married to someone of her own class. There's too much rubbish about equal rights. It hurts me to say this, but men will

185

always be superior. Still, never mind. As long as Miss Nancy's happy, there's nothing we can do but plan for a wedding. I heard Master Gerald saying he was going up to Stone House today, so he might be talking Will Bentham out of it.' She stirred the soup and added salt before trying it.

'What's Master Gerald talking our Will out of?' Alice entered the kitchen. 'What's my brother been up to now?'

'Oh, my dear – I didn't realize you were there. I don't think it's my place to say. You should hear it from your brother first,' Mrs Dowbiggin spluttered as the hot soup burned her lip.

Faulks quickly excused himself, pretending that the shoes he had been polishing were urgently needed. He wanted no part of the cross-examination Mrs Dowbiggin was about to be subjected to.

'What do you mean? You obviously know something I don't, so go on, tell me: what's he been up to?' Alice stood her ground, holding the back of the chair and rising to her full height to slightly intimidate the gossiping housekeeper.

'Well, my dear, I overheard Miss Nancy talking to Master Gerald this morning. It seems your brother proposed to her last night and they're getting married. Miss Nancy is to be your sister-in-law! Now, isn't that grand?' Mrs Dowbiggin watched Alice's face as she absorbed the news. 'I thought that would take the wind out of your sails. I'd have thought one of them would have told you first, but then you were a little busy yourself last night . . .'

'The stupid bloody idiot! What does he think he's doing?' Alice pulled out the chair and sat down, running her fingers through her long hair.

'We'll have none of that language in my kitchen, my girl. But yes, that's what I thought about Miss Nancy. No disrespect, but she is marrying well below her station. Anyway, I've said enough; it's not for me to comment. You know me, I mind my own business, keep myself to myself.' And with that she scurried off to the pantry.

Alice sat at the table, trying to get to grips with the news. Will getting married to Nancy . . . Where would they live? What would become of her? And most of all, how could he afford the wedding that Nancy dreamed of? Oh, why hadn't he talked to her first? She felt hurt and left out. She'd thought she was best friend to both of them, yet they'd not let her into their secret. Even the housekeeper knew before her! How could they? Just how could they!

'Alice! I'm so glad that you are here. I wanted to tell you the news, but by the time I came in from talking to Will, you had gone to bed. Alice, I'm going to get married to your brother. Isn't that fantastic news! Can you believe it? He proposed to me last night. My heart's all aflutter. Tell me that you are happy for us – do say you are happy. To think that you are to be my

187

sister-in-law! I still can't believe it – pinch me, I think I'm dreaming.'

'Congratulations, Miss Nancy.' Alice's voice was cold, without sentiment.

'Oh, Alice, we are going to be so happy. To think that only last year I was convinced that life held nothing for me, and now I'm about to be married. And to make things even better, Gerald is setting up an order for the marble works from the Tsar of Russia! I suspect he will be the next to announce his engagement. You know he's in love with Tatiana, who's in the Tsar's circle of close friends? He's been waiting for her to come of age, and then I'm sure they will be married. I'm so happy.' Nancy smiled and composed herself on the edge of her bed.

'Master Gerald's to be engaged! I didn't know.' Alice could hear herself nearly scream the words.

'Well, not quite yet, but it wouldn't surprise me. They have been close for a while now. Isn't it exciting, all this romance? We will have to get you and Jack together, and then that would make us all happy.'

Nancy carried on prattling happily, but Alice didn't hear a word. She was thinking that, considering it was still only the first day of January, the new year was not treating her kindly. First she'd discovered that her brother had kept her in the dark, and now it turned out that the man she was beginning to admire and have feelings for was virtually betrothed – to a Russian royal, of all people. Why had she even thought she was in his league? He'd been toying with her. She should have realized that behind those smouldering eyes was a menacing, brothel-keeping ogre. A man who was playing games with her. Yet when she looked into his eyes, her legs turned to jelly. Why couldn't life go smoothly? How was it that Will had it all on a plate: never worked hard, gave enough blarney to get by on and everything fell at his feet?

'Of course, Alice, you will still be my companion, won't you? This should make us closer. Alice, Alice, are you listening to me?' The voice was like a distant echo as Alice automatically tidied and put away Nancy's clothes while her mind was racing with all the news.

'Sorry, Nancy, yes, of course I will. I just don't think you will need my services for much longer.' Alice thought that it was best if she tackled her position first.

'Nonsense. I'll need you even more, especially when Will and I have children . . . although the doctors have warned me it could be dangerous for me to bear children. But what do they know? I want to be a mother like my dear mama, perhaps having three or four darling babies. I'm sure Will is going to make a most perfect father; he has so much patience.' Nancy sat in her morning chair, face rosy and happy, wishing nothing more than to be married as soon as possible to the man of her dreams.

'I'm sorry, Nancy, please excuse me – I'm feeling a little faint. I must have tired myself out last night with dancing. Your brother is very light on his feet and I got carried away with the grandeur of the occasion.' Alice had heard all she could take of Nancy's plans, and in truth she was slightly jealous.

She went downstairs and out of the grand front door – the same door that only a few months ago she had been brazen enough to knock on, having no idea then of her place in life. Lifting her skirts, she carefully made her way through the snow, shivering in the cold and wishing that she had picked up a shawl before hurrying out in need of some breathing space. The air was curiously still and not a noise could be heard all down the dale. It was as if there were no other souls on the planet, only Alice, alone in her grief.

Once in the stables, she called for Jack. She didn't think he'd be there; if what Mrs Dowbiggin said was correct, he'd probably have taken Lord Frankland to Stone House. Not a sound: good, she was on her own, exactly what she wanted. She needed time to think things out. She walked past the stalls with the horses munching content on their hay bags or oats, the smell of the animals comforting, reminding her of home. She stopped and stroked the nose of her favourite horse; blowing up its nose to make friends with the creature was a trick her father had taught her. The horse snorted, enjoying the attention as she gave it a handful of oats.

'I don't know, lad, what am I going to do? Nothing seems to be going right for me.' She hugged the horse's neck, expecting no response but feeling better for something to talk to that wouldn't answer back. 'Why does everything go wrong, lad? I've no parents, no real home, and I've just got rid of my baby – poor mite, it had not hurt anyone – and now my brother's lost his senses and is getting married to someone he doesn't really love. And then there's Jack. I know he loves me, but he could do a lot better than me because he's a good man. I don't really love him. I know who I do love, but I can't have him and never will.' The horse munched and gazed at her with its big doe eyes, shaking its head as if in agreement. 'I know, lad, you can't answer me, but I needed to talk to someone.' She patted its neck. Shivering, she folded her arms tight around her, then set off back to the manor.

Up in the hayloft Jack stared at the oak beams, lying on the makeshift bed he used when keeping vigil over a foaling mare. He'd heard every word Alice had said and now he realized it was no good. Whose baby had she been carrying? Whoever the baby belonged to, it was no longer . . . How could she? He would have looked after her, cared for her and the baby, if only she'd said . . . She had broken his heart, if she only knew it. Still, he was going to show her. In another month or two he'd be a man of property. The Alderson family owning two farms in the dale – perhaps that would turn her head.

'Now, Will, I understand you proposed to my sister last night. Did you not realize there is such a thing as protocol? I should have been informed of your decision before you asked for Nancy's hand. Do you really think that she is the right woman for you? And how are you going to keep her in the manner she is accustomed to?'

As he waited for an answer, Gerald studied his soon-to-be brother-in-law. He quite admired the fellow, but Nancy could have done so much better if her reputation and appearance had been up to standard.

'We'll manage, Master Gerald. I do truly love and care for her, and I'm sorry I didn't realize that I had to ask for your blessing first.'

Will had expected this visit all morning and had dreaded it. Of course he had realized he should have asked Gerald Frankland's permission first, but he wasn't about to tell him that. He had known that once Nancy said yes, her brother wouldn't dare say no. He'd been counting on the fact that Gerald would do anything to make her happy.

'Well, I don't know, Will Bentham. I always wanted her to marry someone titled, but true to form, my sister has to go and fall in love with a hired man. No house, not a great deal of money and no title does not place you very high in my society. However, if you truly love her, I can't stand in the way. She deserves some happiness in her life. There's not been a great deal of that since our parents died.' He sat, crossing his long legs, and studied the perplexed face of his employee. 'Now, financial matters, of which my sister knows nothing: she receives a yearly allowance of five thousand pounds from our parents' estate. This is paid into my bank account at the moment; of course, it will be transferred to yours once you have become man and wife. I'm also prepared to transfer the deeds to the marble works to you as my wedding present, which would give you this cottage to live in as your secure home. What's more, I'm in the process of finalizing an order that will give you a great deal of prestige in society – I'll tell you more of that shortly. Now, how does that sound? In return, I want you to promise to look after her. My sister's needs must come first.' Gerald Frankland searched Will's face, trying to read his reaction.

'I don't know what to say, Lord Frankland,' said Will, dumbstruck. 'I didn't expect all that. I just wanted the hand of Nancy. Truly, there is no need for your generosity. And, yes, I will put her before my own life always.'

'In that case, Will, welcome to the family. You must call me Gerald from now on. The one proviso I have is that you must make it a discreet wedding. St John's, I think, not Dent parish church; she wouldn't want everyone gawping at her. She still thinks people look at her as if she were a monster. And then a small reception back at the manor. What do you say. That all right?'

'I don't know what to say, except thank you. I hadn't even planned that far ahead. It's all happening so fast.'

Inside, Will was ecstatic. All that money! He couldn't believe it. And the marble works! He wanted to yell for joy, but knew he had to keep it reined in, at least until Gerald Frankland had gone.

'Well, get on with it, man. One more thing. You might need these – they were Nancy's mother's.' Gerald

Frankland reached into his inside pocket and pulled out a ring box containing a diamond-encrusted engagement ring and a wedding ring. 'They will mean a great deal to her.' Shaking Will's hand, he passed the box to him. 'Good luck, old man. Make her happy.' He patted Will on the back and then left him in a state of shock and ecstasy.

All that money! Not in a million years had he dreamed of owning all this and having money as well. Small price to pay for marrying a scarred, spoilt bitch. Hopefully their night of passion in the stable would have sealed the deal. He hoped that she was pregnant; then there would be no way of getting out of the forthcoming wedding. Yes, things were definitely on the turn for Will Bentham. Why, he was almost related to nobility now.

'Master Gerald needs to see you in the study, Alice. He's back from Stone House – don't know if it's good news or bad news, but he's going through his papers. His desk is in a right mess.' Mrs Dowbiggin placed the tea tray on the table and sighed.

'He wants to see me? Did he say what for, and do you think it's urgent?' Alice quickly checked her hair in the small kitchen mirror.

'How would I know? I'm more bothered about my lumbago – it is giving me jip. Besides, I'm not told anything any more. I've worked for this family more than twenty-five years and I'm not told nothing.' She rattled the dirty teapots in the sink and turned away from Alice, muttering to herself.

Alice smiled. In the study on her own with Gerald . . . perhaps there was hope. She pinched her cheeks and checked her dress; she wanted to look her best.

'Ah! Alice, do come in.' Gerald Frankland fixed Alice with a penetrating gaze, gently rocking in his office chair. 'So, what are we to do? My sister is to marry your brother. Neither can be talked out of it . . . Which leaves me with a predicament: what am I to do with you?'

Alice's face dropped a mile. Was she going to be told to go, to make her own way in the world? She couldn't bear that her life was so hard.

'If we are soon to be related through marriage, we can't have you working for us any more. That would not be correct; family and servants should remain separate. However, it's obvious that my sister adores you, so provided you are in agreement I propose that you leave your brother's cottage and move into the manor. You will occupy one of the good spare bed-rooms and eat your meals with us – after all, we can't have you telling Mrs Dowbiggin all our news around that kitchen table, can we? In return, you must offer Nancy your devoted friendship, help her plan her wedding, go shopping with her, do whatever it is that you women get up to in your spare time. I've told your brother this morning that Stone House is to be his marital home and I am now in the process of signing the whole works and cottage over to him. Your brother will be a rich man, if he plays his cards right. I'm also willing to give you a small allowance, just to help while you are living with us. I want to make everything above board; you know how people talk. So, what do you think, Alice? Does that sound agreeable to you?'

Speechless, Alice could only nod.

He reached across the desk to shake her hand. 'In that case, welcome to the family. I promise that as long as Nancy is happy we will see that you are looked after.'

Tears of happiness in her eyes, Alice shook his hand. Being part of the Frankland family was something she had dreamed about since those early days when she had toyed with the idea of marrying sultry Lord Frankland and becoming mistress of Whernside Manor.

'What are you waiting for? Go and choose which bedroom you want. I'd choose the blue room myself: it catches all the sunlight in the morning. Faulks will help you move your possessions. And, Alice, I enjoyed our few dances last night. Perhaps we can dance together more often, now we are to be related.'

Gerald smiled as he saw the tears again welling up in Alice's eyes before she turned and hurried from the room. He'd always had her down as a fighter; something must have laid her spirits low. Perhaps it was the Christmas period. Everyone missed departed loved ones at Christmas and New Year; it had been years since his own parents died, but he still felt their absence. She would soon cheer up now that she had been relieved of worries about money and work and where to live.

Nancy had made it clear that she wanted Alice to be part of the wedding package. Who'd have thought it, after their first encounter? He smiled to himself at the memory of Alice holding her own against the sneering staff and his raging sister. She'd spoken her mind, too full of pride to be cowed by them. Funny old world: he'd travelled the globe, yet he never felt more relaxed than when he gazed into the cornflower-blue eyes of his soon-to-be sister-in-law.

Alice leaned against the closed study door. Had she heard right? Was she now part of the family? Was Gerald really signing the cottage and marble works over to Will? If so, all their worries were over. In the space of an hour, she had gone from abject despair to elation. A proper home, with money and good food. And she'd be looking across the dining table every day at the man of her dreams. This really was going to be the year all her wishes came true.

When she got to the kitchen, however, she was soon brought down to earth by the sight of Mrs Dowbiggin and Faulks in secretive discussion.

'I don't think you should be with us. Faulks has told me the scenario. You'll be thinking yourself better than us now. Never in all my days have I heard any-thing so scandalous! Take heed, my girl: no good will come of this. If I were you, I'd lock my door on a night and warn that brother of yours what he's really taken on. He'll earn every penny he's got out of Master Gerald; you can tell him that from me.'

'I don't believe it's any of your business, Mrs Dowbiggin. It's between my brother and Lord Frankland – or Gerald, as I'm to call him from now on.' Alice smiled. Now that it had finally sunk in that she had no more worries, she couldn't resist a bit of mischief while at the same time putting the stuffy housekeeper in her place.

'Well, you've changed your colours! The pair of you have worked your way into this family and now you're going to drag it into the gutter. Well, it'll be over my dead body that you harm this family. Nancy was best off left alone in her bedroom with her memories and us to take care of her – no harm would have come to her then.' Mrs Dowbiggin took the copper pan that she'd been waving at Alice as if she wanted to clout her with it and put it on the pan rack.

'Mrs Dowbiggin, please. I've always confided in you, and the only thing my brother has done wrong is fall in love with someone out of his class. Is that such a sin? Please, we all have to live and work together, and I don't want any bad feeling between us. I'm truly grateful for everything that everyone's done for me these last few months. I'll never forget your help, especially.' Alice squeezed the chubby red arm of her accuser with affection. 'I'm lucky, Mrs Dowbiggin, but I'll never forget where I came from and who helped me get this far. All I ask is that you wish Will and Nancy luck. Because, as you say, they are going to need it. Moreover, I'm going to need your help. I've so much to learn – I don't want to let the family down.' Alice smiled at the blustering housekeeper and hope that she'd smoothed her ruffled feathers.

'Aye, well, we'll see. But it's still a rum carry-on.' Mrs Dowbiggin threw her tea towel roughly over her shoulder. 'And I don't know what this useless lump's gawping at – he's supposed to be moving you into your new room.' She deftly flicked the end of the tea towel at Faulks, who up till then had stood on the sidelines, saying nothing.

'Don't bring me into your petty argument. Unlike some, I know my place and keep my thoughts to myself. And kindly refrain from using that tea towel upon my personage.' Faulks rose from his chair. 'Which room is to be yours, Miss Alice? Are we to move your belongings now or later?'

' "Miss Alice" – listen to you! She's Alice, you big galoot,' Mrs Dowbiggin mumbled to herself.

'She is now Miss Alice to me, as I will have to remember when we are in public. Now, which room did Master Gerald want you to have, Miss Alice?' Faulks's face was sombre. Mrs Dowbiggin may not have realized it yet, but changes were afoot at the manor and he had every intention of keeping abreast of the times.

'The blue room, Faulks. And thank you for help-ing me move my few possessions.' Alice smiled at the poker-faced butler; perhaps he was not so bad. Mrs Dowbiggin bullied him something terrible, and yet he never so much as batted an eyelid.

'Good choice by Master Gerald – it gets all the morning sun. Follow me and we will see to it straight away, Miss Alice.'

'Stuffy old cock,' Mrs Dowbiggin muttered as the pair moved out of the kitchen. 'No good will come of this day, you mark my words.'

13

'You've certainly come off well with my forthcoming marriage, Sis. I'm still in shock myself. I can't believe how much comes with our dear Nancy. Hard to believe no one else has picked her up with her being worth all that money.' Will Bentham sat in his usual fireside seat, his shoes practically smoking from the warmth of the fire as he rested them on the trivet. 'She's worth a mint! We'll never want for a penny.'

'Everything comes at a price, our Will. Do you really know what you've taken on? I can't help but think there's something wrong. A woman of her standing should not be marrying one of us. I don't want to see any one of us hurt – I've had enough hurt lately to last me a lifetime.' Alice took her cloak off and sat in the chair next to her brother.

'Give over – we're made! You're always looking at the downside, you are. Here you are living in the fancy house you've always dreamed of, and here's me with my own business, a wife that'll adore me and a nice income – what more can we wish for? All we need to do now is find you a fellow from the snooty circles you'll be moving in and then we've cracked it.' Will grinned at his sister as she played with her fur-trimmed gloves. 'I see you've been spending their money already: new gloves, dress and cloak. That lot must have cost a pretty penny.'

'Nancy said I'd to have them when we went to Kendal the other week. She had a fitting for her wedding dress and while we were there she insisted I should have a new dress and cloak. I don't know how much they cost: it was all billed to the manor.' Alice fumbled with the gloves, embarrassed. She had thought that she would enjoy having clothes bought for her and being treated like a lady, but in all honesty, she wasn't comfortable in her new position. She was neither one thing nor the other, with no purpose in life other than being companion to Nancy. She had also felt extremely uncomfortable when the dressmaker measured her, eyeing her up and down, making her feel like something on the bottom of her shoe. Nancy had assured her that the woman was only doing her job and not to be so silly. But still she felt unworthy of the quality material that was being draped on her.

'Well, we'll have to find you somebody, 'cos I see you and Jack have fallen out, else he wouldn't have had Amy Lawson on his arm in the Moon the other night. Can't say I blame him, like. She is a bonny bit of a thing.' He smiled, remembering Jack giving Amy a kiss outside the pub's entrance.

'I . . . I didn't know Jack had found someone else.

202

Is she all right, this Amy? I don't think I know her.'
Alice was taken aback. She knew Jack had been avoiding her, but she thought that he would have had the decency to tell her that they'd finished and that he had moved on. She missed Jack's company; he was a best friend who always made everything all right, no matter how bad things were. How she wished that he were still friends with her, just for company and for someone to talk to and share her concerns with.

''Course you know her; she's from Bridge End. Her father once sold us a bull – queer old bloke, said he'd come and do the job himself if his bull didn't perform. She's probably like her father. Knowing Jack, he'll be going at it like a rabbit up in that bed over the stables!' Will grinned, oblivious to the hurt he was causing his sister.

'Don't be so vulgar, our Will! Besides, there is no bedroom at the stables, so he won't be doing any such thing.'

'There bloody well is! He uses it when he's got a broody mare or when he wants a bit of peace and quiet, so that nobody knows he's there. Funny bugger, I've often shouted for him at the stable door with no reply, only to find him laying low up in that hayloft, not wanting to talk to anyone. Come to think of it, you two are a lot alike. He goes up in his loft, and you go up the fell. Funny buggers, the pair of you.'

'I didn't know he had a room up there.' Alice now knew why Jack had been avoiding her. He'd been there in his hidey-hole the day when she was upset and talked to his horse. No wonder he was avoiding her like the plague. She had thought it was because of her new position at the manor; she should have known better. Jack wasn't like that. One day she'd tell him the truth, but not yet. 'I hope he'll be happy with Amy. Me and him just weren't meant to be.'

'Come on, our lass, cheer up. Bloody hell, you're hard work today! Another few months and it's my wedding. What do you think our folks would say? I'll never forget that evening when Gerald Frankland brought Father home. God, the old man was drunk. That's when all this started, if you think about it.'

Alice tried to rally her spirits with thoughts of the wedding. For all her faults, Nancy was a good woman who was in love with Will. 'So have you got a new suit? And who's to be your best man? You know I'm your matron of honour, don't you?' Alice grinned at her brother. 'Don't tell me, let me guess: it's Jack, isn't it? I can't understand why none of their family is coming, not even any of Gerald's friends. It's going to be a quiet affair, because there's not many of our side still standing.'

'Never mind, Sis, we'll all be there that counts. As long as I get a ring on her finger, that's all that matters. Don't worry, I'll tell Jack not to rub your nose in it with his latest conquest. I know you think a lot of him really.' He winked. He'd noticed how upset she'd been when he joked about Jack and Amy, but it would never have worked between Alice and Jack. Too much to handle, was his sister. She'd soon have got bored with his steady best friend.

'Don't care if he does. I've got other fish to fry.' Alice wasn't going to let her brother's words hurt her. Besides, when it came to Jack, she was the one who had done all the hurt; she deserved everything she got. But she was damned if she was going to let her brother know that.

'That's it, lass – don't let the buggers grind you down. No matter how bad it gets, keep on fighting, else they've won and that's not what life's about. What's made you come up here today to visit, then? No lords or ladies to entertain or take high tea with?'

'Gerald's going through his tenancies for the year. There'll be tenants going in and out of his office all day today. I thought it would be better if I made myself scarce. We're the talk of the dale as it is, without me being there to add to the gossip. Imagine the embarrassment if Father's friends saw me strutting about, dressed to the nines, when they'd come cap in hand to keep their homes for another year.'

'But we've done nothing wrong, Alice. We've only taken what was on offer to us and made the best of a bad situation. Come on, lass, it's what you've always wanted: big house, good clothes, full belly – a lot more than we've had in the past.'

'You don't understand. We have all the material things that we ever needed, but I realize now it's not them that's important. It's knowing who you are, being

205

your own person and having your freedom. I love being part of the family, but I need that little bit more security, same as you have.' Alice reached for her cloak and put it around her shoulders. 'I've got to go. I'm meeting Mrs Dowbiggin at St John's. We've got to decide how to decorate the church. Thank God you both chose April – at least there will be spring flowers to decorate it with!' She opened the cottage door and smiled at Will.

'Ali, if you don't like it, change it. Set your head and go for it – bring me back my stubborn, headstrong little sister, the one with the attitude, please.' He got up and kissed her tenderly on her cheek. 'Stick me some dandelions in a jam jar – that'll do for their wedding. Let's bring 'em down to our level.'

'Nay, we can't have that, our Will. They'd be wetting the bed all night – isn't that what Mum used to say when we picked dandelions?' Alice grinned and closed the door.

Will was right: she needed a kick up the bum. After all, she was now Miss Alice, not plain Alice Bentham; she had an allowance and was about to help arrange her brother's wedding to Lord Frankland's sister. Enough moaning – time to get on with things.

The walk to the church was exactly what Alice needed. Although it was only the end of January, the weather was quite mild and she enjoyed the two-mile stroll from Stone House to St John's, breathing in the sharp, clear air and seeing early signs of spring all around her.

Lichen covered the tops of the walls and the bark of the bare trees, making everything greener than the grey day should have permitted. In another week or two, the grassy banks would be full of celandines, primroses and wood sorrel and the pungent aroma of wild garlic would fill the air along the riverside. The trees would be filled with nesting birds and the dark nights would soon be gone. It was a time to look forward, to get on with life and stop dwelling on the past.

'Where have you been? I thought me and Faulks were going to freeze to death in this little church. It isn't like the one at Dent; there's nothing grand about this one. There was me getting in a tizz, worrying about all the preparations that needed doing, and Faulks has just told me that there's only going to be ten at the wedding. Lord Frankland doesn't want a big do, doesn't think Miss Nancy could handle it.' Mrs Dowbiggin shook her head. 'It gets stranger by the minute. I always dreamed that a Frankland wedding would be a splendid affair. I was really looking forward to decorating the church and manor, cooking for a huge wedding party and making the finest wedding cake, and now Master Gerald's saying immediate family only. It's a rum do, is this wedding.'

'I like St John's. It's a lovely little church, nestled here among the yew trees and with the river running by. I don't think Nancy and Will would have felt comfortable in anything bigger. This is charming.' Alice surveyed the wooden pews and glittering altarpieces and felt a peace she hadn't known in a long time. 'It's not all about status, Mrs Dowbiggin; it's about being right for the moment.' She watched the old house-keeper wrinkle her nose and run a finger along the altar. 'I hope that they will be very happy together and that their union will be blessed with children.'

'Hold your tongue! That's the last thing we want to hear at the manor – you couldn't have cursed this union more if you tried!' Mrs Dowbiggin's eyes flashed as if Alice had sworn in the house of the Lord.

'Mrs Dowbiggin, enough! Miss Alice only meant well, didn't you, dear?' Faulks intervened.

The two servants exchanged looks. Though no words were spoken, they were remembering Nancy's mother teetering on the brink of insanity after child-birth. It was a curse that had plagued generation after generation of Frankland women.

Observing them, Alice curbed the impulse to snap at the old housekeeper and instead took her by the hand and said softly, 'Of course I meant well. Everyone wants to see children from a marriage. Why do you call it a curse, Mrs Dowbiggin? You seem certain that this marriage is doomed and I don't understand why, especially when Nancy is so happy.'

Mrs Dowbiggin took her handkerchief out of her coat pocket and began patting her eyes. Putting an arm around her, Alice led her to one of the oak pews and they sat down. Faulks, sensing that women's talk was imminent, made himself scarce. He only hoped that he had been sharp enough to stop Mrs Dowbiggin from saying anything out of turn.

'I'm being overprotective, Alice, that's all. The worst pain that any woman can have is childbirth. I'm almost like a mother to that girl and I don't want her to go through that. You know how it is.' Mrs Dowbiggin, obviously flustered, stuffed her handkerchief into her coat pocket.

'But you can't protect her for ever. She's of an age to make her own life, and she loves our Will so much; I hope he returns that love and looks after her. Now come on. With some daffodils and narcissi we'll make this church the bonniest in the dale on their wedding day. And I'll bet you've a cake already made in the kitchen, soaking up alcohol as we speak.' Alice took her hand and patted it and they both quietly walked out of the church and along the pathway to where Faulks stood waiting.

'What do you say, Faulks? Time to celebrate and look forward, eh? How can they not be happy? They have everything and more besides.'

'Indeed so, Miss Alice.'

Alice turned to close the church's black cast-iron gate, just missing Faulks putting his finger to his lips, urging Mrs Dowbiggin not to continue with the conversation.

'Right, I'll not be heading back to the manor with you on the main road. I realized as I came through the dale to meet you that I need some time to myself, so I'm going up there.' Alice pointed to the top of the fell.

'But your clothes, Miss Alice – that beautiful cloak!'

'My sanity is more important. I need my thinking time. I'll see you at suppertime – do lay me a place.'

As she watched the two servants set off along the road, she could imagine Mrs Dowbiggin commenting, 'You can't make a silk purse out of a sow's ear,' as soon as she was out of earshot. Frankly, Alice didn't care. Let them think what they would; she knew what mattered to her and she had just begun to realize that it wasn't money.

Alice hurried up the drive to the manor, her dress hem plastered with mud from taking shortcuts across the fells and a tear in her cloak where she had snagged it on a hawthorn tree in her hurry to climb a stile on the way home. She realized with a jolt of alarm that she'd lost one of her gloves. She resolved to hunt for it later. The light was fading and she could see the candles and gas lamps had been lit in the manor. She decided to chance the front door rather than the back, not wanting to have to explain the state of her clothes to Mrs Dowbiggin. First she stopped to wipe the mud off her beautiful tight-buttoned boots. The leather had been spotless and shiny when she had set out, but now looked in need of at least an hour's polishing if not repair. She wiped them roughly on the grass verge, then brushed herself down. Seeing the state of herself, she felt a little frisson of alarm, but told herself what the hell, she'd only been for a walk. It wasn't as if she'd stolen the Crown jewels. She walked up the steps and quietly opened the front door, wiping her feet on the doormat and hurrying through the hall without anyone seeing her.

'Evening, Alice.' Gerald Frankland was just closing Nancy's bedroom door as Alice, head down, came running up the stairs. 'Nancy's been enquiring as to your whereabouts. I told her that you had gone for a walk after your meeting with Mrs Dowbiggin at the church.'

'Sorry, Gerald, I lost track of time. I'll get changed and go into Nancy straight away.' Trying to hide her distressed attire, Alice brushed past him to get to her own bedroom.

'I trust, by the state of your dress, you enjoyed your walk. It's certainly brought colour to your cheeks. Perhaps you can entertain us at the dinner table by telling us where your walk took you.'

Uncertain whether he was being serious, Alice simply nodded and darted into her room, closing the door behind her. Of all the people to run into! She was mortified that he'd seen her in such an unkempt state, and conscious how ungrateful he must think her, getting her expensive new clothes in such a mess. Anxious not to keep Nancy waiting, she changed clothes, placed her boots outside her door to be cleaned by Faulks, and hurried along to Nancy's room.

'Where do you think you've been? I've been on my own all afternoon, without any company, no explanation, nothing, cast to one side like a disused doll!' Nancy yelled, her hair unbrushed, her scarred face even more distorted with rage. 'I will not be on my own!

211

You are getting paid to be my companion twenty-four hours a day, not just when you feel like it.' She thumped the mattress that she was sitting on with her clenched fists and glared at Alice.

It had been a while since Alice had seen Nancy in one of her tempers. She'd forgotten just how frightening and domineering she could be.

'I was never told I was to be a twenty-four-hour companion. I thought I was to be tret more like family, now you are to marry my brother.' Alice spoke softly but firmly; she wasn't going to kowtow. The few hours that she had enjoyed walking had made her realize that, since New Year's Day, she had not had a single hour to herself. 'I'm sorry, Nancy, I should have asked you first, but I thought you and your brother were busy with the tenants today.'

'Tenants? What do I know about tenants? They are my brother's business. I can't be bothered to sort out rents and finances. I needed you here. I haven't felt well all day and now my bloody brother is threatening me with the doctor.' She pounded the mattress again, then fixed Alice with her blazing dark eyes. 'Whatever gave you the idea you were going to be family? You are Alice, the poor girl we took pity on – nothing more! Now get out of my room. I'm not dining with you tonight. I've told Gerald I need dinner in my room – and you can just go down to the kitchen and see to it. Go on, get out!' Nancy threw her hands up in the air.

Alice said nothing but walked to the door with as much dignity as she could. It was a replay of her first

212

encounter with Nancy, that day when she'd told her she was a spoilt, rich brat and she never wanted to see her again. As she closed the door behind her, she heard the crash of something being thrown against a wall.

So that was how it lay, she thought to herself as she went downstairs: Alice, the girl everyone took pity on, never to be treated like real family. Well, she wouldn't put up with it. Wedding or no wedding, there was no way she would be staying where she wasn't wanted. If she hadn't spent the day getting her thoughts together up on her beloved fells, she would probably have been crying. But no, she was a Bentham, her roots were in the Dales, and she was better than any off-comed family, with or without money.

'You're very quiet tonight, Alice. Is something the matter? I know Nancy is in one of her moods – is that it?'

Alice looked at Gerald. A few weeks ago, she'd have thought it a dream come true to find herself alone in the manor's dining room with the man she was beginning to have feelings for. Now she gave a wan smile and replied, 'I think it'd be best if I left the manor tomorrow. I know you've only taken me in out of pity – Miss Nancy made that clear tonight – and I have my pride.' She carried on eating her dinner, waiting for Gerald to comment.

'Damn that woman! She comes out with such rubbish when she's in one of her moods. I don't know what has come over her – today's episode was one of the worst I've seen.' He cast aside his knife and fork and held his head in his hands. 'We did not take pity on you, Alice. You are her only friend and she is to marry your brother. Sometimes her mouth runs away with her. Forgive her, Alice. She truly does not mean it.'

'I know,' Alice said sadly. 'I went for a walk, but I needed time to think – so much has happened this last week or two. I was only gone a few hours. I'd never hurt Nancy.'

'You are entitled to as much time as you wish to yourself if Nancy is otherwise occupied. She was supposed to be with me at my tenants' meeting today, but she came downstairs barely dressed and started dancing in the hallway in front of my stockman. The embarrassment of it! I had to escort her to her room. We must be the talk of the dale. It's no wonder we have such a bad name.'

Hearing the catch in his voice and seeing the tears welling in his eyes, Alice got up from her seat and rushed to his side. 'Don't worry, Gerald. I'll look after her twenty-four hours a day until the wedding, and even afterwards if Will wants me to.' She squeezed his hand. 'She'll be all right, I promise. I'll stay and keep her mind occupied. It's probably the pressure of the wedding that's getting to her.'

Suddenly remembering whose hand she was holding, Alice hurriedly released it. Blushing violently, she returned to her seat.

'I'd be grateful if you could, Alice. I have a feeling

that this may be the beginning of a very rocky month or two. I hope that your brother knows what he's taking on and that he has a great deal of patience. But let us talk of cheerier things, shall we? Where did your walk take you? You look as if you have benefited from the fresh air. It does one good to have some time to oneself. I sometimes head up to the Occupation Road and sit gazing upon our lovely valley. Makes you forget your worries, those fells rolling gently, dale after dale, until they reach the sea. Have you ever been to the sea?'

'No, I haven't. My father always said he would take me, but we never got to go. The nearest I've been is to the top of Leck Fell, where you can see it in the distance.' Alice cast her mind back, remembering the sight.

'Then we shall go! We'll all go. In the summer, once the wedding is over, we'll have an outing.' Gerald smiled, his mood lightening as he picked up his knife and fork and continued with his meal. 'By the way, Alice, I almost forgot to tell you: Jack is to be the new owner of your old home, Dale End. He made me an offer, and I agreed. It couldn't be in safer hands. Eventually he will be leaving his work here and I'll be sorry to lose him when that time comes. I do believe he must be thinking of settling down. He'll be a good catch for someone.' Gerald smiled and winked, not knowing that Alice and Jack were no longer courting.

Alice's heart pounded. She felt as if she was going to be sick. Jack in her old home – how could he? She had always hoped for Dale End to be hers one day. Only this afternoon she had passed it on her walk and noticed it was still empty. Peering in through the kitchen window had rekindled old memories; she couldn't bear to think of anyone else living there. And now Jack was considering settling down . . . She didn't know what to think. Was it jealousy she was feeling or anguish? If she wasn't careful, she was going to be left on the shelf, and that would never do!

14

'February fill-dyke, that's what it is. Have you ever seen rain like it? How am I supposed to get these sheets dry?' Mrs Dowbiggin moaned to Faulks as she lifted the damp sheets onto the clothes drier above the fire. Pulling at the rope, she wound it tight round the hook before the pulleys let it slip again. 'It's rained all blinking February. What with the weather, my lumbago and her upstairs carrying on, it's a wonder I'm not mad.' She stretched and peered out of the window. 'Anyway, the doctor's coming to see her this morning. Master Gerald says she needs something to calm her nerves. He still thinks it's the wedding that's getting her worked up.'

Faulks grunted while he read his newspaper.

'Morning, another beautiful day.' Alice entered the kitchen carrying Nancy's breakfast tray. 'I thought I'd bring you this, Mrs D – save you entering the ogre's den. I'm afraid Nancy's moods are not improving. If this keeps up, I'm going to lose my temper. I have come so close to telling her what I think of her this last day or two. My mother would have put her over her knee and walloped her, no matter how old she is.' Alice helped herself to a cup of tea from the teapot.

'Get him to serve you – he's doing nothing.' Mrs Dowbiggin kicked Faulks's foot and glared at him. 'Doctor's coming today; she'll calm down once he's been. I must admit we haven't had a session like this for a while.'

'What makes her like this, Mrs Dowbiggin? I used to think it was her scars hurting her, or not having anything to do, but she says she's not in pain, and with the wedding she has plenty to occupy her at the moment.'

Mrs Dowbiggin mouthed some words and pointed downwards.

'What?' Alice was lost.

'Cover your ears, you.' She swiped poor Faulks round his head with a damp pillowcase, then leaned conspiratorially towards Alice. 'Women's problems. Nerves, you know.'

Alice blushed. 'I see.'

'Her mother was the same. Nearly insane with it, she was. Too highly bred, if you ask me,' Mrs Dowbiggin whispered, half covering her mouth. 'Dr Bailey will give her something and then she'll be right again.'

'I'd better go up to her. I said I'd play whist with her until lunch – not that I dare win a game: it'd probably be more than my life's worth!' Alice gave a mirthless laugh and went back upstairs, thinking that if her brother only knew what he was taking on, he'd surely think twice.

She knocked gently on the half-closed bedroom door and then entered. Nancy was sitting in front of the mirror, examining her face.

'Look at me! How could anyone want to marry me? Your brother's only marrying me out of pity; he doesn't love me. I'd be better off dead!' she wailed. Then, wrapping her arms around herself and rocking back and forth, she repeated over and over, 'I'm nothing to no one. I'm nothing to no one . . .'

'For God's sake, Nancy, I've had enough of this self-pity! You're getting married in another month. You should be looking forward to having a new home and a man to love you. I've no man and no real home. Do you hear me complain? Stop this relentless moaning. I can't take it any more. I'm going to my room until your mood's improved!' Then Alice marched out, slamming the door behind her.

Back in her own room, she agonized over whether she should tell her brother how much worse Nancy's moods were becoming, and how she'd inherited them. How near to the edge of insanity had her mother been? Alice wondered. Even though Will said he was marrying Nancy for her wealth and her tantrums were a small price to pay for what he would get in return, would he feel differently once they started married life and he had to live with her? The Stone House works were now safely in his hands, the deeds having been signed over last week, so it was probably already too late for him to back out.

Her thoughts were interrupted by the sound of the doorbell: Dr Bailey had arrived. A few minutes later she listened as Gerald talked to him on the landing before opening Nancy's bedroom door. Then she heard Gerald's tread on the stairs as he left the doctor to examine Nancy. Quietly Alice closed her bedroom door and crept downstairs. Knowing that Dr Bailey would stop by Gerald's study on his way out, she slipped into the adjoining room, hoping to eavesdrop on the doctor's prognosis in case there was anything that her brother should know. Sure enough, she heard him knock on the study door and go in, but when she tried to listen through the wall, it was too thick. She couldn't hear a word.

After a while, the two men left the study together. Gerald was escorting the doctor to the front door. Alice opened the morning-room door a crack and peeked out.

'I'm sorry you have had to come out in such bad weather,' said Gerald, passing the doctor his hat and cloak.

'Not at all, Gerald. Let me know when you come to a decision. As I said, we can do something about it, but it might be as dangerous as seeing things through to their natural term. And you never know, she might calm down in another month or two. I've given her a draught to calm her, so she will probably sleep the rest of the day. You know where I am if you need me.

220

Good luck, old man.' Dr Bailey patted Gerald on the back before dashing out to his carriage in the pouring rain.

'Damn, damn, damn the man. I'll bloody kill him!' Gerald Frankland picked up his riding whip from the hall stand and thrashed the side of his leg with it. 'I'll bloody kill him. Alice, Alice, where the hell are you?' He shouted loud enough for all the manor to hear him.

Alice came out of the morning room and stood in front of him, defiant but frightened by his show of temper.

'Get your cloak on. You're coming with me, else I won't be responsible for my actions when I catch up with your brother.' He thrashed the whip against his side again. 'I'll wait for you outside – and no gossiping with them downstairs.' Then he was gone, pulling the huge door behind him with a bang.

Alice ran and grabbed her cloak, putting her hood up to stop her hair from getting wet. Following the sound of Gerald's raised voice, she caught up with him at the stable.

'Damn it, man, are you going to take all day doing this?' Gerald Frankland was bellowing at Jack, who was harnessing the team to the carriage as fast as he could, his fingers fumbling with the buckles.

At last everything was ready. Elbowing Jack aside, Gerald ordered Alice to get into the carriage, while he sat on the board. He lashed the team with the whip and they set off. The rain was torrential and the horses slipped on the treacherous surface, but Gerald, drenched to the skin and looking like a mad man, drove them faster and faster until they reached Stone House. Pulling the carriage up abruptly at the cottage door, he shouted for Alice to get. Then he stormed up to the cottage door and swung it open, whip in hand, his cloak dripping with rainwater and his eyes flashing with rage. Will was sitting at his kitchen table with his back to them. He turned round in shock at the intrusion into his home.

'Get up! Get up and fight me!' Gerald swung his cloak off and grabbed Will by the neck. 'I'm going to bloody well kill you, you stupid fucking man! The doctor reckons she's pregnant – my bloody sister, pregnant! – and it can only be yours, you bastard.' He held Will by the neck, pinning him against the kitchen wall. 'Couldn't you keep it to yourself till you got married? I'd have told you then that she can't have children. It'll drive her mad; her mind can't take it. Already she's had to be sedated. Now we'll probably lose her, you fool!'

Alice stood watching her brother gasp for breath as Gerald Frankland squeezed tighter.

'You marry her in April, by God. You stand by her and your bastard child, no matter what state she gets into, else I'll kill you.' Gerald's hand shook while he kept his hold tight upon Will's neck. 'And another thing – you can keep the works and the cottage, but you're not going to get a penny of her allowance, nor any more orders through me. Thought me a fool, did you? Thought you'd make sure I couldn't renege on

222

my promise by getting her pregnant? Well, your little plan's backfired. Now you can watch her getting worse and worse with her rages, just like my mother did. You will earn every penny that this place is worth. Not that it's worth a lot – I've been propping it up for years. Italian marble is all the markets want now, not this common black limestone marble.' He sneered at Will, gasping for breath. 'You'll find you're not much better off than you were when you started, but now you'll have a wife and child – and you'd better treat them right.' He released Will, then punched him hard in the stomach.

Will knelt, bent double and gasping for breath, on the flagstone floor. Alice rushed to his side. Even though he had confessed to her that it was only the money he was after, she had hoped that secretly he did think something of Nancy. Now there was a child to consider as well. If only she had known of Nancy's problem, she could have told Will not to bed her and not to use her to get his own back on his employer. He should have been more respectful. He'd seen the agony and torment his sister had gone through at Christmas, after she had destroyed her baby. Will had only to spend an hour with Nancy to realize that her mind was on the brink of a dark precipice. And he was the cause of it.

Gerald kicked Will's crumpled body. 'Get up, you bloody coward! Get up and talk to me. I've done what I wanted to do, without actually breaking your neck. Now we sort it out. Alice, get him a drink of water.

I won't give him the satisfaction of choking to death, because I need him alive so he can stand by my sister.'

Alice passed Will a cup of water. He drank it down and spluttered, thanking her with a hoarse voice. Both men then sat down at the table while Alice stared out of the kitchen window at the incessant rain on the mountainside. She wished herself far away, away from this rain-sodden dale with all its problems, away from Nancy and away from the two men arguing at the table, their voices bitter with the fine line of love and hate running through them, both fighting for what they needed and what they thought was best for them.

'The first Saturday in April, one o'clock – you'd better be there, else I'll come and shoot you myself.' Gerald Frankland rose from his chair, picked up his whip and smashed it down on the table. 'If you lay a hand on her or deny her the attention she deserves, so help me God, I'll break you.' He turned to Alice. 'Are you coming, or is blood thicker than water? You do know Nancy will need you?'

Alice looked to Will. Hands clutching his sore neck, he nodded for her to go. She didn't want to leave her brother; she'd have liked to stay with him – as much to give him a piece of her mind as to make sure he wasn't badly hurt – but she knew her own security depended on the Franklands. Besides, Nancy needed her, and she was carrying Will's baby. That little nephew or niece would be a Bentham, part of her family. Though she didn't know what would happen to her after the wedding, for now Alice would stay by Nancy's side.

She pulled her cloak around her and climbed into the carriage. The horses, drenched and sweating from their chase up the dale, were eager to make the return journey so that they could be unharnessed and get back to their stables. Gerald and Alice rode in silence, their mood matching the weather. Rain pounded the roof of the carriage, competing with the deafening roar of the river as the waters surged, frothing and swirling round the smooth grey limestone formations.

When they finally arrived, Gerald handed the reins to Jack and stormed off across the yard without a backward glance. Alice climbed down from the carriage and followed as Jack led the team into the shelter of the stables. She was in no hurry to return to the manor.

Jack lifted the tack off both animals and began to brush the withers of the first horse. He kept his eyes on the horse, not even glancing in Alice's direction as he spoke. 'He's pushed these horses hard. They've a fair sweat on them, even in this weather. Must have been something urgent that you were both about.'

Alice leaned against the stable door, not knowing what to say. Gerald had warned her against gossip, but Jack could be trusted. 'He'd every right. I don't think I've ever seen him in such a mood.'

'Oh, aye, he's got a temper, has our master. Only once in a blue moon, but when he blows, he blows and there's no holding him back. He once whipped a dog that bit him to within an inch of its life. He'd every right then; according to him it needed to learn a lesson.

225

What's he in a temper for today, then?' Jack carried on grooming, chewing on a straw as he spoke, still averting his eyes from Alice.

'Our Will. I suppose everyone will find out soon enough,' Alice sighed. 'Nancy's having Will's baby and she's going to be real ill while having it – her state of mind can't handle it.'

'Same old story for his lordship then: a dog's bit him again. And you don't bite the hand that feeds you.' Jack led the first horse into its stall and combed out his curry brush. 'Your Will's been a fool. Miss Nancy loved him without him getting her pregnant. He should have taken more care.' Finally he looked at Alice. 'It must be something in the water up at Stone House.'

'What do you mean by that, Jack Alderson?' Alice glared at him in defiance, now certain that he must have heard her talking to the horse.

'Nay, nothing. I'm not saying anything. Next time I see him, I'll tell your brother to keep it in his pocket. Happen he's not the only one who should. By the way, I found this outside Dale End's kitchen window.' He fished out the fur-trimmed glove that Alice had lost the day she went walking up the fell. 'I take it that's yours? I saw you wearing a pair like it on the day you came back with Miss Nancy from Kendal.'

'Thanks. I've been searching for that everywhere. I hear you're buying Dale End – are you going to be living there? It seemed so deserted.'

'Well, you can't live at home for ever and I thought it was time to be settling down and making my own

226

home.' Jack started grooming the second horse. He still couldn't look at Alice; he loved her so much, but when he'd found out the things she'd kept from him – that she'd been untrue and slept with another man, then got rid of a baby – it had caused a hurt in him that was going to take a long time to heal.

'I see. I'm sure it will make you very happy.' Alice could feel a lump forming in her throat. 'Thanks for the glove.' She waved it at him as she turned to cross the yard towards the manor.

If she didn't love him, then why did her heart feel so heavy? And then she thought of the dark and brooding Gerald. Why worry about Jack? He was nothing but a boy she had grown up with, more like a brother than the lover Gerald could be. She swallowed hard, raised her head high and walked into the manor without giving him a backward glance.

Low clouds hung around the small church, wrapping it up in grey cotton wool and making it feel oppressive and dark. It may as well have been the middle of the night, not one o'clock on a Saturday in early April. The church bell, muffled by the low cloud, rang out across the top of the dale. Outside the main door, daffodils nodded in the light breeze as if in conversation with one another about the coming wedding, anticipating the arrival of the bride.

Will, dressed in his new suit, fumbled in his pocket, playing with the family wedding ring. He felt sick with apprehension. If he'd been able to run away, he would have done. But he knew that Gerald Frankland would hunt him down no matter where he went. Jack stood beside him talking to the vicar, who was expressing concern at the size of the congregation. Obviously no one had told him that this was to be a shotgun wedding.

Suddenly the organ sounded the opening bars of Handel's 'Wedding March' and Will, heart heavy with the knowledge that this was his last minute of freedom, turned to see his bride walking down the aisle with her brother at her side. Alice walked behind them with a delicate bunch of primroses in her hand, flashing a reassuring smile at her big brother. Jack nudged Will out into the aisle and encouraged him to take Nancy's hand, while Gerald Frankland stepped to the side of the couple, giving Will a threatening glance as he placed her hand in the hand of her soon-to-be husband. Nancy gave her bouquet to Alice and smiled at Will, her nerves held at bay by the medication the doctor had given her that morning.

With her face covered by a veil and her dark hair standing out in stark contrast against the cream of her wedding dress and flowers, Nancy looked beautiful. If it hadn't been for her scars, she would have been many a man's fantasy: rich, young and with child by her husband-to-be. To Will, she was a millstone. For the rest of his days he would be in service to her, her brother and his unborn child. He'd thought everything he'd ever wanted was being handed to him on a plate, only to discover he was taking a lunatic for a wife, and

228

thanks to her brother he didn't have a penny in the bank to support them. He went through the vows as if in a trance, wanting to run but at the same time rooted to the spot. Never had a wedding service taken so long.

Then finally it was over, and they were walking out of the church, watched by a few curious locals who had gathered on the bridge, wondering who the happy couple might be and wishing them well as they drove off in their wedding coach.

'They're here! They're here! Get a move on – open the doors.' Mrs Dowbiggin was in full cry. Even though it was only a small wedding breakfast, she was determined that it should go exactly the way she'd planned.

Faulks opened the front door and welcomed the new couple in while Mrs Dowbiggin stood clapping in the hall, along with a young servant girl who had been hired for the day. Nancy smiled, happy that everyone was making her day special. There had been a tense atmosphere between her and her brother these last few weeks, but now she had the man she loved and a baby on the way, everything would be all right. She didn't know what everyone was making such a fuss about.

'Congratulations, Miss Nancy. Congratulations, Master Will.' Faulks smiled and led them to their seats, laying napkins out on their laps and pouring a liberal glass of wine for the newly-weds.

'Thank you, Faulks. What a very strange day. I always thought the sun would be shining on my wedding day. Don't you think the sun should be shining?

Instead it's dull and dreary, and I feel quite light-headed.'

'It's spring, miss. Sometimes the sun shines; sometimes it rains. As long as you are happy, miss, you'll radiate sunshine.' Faulks smiled, trying to offer encouragement, but at the same time he cast a worried glance at Gerald.

'That's me, Faulks – a ray of sunshine, shining out over everyone, apart from my sulky brother, who looks like the rain clouds outside. Make him smile, Faulks: he's spoiling my day.'

'He's just concerned for you, miss, as we all are. He knows you are unwell and is worried about your new life.' Faulks moved on to Gerald, his eyes never straying from the wine pouring into the glass – anything rather than meet his employer's gaze.

'My Will is going to take care of me ever so well. Besides, Alice is coming to Stone House with me too. I wouldn't have it any other way.' Nancy beamed at Will and Alice, reaching out for their hands and squeezing them tight.

'Now, Nancy, we haven't decided on Alice yet.' Gerald stirred his soup, which the young serving maid had placed in front of him. 'I'm sorry to embarrass you, Alice, but I'm at a loss as to what to do with you under the circumstances.' He took a long slurp of his soup and gazed across the table at a subdued Alice. 'I'd have thought that you would prefer to stay here at the manor, but my sister seems to think you will be moving into Stone House with your brother and her. I think we had better discuss this after the newly-weds have departed for their home. You can always follow them to Stone House in the morning – that is, if you wish to do so, and if Will is happy with that arrangement.'

Will gave a nod. He'd few words to spare for his new brother-in-law and he was counting the minutes until he could escape the stuffiness of the manor and return to his home.

Alice watched Gerald sitting back in his chair and staring across at the newly-weds, knowing full well he was making Will uncomfortable. 'I'll stay here tonight,' she said. 'It's their first night together – a sister in the next bedroom is the last thing you want.' And then she blushed, realizing she had been forthright. But there was no other way of saying it, as far as she could tell.

'I'm afraid that moment has well and truly passed, Alice, my dear. As we all know, your brother put the cart before the horse, as they say – hence the atmosphere around this table on what should have been a day of celebration.' Throwing down his napkin, Gerald got to his feet and made his apologies, then stormed out of the room.

'I'm sorry, Will, it came out wrong. I shouldn't have said that.' Alice could have kicked herself.

'It doesn't matter, Sis. I've had enough anyway; this food was sticking in my throat. I'm off up the dale and taking Nancy with me. Can you get her things?'

231

'They're already packed and waiting in the front hallway. Let Nancy say goodbye to Gerald before you go, though – it'll only make him worse if you don't.'

They both turned to Nancy. She seemed confused and sad. She was angry with her brother, and couldn't understand what she had done so wrong to upset everybody. All she wanted was to have a lovely wedding day and to marry the man she loved. She knew they were going to be so happy; if only she could rid herself of this feeling of not being in control and stop these anxiety attacks, things would be all right.

'Come on, old girl, go and say goodbye to your brother. I'll wait outside in the horse and trap.' Will helped Nancy up from her chair.

'But the dinner – we've only had the first course.' Nancy was even more confused.

'I'll make you something when we get home, Mrs Bentham.' Will put his arm around her, smiling as he led her out of the dining room.

Alice tugged at his elbow. 'Look after her: she needs your support. And mind you stand by her – she's having your baby, remember.'

'What do you take me for? We'll be all right. Make sure you look after yourself tonight – remember what I've said in the past.' Will winked at her.

'That's the pot calling the kettle black, Will Bentham.' Alice kissed her brother on the cheek.

When Nancy came out of Gerald's study sniffling into her handkerchief, Alice was on hand to give her a hug. 'You'll be fine, Nancy. I'll come and be with you tomorrow, but for now go and be happy with my big brother. And if he doesn't take care of you, he'll have me to answer to.' She walked with her to the manor's steps and waved at the couple as Will whipped the horses into motion.

Behind the study curtains, Gerald watched them set off down the drive. He had lost his little sister to a man he suspected didn't love her. He prayed that she'd survive childbirth. At least once the baby was born, there would be hope.

'Oh my Lord! All this food and nobody to eat it! I've never known a do like this in my life. What's folk going to think of us? Think on, young Betsy, you say nothing to anyone in Dent about this wedding day, 'cos if I find out you've been gossiping, there will be hell to pay.' Mrs Dowbiggin wagged her finger at the poor serving girl as she set off home, her services no longer required now the wedding party had broken up. 'I feel all faint. I could do with some smelling salts, Mr Faulks. What a to-do!' She planted herself in the Windsor chair and fanned her cherry-red face with the tea towel. 'You shouldn't be helping clear away. You're not one of us any more,' she chastised Alice for carrying in the wasted food from the wedding breakfast.

'And who do you think I am? I can't sit about here and do nothing. Besides, it hasn't exactly been the day I wanted either.' Alice was as annoyed as Mrs Dowbiggin. She no longer knew where she stood in life; her brother wouldn't really want her at Stone House, yet there was no reason for her to stay at the manor. It was all very well Nancy saying she needed her, but she didn't realize that Will was going to struggle to feed them all.

Having cleared the kitchen table of food, Alice set about placing it in the pantry and cellar in the hope that it would keep fresh enough for everyone to eat it over the coming week. 'You're all going to eat well, if nothing else,' she said, washing her hands.

'That ham will last longer than a week if there's only us and Master Gerald. What a waste! And all my fancy sweets – nobody even got to see them.' Mrs Dowbiggin held her apron to her eyes, almost in tears.

'Never mind, at least there was a wedding. At one point, I did wonder if my brother would turn up; I was afraid he'd get cold feet. He went through with it, though. Now he'll have to get on with his lot and take care of Nancy and the baby. It'll hit home now he's got responsibilities. There'll be no more spending his spare time having a pint or going shooting with Jack.' Alice shook her head and walked past Mrs Dowbiggin as she headed back upstairs.

Mrs Dowbiggin caught her hand as she passed, gripping it tight. 'Your Will, he will take care of our Miss Nancy, won't he? She may be a handful, but we all think a great deal of her. And you'll be there for her, won't you?' There were tears in the old house-keeper's eyes as she pleaded with Alice.

'I'll be there for her. I'm going to talk to Gerald now, find out where we go from here. I'm neither one

234

thing nor the other, and someone is going to have to make him see sense over Nancy and her baby – they still need his support even though she is pregnant by my brother. He didn't know of her medical problems when he got her pregnant, else he'd not have even touched her.' Alice patted the faithful Mrs Dowbiggin's hand, more resolved than ever to try and salvage something of the day.

Alice knocked gently on the study door. Through the narrow gap underneath the door she could see the flickering light from the open fire, but nobody answered. She knocked harder, knowing that Gerald was in there and not wanting to retreat from the mission she had set herself, even though her stomach was churning. She was about to knock again when the door opened ever so slightly, showing the dark figure of Gerald Frankland. He left the door ajar and Alice went in, following as he returned to his chair by the fire.

'Well, Miss Bentham, have you come to chastise me, to give me the benefit of your considerable knowledge? Because that's what I'm expecting, you and your quick tongue.' Gerald Frankland poured himself another glass of port from the decanter and gazed into the fire.

Alice sat down in the chair opposite, her hands in her lap, trying to remain calm. She could see that Gerald had been drowning his sorrows. 'I'm only making sure you're all right. I know it's been a bit of a day for you, for all of us.'

'A bit of a day? A bit of a day – ha! That's a bloody

understatement.' He swigged his drink. 'It's been a bloody fiasco, that's what it's been. It was like the Mad Hatter's tea party, sitting around that wedding table. My mad bloody sister, not knowing what the hell was going on, and your brother desperate to run away . . . I just want to wipe the whole damn day out. So, yes, it was a bit of a day.' He poured himself another drink and indicated for Alice to get a glass and join him. 'Cheers! Here's to the happy couple.'

'But Nancy *is* happy. Perhaps she doesn't always know what's going on, but she's happy with Will and with the baby coming.' Alice took a quick drink and coughed as the warm port went down her throat. She'd never drunk port before.

'How can she be happy, married to your brother? He hasn't got a penny to his name. She's left here for that hovel at the top of the dale. She's not in her right mind, what with having that bastard baby.' Gerald glared at Alice with his wounded eyes.

'Money isn't everything. Nancy loves my brother. Now, I don't know if he deserves her love, but if she's happy, does it matter? She'll have the baby; things will be all right. Perhaps living up the dale with my brother will do her good.' Alice took another sip of the port; it made her feel warm and relaxed. 'You're going to be an uncle – that's something to be proud of. You haven't lost a sister; you've gained a nephew or niece.'

'She's so ill, I might yet lose her! If she dies, it will be all your brother's fault. I could kill him for what he's done.' Gerald spat the words out.

236

Alice leaned towards him, trying to hold his gaze. 'He didn't know about the danger. The only thing he's done is to love your sister – what's wrong with that? We've all loved someone we shouldn't have.' Words were flowing freely out of Alice as she allowed Gerald to pour her another drink. 'They're going to struggle, though, with no money. But my brother will provide for them. Rabbit stew never hurt nobody.'

She hoped that the mention of rabbit stew would make Gerald realize how tough life was for his workers. Surely he wouldn't want his sister to endure such hardship, regardless of what he thought of Will.

'Don't try and make me feel guilty, Alice; it won't work. I might have had a bit to drink, but I'm still compos mentis. I'll reassess the situation in the morning, when I take you up to Stone House. I might have been a bit hard, especially on Nancy. But can you blame me? My whole family is going to the dogs – even I'm sitting here talking to my sister's maid as if she was my closest friend.' He placed his glass on the table and looked at Alice.

Alice blushed, the warmth of the port making her complexion glow. 'I'm sorry I've overstepped my place. I only wanted to make a case for them both because my brother is hopeless at standing his ground. The port must have given me added courage.'

'Too bloody right! But you never have been one to know your place. To tell you the truth, you amuse me with your forthright ways, but now is not the time. Leave me to my thoughts and this bottle; I'm best sorting my own head out, without a blue-eyed tempt-ress sitting across from me.' He raised his glass and grinned at her. He could see that she knew all too well what she was doing. Alice was not as innocent as she would have him believe. Trouble was, one day he might not be able to resist those cornflower-blue eyes.

'I'll see you in the morning.' Alice smiled and walked past him. Another drink and she would prob-ably have been putty in his hands. There was something about Gerald Frankland that made her lose all control of her feelings. Perhaps he'd come to her later . . . How she wished he would – to hell with reputations!

15

Alice lay back in her bed watching the sun's rays stream through the half-drawn curtains. Specks of dust floated like dancing fairies in the early morning light. She snuggled down under the covers, content with the warmth of the bed and her thoughts of Gerald Frankland. She'd half hoped that she would wake up with him next to her, but common sense told her that it was a good thing she hadn't. Better to hang on to her dignity. Besides, she didn't want him to think she was easy.

She listened to a family of sparrows cheerfully chattering in the wisteria outside the window. They were busy nesting, preparing for their young and enjoying the spring sunshine. It made her think of her brother and Nancy preparing for the new arrival. Would Gerald have changed his mind and decided to give Nancy her dowry? Alice hoped so; there was not going to be enough business at the marble works to keep the labourers and the foreman's new family fed.

Throwing off the covers, she got up and pulled the

curtains fully open. It was a beautiful day. The sun was shining, the sky was blue, and the surrounding fells were turning green again after the long, hard winter. They beckoned Alice. She longed to go walking from dale to dale until her legs ached and her stomach needed food. But there was no time for that today; she was off to Stone House, to join her brother. Conscious that she might never again wake to the luxury of her bedroom at the manor, she lingered by the window, making the most of the view.

Downstairs, the clock in the hall chimed six o'clock. Not a soul was stirring; it would be another hour before Mrs Dowbiggin started making breakfast. That left Alice with time enough for a quick walk. She washed and dressed, tiptoed downstairs and out through the front door, then across the stable yard to the path that led to the fellside. The hedgerow along the bottom of the fell was filled with the new buds of spring, with violets, wood sorrel and primroses in bloom along the grassy banks. The fresh morning air was clear and sharp and Alice breathed it in as if it was the elixir of life as she made her way to the stone wall that separated the meadowland from the rough grassland of the fell. It was the perfect vantage point from which to gaze down on the valley below while she pondered what life was going to throw at her. She sat on a stone next to the gateway to the fell, watching the hazy mist that lay along the river evaporate in the heat of the sun, leaving the river glittering like a silver ribbon as it meandered down the dale. She was sitting there, basking in the sun and daydreaming, when she heard the chain on the gate being opened. It was Jack, leading one of the horses that had been grazing on the fell.

'You're an early bird. I never usually see a soul up here at this time.' Closing the gate behind him, he tied the horse to one of the crossbars. He pulled a packet of cigarettes out of his pocket and lit one, then leaned on the wall next to Alice.

'I couldn't resist. It was as if the sun was calling me. Besides, I needed to think things through before I go up to Stone House this morning.'

'Aye, I reckon your lad's taken on more than he can chew. He'll not be happy with that one. She's used to getting her own way, whereas he's like me and you – bit of a free spirit. Wild birds die if you cage 'em; he should know that.' Jack took a long drag on his cigarette.

'I'll remind him, but it's too late now. He should have thought about that when he was busy plotting how to get his hands on Nancy's money.' Alice couldn't help but confide in Jack that she knew Will had only married and got Nancy pregnant for her money.

'I thought this baby was an accident. Has he got her in the family way on purpose? By 'eck, my father would kick my arse if I'd have done that.'

'Now you know why there was such an unwelcoming feel about the wedding. He'll be right with Nancy, but it's her brass that he's after. I don't know what's got into our Will. He's changed since Mother and Father died.' Alice picked up a pebble and threw it hard, watching it bounce and settle on the stony path.

241

'Aye, well, I haven't seen him much this last month or two – haven't had much time for owt lately.' He untied the horse and stamped out his cigarette with his boot.

Alice stood up, brushed her skirt and linked her arm with Jack's. 'I'll walk with you. They'll be waking up at the manor now. How's that girlfriend of yours – Amy, is it? Must be serious if you're thinking of settling down.'

'Nay, I've given over taking her out. She was costing me a fortune and she couldn't bake. What I need is a lass that's good with money and can make something out of nowt. Amy was no good for me.'

Alice smiled. She'd had a narrow escape from thrifty Jack; she wanted a bit more from life than working and she'd had her fill of having to make something out of nowt.

Mrs Dowbiggin was busy lighting fires and getting the kitchen going for breakfast when Alice walked in.

'What on earth are you doing up and about this hour of the day? I've only just got dressed myself!' She pulled a new tablecloth out of the large oak drawer and shoved it into Faulks's hands so that he could set the breakfast table in the dining room.

'It's such a beautiful morning, Mrs D, I couldn't waste it lying in bed. I needed to get out while I have the chance. Once I'm up the dale, I'll not have much time to myself.' Alice helped herself to a glass of water, sipping it while she watched Mrs Dowbiggin stir the porridge.

'Must be something in the water, because his lordship is up and about too. He's just demanded a cup of tea in his study. I told him he'd have to wait until the kettle's boiled and I've only one pair of hands.' Wiping her fingers on her apron, she began getting the breakfast crockery out.

'Leave that to me. I'll take it through to him. I need a word with him anyway.'

Alice put a cup and saucer and teapot on a tray; then, while she waited for the kettle to boil, she ran outside and picked a small bunch of violets. Mrs Dowbiggin tutted as Alice arranged the violets in a small vase and put it on the tea tray before carrying it off to Gerald's study.

As soon as Alice was out of earshot, the housekeeper shook her head and said, 'I don't know what's going on in this family any more, Mr Faulks, I really don't. Perhaps it's best that we are where we are in life, 'cos I wouldn't want to be young again.'

'Morning. Isn't it a beautiful day? It'll be a nice ride up the dale this morning.' Alice breezed into Gerald's study, placing the tray of tea in front of him.

'I suppose it is, but my head doesn't think so.' Gerald squinted at Alice. 'I'm afraid I drank too much last night and now I'm suffering, hence the tea.' He took a deep slurp of tea and eased into his chair.

'Having drunk myself stupid and considered the matter from every angle, I've come to a decision. I will give them Nancy's allowance – they'll need it to bring the baby up. But I want your assurance that you will be there for her, no matter what. She trusts you and I know that she's going to need all the help she can get in the next few months. No taking sides, Alice; you do right by me and mine, because you know your brother's plotted his way into this family and I'll not fall for any more schemes.' He looked intently into Alice's eyes, as if questioning her motives.

'I'll be right with her, Gerald. I'll be there when she needs me, and I promise neither Nancy nor the baby will come to any harm if I have a say in it.'

'Right then, let's wish them all the best this morning when we go to Stone House. I'll drop you off at the cottage and then I'll look around the works with Will. I've been going through the books and, to be honest, I don't know what we are going to do. We can't compete with these foreign imports. Bloody Italians – thanks to them, our marble's worthless. For a month or two I thought we were doing well, but orders have dropped off. I need to discuss it with Will.' He flicked through the accounts book and sighed.

'Thank you, Gerald.' Alice smiled at her new brother-in-law, glad that she'd secured her brother a decent living. 'Don't worry, things will come right in the end.'

'Go on, go on, get your breakfast.' He waved his hand at her. 'And, Alice, I like the violets.' He smiled, leaning back into his chair as he watched her leave his study, inspired by her determination. She wasn't one for giving in; that he was sure of. His sister would be in good hands as long as Alice was with her.

The ride up to Stone House was pleasant, the team of horses trotting steadily while the early spring sun shone down on Alice and Gerald. There was little conversation between them; both were lost in their own thoughts. Alice had packed a small bag with a few possessions to take with her and then closed her bedroom door with a long backward glance, not wanting to leave the comfort of the manor for the spare room at Stone House. She had to go; that she knew. She owed it to Nancy and her baby; and her brother, who until now had had no idea how much his new wife was suffering from her nerves, was going to need her support.

She looked at Gerald, his eyes on the road ahead as he sat next to her at the reins. This was the man that she had been warned about, the man who ruled her life, and now he was her brother-in-law and she felt at ease with his charms. In fact, she could honestly say that there was not a minute in the day when she did not think about him. His dark hair, his dry smile and his smooth voice . . . Yet below the gentle side to him Alice could see there was a man of passion, the side that one day perhaps she would see more of. She gathered her thoughts as the trap went over the small arched stone bridge that had crossed the River Dee for centuries and up the short path to her new home. Gerald held her hand as he helped her to alight; then she hurried to the open kitchen door, where Nancy was standing with arms outstretched.

'Will said you were coming, but I thought he was teasing. He's even put some of Mrs Dowbiggin's cakes out on a plate for us. I don't know how to make cakes. Do you, Alice? I fear I'm not going to be a good wife and mother; I've so much to learn.' Nancy sat down and fidgeted with her fingers, a look of hopelessness on her face.

Alice removed her hat and shawl and took Nancy's hands in hers. 'That's why I'm here: to take care of you and the baby, to make sure you eat and get enough rest. All you have to do is take care of yourself and Will and be happy.' She smiled reassuringly at her sister-in-law, who looked as if she had finally realized what she had let herself in for.

'Aye, our Alice will look after you, lass. She can cook, so tha needn't bother your head over that.' Will put his hand on Nancy's shoulder just as Gerald came into the room.

'Will, you and I need to make a fresh start. You're married to my sister now; I might not agree with it, but as long as you promise to stand by her and care for her, then you'll have my backing, along with the allowance that we originally talked about. You can thank your Alice for that.' Gerald looked at Alice as she knelt on the floor next to Nancy. 'She made me see sense last night. We've got to take care of this baby now it's on its way.'

'Well, that takes a weight off my mind.' Will's face lightened. 'I can't thank you enough for helping us out. I didn't know how we were going to manage; the stone works is not doing much at the moment and the men are all grumbling. We need to find a better seam of marble soon if we are to keep working.'

Will had been dreading seeing Gerald Frankland all morning. One night of being with Nancy had made him realize just how bad she was, but at least the money gave him some hope.

'Right, let's go and take a stroll up to the works so I can take a look around. How many men have we working for us at the moment? If you haven't the work for them, perhaps you could get rid of one or two – that's what I advise, anyway.' Gerald danced around his words, remembering that he no longer actually owned the marble works.

'Aye, well, any advice you can give, I'd be grateful. You'll have seen by my accounts that we aren't breaking even at the moment. The market's just died.' Will was clearly uncomfortable.

'Nancy prompted me a while ago to secure you an order from the Tsar of Russia – I have contacts over there, as you know. However, there is turmoil in the country at the moment and I'm sure that ordering a fireplace from Dent would be the last thing on their minds. For the time being we will have to come up with another way of boosting profits.'

Alice was struck by the words 'turmoil in Russia'. So things were not going well over there. Come to think of it, she hadn't seen any letters arriving with the delicate feminine handwriting on the envelope; perhaps that was one of the reasons Gerald had been so moody lately. She felt herself looking at him and blushing at the thoughts that were going through her head. Perhaps he was fair game after all. With his beloved Tatiana off the scene, she could woo him and keep his attention. How she hated the sound of that Russian woman's name. If as a result of this turmoil she were to vanish from Gerald's life, Alice would be a happy woman.

'Do excuse us, ladies. We are going to take a stroll to the stone works so we can draw upon one another's knowledge and see what can be done. Nancy, dear, I'll have a talk with you later, but I'm sure you and Alice have plenty to catch up on in the meantime.' Gerald put on his hat and stepped out, followed by Will, who turned to wink at them as he closed the door. There was a broad smile on his face; he felt much more comfortable not being at loggerheads with his brother-in-law.

Alice bustled around the kitchen, tidying up and sweeping the hearth, then filling the kettle before placing it over the fire to boil.

'I'm so useless. I'm Will's wife – I'm supposed to be doing this, but I don't know what to do,' Nancy wailed as she watched Alice scurrying around.

'And as I said that's precisely why I'm here: you and your baby will be wanting for nothing. Talking of babies, you need to stop wearing those corsets. The poor mite will be getting squashed in there.' Alice nodded to Nancy's cinched-in waistline. 'You need some loose-fitting clothes. Tell our Will to put his hand in his pocket and take you to Kendal. You need to be comfortable, not make a fashion statement.'

Nancy's face immediately clouded over. 'I don't want to lose my waist. It'll have to be squashed – I'm not spoiling my figure for a baby.' She pouted and launched into a tantrum that a ten-year-old would have been proud of, screaming, 'I wish it was dead. It has spoilt everything!'

Alice did her best to calm her down. 'You don't mean that, Nancy. Why, only the other week you were saying how much you were looking forward to being a mother. In five months you'll be wearing the tightest corsets you can find. Don't wish the baby ill; it'll bring a lot of joy to you both – a new baby always does.' She could see that Nancy was struggling to come to terms with the course her life had taken and that she didn't really wish any harm to the baby.

Nancy sobbed, 'I've made a mess of my life. What am I doing here instead of at the manor? Look at it – a worker's cottage – and me four months pregnant the day after a shotgun wedding. My life's a mess, a horrible mess.'

Alice put a comforting arm around her. 'We all make mistakes. I should know – I've done things that I'm really ashamed of. But you have so much to look forward to. You've got money, a good cottage, a man who loves you and a baby on the way – and when he or she is born, I'm sure you'll love that baby with all your heart. Things will get better. You've just to get on with it. I'm here to do all the work and take care of you both and I'll not let you down.' She rocked Nancy's trembling body, gazing over her shoulder at the beautiful spring day outside the kitchen window. It was going to be a long five months, and even then she didn't know how things would be. She only hoped and prayed things would improve.

16

It was payday and the burly marble workers formed a line at the doorway of Stone House Cottage, collars turned up and caps pulled down to protect them from the fine drizzle. The grey skies matched their mood.

'I've not had to carve anything for over a month now,' said the oldest man in the group. 'I can't see us carrying on. There's no work, and we can't go on like this for ever.'

Josiah Middleton nodded in agreement and carried on trying to wind the men up. 'If O'Hara had still been here, we'd have had full bellies and full pockets, but this arse-licker only looks after himself. I tell you, O'Hara might have been turning Frankland over, but he took care of his own. With this 'un we'll get bloody nothing, 'cos he's neither one thing nor t'other. The man's a traitor to his own kind!' Middleton shoved his hands in his pockets and spat on the clean step of the cottage. 'Come on, you bugger, open up – we want our brass,' he brayed at the kitchen door.

The green-painted door opened and Alice stepped

out, wiping her hands on her pinny. She glared at the great hulk towering over her in the doorway. 'Will you be quiet! Miss Nancy is resting and my brother's trying to count out your wages. You'll not get them any sooner by bellowing.' There was no trace of fear in her voice, but inside she was quaking. The huge man could easily have picked her up off her feet, and well he knew it.

'Oooh, lads, did you hear that? Miss Nancy's resting. From what I hear, both these so-called ladies are at their best on their backs,' Middleton roared at his workmates, who rewarded his wit with rumbling laughter.

'Don't you make fun of me, Mr Middleton, or you'll live to regret it.' Alice could feel her temper rising. Her face was flushing not with embarrassment but with fury. How dare he, the crude, vulgar man. 'I'm warning you, mind who you are talking to.'

'And who's that, then? A lady's maid – if you can call that wild thing a lady. As for the "maid", why she's no better than a prostitute, or so I've heard.' Middleton continued playing to his admiring crowd, unaware of Will coming to the door.

'Middleton, you've insulted my family enough – get yourself in here now, and close the door.'

Will was sharp and hard with his words; this troublemaker had riled him once too often. He went and sat behind the kitchen table, where the allocated wages and his accounts were all laid out, and began counting out a few extra shillings alongside Middleton's wages. The man had taken his cap off and relaxed his stance in anticipation of receiving his week's pay. Alice looked on, her eyes burning into Middleton's back. Her hands were clenched into fists by her side; she was so angry she wanted to lash out at him for calling her those things.

Will counted the money out as he placed it in the big man's outstretched palm, and carried on counting until the man was holding two weeks' wages. Then he rose to his full height and looked the grinning man straight in the eye. 'Middleton, you're fired. I've had enough of you and your troublemaking. I don't need your sort round here. There's an extra week's wage in your hand. Now, I want you off my property by the end of the day.'

'You dirty rotten bastard – you can't run that works without me. You're nothing, you jumped-up piece of shit.' Middleton grabbed Will by the collar, pulling him halfway across the table and sending the rest of the wages scattering across the floor.

'Oh, but I can,' said Will, breaking free from his aggressor's grasp. 'There isn't going to be a marble works any more – I've just closed the place down and now you're all out of a job. So you can threaten me all you like but there's nothing you can do about it.'

'You bastard! You've sold us all out! Taken care of yourself, haven't you? Made sure you're all right, but you don't give a damn about the rest of us – we're nothing to you.' He made a fist and was about to throw a punch at Will when he felt something poke him in the middle of his back.

'I wouldn't do that if I was you. Now you'd better calm down, walk out that door and keep on walking else I'll pull this trigger – and believe me, my brother taught me how to handle a gun real well. I don't just lie on my back, as you so quaintly put it.' If Alice could have pulled the trigger without fear of being prosecuted for murder, she would have done it. She hated the ugly brute of a man.

Middleton went quiet, bent down to pick his cap up and slowly made his way to the door. The whole time Alice held Will's shotgun to his spine. He opened the door, spat once again, put his cap on at an angle and walked out of the yard without so much as a glance at his fellow workers. Alice and Will stood on the door-step watching him, his coat flapping and arms swinging as he turned the corner and disappeared from sight.

Having heard every word of what had gone on inside the cottage, the rest of the men stood silent, their faces sombre as they awaited their final paypacket. They were regretting the times that they had moaned about their work; it might not have been up to much, but at least it put food on the table and a roof over their heads. Now things looked bleak. As each man emerged from the cottage clutching his money, he paused to solemnly shake hands and mutter promises to stay in touch. In reality they didn't know what the future held for them.

Once the last worker had left the kitchen, Will breathed a sigh of relief. It had been the worst day's work he had ever had to do and he felt sorry for his ex-workers. Work was hard to come by and he didn't know where they would end up.

'Thank God that's over,' said Alice. 'If that Middleton had said another word, I swear I'd have shot him. Ignorant brute.' She was sweeping the kitchen floor, pushing the broom with a vengeance as she cleaned up all traces of the muddy boot prints that had been left on the stone slabs. 'I'm glad Nancy didn't wake up when he started losing his temper and shouting: it would have made her nervous and upset her.'

'Aye, he's one that I'll not be sorry to see the back of. I'll miss some of the others, though. Still, if all goes well, I might be able to rehire them.' Will took his accounts book and the few pounds he had left over and locked them in his sturdy sideboard.

'That was a good idea the pair of you came up with. Shows what you can do when you put your heads together. Once the conversion's done, the marble works will make two good houses. And as soon as they're sold, you can build them two new houses. All in all, it should make a good investment for the both of you.' Alice set aside the broom and busied herself washing dishes.

'Aye, I can't wait. Starting next week, I'm going to have a hell of a tidy-up. I need to get hold of the scrap man first – might as well get what money we can from the old machinery. But that's all I can do for the time being. I wish that architect friend of Gerald's would get a move on with the plans. Last thing I want is to be sitting around here with nothing to do.'

Alice turned from the sink to look at her brother. 'Nancy will enjoy having you around. She needs your support.'

'Aye, but do I want to be around her? She's near driven me mad of late. I tell you, lass, if she hadn't any brass, I'd be thinking about doing a runner. I didn't know what I was taking on – why didn't you tell me how bad she was?' Will was standing in the kitchen doorway, staring out at the drizzle and the mist that was starting to form around the fell.

'She'll get better once the baby's born. Not long to go now, so be patient; you'll soon be a dad and that will change everything.' Alice went to her brother and put an arm around him. 'With all this money you and Gerald will be making from your new project, you'll be lord of your own manor before you know it.'

'Aye, well, we'll see. It'll take a while to get everything in place. In the meantime, we'll have to live on Nancy's allowance and be content with that.'

'Is someone talking about me?' Nancy, fresh from her afternoon nap, entered the kitchen.

'No, Nancy. It's been a bit of an afternoon, that's all. Will's just laid off the workers – I'm surprised the shouting didn't wake you up.' Alice beckoned for her to sit down. 'Will was only saying it's a good job we have your allowance to live on, until the houses get built.'

'What houses? What are you talking about? Nobody ever tells me anything!' Nancy demanded in an aggravated tone.

'You were there when Gerald and Will talked about closing the marble works and changing it into houses. That way they can keep Stone House turning a profit for them.' Alice squeezed her hand.

'I can't remember. I can't remember anything. My head feels all fuzzy. I can't think straight any more.' Nancy turned to Alice, her eyes pleading for an explanation.

'Don't worry, love. You let us worry about that. We'll take care of things, won't we, Will?'

'Aye, nothing to fret about, all's in hand.' Will grabbed his coat and cap from the hook by the door. 'Right, I'm off up to the works to make sure all's straight. It'll be funny to walk up there and not have any workers around.'

In truth, it was just an excuse to get out of the cottage. Will was fed up with humouring his new wife and listening to baby talk, and having to endlessly repeat things because Nancy couldn't remember having been told. Already he was sick and tired of this being-married lark. Given the chance, he'd welcome being free and single again.

17

'Are you ready, you two? The horse and me are waiting. I don't know why you women take so long. God only knows what you get up to.' Will waited in the bright sunshine, impatient to set off. He was meeting Gerald at the manor to go over the plans that had been drawn up for the new houses.

'We're coming. You should know better than to rush a pregnant woman – we had to make sure we looked our best, didn't we, Nancy?' Alice helped her sister-in-law into the trap, Nancy's swollen belly showing that the unborn baby was growing. 'You're going to have to be more patient when you're a father, what with all the sleepless nights and nappies. But I'm sure you'll cope.'

She climbed in and sat opposite Nancy in the back. Behind her she could hear Will grunting and mumbling under his breath in response to her dig at him.

'We do need to get there for dinner time, not supper – get a move on,' Alice prompted.

Will finished lighting the cigarette that hung from

the corner of his mouth and whipped the horse into motion.

With the trap finally moving, Alice and Nancy sat watching the countryside go by and listening to the steady pace of the horse's hooves. In the dale, farmers were cutting the grass to make into hay and the warm air was filled with the smell of sweet grass drying. It was a beautiful day and even Will began to relax a little, breaking into a merry out-of-tune whistle.

'It's nice to see home.' Nancy gazed at the manor with tear-filled eyes as the trap slowed to a halt by the front steps. 'I forget how much I love this place. Not that I don't want to be with Will, but it would be nice if the cottage was a little larger.'

'It won't be long now. Gerald and Will have agreed that the first house to be built will be for the two of you and the new baby to live in. Then you can rent your cottage out.' Alice knew Nancy had been missing the luxuries of the manor and she could understand how she felt. She had forsaken so much for the love of Will and he did not appreciate it.

'Nancy, my love, you're blooming!' Gerald took hold of his sister's hand to support her as she alighted the trap.

'Thank you, Gerald. I feel fine sometimes, but how I miss this place.' A tear rolled down her cheek.

'Now, don't get upset. You know we are always here and that you are always welcome.' He escorted her into the manor, then turned to help Alice alight. 'Alice, how are you keeping? I see you've brought the sunshine

259

with you.' His eyes twinkled with mischief, but he lowered them when he noticed Will watching him.

Alice couldn't take her gaze off Gerald as he escorted her up the steps. It had been a few weeks since she had seen him and every day she had fantasized about his dark features. Crossly she reminded herself that she had no business thinking about him in that way. So far as he was concerned, she was just a servant girl. She chattered brightly in an effort to cover her inner turmoil.

'Thank you. It's such a beautiful day, we had a lovely journey, and Nancy's been coping ever so well. She just got a little tearful when she saw the manor. You must admit, there is quite a difference between this and where we live.'

'Ah, but that will soon change. You should see the plans I've had drawn up; the new family will not want for anything with the house we are to build. Come on, Will, leave that animal to Jack and come and join us in the study.'

Once the men were engrossed in their discussion of the plans, Mrs Dowbiggin came in with a tea tray and began serving the two women. 'Miss Nancy, it's lovely to see you.' She gave Nancy a hug and fussed over her as she poured tea and passed out the cups. 'How's things with the baby?' she whispered, not wanting the men to overhear 'women's business'.

'Mrs Dowbiggin, I miss you. Are you taking good care of my brother? And where's Faulks? Is he well?'

Nancy, shaking with emotion, clutched Mrs Dowbiggin's hand.

'We are fine, Miss Nancy, so stop bothering about us and just look after yourself and that baby. That's all that matters now.'

Mrs Dowbiggin blew her nose on a lace-trimmed handkerchief, disguising the fact that her eyes, too, were brimming with tears. Having looked after Miss Nancy since she was a girl, she had missed her terribly. At times she'd even found herself missing the tantrums, wishing she could hear her screaming upstairs and smashing ornaments. Life had been so quiet without her.

Putting on her cheeriest voice, the housekeeper brushed Nancy's arm and said, 'Not long now – another three months and we'll be hearing the patter of tiny feet. Your mother would have been so proud. I'm knitting, you know – it gives me something to do of a night.' And then she began sniffing into her handkerchief again, upset but trying not to show it, as she shuffled out of the room.

Alice sipped her tea and watched the two men reading the plans in the bright light that was streaming through the open study windows. She liked the study, with its green walls lined with bookcases; it gave her a secure feeling. Seeing Gerald seated at his desk like a proud statesman, she couldn't help but think how things had changed since her first meeting with the Frankland family. Then her mind returned to the present as she observed Nancy, her features drawn and tired. Thankfully, this was one of her better days. There were times when it was all she could do to remember her own name, let alone anything else. The sooner the baby was born, the better for all concerned.

'Beg your pardon, sir, but I thought you might want to see this.' Faulks entered the study waving a crisply ironed newspaper. 'The paper boy sends his apologies at the lateness of his delivery, but as you can see by the headlines it could be grave news, especially for your Russian colleagues.' Flustered, he set the paper on the desk in front of his employer.

'What's all this fuss, Faulks? What on earth are you talking about?' Disgruntled, Gerald picked up the paper and scanned the front page. The colour drained from his face as he read.

'What is it? What's wrong?' said Will, seeing his reaction.

'Archduke Franz Ferdinand, heir to the Austro-Hungarian throne, has been assassinated in Sarajevo by a Serbian nationalist. This could have terrible consequences if the Austrians retaliate by attacking Serbia. Russia is sworn to defend the Serbs, while Austria will turn to their German allies for support.' Gerald placed the paper on his knee, his face grim as he contemplated what would happen if, as he feared, the great powers of Europe went to war.

'Oh, so it's nowt for us to worry about, then, just a load of foreigners fighting among themselves. From the way you were looking, I thought good old King George had died! Come on, let's get back to these plans; never mind the paper.' Will leaned over the architect's drawings, trying to make sense of them all.

'For God's sake, man, there are people I love in Russia! If war breaks out, their lives may be in danger. And you expect me to put all thought of that aside for the sake of building a few houses? There are more important things in this world than making money.' Thrusting the plans away, Gerald sprang to his feet and went to the window, the newspaper still clutched in his hand. 'A beautiful day like today, sun shining, family all around me, but I feel a dark cloud blotting the horizon.'

Nancy went to her brother's side and laid her hand on his shoulder. 'You've always got us, dear. It's better we forget our ties to Russia. The time has come for us both to move on and find happiness here.' Smiling, she kissed him lightly on his cheek before returning to her seat next to Alice.

'Aye, come on, man, nothing's happened yet. Don't go looking at the black side. These bloody foreigners always kiss and make up; the whole thing'll have blown over by next week.' Will patted him on the back.

'I hope you're right, old man. I pray that you're right and I'm wrong, because otherwise we'll be building these houses for nothing.' Gerald came away from the window and poured two whiskies from the decanter on his desk. He handed one glass to Will and downed the contents of the other in a single gulp.

Will looked at the crystal whisky tumbler filled with golden liquid. Never having drunk the stuff before, he followed Gerald's example and threw it back in one gulp. Coughing and spluttering, eyes watering and cheeks turning red as the spirit warmed his insides, he wheezed, 'Now I know why they call it firewater! Give me a pint of best bitter, any day.'

Gerald patted him on the back and laughed. 'It's a taste that grows on you after a while. Same thing's true of bloody foreigners.'

'Aye, you can keep them and all. Nearest thing to foreign I've ever seen is Lancashire, and that was enough for me.' Will laughed and coughed again as he leaned over the desk.

'Let's hope, for all our sakes, that you never go any further,' said Gerald, pouring another drink. This time he sipped it slowly and thoughtfully.

'Gerald seemed to be very worried by the news. I think he might know more about it than he let on.' Alice was sitting with Will on the wooden bench outside the cottage watching the sun set over Combe Scar. For fear of upsetting Nancy, they had not spoken of the incident in the study while in her presence; the journey home had been spent chatting about the new houses and their visit to the manor instead. Only now that she had retired to her bed, leaving brother and sister to sit outside until it was time for them to sleep, were they able to discuss it.

'It'll be nothing. I've never even heard of this fellow that got killed, so how could it make any difference to us that he's dead? We'll get them houses built and we'll make as much brass as Gerald. Then we'll give everyone a run for their money.' Will finished cleaning his shotgun and blew down the barrel. 'It's a grand night. I'm just going to have a wander up the fell and pot a rabbit or two. Are you coming with me?' He jangled some cartridges in his pocket and put his cap on.

'No, I don't think I will. I want to sit here a while longer and mull things over. Nancy's been good today, but who's to say what she'll be like tomorrow? She wears me out some days.'

'Aye, that's why I'm going up the fell – need a bit of time to myself. I tell you, Sis, it's a high price I'm paying for a bit of extra brass.' He put his shotgun over his shoulder and walked away.

'You've only yourself to blame,' she retorted, but he didn't hear her. Alice shook her head. Will had everything to look forward to – new big house, doting wife, a baby on the way – and he still wasn't satisfied. He'd only been married a couple of months and already his patience with Nancy was wearing thin. Hopefully, when the baby came along, things would be different.

Her thoughts returned to Gerald and the expression on his face as he studied the newspaper. Something had disturbed him a great deal, and that worried Alice. Unlike her brother, Gerald knew all about politics and world affairs. Not only had he travelled the globe and lived in Russia for a while, he'd attended Sedbergh School and been a cadet. He wouldn't have been alarmed without cause.

265

The glorious sunset soon made her forget her anxieties, bathing the countryside in shimmering hues of gold and orange. The screeching of diving swallows made way for the high-pitched squeak of bats as they clambered out of their daytime hiding places to glide through the dusky skies on dark, leathery wings. Alice shivered as the temperature fell with the disappearance of the sun. It was time to go in and wait for Will's return, although, knowing him, it could be early morning before he ventured home.

She lit the oil lamp and placed it in the window, catching sight of her reflection in the glass. What a state she was in! Alice took a loose strand of hair and twisted it behind her ear. She'd gone to the dogs since moving out of the manor. Maybe now that plans for the houses were coming along, she could convince Will to buy her a new dress and perhaps a hat to go with it. Tomorrow she would suggest that they take a ride into Kendal for some baby clothes and then she would try and steer Nancy past that shop she liked, the one on Stramongate. They always had such beautiful materials in the window. Yes, that would be the best way to go about it: once Nancy came around to the idea, Will wouldn't be able to say no. She hummed to herself as she sat at the table darning Will's socks. When they visited the manor to show off the new baby, she'd be all dressed up in her new dress, new hat, maybe even new shoes. She wanted to look pretty next time she saw Gerald, because it would be her he'd be looking at, not the baby.

18

'Gerald, good to see you.' Colonel Fredericks stood up from behind his desk and shook Gerald's hand firmly. 'I wondered if you would be showing interest. I take it you've heard that Germany declared war on Russia yesterday? It's only a matter of time till good old Blighty gets pulled into it. Damned shame, but we'll soon show them.' He indicated for Gerald to take a seat. 'So, what can we do for you, old man? D'you fancy a posting?'

'That's what I was hoping for, sir. I reckon I'd be more use with a gun in my hand fighting for my country than potting the occasional pheasant or rabbit.' Gerald had thought long and hard before catching the train to Carlisle and requesting an interview with his father's old friend, the colonel of the Border Regiment. The news that Germany and Russia were now officially at war had made up his mind.

'Seriously, lad, do you really want to risk everything to go and fight in some foreign field?' The colonel's usual bluff manner was replaced by a much more

267

serious tone. In the days when Gerald's parents were alive he had attended many dinner parties at Whernside Manor; fascinated by his dress uniform, the young Gerald would follow him around, begging to be allowed to play with the sword that hung by his side. 'I owe it to your father and mother to warn you, Gerald, that this could turn out to be the war of all wars if England does get involved. You've a lot to lose. And then there's that sister of yours . . .'

'What's the point of wasting my training sitting in the Dales, pretending to be lord of the manor, when everything I know is changing?' Gerald looked the colonel in the eye. 'As for Nancy, she's now married and is expecting her first baby.'

'Is she, by God! Then congratulations are in order. Who's the lucky fellow? Anyone I know?'

'No, Colonel, he's no one you would know.' Gerald wasn't about to tell him that his sister's new husband was just some local and that it had been a shotgun wedding. Impatient to return to the matter at hand, he declined the colonel's offer of a celebratory cigar and pressed on: 'Do you think you can find me a commission?'

'If that's what you want, I will write a letter of recommendation to the War Office informing them that one of the finest cadets Sedbergh ever produced is applying for a commission. They'll want to see your birth certificate and a medical certif—' He broke off as Gerald produced the documents from his pocket and handed them over. 'Well, my boy, you really are determined, aren't you? With these I can get you gazetted more quickly. But, Gerald, you take care. I wouldn't want the son of my dearest friends to end up dead because of me.' He smiled at the serious-faced young man sitting across from him.

'Thank you for your concern, Colonel, but I am determined to volunteer. When this country does get drawn in, I want to be one of the first to take up arms. There's far too much at stake for me to ignore my obligations.'

The two men got to their feet and shook hands. The colonel looked tired and too old to take on a new war. But Gerald couldn't wait for his papers to come through so that he could do the job he'd trained for as a cadet at Sedbergh and fight for King and Country.

'Read all about it, read all about it! Britain declares war on Germany.' The newsvendor on the corner of Stramongate was doing a roaring trade, barely managing to give out the papers and take the money fast enough. People were clamouring to get their hands on the latest edition with its shocking news of Britain's entry into the war against Germany and its allies. Will, Nancy and Alice dodged the throng and crossed the road to the haberdasher's, the bell above the door chiming loudly as Will ushered his womenfolk into the shop.

'I've never known a morning like it,' said the shop-keeper, turning from the window where she'd been watching the commotion. 'That's the second printing of papers that young lad has sold today. Folk are carrying on like they've been given a pot of gold 'stead of getting into a war. I can't see any sense in it, myself. Why should we go and rescue those Frenchies? The world's gone mad.' Observing Nancy's bulge as the three drew closer, she added: 'Just be glad that you're married. At least you won't be going to war. And you won't be letting him go, will you, love, not in your condition?'

Already unnerved by the hubbub in the street, Nancy became even more confused and scared at the mention of war. Alice hurried to reassure her as Will stared through the glass door at the crowds still gathering.

'Here now, take the weight off your feet.' The stout middle-aged shopkeeper came out from behind the counter with a chair and set it down beside Nancy. 'I remember when I was having our Alf – by 'eck, I was tired and my feet ached. I used to say to the old man he had no idea what I went through to give him a son. They've no idea, haven't these fellows, no idea whatsoever what we women go through.' Catching sight of Alice casting an admiring glance at a ream of delicate pink calico, the astute saleswoman swiftly changed topic: 'Now that is a lovely bit of calico, just come in from Liverpool docks last week. I can give you a good deal on it if you buy two dress lengths, and it'll last well.'

'Thank you, but we've come for some of your baby

clothes. We noticed them in the window last time we were in Kendal.' Alice spoke on Nancy's behalf.

'Aye, I've a good stock in: wool vests, liberty bodices, nappies . . . and I've some lovely flannelette nighties – any baby's right in them until they start crawling. Is this your first?' She turned to Nancy, studying her with enquiring eyes.

'Yes, it's my first.' Nancy looked down at the floor, not wanting to engage the old woman's stare.

'Well, I hope it's a lad, for your sake. Then you mightn't have to go through it again. The pain when I had our Alf was unbearable. I vowed I'd never have another after that. I tell you, these fellas take their pleasure but don't know the other half of it.'

'Can we have a look at the vests, please?' Alice cut in, hoping to get the shopkeeper off the subject. She didn't want Nancy subjected to a long drawn-out description of the agonies of childbirth. From the look of the woman, the son whose birth had proved so much of an ordeal must be a grown man by now.

'I'll just get my steps – the vests are up there on the top shelf. Do you want a fairly big size? You can make them do for six months if you get them big enough. Same with the liberty bodices. Little mites are better warm than cold; they need at least three layers on, even in this grand weather.' She pulled out some rickety wooden steps and climbed slowly up. Balancing three flat cardboard boxes under her chin, she made a wobbly descent with one hand on the steps. 'These are our finest wool vests. Now, I'm only advising, but if I were you, I'd take three of them.'

Alice took one out of the box and passed it to Nancy, who held it up and then squeezed it tight to her face, feeling the softness of the wool and playing with the tiny drawstring ribbon round the neck. 'Will, darling, come and look at these – aren't they adorable?' Nancy's eyes filled with tears as it suddenly dawned on her that she was about to be a mother.

'I'm just watching these crowds, Nance. I've never seen anything like it in my life.' Will walked reluctantly from the shop doorway, glancing over his shoulder, unable to take his eyes off the crowds gathering around the newsvendor.

'What do you think? Aren't they sweet?' Nancy held a baby vest up for Will to inspect.

'Aye, aye, you get whatever you want, lass, and I'll settle the bill when you're done. While we're here, might as well treat yourself an' all. And knowing our lass, I'm sure she'll have her eye on something too. Just pick out whatever you want and give me a shout when you're done – I'm going to nip outside, see what's going on. It's like Christmas out there.'

Alice winked at Nancy as Will walked out of the shop. Time for them both to get what they wanted.

'We'll have half a dozen of the vests and the same of the liberty bodices . . .' Alice took charge of the orders as Nancy admired the ribbons and small buttons that fastened the tiny garments. 'Two dozen nappies ought to do it, and can we see those nighties that you

272

were suggesting? After that, we'd both like to look at some material. Do you do dressmaking as well?' The woman nodded. 'Oh, good, that makes it easier all round. Can you take our measurements before my brother comes back – it's a case of what the eye doesn't see, the heart doesn't grieve, if you know what I mean.'

'Anything you want, we can do it,' said the starry-eyed shopkeeper, overjoyed that she'd had second thoughts about opening up that morning. Because the way these two were spending, there would be no need to open for the next month. 'Would you like your order parcelled and sent to you? It'd save you both any awkward questions. Now, what about a pair of these pink gloves? They would go lovely with that calico you had your eye on . . .'

Soon the shop counter was covered with goods as Nancy and Alice took Will at his word and picked out whatever they wanted. It was like turning two children loose in a sweetshop.

'By 'eck, I didn't realize a baby could cost so much! Does it really need all that? We'll be living on bread and dripping with the money I've spent today.' Will shook his head as he put the receipt into his pocket.

'You want your son to be dressed right, don't you?' Alice replied, giggling at her sister-in-law. Nancy was smiling, enjoying a good day out shopping.

'And how do you know that it's going to be a lad? Mind, I hope it is a lad, 'cos God help us if it turns out to be a lass that takes after her aunty Alice.' Will grinned at Alice as they walked through the crowds. 'I bought a paper off that lad. I thought we could drop it off at the manor, show it to Gerald. Looks as though he was right – all hell's going to break loose. But the folk I were talking to say it'll be over by Christmas. Won't take us long to teach Kaiser Bill a lesson and send him running home with his tail between his legs. Nancy, are you up to calling off at your brother's? You're not too tired, are you?'

'No, it'll be good to see him. Then I can tell him about the sweet little baby clothes.' Nancy glowed as if it would make her day complete to see her darling brother.

'Right, let's get out of this madhouse and go see what Gerald makes of the news.' Will untied the horses and, realizing that they'd been spooked by the hullabaloo, led them away from the bustle of central Kendal. As his womenfolk chattered happily in the back of the trap, he posed a question, keeping his voice low so only the horses could hear: 'War declared – what the hell is that going to mean to all of us?' Then he mounted the trap and drove them slowly home.

'I tell you, Gerald, all hell's broken out in Kendal. The papers are stirring everybody up – the place was full of crowds cheering and young lads lining up for a chance to take on the Hun, and their mothers were crying, not wanting them to go. I've never seen anything like it.' Will was pacing up and down the sitting room of the manor, trying to describe the atmosphere in Kendal.

'I read it this morning.' Gerald sat stony-faced until

his brother-in-law had finished, then he knelt beside his sister and took her hand in his. 'Nancy, love, forgive me, I should have told you earlier: I've signed up and am about to join our gallant lads. I'm so sorry, but I have to go – not only am I fighting for England but also for our friends in Russia. I join my regiment next week. They've appointed me second lieutenant – I'll be shipped out to France straight away.' His eyes pleaded with Nancy as she started to tremble and sob. 'Try to understand, Nancy, I must go. You've got Will and Alice to look after you, and if, God forbid, anything happens to me, the manor and everything that's mine will be yours.'

'Don't leave me. Please don't leave me. You are all I've got in this world.'

'Nonsense, you've got Will, who loves you dearly, and faithful Alice, who is always by your side. And soon there'll be the little one as well. I'll come home to find you with a bouncing baby on your knee and probably another one on the way. And I will come home, you know me – just like a bad penny.' Gerald smiled at his sister, fighting back the tears that were beginning to well up in his eyes.

Nancy cried inconsolably as he rose from his knees and walked over to Will. 'I'm afraid the build will have to go on hold until I return, old man. You understand, don't you?'

'Aye, I understand. If you feel it's your duty, you must go. No doubt you'll be the first of many. To be honest, I wish I were coming with you – see a bit of other lands, shoot a Hun or two. It'd only be like potting rabbits.' Will slapped him on the back. 'She'll be all right, don't worry.' He nodded in the direction of Nancy. 'Me and our lass will take care of her.'

'Alice, will you wish me luck and look after my little sister and her new baby?' Gerald turned to Alice, who had remained silent when he made his announcement.

'I'll wish you luck and I'll look after Nancy, but I think you are wrong to go and leave us all. We need you here. Let someone else fight this war; it's nothing to do with us here in Dent.' Alice's blue eyes blazed with fear and hatred of the war that was going to take Gerald away from her.

'My dear Alice, the world is a much smaller place than you think. I'm going to fight for all of us, to make our lives safer and to let people like you say what they think. I know you're angry with me – those blue eyes give you away – but I have to go.'

As Alice looked up at him, silhouetted against the evening sun shining through the sitting-room window, it seemed to her as if a cloud of darkness enveloped the room. The war had come to Dent and nothing was going to be the same.

19

Alice sat on top of the limestone wall, resting from hoeing the small piece of earth she called her garden. She'd claimed it from a strip of land between the stream that ran by the side of the cottage and the lane down to the main road. All spring she'd dug and weeded the long strip of rough land, and now with summer drawing to an end her labours had been rewarded with a display of vibrant dahlias and chrysanthemums flowering in one part of the garden while a thriving vegetable plot occupied the remainder.

The weeds didn't stand a chance with Alice venting her anger on them in the early morning sunshine. The lettuce, beetroot and cabbage patches had never been weeded so fast; while her brain had been doing overtime, her body had mechanically gone on with its chores until there were no more weeds left. Still gripping the hoe, Alice stamped it on the ground, shaking her head in disgust at herself for not saying goodbye the way she'd wanted to. She'd stood there on the platform, waving as Gerald boarded the train in his smart army uniform, when what she should have done was taken him to one side and told him how she felt. But that class thing had got in the way as usual: she was a maid and he was her master, and no matter how much she wanted to show her feelings, she was afraid of showing herself up if he refused her advances.

Alice stamped the hoe down once again, this time slicing an earwig in two. Alice watched its death throes, the life ebbing from its body. Normally she'd have been satisfied with flicking it off the dahlia it was making a meal of, but today she needed to vent her wrath on something.

The previous morning they'd taken the winding hill road to the station. The fell was shrouded in fog that clung to the landscape like a damp cobweb, obscuring the view. Nancy had sobbed inconsolably as she clung to Gerald in his khaki uniform, his cap and stick making him look every inch the officer and a force to be reckoned with. The steam train had come shunting out of Rise Hill tunnel, puffing grey smoke as it made its way on the upward line to Settle and then on to Leeds. The claret-coloured carriages were packed with khaki-clad troops from the barracks at Carlisle and with enthusiastic volunteers eager to go and teach the Hun a lesson.

As the train had drawn in, Will had shaken Gerald's hand, promising to take care of Nancy and her new-born. Then he'd prised Nancy's fingers from her brother's uniform and dragged her away, still frantically pleading with him not to go. It was then that

Alice had stepped forward, wanting to put her arms around him and tell him of her feelings, but unable to say the words. Even when his dark brown eyes had looked into hers and his soft voice had murmured, 'Alice, take care,' as he kissed her on the cheek, she'd remained silent. Not so much as a 'Take care. Keep your head down' – not a word, let alone 'I love you'. She had stood on the platform as he boarded the train, cheered on by the occupants, and slammed the carriage door. She'd gone on standing there as the train pulled out with him waving from the window. Then she had turned to Will and told him that she would walk home rather than ride with them in the trap. The fog had lifted by this time, and from the first bend of the road on the hill she could just make out the last carriage going over the top viaduct at Dent Head before disappearing into Blea Moor tunnel. There she had stood, tears in her eyes, whispering, 'Take care, my love.' Then she had picked a bunch of heather from the roadside in remembrance of the day.

A cry of 'Delivery for Will Bentham!' brought Alice back to the present with a jolt. The post lad was coming up the road with a huge parcel balanced on the front of his bike. 'Can you sign for it, miss?' Alice looked at him with her blue eyes but said nothing. 'Miss, can you sign for it?' He puffed and caught his breath as she took his board and pencil from his hand and signed, then returned it without saying a word. He untied the string that held it secure on his bike and passed it to her, hesitating for a minute or two, expecting a tip, for it was a long, hard pedal up the dale from Dent to Stone House and he'd hoped to be given something for his trouble. But seeing that nothing was forthcoming, he mounted his bike and carefully picked his way past the larger stones on the path to the main road, then freewheeled most of the way back to Dent. Some folk just did not appreciate his deliveries, and it was usually the same lot, the snobs.

Alice wiped her hands on her pinny and carried the parcel into the kitchen, placing it on the table and cutting the string tie with a carving knife. It was the baby clothes and the dresses that they had ordered on their visit to Kendal. She examined the tiny baby clothes, smiling at the smallness of the garments and feeling a twinge of guilt at having ended her own baby's life so cruelly. Surely the delicate, beautiful clothes would make her smile. She then unfolded the floral-patterned dress that Nancy had ordered; it was pleated and loose-fitting, which should make her more comfortable in the last months of pregnancy. At the bottom of the pile were the pink dress and gloves. The dress was beautiful; the seamstress had done an excellent job. Alice held it to her waist, twirling round the kitchen table with it held close to her. What a pity there wasn't going to be a single man left in the dale, let alone Gerald, who would surely have admired her in this. Bloody war, spoiling everything. The sooner it was over the better!

*

280

Will leaned on the oak table in the Moon and took a sip of his pint, the frothy white head giving him a creamy moustache, which he wiped off with his jacket sleeve. 'So, what do you reckon, Jack? Are you going to join up and see a bit of action?'

'I'm not off anywhere. I'm farming with my father and that's where I'm stopping. I'm not going to be cannon fodder for the toffs, bugger 'em. I'm best off at home, same as you are.'

'Aye, but haven't you ever wondered what it'd feel like to shoot a fellow dead? I nearly did – remember t'other spring when I shot O'Hara? It was such a feeling, I could hear my heart beating. Nothing like shooting rabbits: they just sit there and let you pull the trigger.' Will downed his pint and got to his feet. 'Another, Jack?'

'OK, one more, then I'm off home.' He set his pint glass down on the table and watched Will head over to the bar. He remembered all too well the day that Will shot Sean O'Hara. The man had been an evil bastard, and after the way he treated that horse he deserved everything he got, but Jack wouldn't have wanted to be the one to pull the trigger.

Will returned with two frothing pints. 'Here you go, lad. What's all this talk of "One more, then I'm off home"? It's not that late – sun's not even set yet.'

'I've a cow that's about to calve, so I'll need to be up early in the morning. I'm not like you, a man of leisure.'

'Nay, be fair – I've been busy tidying up at the mill the last few weeks. I'd be helping dig the foundations out for the new buildings, but everything's on hold now until Gerald gets home from playing soldiers. To be honest, the last thing I want is to be a man of leisure – bloody Nancy is starting to turn me mad, never mind herself.'

'Well, you've only yourself to blame. Back when we were both working at the manor, how many times did we hear her screaming and carrying on? You knew what you were taking on. We always used to joke that she was mad – well, now you know she is.' Jack took a mouthful of his fresh pint and looked at his friend. He had that faraway expression on his face that he always got when he was plotting something.

'Did you know Gerald got fifty quid to fit himself up for his new uniform? All the officers get that. He went to Moss Bros in Leeds with his allowance. Fifty quid – that'd last me a lifetime in clothes.'

'Aye, they might last his lordship a lifetime – the way he shoots, he'll be lucky to last a week. You should know what he's like with a gun: can't hit a pheasant, let alone a Jerry.'

'Jerry who?' Will frowned, his pint stopping midway to his mouth.

'That's what the papers are calling the Germans on account of their helmets are like Jerry pots that you put under the bed.'

Will spluttered into his pint. 'Fancy having helmets like pisspots! We're bound to kick their arses. I tell

282

you, Jack, it'll all be over by Christmas and life will get back to normal. Still, I wouldn't mind having a pop at one or two of them. I'd soon get their numbers down.' Will mimed shooting Jack with his fingers.

'Don't even bloody well think about it – you've a baby on the way and your Alice will need you,' Jack growled.

'Our Alice, need me? She doesn't need anybody, that one. She's as hard as nails and feisty with it. You should know – you've had plenty of do's with her!' Will grinned cheekily.

'She'll more than get feisty with you if she hears you talking about going off to fight. Just behave yourself and keep out of trouble for once in your life.' Jack drained his pint and stood up. 'Right, I'm off. Knowing my luck, I'll get home to find this cow will have started to calve.' He pulled his cap low over his eyes and walked out of the Moon.

Will watched him go. There had been a time when the two of them had dreamed of going off to see the world. No way Jack would be doing that now – he was too content with his lot. Still, it might not be too late for him. And perhaps now was the time to do something about it.

Will wrote his note quickly and left it on the kitchen table in clear view for Alice to find it. He cut himself a slice of bread, spread it with butter and ate it while he gazed around the kitchen. God, Alice would go mad when she found out he'd left, but he couldn't take living with Nancy any more. Besides, she'd be all right: she had money, and Alice would take care of her and the baby. He swigged a pint of milk to wash down the bread. Then quietly closing the kitchen door behind him, he led his saddled horse down the lane.

An early morning mist hung over the river and the smell of autumn was in the air, with a hint of frosty days to come. He turned to look back at the huge pillars of Stone House viaduct and the cottage that had been his marital home. A wave of guilt washed over him: was he being selfish? It couldn't be helped. He had to get away. As he'd crept out of bed, tucking his shirt in and pulling on his braces, he'd watched Nancy sleeping peacefully. Another month and the baby would be here, and then it would be too late to leave. He didn't love her, he never had. How could anyone really love someone whose moods changed like the weather? She had worn him out. No, it was definitely time to go. He mounted his horse and kicked its sides. He had an urgent appointment with a recruitment officer and after that . . . who could say?

Alice sat at the kitchen table, her hands shaking, tears dripping from her cheeks onto the brief note until the ink ran down the page. How could he? The stupid bloody idiot, how could he walk out on his wife and soon-to-be-born child? And how could he leave her with all the worry of looking after them both? She screwed the note up tight in her hand. Selfish bastard!

He wasn't going to join up because he was patriotic; he was running away from his responsibilities. Her heart ached, with sorrow at not having a chance to say goodbye to her brother, but also with worry at the thought of how strong she was going to have to be. Would she ever see him again? She prayed to God that for once he would do the sensible thing and keep his head down instead of trying to prove himself.

Her first problem was how to break the news to Nancy. How do you tell an eight-month-pregnant woman that her husband has gone to war rather than standing by his family? This poor baby was already facing the prospect of being born to a mad mother; now it looked as though it might never know its father. And with the war raging in Europe, who knew what the future might hold for the poor little mite? Alice vowed that, no matter what anyone else did, she would stand by the baby. This little niece or nephew would need her, and she needed him or her; by caring for this child she would make up for what she had done to her own baby.

The sound of Nancy moving about upstairs brought Alice to her senses. She sniffed and wiped her eyes on a tea towel, putting the kettle on to boil before trying to deal with the mess Will had left her. Best she told Nancy of Will's absence straight away: it would have to be done sometime. She'd make a pot of tea for them both and then show her the letter. Alice felt so sad for her; it was bad enough that Gerald had gone to war, but for her husband to abandon her when she was eight months pregnant . . . that would no doubt tip the poor girl over the edge.

Hearing footsteps on the stairs, Alice took a deep breath, stuck her chin out and dried her tears, and then turned to face Nancy. The weight of the baby slowing her down, she entered the kitchen and smiled at Alice as she pulled out a chair and sat down. She took a long sip of her tea before speaking.

'That's good – just what you need to start the morning off. Do you know where Will is? I woke up this morning and his side of the bed was empty.' She peered at Alice over the edge of her teacup. 'I expect he's gone out with that terrible gun of his. I do wish he'd realize that he no longer has to kill things to keep us fed.' She took another sip of tea, and only when there was no answer from Alice did she look at her face and see the tears welling up in her eyes. 'What's wrong, Alice? Why the long face?'

Alice didn't say a word. She couldn't – the words wouldn't come out; instead there was this huge lump in her throat that she kept forcing down, along with the tears. Silently she passed Nancy the letter with a trembling hand and then wiped the escaping tears from her cheeks.

Nancy read the letter. She read it once and then she read it again, trying to take the news in. Not believing that her husband would rather go to war than be with her, would rather be killed on some foreign battlefield than hold his newborn baby.

'No, no! I don't believe it. He wouldn't leave me, he wouldn't walk out on me in this condition, he wouldn't, he just wouldn't. Help me, Alice, help me! I don't want to be left on my own. I've nobody, nobody, and I hate this baby and what it's doing to me.' She rocked her body, screaming and yelling with the grief of Will leaving her.

Alice hugged her sister-in-law, tears running down her face as she comforted her. What had he been thinking? How were they going to cope without a man about the house? Desperate to calm her down, she offered her an arm to lean on and suggested that she return to bed, murmuring words of encouragement as they climbed the stairs to the empty bedroom. The last thing they wanted was for the upset to result in the baby being born early. As she mixed her a tonic to help her sleep, Alice caught sight of yesterday's newspaper by the side of the bed, its front page full of news of the war and of patriotic propaganda, with Lord Kitchener pointing his finger and declaring, 'Your country needs you.' Alice pulled the covers over a sobbing Nancy and grabbed the paper. Well, that can go on the fire, she thought; it's done its job! And now because of it there were two heartbroken women and a baby about to be born without its father present. She pulled the bedroom's curtains and stroked Nancy's hair as she sobbed into her pillow.

'Hush now, we'll be all right. You know Will – he had to go. Where there's trouble, that's where he's got to be. I know he loves you – he's always telling me

287

that he does and he'll always be there for you and the baby.'

She kissed Nancy's forehead, then left the room and went downstairs. She was fed up with lying, especially for her brother. He didn't love Nancy, he never had done, and he would never be satisfied with life. Well, there was only one thing to do and that was to get along without him. Somehow they'd get by – who needed a man anyway?

20

Gerald lit a cigarette and leaned back on a wooden crate, exhausted. Since the moment he had disembarked from the troop ship at Le Havre, he'd been on his feet virtually twenty-two hours a day. What little time he did get for sleeping was interrupted with the constant sound of shellfire and gunshots. He remembered the Channel crossing: the waters had been so rough that everybody had been sick and what had started off as smart uniforms were mostly covered with vomit by the time they reached the shores of France. Then there was the marching: a fifty-pound backpack plus weapons and ammunition to be carried all the way to the Belgian border. And on their arrival they'd taken a pounding from a gun that the soldiers had nicknamed Little Willie. Gerald remembered throwing himself on the ground as he heard a shell whistle overhead. All the soldiers who'd been stationed there carried on as if nothing had happened and didn't give the new officer a second glance. Since then he'd got used to gunfire, exploding shells and the never-ending casualties and deaths. Some of the young comrades he lost were as young as eighteen. These young officers, fresh out of Eton and Uxbridge, had arrived at the front line full of patriotic fervour and eager to fight for their country. Now, those that survived looked like him: gaunt and weary. Any illusions that dying for their country would be a glorious thing had vanished like the smoke that hung over the mud-laden fields of war.

Gerald drew on his cigarette and decided it was time to write home. He wondered whether Nancy was a mother by now and hoped that things were going well for her; she'd been so upset when they had parted that early morning at Dent station. He remembered kissing Alice on the cheek, and her standing watching the train pulling out of the station. What a fool he had been! He should have taken her in his arms and kissed her properly to say his goodbyes. Life was too short to abide by formalities. There were boys dying around him who had never kissed a girl, lads so young that they had only known their mother's love. And there he'd been with a beautiful young woman under his roof, ignoring her because of her class! Life was stupid. Death was stupid.

He cast aside his cigarette butt and dragged his boots through the mud-filled trench to the officers' dugout. There he found a pen and some paper and sat down to write home. How he missed home! What he wouldn't give right now for the comforts of the manor and his evening meal with a good glass of port . . . He must not think about it; Blighty needed him to fight and he was here to do his bit. Picking up his pen, he wrote:

My dear loved ones,

It has been some weeks since we said our goodbyes and I think of that moment with great tenderness. You really have to be here to understand what it's like, and I don't want to be too graphic about what goes on out on these flat French fields. However, I will tell you about my billet. I am sitting in a hole dug in the trench, five feet by three feet, with a board stuck up in the middle to support the roof. At present there are two of us in here. Later on, I will try to get my other officer in. It is raining and the mud at the bottom of the trench is a foot deep – in some places it's so deep it goes over your knee. Across the entrance of the hole is waterproof sheeting, now daubed with mud like everything else around here, but it provides some shelter. We are continually under bombardment and the earth vibrates with the big shells the Boche keep chucking at us. Despite this, morale is good. We are supplied with cigarettes, port and brandy, and reasonable food. The one thing that is not so good is the water. It is transported in petrol cans from our stores and they sometimes forget to clean the cans out before filling them with water. Tea flavoured with petrol is not to be recommended.

I'm sitting here wondering if I'm an uncle
yet. Promise you will write and tell me – some
good news would be cheery. Give my best to
Mrs Dowbiggin and Faulks. I know the manor
is in good hands while they stay there. I miss
you all greatly, but it won't be long before
I'm home.
    Your loving brother,
    Gerald

He sealed the letter and put it in the pile of documents to be posted. Hopefully it didn't sound too downbeat. He didn't want Nancy to worry about him: she would have enough on with the baby. A shell exploded directly overhead and a whistle sounded; time to organize his troops and go over the top. How many would die this morning?

A fortnight of hard training had taught Will that, wherever he was going, it would be no picnic. He'd excelled in gunnery, but he was finding it hard to follow orders. If he could have rammed a grenade down the sergeant major's throat, he would have done. He was sick of training with full kit on, saluting and being shouted at. Now the order had finally come through: they were being shipped across to help hold the line at Ypres. Instead of bayoneting straw men and yelling at the pretend Hun, they'd be let loose on the real thing. At last they could do their bit for King and Country.

'Give us a light, mate.' The young lad next to him was trembling as they neared the shores of Calais. He seemed so young, Will wondered if he'd given the recruitment officer his true age. They'd heard the guns as they stood on the docks at Dover and now, as they were nearing French soil, they sounded even louder. The young lad's hand shook as he held the match to Will's cigarette. He flinched as an extra-loud shell exploded somewhere on the Belgian border.

'You're going to have to get used to that, mate. We'll be right under them in twenty-four hours.' Will winked at the young lad.

'I know. I just can't do with the noise. I've never heard anything so loud. I didn't think it'd be like this.' His face was strained and frightened.

'What's your name, and where you from? I'm Will, come from a little town called Dent in Yorkshire, which seems a million miles away now.' Will held his hand out.

'I'm Billy, from Buxton in Derbyshire. Me mam and dad farm, but I'd had enough, wanted to see the world.' He smiled and shook Will's hand.

'Well, Billy, you stick next to me and we'll get through it together. We'll show these bastards not to take us farm lads on. We'll make your mum and dad proud of you.'

Will looked at young Billy, still wet behind the ears, yet desperate to prove himself. How could he have envisaged what he was going to be up against? The way the lad was quivering every time a shell went off, he'd be a sitting duck on the front line. Will decided he'd make it his business to keep an eye on the young lad, keep him alive as long as possible. For the sake of Billy's mam and dad, who must be going out of their minds with worry, he'd be the lad's guardian angel without letting him know it.

His thoughts returned to his own life and the way he'd walked away from his responsibilities. By now things should have calmed down. Alice would have cursed him, and Nancy would be doing her usual wailing, but she'd soon have a baby to keep her busy. His thoughts were interrupted as the sergeant major gave orders to get ready to disembark. The clank of rifles, ammunition and backpacks being gathered up by hundreds of intrepid soldiers echoed around the ship. The atmosphere was so laden with fear, you could almost taste it and smell it as the aged troop ship docked.

'Stick with me, lad – I'll look after you. Keep your head down and your mouth shut and we'll make it.' Will pushed his protégé down the gangplank in front of him.

Orders were being yelled out left, right and centre as they marched out of the docks and down the road that led to the Belgian border at Ypres.

Ten miles from the Allied trenches, the troops rested for the night in a holding camp; even that far back from the front line, they could smell gunpowder and hear the pounding shells and gunfire. Will could hear Billy in the bunk above him sniffling and crying.

'Quiet, lad, you can't go home to your mother now

– it's too late. You'll have to grow up and be a man. Get some sleep, 'cos this will be the last good night's kip you'll have for a long time.' Will looked up at the wooden boards of the bed above his head and heard the young lad turn over. Not another word was spoken as Will gazed into the night. In truth, he too was frightened. He longed to be back at the little cottage in Dent, even if it meant putting up with Nancy's screams and his sister's caustic tongue. He knew now what a fool he'd been.

'For fuck's sake, Billy, keep your bloody head down – a good sniper could pot you off as easy as shaking hands.' The two men lay with their backs against the trench wall, both caked with mud, breathing heavily after making a dash from one trench to another. Will watched a rat run along the trench wall, squeaking as it went. It had no fear of the two men watching it; there were rich pickings among the dead and dying and it knew how to survive. 'Bloody flea-infested things! I woke with one of 'em running across my face t'other night.' Will lit a cigarette and offered it to Billy before he lit one for himself.

Billy inhaled the smoke and then exhaled slowly, watching the smoke rise above the edge of the trench. 'I hate 'em an' all. We used to have them on the farm, around the pigpens mainly, but never as big as this. These French rats are nearly as big as dogs.' Billy turned on his side and examined his canteen. It had taken a battering as he flung himself into the trench.

'Well, that looks knackered to me. We'll pick one up somewhere en route, or Sarge will issue you with one.' Will threw his cigarette stub into the filthy mud. 'Give us ten minutes and then we'll make our way over the top, back to our own trench. I'm a bit like your canteen – knackered. It's hard keeping alive with them bastards always taking a pop at you.' Will shut his eyes and pulled his cap down.

As he catnapped in the wet and filthy trench, Billy sat watching him. Will had found out everything there was to find out about him, even down to the name of his pet dog. But Billy knew nothing about Will, apart from the fact that if he hadn't had him as a guardian angel, he'd have been killed fifty times over. The rough Yorkshireman was a crack shot and a good comrade, but he kept himself to himself, never talked about his family or home. Billy closed his eyes; he couldn't sleep, but he might as well rest while he could. The non-stop pounding of the big guns and the cracking of rifle fire meant someone else was probably meeting their death right this minute. How he wished he'd not joined up. He'd seen things this last fortnight that a man his age should never see. His mind raced with faces that he'd never see again and the cries of dying men. Then a hand grabbed his shoulder.

'Some guard you are!' Will was shaking him awake. 'Come on, get ready – we'll make a run for it. All's a bit quieter at the moment.' He adjusted his tin helmet and stood ready with his rifle. 'You make the run first and then I'll follow. I'll cover you, but be bloody quick

296

– no dawdling like an old fellow.' Will raised his head over the trench. 'Go on, then – there's nothing about. It must be Jerry's tea time.'

Billy's heart was pounding; he hated these desperate scrambles between trenches where you felt like one of those ducks in the shooting gallery at the fair. He climbed the wooden ladder up the side of the trench, his boots slipping on the mud-covered rungs and his hands shaking as he hauled himself to the top.

'Go on, fuck off then, else Jerry's going to blow you to bits,' Will urged.

He gave Will a quick glance and then scrambled the few yards to his battalion's trench, heart pounding, running half bent to dodge any bullets aimed for him. Overcome with relief, he threw himself into the relative safety of his unit. He'd just picked himself up and was about to peer over the trench wall when a shot rang out. So distinct and clear, it was a shot that would be with Billy for the rest of his life. As he stuck his head above the wall, Billy saw Will sink to the ground, a bullet hole straight through his head, blood streaming down his face. His eyes were wide open, staring at Billy as he fell with arms outstretched, trying to reach for the safety of the trench. He was dead; Billy's guardian was dead. The young man slid down the side of the trench, curled up in a ball and sobbed, every bone in his body aching and shaking. Why couldn't it have been him? Why Will? He'd always been able to hold his own, he didn't fear anything, and now he'd left him on his own.

Will's body lay on the sodden, mud-covered ground of no-man's-land until nightfall; then he was retrieved along with the other fallen, his details noted and his corpse buried in a mass grave. No ceremony, just another statistic, another life claimed by the endless pounding of the guns of war.

21

Alice sat at the kitchen table, Gerald's letter in her hands. She'd just finished reading it aloud to Nancy and was trying to head off the inevitable flood of tears by playing up the few positive points: 'At least he's well, Nancy, and he sends us all his love. It doesn't sound too bad: he's got food and drink and—'

'He's going to die! They are all going to die! He'll never come back. I'll never see him again. He'll be buried out there in one of those filthy trenches stabbed by a Hun carrying a bayonet just like Will will be and all because of me.' Hair uncombed and still in her nightgown even though it was mid-morning, she began rocking herself backwards and forwards in her chair. 'Everyone who loves me dies! I'm cursed!' she wailed, tugging at her hair.

'Nonsense! Lots of people have bad times in their lives, and right now there are thousands of young men out on the front lines. The one I can't forgive is my brother – trust him to take care of himself, leaving us like this with his baby due any minute.' Alice put another log on the fire. It was a cold, frosty day and the autumn leaves were falling from the trees. 'Go and get some clothes on – you can't sit around like that all day. We can't have the local gossips thinking that you are going around half dressed.'

Alice was at her wits' end. Ever since Will had absconded to join the army, Nancy had been impossible. If it hadn't been for Jack occasionally popping in on his way up the dale to see his dad, she was sure she would have gone mad. It was Jack who'd brought the mare back after a traveller who'd been staying at the Royal Shepherd in Kendal delivered Will's message saying that he'd stabled the horse at the inn and asking Jack to come and collect it. He was the one who listened as she poured out her worries and cursed her brother for leaving them and going to fight in a war that had nothing to do with them. The rest of the time she kept her worries to herself, knowing there was nothing she could do and that sitting around moping would get them nowhere.

'Come on, let's get you up those stairs so I can brush your hair and make you look respectable.' She pulled at Nancy's arm to ease her up out of the chair.

'Alice, I don't feel well today. I keep getting a pain in my stomach. I've been feeling it for a while. I didn't want to say anything when you were reading the letter, but now I think I better had . . .' She looked down at her wet nightdress and the puddle of fluid that had appeared on the floor underneath her chair. Then she screamed, not knowing where it had come from.

300

'Shh, shh, keep calm, your baby's on its way. Now, let's get you up those stairs and in bed while we can.' Though her voice remained calm, Alice was filled with panic as she ushered her screaming sister-in-law up the stairs. She needed the doctor, or at least old Mrs Batty, but the thought of her entering the house made her skin crawl. 'We'll get you into bed and then I'll have to run and ask someone to go and get the doctor.'

'Don't leave me, Alice, please don't leave me – the baby's coming,' she cried, grabbing Alice by the neck.

'Stop it, Nancy – it takes hours for babies to be born. My mother was on three days when she had Will, I remember her telling me. It'll not come yet, don't worry. Now that I've got you settled, I'll go and put some hot water on – we'll need it to wash the baby.' She paused until Nancy, gripped by another spasm of pain, had finished screaming. 'I'll not be long. Stop in the bed until I come back up and you'll be all right.'

She rushed downstairs, grabbing her shawl from behind the kitchen door, and ran as if the devil himself was after her across the fields to the neighbouring farm of Cow Dubb. Banging on the door and fighting for breath, she pleaded with young Ben Harper to go get the doctor from Dent and to be quick about it. As she raced back across the fields to Stone House, Alice looked over her shoulder and saw Ben galloping round the first bend in the road, his jacket flapping around him. By the time she reached the lane end she could hear Nancy's screams. It was all she could do to keep going. The muscles in her legs were burning as if they were on fire, her heart was pounding, and her lungs were struggling to take in air.

Somehow she found the breath to yell up the stairs between pants: 'I'm coming, I'm coming, Nancy. I'm just putting some water on.' Hurriedly filling the kettle and putting it on to boil, she hauled herself upstairs to Nancy, who was screaming so loud Alice thought her eardrums would burst.

'The baby's coming, the baby's coming,' Nancy panted, perspiration running off her brow.

There was nothing else for it: Alice was going to have to deliver it as best she could.

She grabbed some towels from the bathroom and arranged them under Nancy. 'Breathe, Nancy, breathe. Try not to scream . . . I think I can see it coming . . . That's right. I think I can see the head . . . Push, Nancy, push . . . One more big one . . . Go on, you can do it.'

With an almighty scream from Nancy, the baby was born, its red face all screwed up and angry-looking. Alice wrapped the little mite in one of the towels, hoping that her attempt at cutting the umbilical cord would be acceptable to Dr Bailey, who was hopefully on his way. Exhausted and soaked with perspiration, Nancy lay back, grateful that the ordeal was over. Alice wiped the newborn's face and handed the swaddled bundle to its mother.

'You have a little girl, Nancy, and she's beautiful – just look at her!'

The new arrival's eyes were closed tight, as if she had no desire to see the world she'd been thrust into.

'She's beautiful, and she's all mine.' Nancy gazed down at her daughter with tears in her eyes. 'I wish her father was here to see her. Will he ever be able to see her, Alice?' A tear dropped onto the new baby's head, christening her with love.

'I don't know, Nancy. I really don't know. But she will always have us two, and we are all she needs.'

'I'll call her Alice – after all, you've brought her into the world. Alice Rose. Rose was my mother's name.' Nancy bent and kissed Baby Alice on the head. 'Hello, Alice Rose. I'm your mother and this is Aunty Alice.' She smiled at Alice and yawned.

'I'll go and get the cot; then we can wrap Baby Alice up and put her in it. The doctor's on his way – no doubt he'll want to check you over on his arrival.' Alice dragged the heavily draped cot next to the bed and gently placed the sleeping baby inside. 'Now then, let's tidy you up a bit, and then you can have a little sleep. You'll need all your strength with a new baby to feed.'

She helped Nancy into a clean nightdress and changed the bloodstained sheets, then lit the oil lamp in the window before leaving the new mother and baby. As soon as she got to the kitchen she threw the soiled sheets on the floor while she poured boiling water into the dolly tub, adding a good handful of soda crystals. Then she put the sheets in to soak. Once that was done, she sank into the kitchen chair. What a day! Screams, tantrums and now a new baby. Wherever Will was, she hoped he was paying for the sin of walking out on them.

The knock on the door gave her a start. She must have dozed off in the warmth of the kitchen. Alice stirred herself, checking in the mirror to make sure that she looked presentable before opening the door to Dr Bailey. The colour drained from her face when she saw it was not the doctor but the delivery boy from Dent post office. In his hand was a black-edged envelope.

'Beg your pardon, missus. Message for Miss Bentham.' The boy looked down at his shoes, his face red. Then he turned and mounted his bike in a bid to get away as fast as possible. This one wasn't the first he'd delivered and he didn't want to be around when the contents were read.

Alice was shaking as she opened it. She read the message once and then she read the message again.

It is my painful duty to inform you that Private William James Bentham, No. 289645 of the Northumberland Fusiliers, was killed in action on 4 October 1914.

By His Majesty's command I am to forward the enclosed message of sympathy from Their Gracious Majesties the King and Queen . . .

Not Will. It couldn't be Will. He'd have kept his head down. He thought too much of life to get killed!

304

Then Alice thought of the new life asleep in the cot upstairs, oblivious to the cruel world she had just been born into. Poor little thing, she'd never know her father.

Alice sank into the chair, trembling as she read the lines over and over again. There'd been a mistake. Surely there had been a mistake? Will had not long gone. Surely they meant Gerald? Why had it been addressed to her? Nancy was his wife and next of kin. Alice lay her head on her folded arms, the message crumpled in her hand, tears rolling down her face and her small frame heaving with sobs, oblivious to the fact that she'd left the kitchen door open. She felt a hand on her shoulder and lifted her tear-stained face up to see the doctor standing by her side.

'Alice, are you all right? I met the telegram boy on the road up here.' Dr Bailey spoke kindly to her in a soft voice. 'Is it Gerald . . . ?'

Alice rubbed her red eyes and blew her nose. 'It's Will, Dr Bailey. He's been killed in action.'

'My dear, I didn't even know he'd gone to war! My condolences. I always seem to be bringing bad news to your door. Now, I must see Nancy, but I will talk to you once the baby's been delivered.' Dr Bailey was already on his way to the stairs, upset to think one of the local lads had become a war casualty.

'The baby was born about half an hour ago. Both mother and baby are doing fine. Nancy's exhausted – you'll need to take a look at her – and the baby's tiny, but she's all in one piece. I delivered her.'

'Does Nancy know about Will?'

Alice shook her head. How could she tell her on the day their baby had been born?

'It would seem you have had your fair share of worry today, my dear.' He patted Alice on the shoulder. 'Put the kettle on and we will have a talk once I've examined mother and baby. I'm a good listener!' He smiled and picked his black bag up, taking his time as he climbed the stairs. He was beginning to feel his age and the cold northern climate was not kind to his rheumatics.

By the time he came down, Alice had stoked the fire and made a fresh pot of tea.

'Mother and baby are fine, Alice. You did a good job. Now, what are we to do with you? Are you all right, my dear? Life does seem to be throwing everything at you.' He pulled a chair up to the table and stirred a spoonful of sugar and a dash of milk into his tea while studying Alice's face. 'Will you be able to manage tonight with all this responsibility? The death of your brother is bound to take its toll, and on top of that there's the baby – I doubt Nancy will be able to cope with her. I'd keep the death of your brother to yourself as long as you possibly can. It's liable to send Nancy over the edge, and we want the baby to have the best start in life now, don't we? After all, she may well be the next heir to all the Frankland estates. God willing, Gerald will come back in one piece, but if he doesn't, that little girl will be worth a fortune. Of course, I shouldn't be commenting on this, but it would be in your interest to look after the baby, keep her safe, and one day you'll get your reward.'

Alice was taken aback. She'd known Dr Bailey was the Franklands' family doctor, but she didn't realize he knew so much about the family's affairs.

'I'll take care of her as if she was my own. And I'll break the news to Nancy when I think she can handle it.' Alice offered him another cup of tea.

'Good girl, I knew I could count on you. Now, I've given Nancy a sleeping draught for tonight. Have you everything you need to feed the baby by bottle? Ben Harper's cows give good creamy milk; it'll not hurt her to be on that for a day or so. It'll take a bit of pressure off Nancy – that is, if you think you can cope with giving the baby her night-time feeds? You don't want Nancy up and about, wandering on her own in the early hours.'

Alice nodded. She'd rather be in charge of the baby; at least that way she'd know that it was getting fed.

The doctor rose and put his hat on. 'Take care, Alice. I'm so sorry for your loss. I have a feeling there will be many more to follow, leaving behind a lot of broken hearts. I'm getting too old – I know what this world is capable of.'

Alice watched the aged doctor mount his horse with some difficulty. As he trotted off down the lane, her eyes filled with tears. She needed peace to mourn her brother. She longed to go up and talk to her

Maker on the wild fell, but instead of the balm of fresh mountain winds on her tear-stained cheeks she would have to make do with the snug warmth of the kitchen.

22

Alice held the letter from the solicitors in Kendal in her hand, shaking her head in disbelief. What a state of affairs! She couldn't believe how men ruled the world when it came to money. She'd had a much better business brain than her late brother, yet here she was, left with nothing. Worse still, Nancy was penniless too. On Will's death, Nancy's inheritance had reverted to Gerald, leaving them with nothing to live on except the vegetables in the garden. What were they going to do now?

She stared out of the kitchen window, trying to organize her thoughts and come up with a plan as to what to do next, but it was impossible to think with Baby Alice screaming the house down. It seemed to Alice that her namesake had started crying the moment she was born and hadn't stopped since. Perhaps the baby could pick up on the tension that was building in the cottage. Alice clenched her hand in anger, screwing the letter into a tight ball. Shut up, just shut up for one hour, just sleep!

It looked as though she was going to have to pacify the screaming baby, because as usual Nancy was oblivious to the child's needs. She seemed to be oblivious to everything since the baby's birth. All she did was sit in front of the dressing-table mirror, staring at her reflection as she combed her hair. When she could be bothered to come downstairs, she'd sit gazing out of the living-room window. Although a month had passed since Alice had learned of Will's death, she still hadn't got round to telling Nancy. Given her current state of mind, it was too risky. For the time being, she was better off living in her own world and not knowing the truth. Oh, that dashed baby and her screams! There was nothing else for it – she'd have to go and get her.

'Now then, you awkward little devil, what're you screeching for?' She lifted the angry, red-faced bundle of noise from her cot. 'You've come to test us all round, haven't you, Baby Alice? I see – or should I say, I smell? – that we need our nappy changing. Where's your mother at? I'm sure she could do this – let's find her.'

The baby continued to scream as Alice carried her downstairs. A cold blast of air greeted them as they entered the living room. Nancy was sitting in her usual place, with the top sash window wide open and the wind blowing the curtains wildly about as she stared unseeing at the outside world.

'What are you up to? Shut that window. It's the end of November, not the middle of the summer! Here, take the baby while I close it.' Alice passed the baby to Nancy, making sure she was wrapped up warm in the cold of the living room. She slammed and fastened the window. 'What's the point of wasting money on coal for the fire if you're going to have all the windows open? Anybody would think we'd money to burn. I had to go scavenge the bit of coal we have off the railway batters as it is. Give me Alice back – she needs her nappy changing. Do you want to watch again? Then perhaps you can do it next time.'

Alice looked at Nancy as she took the baby from her, the little mite still screaming and yelling for attention. There was no response; Nancy acted as if she hadn't heard.

'Go and put some more clothes on, Nancy. You must be freezing, sitting in that draught with that thin dress on.' Alice lifted the baby over her shoulder and patted the screaming child on her back, hoping that she would stop screaming just long enough for her to get Nancy to put more clothes on.

'Did you not hear him?' said Nancy, as if in a trance. 'Did you not hear him shouting my name? I heard it on the wind. I've seen him walking up the path on a moonlit night as clear as day.'

'Who? What are you talking about? It's just the wind. It's blowing a gale.' Alice rocked the baby and patted her as she watched Nancy with her wild eyes.

'I'm not telling you! I'm not sharing with you. He's always been closer to you than me! Well, not this time;

311

this time he's mine.' Nancy laughed a strange laugh and rose from the chair. She seemed to float past Alice, her silk dress swishing softly as she left the room.

'Since she had you, little woman, your mother's been getting worse, not better. I swear some days she acts as if she doesn't know you exist.'

Alice took the baby into the warm kitchen and removed her full nappy, replacing it with a clean one from off the airing rack. While the baby lay on the table kicking her legs, she filled a bottle with warm, creamy Jersey milk. Sitting on Alice's knee in front of the kitchen fire, the angry little body relaxed and suckled contentedly. 'You don't like being ignored by your mother, do you? That's why we have these tantrums. I'd be the same if I was in your shoes. I was lucky: I had a perfect mother. She was my best friend, my guardian and a wonderful mother, and I didn't even have the manners to say goodbye to her as she lay dying. How I regret that. No matter what your mother's like, she's still your mother.'

She stroked the little girl's rosy cheeks until she fell asleep. Alice gazed at her, thinking of the baby she'd lost, her mother and father dying, and what her brother must have gone through on the battlefield. Now he lay buried in a foreign land. Life had dealt her some hard blows in the last two years, but each time she had managed to bounce back. And she'd go on bouncing back. Somehow she would sort out the money problem. Gerald would surely have made some provision for the baby his sister was carrying before he went to war. She would book an appointment with the solicitor in Kendal, see what he had to say. Once she told him what had happened, Jack would probably offer to take her. She'd mention it to him when he next called by.

'Don't you worry about a thing, Miss Alice. They'll both be all right with us. I'm fair looking forward to having this little mite for a day.' Hilda Dowbiggin was cuddling the baby so tight it was a wonder she could breathe. 'And Miss Nancy will enjoy the change, so don't you worry, we'll be just fine.'

Alice looked over her shoulder at the plump housekeeper waving them off from the steps of the manor.

'I hope they know what they're in for with Nancy. Instead of getting better she's been getting worse since the birth of the baby.' Alice shuffled her clothes and made herself more comfortable next to Jack.

'Aye, she's in a bit of a state. I can see why you've not told her about Will yet. That would push her right over the edge. It's taken me a week or two to realize that I'll never see him again. I keep going over and over our last night in the Moon. If I'd known the silly bugger was serious about wanting to shoot the Huns, I'd have played hell with him. I thought it was all talk.' Jack flicked the reins and the horses broke into a canter along the flat road under Helmside and on towards Kendal.

'I miss him so much, Jack. He was the only one I had left. If it hadn't have been for Baby Alice being born on the day the news came, I think I would have probably fallen to pieces myself.' Alice smiled at Jack. She'd come to appreciate his company more and more, regarding him as her closest friend.

'I know, lass. I miss him too. I've no one to have a pint with or go shooting with now. He may have been an awkward bugger, but he isn't half missed.' He squeezed Alice's hand with his free hand and gazed longingly at her. 'Do you mind if we pull in for a minute or two when we get to the Black Horse under Killington Fell? I'd like to give these two a bit of a break before climbing the fell road.' He nodded at his team of horses.

'No, that'll be fine. I haven't set a time with the solicitor. I only hope he can see me today, else it'll be a waste of our time.'

'No, Alice, I don't call it a waste of my time. We're back talking. Just like I miss Will, I've missed you all this time. You don't know how much I've missed you. I've never let on until now, but I heard you that day talking to the old horse in the stable.' Jack couldn't bring himself to look Alice in the eye while he confessed. 'I wish to God that I hadn't overheard – it broke my heart to think what you'd done with that baby.'

'But . . . but what you heard wasn't anything to do with you. I'm so sorry I hurt you, but believe me, the baby couldn't be born. Every time I saw it I'd have been reminded of the shame of that night . . .' Alice's eyes filled up with tears. Had he really thought she was capable of destroying a baby she could have loved? As it was, the father would never have loved it, and she

314

doubted that she could bring herself to love a baby if she couldn't even look at it without being reminded of the humiliation and hurt of being raped.

Jack reined in the horses. 'What do you mean, "the shame of that night"? What happened, Alice? I thought you'd just been carrying on behind my back, like a bloody floozy. What happened? Tell me!' His face was red with anger as he looked at her tearful face.

'You don't understand,' Alice sobbed.

'Too right I don't bloody understand. I don't understand how a grand farm lass can turn into a common hussy!' Jack glared at her.

'I was raped, Jack! I was raped by Uriah Woodhead while his wife went to see her mother. Now do you understand?' Burying her head in her hands, Alice sobbed uncontrollably. She had been carrying her secret for so long, it was a relief to get it off her chest.

Jack jumped down from the trap, steadied the horses and went to help her alight. 'Oh, lass, I didn't know. I'll kill that bloody Uriah! He's always had a wandering eye, the dirty old bastard. It's the last bloody time he'll get my trade. I'll swing for him, so help me God. Why didn't you tell me earlier?'

Alice stammered: 'Because I didn't want anyone to know. I felt so dirty, so vulnerable – and who'd take my word against his?' She sobbed into Jack's jacket.

'Everybody would have listened to you! He'd done it before, with a lass from Gawthrope. He's a mucky old bugger when he's had a drink or two, and Annie does nothing about it except cover for him. She daren't do anything else.' Jack held her tight and gave a mirthless laugh. 'Like, I knew it wasn't mine, seeing you wouldn't let me get that far, but raped – I never dreamed that. The bastard!' He hugged Alice tighter still. He still loved her; if anything, he loved her more than ever now he knew she'd been faithful to him.

Alice held him close, loving the feel of the tweed material of his jacket on her skin and the security of his arms around her. She had even missed the smell of the carbolic soap that his mother washed his shirts in. He was all she had left of her old world and she was so glad that he was there. She held him tight while the cold November winds blew around them, glad to have him back as a friend.

23

'Now, Miss Bentham, how can I help you? Does this have something to do with your late brother?'

The solicitor's offices were dark, the green velvet curtains blocking most of the faint November light, and the air was filled with the smell of musty papers and books. Alice was nervous; she had never dealt with someone in authority before.

'Yes, that's right, sir – my brother, Will Bentham, and his brother-in-law, Lord Gerald Frankland.'

'I see. Well, carry on, Miss Bentham.' He looked at her over the top of his spectacles, eyes burning through to the bone, judging her character.

'My brother, as you know, was the beneficiary of his wife's allowance, set up by her brother, Lord Frankland. Since my brother's death we have not been receiving any payment because it has been withdrawn, yet I'm sure that Lord Frankland would want it to continue, especially as he is now uncle to a baby girl.'

'I see . . . Please give my congratulations to, er . . . Nancy? Is that correct? I see your brother was put in

317

charge of the allowance because Nancy is not able at the moment to look after her own affairs. Is that still the case?' He flicked over page after page of documentation with his bony fingers.

'Yes, that's correct.' Alice felt as though she was being cross-examined in court.

'And am I also correct in thinking at this moment in time you are looking after her and the infant's welfare?' Once again he peered at Alice over the top of his spectacles.

'Yes, I am.'

'Would you give me a moment to read these notes? There may be something in here that will help with your request. I see that Lord Frankland does mention you in his instructions, so please bear with me for a moment, Miss Bentham. Unfortunately this war is making extra work and I've had no time to acquaint myself with these documents.'

He studied the folder while Alice surveyed the dreary office with its stacks of files and documents.

Eventually the solicitor looked up from the papers in front of him. 'Well, Miss Bentham, you are indeed mentioned – I have here a note in Lord Frankland's own hand assuring me of your good character and your dedication to his sister's interests. He has made provision that, in the event of his or your brother's death, Miss Nancy's monthly allowance should be issued to your good self. Thankfully, we have had no notice of Lord Frankland's death. Rather than wait for communication from his lordship, I think we can act on his behalf – after all, he has quite enough to be getting on with, fighting for dear old England.'

He signed a note to that effect and passed it to Alice, who took it gladly with shaking hands.

'Give this to my secretary downstairs and she will see to it that the allowance is paid to you. You may also be interested to learn that Lord Frankland states that, in the event of your brother's death, Miss Nancy, her baby and your good self are welcome to live in Whernside Manor. He must value your services highly, Miss Bentham.'

Conscious once more of coming under scrutiny from those penetrating eyes, Alice got to her feet. 'Thank you, sir. Thank you for your help. You don't know what a relief this is.' She couldn't believe it – they could live at the manor! She could have her old room back, and Mrs Dowbiggin and Faulks would be able to help with Nancy and the baby.

'Thank you, Miss Bentham. Regards to your sister-in-law and her child.' The solicitor busied himself with his paperwork, not even opening the door to show her out. After she had left his office, he sat back in his captain's chair and stared at the door. A young slip of a thing – working class, too, from the sound of her – and he'd just handed her the keys to the best house in Dent, and a good monthly allowance to boot. Some people had all the luck.

'Well, how did you get on?' Jack was waiting outside the solicitor's when Alice emerged.

Alice grinned. 'Let's just say I can afford to buy you a cup of tea and a cream cake at Simpson's café, if you wish, kind sir?' She gave a playful curtsy, happy with her good fortune.

'Too right, lass – I'm blinking frozen. I'll not say no to a warm-up, and then we'd best get back. Looks like rain's going to set in and it's nothing of a job sitting sodden on this buckboard for twelve miles.'

'Right, take my arm if you wish, kind gentleman.' Alice linked arms with Jack and they walked across the road to the tea shop, giggling all the way.

'I have missed you, you know that, Alice, and I do still love you.' Jack leaned across the table where they were now seated and took her hand.

Alice blushed. 'Jack, we are in company – don't be silly.'

'I don't care if the whole world knows it. You've always been the one for me, ever since we were little. I'm sorry I weren't there when you needed me most. You promise me you'll come to me if there's anything you want.' He squeezed her hand tightly.

'I promise.' Alice smiled. It was good to have him back in her life. 'Come on, let's go – it'll be dark before we know it.' She linked her arm through his again as they left the shop, making their way to the horse and trap.

'Who's put that there? Who's dared to put that there?' Jack was visibly upset as he pulled a white feather from

320

the tied-up reins. 'I'm no coward! I'd fight for my country if I really had to.' He squashed the feather in his hand, disgusted at being branded a coward. He was doing his bit for the country by farming and making sure local shops were supplied. He glanced around the marketplace but no one met his eyes.

'Hush now, Jack, they don't know what you do. Whoever left it obviously watched us go into the café and assumed the worst. Forget it.' Alice pulled on his arm as the crumpled feather was thrown down in the road. 'Come on, it's been a long day and I want to get home. Things were going so well; let's not let a stupid feather spoil it.'

Jack spat in the street, then climbed onto the trap, pulling Alice up next to him. 'Isn't it enough I've lost my best friend, my boss is on the front fighting, and my father has made me go back farming? Mind, I'm not about to be made into cannon fodder, so perhaps a white feather is right.'

He whipped the team into action and drove them hard out of Kendal and across the wild moorland up to the Dent road. He was silent all the way, never looking at Alice, who felt that a good day had been ruined by a stupid, unthinking gesture by a total stranger. By the time they arrived at the manor it was pouring with rain and the grey clouds had come down the fellside, turning late afternoon as dark as night.

'You'd be best stopping the night here, if you can. You don't want to take the baby out in this weather –

321

it'll catch its death. I'll come and take you all back up to Stone House in the morning.' Jack barely glanced at Alice as she alighted from the trap.

Her clothes sodden, hair dripping down her face, Alice looked up at him. 'Jack, please stop worrying about that blasted feather – it means nothing. You're doing enough for the country without having your brains blown out.' She shook her wet hair out of her eyes and gave him a smile. 'I'll see you in the morning, and thanks again for taking me – it's been a good day.'

Alice watched Jack ride off, his hand waving to her as he turned the bend of the path and went out of sight. She stood leaning against one of the pillars of the grand porch for a while, just watching the rain pelting down. So Jack still loved her! It was a good feeling to have. Trouble was, it didn't feel good enough. There wasn't that flutter that she got when she talked to Gerald, but since he would never be hers, perhaps she had better set her cap at Jack. At least he was a safe option. Was he the right one? Oh, she just didn't know! Her heart said one thing and her head another. With a sigh she turned and went into the manor.

'Aye, lass, you're soaking! Let's have them wet clothes off and get you into fresh ones. There's one of your old dresses still upstairs in the blue bedroom.' Mrs Dowbiggin passed her a warm towel from out of the airing cupboard and escorted her upstairs.

Having tousled her hair dry and got out of her wet things, Alice felt much better. She put on the dress and pulled a woolly cardigan over it. 'Where are Nancy and Baby Alice?'

'Miss Nancy's in her old room and the baby is asleep. Pretty as a picture, she is, the image of her mother.'

'Thank you, Mrs Dowbiggin. Have they both been all right for you? Baby Alice can be a bit demanding and, well, you know how to cope with Nancy.'

'Aye, well, I thought I knew how to cope with Nancy, but she's terribly confused at the moment, doesn't seem to want to settle to anything. I even read her a letter that we got from Gerald, but she wouldn't sit and listen.' Mrs Dowbiggin picked up Alice's discarded clothes. 'I'll put these on the airing rack. They'll be dry by the morning.'

'You've got a letter from Gerald? We haven't heard from him in weeks. Is he all right? Is he injured?' Alice couldn't ask the questions fast enough.

'He's fine – or rather, he's tired, fed up of fighting and complaining of the food, but he sounds cheery enough. I'll give you it to read later. I thought you'd have received one from him. Although, I have to say I'm glad that you haven't, just in case he mentioned Will dying and Nancy read it.'

'It's so difficult trying to keep it from her. I've been waiting and waiting for the right moment, but she's so fragile. I dread to think what it will do to her.' Alice sat down on the edge of the bed and sighed.

'Aye, I'm sorry, pet. For someone so young, you

haven't half been through the mill. Come on, come down into the kitchen while all's quiet and read Gerald's letter. I'll make you a nice cup of tea before we serve dinner. It'll be a novelty for me and Faulks looking after folk again. Since his lordship went to war, we haven't been standing on ceremony round here. The old devil and me have lived in the kitchen. I doubt things will ever be the same after this blasted war.'

Alice settled in a chair by the kitchen fire and began to read the letter. Before long her face was glowing red with the heat of the blazing fire and the passion that she felt as she hung on every sentence of the precious letter. When she came to the line *Remember me to Alice and thank her for looking after Nancy – I really do appreciate her*, she stared at the letters on the page so hard it seemed they would be engraved on her memory for ever. She prayed that he would stay, keep his head down and come home soon. If only he would return to her, she might pluck up the courage to tell him how she felt. To hell with the consequences.

24

'Marry me, Alice, please marry me. I've loved you since we were little. There will never be anyone else but you for me; I know that now,' Jack pleaded with a dumb-founded Alice over the kitchen table as she nursed the baby. Baby Alice gurgled contentedly, granting her permission.

'Oh, Jack, how can you ask me to do that when you know what I've done? You know I'll always love you, but as a friend. You deserve better than me.' Alice blushed and played with the baby's rattle as if trying to draw attention away from her embarrassment.

'You know I'm a man of few words. I wouldn't be asking you if I wasn't true with my feelings. I can provide for us well. You know I've bought your old home and, after my father's and mother's day, I'll have my home and all. I'm worth a bob or two, lass, if it's brass you're worrying about.' Jack leaned over the table and then sat back, rubbing his head with his cap in frustration.

'It isn't that.'

'Then marry me. We are made for one another.' Jack was not for giving in.

Alice didn't know what to say. She didn't want to hurt his feelings by saying no, and she knew Jack was a good safe catch. But in her heart of hearts, she wasn't truly in love with him. He was too much like part of the family. She had grown up with him and he was beginning to be like a replacement brother to her.

'Give me till Christmas to think about it – it's only a month away, not long to wait for an answer.' Alice smiled at crestfallen Jack. 'I just want to be sure. Everything is happening so fast and I'm not over losing Will yet.'

'Sorry, Alice, I wasn't thinking. 'Course you're still in mourning. Still, I've got to say, Christmas can't come quick enough. Aye, lass, make it a yes and I'll be the proudest man up the dale.' A huge smile lit up Jack's face. 'I'd always be right with you, you know that.'

'I know, Jack. I just need time. I don't know what I want myself – all's wrong in the world. All of them young men fighting and dying for our country and here am I looking after Nancy and this baby here. I can't leave them – what would become of them? Mrs Dowbiggin and Faulks couldn't manage; neither of them is getting any younger. Give me until Christmas; by then we'll have moved back into the manor. And who knows, Gerald might be home by then and the war might be coming to an end.' Alice felt quietly ashamed of herself, making up any excuse rather than saying no.

'Right, Christmas it is. And if you say yes, we'll get

married on New Year's Day, 'cos I'm not going to give you time to change your mind. Until then, I'll leave you in peace.'

Jack opened the door and Alice could hear him whistling as he walked down the lane. She didn't want to break his heart again, but while Gerald remained alive, there was still hope of her winning his affections, she just knew it – how could he resist? The thought of marrying Jack when she knew it was Gerald she had feelings for filled her with dread. Come Christmas, she was going to have to tell Jack the truth and hurt him. She'd written to Gerald, giving him the good news that he was now an uncle, and then informing him of Will's death. She'd cried as she'd written the letter, thinking of her father's saying 'One going out of the world and a new one in, always happens like that.' How true it had been that day.

She'd come to a decision about Nancy, too. By the end of the week, she'd break the news about Will's death. How she'd take it, Alice didn't know, but it had to be done. Alice could not carry the burden any more; she was worn out with their endless conversations about what a dead man might be doing in far-flung fields.

Nancy sat motionless. Not a tear, not a whimper, just a constant to and fro of her body, swaying in her chair as Alice told her of Will's death. She twisted her handkerchief tighter and tighter in a knot and gazed out at the rain trickling down the glass panes of the window.

'Do you understand, Nancy? You do know that Will's not going to be coming home to us, that we are on our own now?' Alice put her arm around Nancy as she stared out of the window.

Nancy lifted her hand and traced the downward path of a raindrop on the glass with her finger. She didn't say a word, but a trail of tears ran down her cheeks, mimicking the raindrops on the windowpane.

In the end, Alice left her there, not knowing what to say. It had been bad enough when she was heartbroken over Will choosing to go to war. Now she had to mourn his death and face the fact that she would never see him again.

The shells had pounded all morning, the constant barrage of guns and noise sending men almost to the edge of insanity as they wallowed in the thigh-high mud amid the dreaded lines of barbed wire strung out between the trenches.

Gerald Frankland was leading an attack on a patch of land just the other side of the Belgian border. It was only a few yards, but if they could gain it, the morale of his men would be lifted. A few yards meant a lot in this war.

'Right, men, listen for my whistle. On my signal, we go over the top.' Gerald lined up his exhausted and battered men. Their eyes betrayed the fear they were feeling; while some prayed to their Maker, others took deep drags on their cigarettes in an effort to combat nerves.

Gerald blew loud and clear on his whistle and the assault began, men scrambling over the trench, bayonets fixed, voices screaming and guns firing, both sides refusing to give an inch. Shells exploded, sending limbs and bodies flying. Smoke hung all around, and the smell of sulphur and the blood of dying men mingled in the air.

Gerald charged forward, yelling at the top of his lungs, bayonet drawn, leading his men into battle. He stumbled, only to get up again, yelling all the while. Then the ground gave way beneath him as a shell exploded inches away. Bleeding, injured and half buried, he lay fighting for his life in no-man's-land, while all around him his men were falling one by one. Consciousness came and went, and Gerald found himself crying out in pain with no one there to hear him apart from his dying comrades. The last thing he saw was the grey gun-smoke skies clearing and the blue of a frosty December morning shining through. The clear, sweet voice of a skylark trilled its song over the devastated battlefield. For a moment he smiled, remembering the clear blue skies of the Yorkshire Dales, and then darkness fell, his pain winning the day.

25

The rain had fallen every day since the trip to Kendal, never giving anyone the benefit of seeing a clear winter's sky for more than a few hours. The streams down the fellsides were in full flood with waterfalls splashing into deep pools and entering into the River Dee with force. The river had risen well above its banks, surging through the dale, uprooting small trees and dislodging boulders in its urge to get to the sea.

Alice stared out at the rain, unwittingly rocking the baby to and fro in her arms. She was turning out to be more of a mother than Nancy. Since learning of Will's death, Nancy had barely left her bed.

'I don't know, little one, this weather's getting worse. It's the first time I can remember hearing the river from here – it must be terribly high. It'll do some damage if it's not careful.' She folded the blanket around the baby's head and gently placed her in her cot. Baby Alice chortled happily, gazing at the woman she thought was her mother.

'That wind's getting up – just listen to it blowing

down the chimney. We'd better get some coal in from outside before it gets dark. We're going to have to keep that fire going tonight, aren't we, my darling?' She tickled the smiling baby girl under her chin, then picked up the coal scuttle and went outside.

Leaving the door ajar behind her, Alice ran through the driving rain to the shed where the coal was stored. Behind her, the wind caught the back door and slammed it with an almighty bang. Moving as fast as she could with the full scuttle, Alice returned to the house and closed the door behind her.

'There, my love, we can close the door on the world now.' Grabbing a towel, she went to stand by the baby's cot so she could carry on talking to her while she dried her hair. When she lifted her head, Nancy was standing in the doorway, looking at the pair of them.

'Nancy, love, come and sit by the fire – you must be cold in that nightdress. I'm sorry, did I wake you up with the door banging? I've been out for some coal. It's such a wild night out there. Just listen to the wind blowing down the chimney! I wouldn't want to stop out in this.' Taking Nancy gently by the arm, she guided her towards the warmth of the fire. 'Why don't I make us something to eat? Would you like Baby Alice to hold?'

Nancy shook her head as she sat next to the fire.

'Here, let me put a blanket around you. There's a real draught blowing through them windows, even though I've closed the curtains.' Alice pulled a blanket from the old oak bedding box that had belonged to her parents and wrapped it around Nancy's shoulders.

'Have you heard the voice? I heard it as plain as day when I was lying in bed. It called to me from outside. Did you not hear it? It called my name.' Nancy gripped Alice's hand hard.

'Don't be silly, Nancy, there's nobody out in this. It's the wind you're hearing, that's all. There, do you hear it whistling down the chimney?'

Both women jumped as a loud knocking was heard on the door. Nancy shrank back in terror as if it was the devil himself knocking.

Alice hesitantly went to answer, nerves on edge after listening to Nancy and her story of voices calling for her.

There in the pouring rain was the telegraph boy. 'Sorry, missus, but I've got a telegram for Mrs Bentham. I had to deliver it even in this weather.'

The wind howled around him and the battered winter leaves blew into the house as the drenched telegram boy stepped over the threshold, his dripping waterproofs leaving puddles on the floor as he fished inside his leather bag for the all-important telegram.

'We don't want it! Whatever you've got for us, we don't want it – you must have the wrong house!' Alice didn't want to take the envelope from the boy: she knew what it would contain.

'Give it to me. It's addressed to me – I'll read it.' Nancy snatched the telegram from the boy's hand and went into the front room, clutching the rain-soaked telegram in her hand.

Alice looked at the shivering young boy standing on the flagstone floor of the kitchen. She knew what he'd brought and she didn't want him in the house a moment longer, but at the same time she couldn't send him back to Dent in this weather.

'Do you want to stay? It's not fit to return to Dent tonight – that river sounds really swollen.' She looked at the shivering, white-faced boy. He could only be twelve or thirteen at most; his mother must be worrying where he was.

'No, me mam said I'd to get home and not go near the madwoman. I'm more frightened of her than the weather.' He reached for the door handle, job done and his instructions from his mother calling him home, no matter how bad the weather was.

'Just a minute, I'll give you something for coming out.' Alice went to the kitchen drawer to get her purse. As she did so, a blood-curdling scream came from the front room. She turned to the ashen-faced boy.

'Thanks, missus, but I'm off. Me mam said the madwoman'll have me if I don't get home straight away.' Banging the door behind him, he disappeared into the wild night before Alice could give him anything for his bother.

Replacing her purse in the drawer, her heart heavy, she went to join Nancy in the living room. The baby had joined in with the cries of her mother, but

Alice was more concerned with the contents of the telegram.

'What does it say, Nancy? Give it to me.' She snatched the paper from her.

'I told you I could hear him crying out my name! He's on the wind. I can hear him calling me.' Wild-eyed, Nancy got up, pulled the curtains back and looked out of the window, the palms of her hands flat against the windowpane.

Her hands shaking so much it was all she could do to focus, Alice read the telegram:

It is my painful duty to inform you that Second Lieutenant Gerald William Frankland No. 598624 of the Border Regiment is missing in action and presumed dead.

Please accept our sincere sympathies in your loss.

How many of these letters did the armed forces send out? Alice looked at the telegram, thinking about the wording and how the people who sent them must be almost immune to the constant stream of grief that they wrote every day.

'Nancy, he's missing in action; they are only presuming he's dead. It's not the same as the one I received about Will – Gerald might still be alive.'

'He's dead. I know he's dead. Can't you feel it? Something's wrong. I keep hearing his name.' Nancy made no effort to soothe poor Baby Alice, so Alice picked her up and rocked her in her arms as tears rolled down her own cheeks.

'He can't be! Both our brothers can't be dead; he's just missing.' Alice hugged the baby tight, needing a cuddle in her grief and the baby giving her some reassurance. 'Nancy, come and sit down. We don't know that he's dead. They will surely write again and confirm his death or tell us that he's been found safe and alive.'

She put the baby back in her cot and guided Nancy to the fireside, settling her in a chair and stroking her long black hair. All the time she was trying to comfort her sister-in-law, she wept silent tears. Two deaths in two months; this was the second time in Alice's short life that two deaths had come close together. What had she done to deserve all this sadness?

That night she lay in her bed exhausted by grief yet unable to cry herself to sleep with the wind gusting around the chimney and the rain pelting down on the tin roof of the stables. It was the wildest night she could remember. Seeking the comfort of Baby Alice's presence, she crept to the cot, smiling at the sight of the perfect little girl with her arms stretched above her head, content even though a force-ten gale was blowing outside. Suddenly she heard the familiar creak of the top stair: Nancy must be awake. Alice opened her bedroom door and got to the stairs just in time to see her sister-in-law going into the kitchen. Perhaps she, too, was unable to sleep for thinking of her loss.

By the time Alice got to the kitchen, Nancy was unbolting the back door. 'What are you doing? You can't go outside in your nightdress in this weather!'

'Can't you hear him? He's up at the old marble works and he's calling for me to come. Will's there too – can't you hear them?' Nancy turned wide-eyed, then carried on pulling the bolt and lifting the latch.

'Nancy, come back. Don't be so daft – it's the wind! It's only the wind you can hear.' She snatched at Nancy's nightdress, trying to pull her away as she opened the door, the wind and rain gusting into the cottage, snatching at the curtains and the clothes on the airer.

'Don't stop me, Alice. I must go – he needs me; he needs my help.' She pushed Alice aside with all the force of a madwoman, but Alice stood firm.

'Nancy, come, my love, come to bed. There's no one there; it's only the wind. Let me close the door and we'll go to bed.' Holding Nancy tight, she leaned against the back door, closing it on the wild night outside. 'Here, carry a drink of milk upstairs and let me tuck you into bed. There's no one there, believe me.'

'But I heard him! I heard him, Alice – he's out there in the wind and rain.' Nancy stared at Alice, eyes wild and tearful as she climbed the stairs to her bedroom.

'Shh now . . .' Alice stroked Nancy's long black hair and pulled the sheets up to her chin. 'See? Nobody's there.'

Nancy lay in the bed and closed her eyes. Alice could hear the baby moving and the familiar muffles that usually turned into tears. She prayed that Baby Alice would hold on another minute or two before she started crying; she daren't leave Nancy till she was certain that she had settled. Thankfully the little one obliged.

By the time she crept out of the room a few minutes later, the first splutters of a cry were erupting.

'Now then, young lady, I've had quite enough of your mother tonight, without you starting as well.' She hugged the baby to her, the warmth of her body and the security of being held quietening the little mite. It wasn't long before Baby Alice was fast asleep, and Alice herself began to drift in and out of sleep, trying hard to stay awake but finally succumbing to exhaustion.

She didn't know how long she'd slept when she was jolted awake by a loud bang. Was that the back door slamming? She quietly withdrew her arm from around the baby and went to the top of the stairs. The kitchen appeared to be empty and everything was quiet. Then she crept along the landing and peered into Nancy's bedroom only to find the bed empty and Nancy gone.

Out into the wild, dark night Nancy ran, her sodden nightdress clinging to her skin, the voices urging her on. Through howling wind and driving rain she ran and ran . . .

Alice tore down the stairs, stumbling and banging her head hard against the banister in her haste. Light-headed and with blood trickling down her face, she pulled herself upright and continued to the door. Supporting herself against the doorframe, she stood yelling

337

into the night: 'Nancy, Nancy, Nancy . . .' She kept on yelling until her voice was too hoarse to continue. Blood from her head wound was dripping down the back of her neck, and her body and face were drenched from the rain and battered by the wind. Upstairs she could hear Baby Alice crying. Reluctantly she closed the door, giving up on Nancy returning. Hopefully she'd have taken sanctuary in one of the old workmen's huts, but only daylight would reveal that. The baby was yelling loudly now, demanding attention. Alice hauled herself up the stairs and looked at the little one's angry face. As she leaned over the cot, she realized that she was dripping water on the baby. She pulled off her soaking nightdress and put a clean one on before picking the screaming bundle up.

'Hush, little one. Quiet now. Your mam's gone to look for your pa, but you've still got me. You'll always have me.'

26

When morning came, the skies had cleared and the wind had dropped. Her head aching, her eyes red and sore from the tears she had wept over all she had lost, Alice went to the kitchen window and looked out. Storm debris lay scattered on the ground, and the sound of the river in full flood filled the air. The sun was rising over Whernside, its weak rays caressing the reddish-brown tops of the fells.

After feeding the baby, Alice had spent the rest of the night in the kitchen, sitting by the dying embers of the fire and anxiously watching the back door, hoping that Nancy would return. She thought of Gerald and Will, both lost to the war, and the promise she had made Gerald: that no matter what happened, she would look after Nancy. She cursed herself for not looking after her, and not stopping her from going out into the night.

Wearily she climbed the stairs and tiptoed to the cot. Baby Alice was breathing heavily, fast asleep. Alice got dressed and put her boots on, then set off in the direction of the viaduct. From up there she would have a view over the marble works, maybe see where Nancy was. Leaving the back door open so she would be able to hear if Baby Alice awoke, she ventured up the hillside. The cobbled path was awash with small tributaries flowing downhill into the swollen River Dee, and the stream that powered the polishing machine for the marble works had turned into a full-blown river. As she climbed, Alice called Nancy's name over and over, and when she came to the remains of the marble works, she searched the remaining workmen's shed, in the hope of finding her there. Not a sign.

She carried on up the slope until she reached the arch of the viaduct. From there she could see right to the far end of the dale. Somewhere out there was her sister-in-law; she only hoped she was safe and not, as she had feared in the middle of the night, lying dead and alone. The chill December air was crisp and pure, and the smell of fresh water cleared her heavy head. Alice gazed around her: even the sheep had gone, deserting the fell for lower ground where they might find shelter from the pounding rain that had fallen for the last few days. It was time to head home; Baby Alice would be waking soon, and her needs must come first. She picked her way down the rough cobbled road, her skirts getting wet and dirty. As she reached the final few yards, she saw a figure emerging from the kitchen doorway.

'Jack! I'm here, Jack, I'm here!' Alice yelled to him, desperate to stop him before he disappeared.

'By God, I thought you'd done a runner on me, but then I heard the baby making a noise upstairs.' He began to walk up the slope towards her. 'I was just checking the sides of the river – I've lost some sheep; silly bloody things crept down here to get away from the storm and ended up drowning – and since I was almost at your bridge, I thought I'd pop my head in to see that you're all OK after last night's storm.'

Hearing Jack rambling on about lost sheep, Alice covered her head in her hands and began sobbing uncontrollably.

'What's up, lass? Whatever's wrong?' Jack ran to her and put his arm around her. Only then did he see the cut on her forehead. 'Are you all right? Did you bang your head? What happened?'

Alice buried her head in the familiar smell of his tweed jacket, sobbing and pouring her heart out, telling him of the past night's events, of Gerald going missing and of Nancy running out into the night.

'Are you sure you feel all right after that bump on the head? In that case, go put the kettle on and make a brew. Get that young 'un upstairs fed and this house warmed up. I'll organize a search party – she can't have gone far. And stop fretting. You couldn't have stopped her: she's been off her head for months now. The news of Gerald must have been the last straw.' Jack gave Alice one last comforting hug as she sniffed and filled the kettle with brown floodwater from the tap, ready to boil for tea. 'As soon as I've got any news, I'll come back and tell you.'

Though he managed a smile for Alice, in his heart he feared the worst. Nobody could survive out in the open on a night like this. He only hoped that Nancy had found shelter.

It was nearly dusk by the time a weary and down-hearted Jack entered the kitchen at Stone House. He didn't want to break the news; he felt sick with the day's findings.

'Well, did you find her? Has anyone seen her? Please, Jack, tell me. I've been going out of my head with worry all day. I've felt so helpless, stuck in the cottage with the baby, not able to do anything.' Alice tugged at his jacket as he steered her to the chair next to the fire and sat her down.

'Aye, we found her. I'm sorry, Alice, I don't know how to tell you . . .' He bent over and gazed into the fire, rubbing his head with his hand. 'There's no easy way to say this: we found her drowned, in the river at Cow Dubb. She was washed up, tangled in some tree roots. She must have fallen in last night. She wouldn't have stood a chance: the river's still in flood today and it was a torrent last night.'

'No, she can't be! She just can't be! That's everyone gone. There's nobody left.' Alice crumpled in a heap on the pegged rug in front of the fire and wept. 'I'm so fed up of fighting, of being strong. Now I've no one.'

'You've still got me, lass. I'll always be yours, you know I will. I'm not sure what to do for you, but I promise you I'll always be there.' Jack sighed, looking

342

at her distraught face. 'To make matters worse, they've found young Tommy Goad, the telegram boy, just below Bath Bridge. He must have tried to take a shortcut home down the back lane and been swept off his bike. His mother will be heartbroken too. It's a right do. I've never known anything like it.' Jack put his arm around Alice as she rested her head on his knee, sobbing and wishing that she had persuaded the young lad to stay, regardless of what his mother thought of Nancy.

'Where have you taken Nancy's body?' Alice wiped her eyes and raised her head. 'Did you not think to bring her back here?'

'Nay, lass, you wouldn't want to see her, the state she was in. We took her to old Mr Batty's. He'll see to her. No doubt he'll be coming to see you once the river subsides a bit. Old devil will be rubbing his hands, thinking of the money he can make with this funeral. I shouldn't say it, but you know what he's like.'

'Well, he needn't bother. Nobody bothered with her when she was alive, so they'd only be hypocrites if they turned up for her funeral.' Alice was angry that she would once again have to do business with the Battys. She hated them, and even in her grief she was determined that they were not going to get the better of her.

'Now, what are you going to do, lass? You're in a funny position. I suppose if Gerald is missing, presumed dead, Baby Alice is the rightful heir to all his estates. Poor little mite, good thing she's too young to know of all these carryings-on.'

'I don't know . . . Gerald's solicitor will have to be informed of Nancy's death and Gerald being declared missing. We were going to move into the manor before Christmas, and I think I will still take Baby Alice there. It's where she belongs and, besides, I don't want to stay here. There's too many bad memories here for me.' Alice rose up from her knees. 'We'll manage – you have to; no matter what life throws at you, you've got to get on with it.'

Alice looked at the concentration on Ernie Batty's face as he bent over his notepad writing down her wishes for Nancy's funeral.

'Satin inlay, did you say, Miss Bentham?' He had his professional slimy voice on and he smiled at Alice, showing his black stumps of teeth to her.

'Yes, we agreed on that – bright red, if we could, Mr Batty.'

'Oh! But, Miss Bentham, I don't know if that's proper in a coffin. I've a lovely shade of oyster silk that would be more fitting.' He rubbed his hands, thinking of the price he could charge.

'Red was her favourite colour and it showed her hair off so nicely. I want red, Mr Batty.' Alice returned his sickly smile, gazing innocently at him, while what she really wanted was to scream.

'Right, red it is. Horses, Miss Bentham – do you need a horse-drawn hearse? Nothing looks finer than horses with plumes . . .' His hand made waves in the air, conjuring the forms of fine horses.

344

'Mr Batty, she's lying in your mortuary not twenty yards from the church. Do you honestly think I need horses and a hearse? Four bearers will be sufficient, thank you.'

'And finally, how many are you expecting for the funeral tea, and where would you like it arranging? Should we say tea for a hundred to a hundred and fifty?'

'Mr Batty, I don't know where you are getting those numbers from, but there will be four of us there. And what tea we will be needing will be ready and waiting for us at the manor.'

'I thought that you'd wish for her to have a funeral that befits her brother's title; that's why I came up the dale to sort it.' His smarmy act was starting to fail as he realized that there was not going to be a lot of profit to be had.

'Aside from her brother and husband – one of whom lies dead in France, the other missing and presumed dead – Nancy Frankland was loved by two good friends and two faithful servants. Those four were the only ones who really knew her, so those are the ones whom she would want at her funeral, no one else. We wouldn't want to be seen as hypocrites now, would we?'

'Certainly not, Miss Bentham. I'll see to it – her funeral will be small but professional.' He rose from his seat and put his tall black hat on. 'Thank you for your time. Your wishes will be carried out.' He grimaced a smile as he reached for the door.

'Just one more thing, Mr Batty – please send your bill to Bramble & Partners Solicitors. Their office is on Stramongate in Kendal. They will settle with you once they have dealt with Miss Frankland's estate. I'm afraid you might have a wait, as they are busy with a lot of estates given the times we are living in.' Alice couldn't be certain, but she was sure he swore as he closed the door behind him, mumbling under his breath.

She leaned against the door and surveyed the empty kitchen, remembering how Ernie Batty had asked for money up front from her heartbroken father after the death of her mother. She could still see her father throwing the few pence that they had onto the table for the money-grabbing couple to put into their pockets. Well, at least she had given Nancy the coffin she deserved and not the flimsy board one that her mother had been buried in.

She moved away from the door: time to pack. She was looking forward to moving into the manor with Baby Alice. The prospect was a ray of sunshine in the gloom. If she never saw Stone House again it would be too soon; there had been nothing but heartache since the day she'd moved in.

'Oh, Alice, it's so good to see you and the baby! At last you're back where you both belong. I just wish Miss Nancy was with you. We'll miss her so much.' Mrs Dowbiggin dabbed her tear-filled eyes. 'It's such a terrible, terrible time. Have you any news of Master Gerald? Is he still missing?'

Alice and the baby couldn't get into the manor for the endless questions that were being thrown at her as she climbed the front steps.

She gave Mrs Dowbiggin a kiss on the cheek and then passed the sleeping baby to her before taking off her black hat and hanging it up on the hall stand.

'We've not heard a thing, Mrs Dowbiggin; I only wish we had. It's the not knowing that's the hardest part.'

'Aye, and this little one's left all alone in the big bad world.' Hilda Dowbiggin smiled and tickled the chin of the dark-haired baby. 'It's a good job she's too young to know owt about it all. Now, I've put you in your old room and I've made what used to be the nursery up for this little one.'

'That's lovely, thank you. I'll just say goodbye to Jack and make sure he's all right for Friday and the funeral, and then I'll catch up with you and Faulks over a cup of tea.' Alice left Mrs Dowbiggin holding the baby and went outside to thank Jack for bringing them and their belongings down to the manor.

He was unloading the last case as she caught him.

'I suppose you're glad to be back here. You always wanted to live in a big house; that's what you used to dream of.' Jack looked at her, dressed in her mourning outfit; even in black she was beautiful.

'It's not for ever; it's only till I know what's going to happen to the baby. Are you all right for Friday? Can you still pick us all up and take us into Dent for the funeral?'

'Aye, I said I would. I'll pick you all up about eleven. I hope it's reasonable weather, I've had enough of this wet stuff. It's no good for nothing.'

Alice planted a kiss on his cheek and he returned with a kiss on the lips, holding her close and looking into her blue eyes.

'See you Friday. Behave yourself.' With a smile he climbed into the trap and whipped his horses into action.

Alice watched him go. He would want to know where he stood with her before long. Trouble was, she had no idea what she wanted: her head said marry him, but her heart said no.

The cobbled streets of Dent were empty as the small procession walked the few yards to the church, following the beautifully carved coffin along the iron-railed path, passing the ancient tombstones inscribed with the names of people long since gone. Mist gathered around the fells, making the air heavy and dank as the small funeral party entered the church. The vicar, who had never met Nancy in her lifetime, preached a quick sermon on good morals and the way to lead a decent life. The few mourners bowed their heads and listened as his voice echoed from the pulpit.

Alice sat staring out of the window. She'd no time for religion: God had not been kind to her, so why did she need Him? But at the same time there was something inbred in her that made her still respect the church. She bowed her head as the Lord's Prayer was said; she'd been taught the words as a child, but she was too bitter to say them. They meant nothing to her. If God was so good, why had He taken so many people away from her? Jack squeezed her hand and sneaked a quick look at her as the vicar came to the end of his prayers. She smiled bravely and stood up, ready to follow the coffin out into the graveyard. Faulks put his arm around Mrs Dowbiggin, steadying the distraught cook, who had been more mother than housekeeper where Nancy was concerned. They walked, the vicar continuing the prayers, down the grassy bank to where Nancy's final resting place was going to be, and there they gathered around the grave watching the bearers gently lower the coffin into the deep, dark hole.

As the coffin disappeared into the depths, Alice turned her eyes to the surrounding fells. She'd done this too often; she didn't want to be here again. Once the coffin had been lowered, she walked over to her mother and father's grave, knelt down and said a few words to both, tears in her eyes. There would never be a grave for Will; he'd never be with his family, where he belonged, under the home turf of Dent. Instead he was lost on the battlefields of France, buried with hundreds of unknown soldiers. She got to her feet, crying, Jack by her side. Once again she turned and sobbed into the comfort of his jacket, but at the same time she was angry, she was so angry. Why had life dealt her such a bad hand? Perhaps it was time to play it at its own game. She'd had enough unhappiness; that she was sure of.

'Come on, pet, there's nothing you can do about what life throws at you. Time to move on.' Jack put his arm around her and walked with her out of the churchyard and across to his horse and trap.

Faulks and Mrs Dowbiggin were waiting, both looking sombre as Jack gave Alice a hand up into the trap, making sure that her black skirt was all gathered in and that his two extra passengers were sitting comfortably.

'I never want another day like this one. My nerves couldn't stand it.' Mrs Dowbiggin dabbed her eyes with her violet-scented handkerchief. 'And to think it's Christmas Day in a week! When I think back to last year at this time, everything was so different. This blasted war is to blame for everything. I still can't understand why we are in it!'

'Hush now, Hilda, don't you go having one of your do's. We've tea to serve when we get back to the manor.' Faulks kept his cool as he tried to stop Mrs Dowbiggin from getting in a fluster.

Alice watched the familiar countryside go past as Jack's team of horses made their way quietly home to the manor. She looked around her at the bare brown fields and dark silhouettes of the trees in winter. It'd soon be spring and the vibrant greens of the new season would be showing through. With the new year would come new hope and new aspirations. She just needed to get over the next few weeks and then things would seem better with the spring sun shining. She sighed and folded her gloves, which caught Hilda Dowbiggin's attention.

'Are you all right, my dear? It's been a terrible time for you, more so than for any of us – you've been in the thick of it.' She reached across and patted Alice's knee.

'Yes, I'm fine, thank you, Mrs Dowbiggin. Just wondering what the next year will bring. Surely it can't be as bad as the last two.'

'Well, let's hope not, my dear. Do you think Baby Alice will have behaved for her new nursemaid? It was good of Mr Bramble to engage one so fast on behalf of Master Gerald. At least it gives you your life back, my dear. What will you do with yourself now?' Hilda Dowbiggin enquired, her curiosity getting the better of her as they pulled up at the steps of the manor. Jack opened the trap door and gave Mrs Dowbiggin his hand.

'I tell you what she's going to do, Mrs Dowbiggin – she's going to wed me, that's what she's going to do.' Jack looked up at Alice as the stout housekeeper sat gaping at him. 'I've waited long enough for an answer, Alice. Now marry me, and come and live back at your old home, back where you belong.' He stood his ground, waiting for Alice's answer, taken aback by his own forthright manner.

Alice looked at him. Should she? He offered stability; he was worth money; she knew all about him . . . There was just one thing wrong: he wasn't the dashing Gerald! She looked at the two elderly servants standing on the steps like a pair of statues, waiting for her answer. She blushed and fiddled with her bag, not knowing what to say.

'Well, what's your answer?' Mrs Dowbiggin prompted her.

Alice looked at the three faces beaming at her. 'Yes! My answer is yes, I'll marry you, Jack Alderson, and we'll make Dale End our home.' She could feel a lump in her throat and wanted to burst into tears. She'd no option but to marry him: it was security and he was a good man.

'You will? You've said yes! I can't believe it! I'll turn the trap round and set a date with the vicar straight away.' Jack was over the moon with delight.

'You will not, Jack Alderson – we've just come away from a funeral; show some respect,' Alice chastised her husband-to-be. 'We'll both go and see him after Christmas when we have finished mourning and have shown respect to the ones we have lost.'

Jack held her tightly around the waist and kissed her on the cheek, nearly making Mrs Dowbiggin faint with the sight of him being so forward. 'We'll be happy, my love. I'm sure we'll be happy.'

'Aye, well, that's enough of that. Remember we've just come back from a funeral and there's a baby in there without a mother. Keep the celebrations quiet for now.' Alice climbed the steps and watched Jack as he led the horses away. She sighed. She'd said it now: she was going to have to marry him. For better or for worse, she was getting married.

27

'Come on, Miss Alice, you're going to have to get a move on – it's ten o'clock already. Another two hours and you'll be walking down the aisle. Just look at the garden; you can tell it's the first day of spring. I've never seen as many daffodils. The lawn is covered with them.'

Mrs Dowbiggin bustled around as Alice gazed out across the grounds of the manor. It would be the last time she looked out of the huge bay windows and admired the well-kept grounds. After today she would be back to low ceilings and the small windows of Dale End, with no beautiful garden or wallpapered walls. Ah, well, she should have known that none of this could ever be hers. She ran her fingers over the back of the leather Chesterfield suite and made her way up to her room to change into her wedding dress. It was all laid out for her on the bed, simple but beautiful, with small satin buttons that fastened the high neckline round her slim neck and circled her dainty wrists, every inch of her body being flattered by the elegant design.

The dressmaker had said she was a dream to make a dress for because of her slight figure. She'd stood while pins had been stuck into her and tucks had been made at strategic points until the beautiful dress had been finished and everyone had stepped back and admired the craftsmanship that had gone into it and how beautiful she looked.

To Alice, it felt more like dressing in slave chains. She didn't want to go back to farming, getting up first thing in the morning to milk cows, and having to eke out a meagre existence on a bleak fellside. She'd enjoyed the few months she had lived at the manor. Baby Alice had settled with her nursemaid, leaving Alice with time on her hands – perhaps not a good thing, as her mind had been doing overtime. The devil making work for idle hands, as her father once said when she'd done something wrong instead of helping him.

She pulled her silk stocking up her leg and fastened her suspenders, slipped her silk cami down over her body and studied herself in the mirror of the wardrobe. She looked tired; after all, she hadn't slept for a night or two, wondering if she dared go through with the wedding, wondering whether to pack a bag and walk over to the next dale, where nobody knew her. But that wasn't her style. She'd never walked away from anything, and she couldn't break Jack's heart again. He was a good friend; happen in time she'd grow to love him. She slipped the wedding dress over her head and did up all the buttons, then sat on the edge of the bed to put on her shoes.

There, she was dressed. She just needed the hat from downstairs and the bunch of primroses and violets that Jack had picked for her. She flicked her long hair over her shoulder and walked down the sweeping staircase. She remembered the first time she had walked down those stairs, conscious of the stares of all the Frankland ancestors in their picture frames, watching the young country lass with attitude, saying what she thought, regardless of her class. She'd learned a lot since then.

'Miss Alice, you look beautiful, absolutely beautiful! We are so proud of you.' Mrs Dowbiggin brushed tears away as she watched Alice glide across the hallway. 'Say something, you big useless lump.' She dug Faulks in the ribs as he stood next to her.

'You do indeed, my dear. I don't think I've ever seen a more beautiful bride.' He smiled at Alice and then scowled at Mrs Dowbiggin. 'I believe your carriage awaits outside, Miss Alice. There is a stable boy with a decorated trap. I understand your husband-to-be has sent it for you.'

Alice couldn't resist opening the front door for a quick peek at her transport before putting her hat on. Standing in the courtyard was Jack's trap, decorated with white blossom from the hedges, and his team of horses had their manes plaited with blossom threaded between the braids. It must have taken him ages.

'Good morning, Miss Alice. Mr Jack says he hopes that you like the trap and he's waiting for you at the church.' The young stable boy smiled and pulled at the horses' harnesses as they reared their heads.

Alice blushed and closed the door, checking herself in the hall mirror and arranging her hat so that the white veil from around the large brim fell about her face.

'Here's your flowers, love. I've put a bit of ribbon round them and tried to make them look posh.' Mrs Dowbiggin passed her the posy and squeezed her hand, and then Faulks opened the door for her to mount the trap.

'I'll miss you both, you know that.' Alice hugged the stout figure of Mrs Dowbiggin and kissed Faulks on the cheek. 'You've both been good to me.' Her eyes were filled with tears.

'Get away, go on, be gone with you – your man's waiting. You know where we're at. You know you can always come and see Baby Alice at any time. Now go on, get gone, before I start crying.' Mrs Dowbiggin shooed her out of the hallway and down the steps.

It was too late to turn back. Alice could hear the church bells ringing out in the distance. It was her wedding day and Jack was waiting.

Alice stepped out of the trap onto the cobbled street of Dent. A few locals were gathered around the church gate to wish the new couple well and they watched as she nervously walked up the path. Her stomach was churning and her heart was still asking her head why she was going through with the marriage. She reached the porch entrance and swallowed, keeping her stomach in check, then stepped up to the doors of the church. Jack's father took her arm as soon as she entered. He was a man of few words and just smiled as he offered her his arm. They walked up the aisle to the traditional wedding march until she was at Jack's side. He looked nervous, scrubbed to within an inch of his life, with shiny cheeks and pink blossom in his buttonhole that matched them. He smiled and shuffled his feet, looking at his beautiful bride.

The vicar smiled at Alice, his long, thin body towering in front of them in his white surplice.

'Please be seated.' The few people present duly sat, and then he cleared his throat and continued with the service.

Alice glanced nervously at Jack as the congregation rose to sing the first hymn. The notes from the ancient church organ were not quite in tune with the congregation as both organ and vicar sang in a higher key.

It was at the end of the last verse of the hymn that everyone turned their heads when they heard the church door open. Slowly a figure entered, gradually emerging from the shadow of the clock tower and into the spring light that was streaming through the windows. Thin and unsteady on his crutches, Gerald Frankland walked up the aisle, his face scarred and drawn. He stopped three pews away from the couple, just standing in the aisle, before sitting awkwardly down.

Alice couldn't believe what she was seeing. Forgetting where she was, she dropped her wedding posy and rushed to his side, dropping down on her knees, speechless, with tears in her eyes. Jack just looked on, not knowing what to do. The vicar tactfully gave a small cough, urging Alice to rejoin her husband-to-be. She rose to her feet, tears streaming down her face. Gerald was alive! The man she secretly loved and adored was back, and there she was, getting married to a farmer's boy.

'Ladies and gentlemen, I want to remind you that we are gathered here today to join together John Richard Alderson and Alice Bentham in holy matrimony.' The vicar looked down into his prayer book and coughed.

'Just hold on, Vicar.' Jack looked at Alice, her eyes red with tears. Then he lifted her veil and kissed her.

'This is highly unusual! You can do this after the marriage, Jack.' The vicar looked displeased.

Jack blushed, uncomfortable. 'There's not going to be a wedding. I'm not going to be second best and marry a lass that doesn't love me. I don't think she ever has. She's never looked at me the way she looks at Lord Frankland there. And I don't blame you, lass. I'm just an ordinary fellow that does his best, but you will always want more than I can give you and he's got everything I haven't got.'

Alice sank into a heap, still clutching her posy, and

wept. He was right: she didn't love him. She was marrying him for security, but now Gerald was back and everything had changed.

Jack reached for his cap and put it on. Placing his hand on Alice's head, he whispered, 'Don't cry, lass, you'll be all right. As for me, I'll just stick to my horses in the future.'

He walked down the church aisle past Gerald and his family and out into the spring sunshine. The congregation listened to the sound of his horses and trap driving off across the cobbles, whispering and feeling uncomfortable at the unfolding event.

'I'm sorry, ladies and gentlemen, I'm afraid there will be no wedding here today.' The vicar walked down the steps. 'It seems that I nearly undertook a most unwanted service by one of the party.' He ushered the congregation out of his church, leaving Gerald and Alice alone.

Gerald gripped the pew and pushed himself up onto his feet again, making his way towards Alice.

'I'm sorry, Alice, I've ruined your wedding day. I shouldn't have come, but I had to see you. Every day when I was fighting for my life in that awful Red Cross hospital I thought of you – your blonde hair, those blue eyes, that mischievous smile and the way you can make me lose my head, like drinking the most exotic wine. When I went home to the manor and Mrs Dowbiggin told me you were here, getting married, I knew that I had to make speed and stop you from making the biggest mistake of your life.'

Alice sniffed and wiped her eyes, then looked at Gerald's face and smiled.

'That's better! Where's my feisty Dales lass?' Gerald made fun of her Yorkshire roots. 'Don't you know how much I love you? It's taken a bloody war to make me realize it and to know that class is nothing.' He hobbled forward on his crutches, then lifted her chin and kissed her on the lips. 'Come on, Miss Bentham, let's go home. I know at least three bodies who will be pleased to have you back where you belong, and Mrs Dowbiggin is going to be so busy with a proper wedding to plan, she isn't going to have time to gossip with Faulks.'

'Do you really feel the same way as I do, Gerald?' Alice lowered her tear-filled blue eyes, not daring to look him fully in the face. She felt sick with happiness and relief. She had almost settled for second best, until Gerald had rescued her. Poor Jack – she hoped he'd understand.

'If you'd been through what I have been through, you'd know just what you wanted. I know I love you with my every breath. Now, where's that reprobate brother of yours and my sister? I didn't see them as I entered the church.'

'Didn't Mrs Dowbiggin tell you?'

'Tell me what? I didn't stop. I had to get here and see you. What is there to tell? Is there another baby on the way?'

'Oh, Gerald, if only there was, if only it was such good news. I'm afraid both Will and Nancy are dead.'

'Dead? No, they can't be; they were both safe here in Dentdale. It was me who went to war to give them life and hope.'

Alice held his hand while she sat with him on the church pew and told the sorry tale of the two deaths. Then they walked out into the spring sunshine and she showed him Nancy's grave. Gerald bent down, his army cap in hand, and prayed for his lost sister. The newly sprung yellow cowslips nodded on the earthy grave in agreement with his prayers as a low cloud passed over the spring sun in keeping with the mood in the little village churchyard.

28

'Well, I nearly dropped down dead when I saw Master Gerald on the step. I hadn't time to tell him anything – he turned round as fast as he appeared soon as I said everyone was at Miss Alice's wedding. It wasn't half good to see him. Looks frail, mind you, but we'll soon build him up now he's home.' Mrs Dowbiggin kneaded the loaf of bread that was going to be wanted now that Gerald Frankland had returned. 'That poor horse of his got the biggest whip across its backside I've ever seen. I suppose he wanted to see Alice getting married. It'd be a change after dreary army life.'

'I'm just glad he's back – a fellow man in a house full of women. We can stand together against you females.' Faulks folded his newspaper.

'You, classing yourself in the same bracket as Master Gerald? He's twice the man you are, you old goat.' Mrs Dowbiggin patted her hands against her apron, causing a dusting of flour to cover the kitchen floor, before putting the loaf of bread to rise next to the open fire.

'You'd be lost without me, you know you would, you old fool.' Faulks winked at the blushing Mrs Dowbiggin, then buried himself in his newspaper.

'Happen I would. We go together like a pair of well-worn shoes. Life wouldn't be the same without you.' She busied herself and cleaned the pine table, not looking at the smiling Faulks. They'd been in service together for years and she was content in his company.

'Put the kettle on, Mrs D – we are home,' Gerald Frankland yelled across the hall after slamming the front door. 'We'll be in my study.'

'We? Who's we?' Mrs Dowbiggin looked at Faulks in puzzlement. 'Well, go and see who's with him. You need to welcome him back; that'll give you an excuse to see who's there.'

Faulks folded his paper, rearranged his waistcoat and solemnly made his way to the study. He coughed before knocking on the door and entering.

'Come in, Faulks. How have you been, old man? There was many a day when I could have done with your service, when my boots needed cleaning and my buttons shining.' Gerald Frankland held his hand out to be shaken by his trusted old butler.

'It's good to see you, sir. May I say it's a pleasure to see your smiling face. It seems a lifetime ago that you left us for the front. Was it terrible out there, sir? From what I understand, we've suffered a shocking loss of young life.'

'I prefer not to talk about it, Faulks. I'm trying hard to forget the whole terrible episode.'

'Of course, sir. I understand.' Faulks coughed politely. 'Did sir say he wanted tea? One cup, is it, sir?' Faulks had spotted the delicate white lace of a woman's dress from behind the winged chair that was facing out of the study window.

'No, Faulks – allow me to introduce my wife-to-be. I'll be needing two cups of tea and, I suspect, smelling salts for Mrs Dowbiggin. Alice, take my hand, my darling. Rescued in the nick of time, Faulks: the woman who kept me alive. All those months in those dreaded trenches and hospital, this face of an angel kept smiling at me and I knew I had to survive to marry her.'

Alice stood up, bashfully holding Gerald's hand, not quite knowing what to say to the gobsmacked Faulks.

'But Miss Alice was marrying Jack. I don't understand.'

'She was, Faulks, but I saved her and now we are to marry. Go! Go and tell Mrs Dowbiggin – no doubt she will have something to say. And ask the nursemaid to bring me my niece. I want to see who she takes after. If it's her delightful aunt, then I'm doubly blessed.'

Alice smiled at Faulks as he walked out of the study door. Gerald grabbed her by her waist and held her tightly in his arms. 'I see nothing's changed here: the servants still need to be the first ones to know the news.' He smiled and kissed her hard on the lips. 'That tastes good. You don't know the times I've

364

dreamed of that when I was lying in that dreadful hospital bed.'

'Gerald, behave yourself! What would Faulks think if he walked in? Besides, they have been wonderful to me since Nancy and Will died; they've always been there for me.'

'To hell with them. I'll kiss you when I want. You're mine now and I want everyone to know it.' Gerald's dark eyes flashed as he held Alice tight and kissed her more firmly. 'Tonight you'll sleep with me. I've needed company for so long.'

'Gerald, I can't, it wouldn't be right. This was supposed to be my wedding night, in case you've forgotten.' Alice was horrified. 'We need to take things slower, do this the right way.'

'Nonsense. Just pretend it is your wedding night, that I'm your husband. I assure you I won't be as disappointing as your farm boy.'

Gerald released Alice when the nursemaid knocked on the door and entered the study carrying Baby Alice in her arms.

'So this is my niece.' Gerald peered over the cream lace blankets at the dark-haired baby.

'Would you like to hold her, sir?' The portly nursemaid offered the gurgling baby for him to hold.

'Oh my God, no. Babies are for women. You won't catch me holding one. Is she perfect? Nothing wrong with her? Is she showing signs of having all her faculties?'

'She's perfect, sir. Aren't you, my little angel?' The

nurse tickled under Baby Alice's chin, making her smile and blow bubbles.

'Good, good, I'm glad to hear that. I was worried, you know. You can't be too sure. Er, now I've returned and Miss Alice is to be my bride, I'm afraid I won't have need of your services.' He looked at the distraught nursemaid and then at Alice. 'Of course, I will pay you to the end of the week, and then Miss Alice will take charge of your ward.'

The nursemaid fought back tears. She had been so contented looking after the beautiful little girl and it had given her a purpose in her life, but now she was without a home and pay.

'Thank you, sir. I'll pack my bags and be gone by Friday.' She curtsied with the baby still in her arms and left the room.

'Gerald, that was hard. Of course I'll be glad to look after Alice, but an extra pair of hands would be useful around the place.' Alice frowned, wondering what was going on in Gerald's mind.

'We don't want a nursemaid wandering around the place. Besides, she isn't exactly an oil painting – a bit dour in that black dress.'

'She's just lost her husband: he was killed at the Somme. I thought you'd be more understanding of a war widow who was trying to make a living.' Alice turned and stared at Gerald. Even in the few hours that she had been with him she'd realized that he'd changed since he'd come home from the war.

'She'll make a living somewhere else. Now, where is

that blasted Faulks with our tea? I could have made it myself at this rate.' Gerald stormed out of the study in pursuit of his elusive cup of tea, shouting for Faulks as he crossed the hallway.

Alice flopped into her chair. Had she done right? She did love him, but she wanted to take things more slowly, not be bedded on the first night of his return. Perhaps she could talk him out of it. Besides, her mind would only keep wandering to thoughts of Jack; after all, it was his bed she was meant to be in. Poor Jack, he'd been a good friend and always would be. She only hoped that he'd forgive her for the way she felt about Gerald. He had to be the one: he had the looks, the charisma and most of all the money – what else could a girl want?

Gerald sat in his study before retiring to his bed. Will was dead, likewise Nancy. Leaving just Alice, his flight of fancy, the one he had to have. Just why he had become obsessed with her when he was in the trenches, he could not understand. A waiflike commoner, yet she'd been the fantasy that had kept him alive through the fighting. What a sight she'd looked, marrying that oaf of a farmer. Gerald swilled the last dregs of brandy around his glass and smiled. He'd enjoy bedding her. The ever-willing Alice was waiting and he could resist no longer.

Alice lay back beneath the crisp sheets of the master bed, the morning's sun shining through the windows and an early visitor of a swallow was tweeting outside. She sighed and ran her fingers through her long blonde hair, feeling the warm imprint of where Gerald had lain. It had been a night of lust and passion, neither of them holding back their hunger for sex. Alice had soon forgotten that she should have been in the arms of Jack as the experienced hands of Gerald held and caressed her most intimate parts, making her feel more pleasure than she ever had in the hands of a man. At first she'd been frightened, remembering the feeble fumblings of Old Todd and the aggression Uriah Woodhead had shown her when she was raped in the bedroom of the Moon, but these memories had all faded into insignificance as Gerald held her close and spoke his words of magic.

He must have woken early and crept out of the bedroom; it was still well before six and the manor was silent. Alice sat on the edge of the bed looking at herself in the full-length mirror for a moment, then pulled her dressing gown around her. On her way to the bathroom she saw Gerald in his nightshirt, leaning over the baby's cot in the adjacent bedroom. Not a sound did either of them make; he was just staring at the sleeping baby. She walked into the room behind him and slipped her arms around his waist.

'Penny for them?' Alice smiled and kissed him behind his ear.

'What's that? What did you say?' Gerald spun round and faced her. 'Don't you ever sneak up on me again.'

'I only meant a penny for your thoughts. You

looked so intent as you stared at little Alice. I'm sorry if I disturbed you.' Alice loosened her grip as Gerald turned back to the sleeping baby.

'I thought I heard her screaming, but she's asleep. I must have been dreaming. Do you think she's all right, Alice? She isn't showing signs of being like her mother, is she? I worry for her.'

'Don't be silly – she's perfect in every way. She's got her mother's good looks with that mop of black hair, but she's as bright as a button.' Alice stroked the sleeping baby's cheek and linked her arm into Gerald's. 'Come on, come back to bed. Mrs Dowbiggin's beginning to stir and here's us in our nightclothes.'

'No, I'm getting up. I need to have a ride around my land before breakfast, see what's been going on while I've been away. So stop tempting me, woman, I've things to do . . . but tonight is another matter.' He slapped Alice firmly on her buttocks and chased her back to his bedroom. Then he quickly got dressed and set off, slamming the front door behind him.

Alice lay in bed listening to the horse's hooves clattering across the gravel and down the rough path. She'd got her man and a family. For the first time in her life she felt content; this was where she belonged, warm and secure in the fine bedlinen of the manor with the sun shining through the windows and breakfast being prepared just for her. Life couldn't get any better.

'Well, I don't know what on earth he's thinking about. He must have lost his senses – and she hers: fancy sleeping with another man on what should have been your wedding night! As for him, he's only having his bit of fun.' Mrs Dowbiggin was turning the spitting bacon in the huge frying pan as she shouted to Faulks, without realizing Alice had appeared in the room.

Faulks's muffled cough made her aware of Alice's presence.

'Please don't stop on my account,' said Alice. 'You're entitled to your opinions. But let me make one thing clear: Gerald and I are to be married, so you will soon have to give me some respect as I will be the lady of the house.' Alice turned, her skirts rustling as she marched out of the kitchen, calling over her shoulder, 'I'll have my breakfast in the study, please, Faulks. Master Gerald's gone out on his horse and he may be some time.'

Alice was angry. How dare they gossip about her as if she wasn't there? She'd show them. She'd ask Gerald for an engagement ring and then they'd know he was serious. Maybe that would make them respect her.

'Mrs Dowbiggin didn't mean any harm, Alice. We both think a great deal of you. She was only trying to protect you. You see, we know Master Gerald, and he has always been hasty in his actions, especially when he sees someone else getting something he wants.' Faulks put the tray down next to Alice as she looked out of the window.

Alice was still angry as Faulks made his apology. 'That's just it, Faulks: he wants me and he is to marry me. Tell Mrs Dowbiggin I need to see her. We'll start talking about wedding plans this afternoon. I'm sure Gerald will agree. I think Midsummer Day will be ideal, don't you, Faulks? That is my birthday, after all.'

'I'm sure it will be ideal, Miss Alice. And once again I'm sorry if we were talking out of turn. I'll tell Mrs Dowbiggin to start thinking of some plans for your wedding day.'

He closed the door firmly behind him, leaving Alice playing with her scrambled egg like a sulking toddler, pushing it around the plate, uninterested in eating it. She would have the perfect wedding. He did love her – it was so obvious to her. Why could no one else see it?

It was nearly noon before Gerald arrived back at the manor. Alice had been wearing the carpet thin pacing up and down the study, preparing her instructions for Mrs Dowbiggin and her questions for Gerald.

'Gerald, you've been ages. I've been counting every minute.' Alice rushed to his side as he entered the study.

He poured himself a drink and sat down heavily in his chair. 'Bloody hard morning, Alice. I've called in at my lettings – nearly all of them have a lad missing or still over there fighting. I feel a fraud being discharged and back in my old life. You know half of them could have stopped at home; all they had to do was say they were needed by their fathers to keep the farms going. But instead they've chosen to fight. And for what? A

bloody government that's using them for cannon fodder.' He swigged the last of his port and rose to pour
himself another.

'I'll ask Mrs Dowbiggin to make us some lunch.
You'll feel better once you've eaten.'

'Better? You think a bit of lunch is all it will take to
make me feel better? Nothing's going to make me feel
better, stop me hearing the screams and the faces of the
dead, the rats and the squalor of the trenches. Yet here
I am, safe and secure, lying to those poor, blissfully
ignorant tenants of mine, telling them their sons and
brothers will be fine, that they should be proud that
they are fighting for their country.' He swigged his port
and idly twisted the glass in his hand.

Frightened, Alice slipped out of the study. Gerald
had changed; the war had left its mark on him.

'Are you all right, Miss Alice?' Faulks appeared, on
his way to the study.

'Yes, thank you, Faulks. Could you take Master
Gerald some lunch, please? And can you tell Mrs
Dowbiggin that I won't need to see her this afternoon?
I'll make it another day. Master Gerald isn't up to
discussing weddings at the moment.'

'Very well, Miss Alice. Will you be partaking of
lunch with Master Gerald?'

'I won't, thank you, Faulks. I'm going for a walk.'
Alice thought she detected a smirk on the butler's face,
but she wasn't going to rise to it. She knew why she'd
cancelled and it had nothing to do with servant
intervention.

372

She climbed the stairs and went into the makeshift nursery. Baby Alice was asleep in her nursemaid's arms.

'I was hoping to take Alice for a walk. Would that be all right?' Alice leaned over and kissed Baby Alice on her brow.

'She's due for her bottle in half an hour, ma'am. I reckon she'll scream all the way without her feed. She likes her food, does our Alice.' The nursemaid smiled at the rosy-cheeked infant as she slept content in her arms.

'I'm sorry that Master Gerald said we could manage without you. Will you be able to find work elsewhere?' Alice looked at the nursemaid; she was good at her job.

'I'll go back to Sedbergh. I'm sure I'll find some job in service, or perhaps at the private school there. I will miss this little one, though. She keeps my mind off things.' She smiled and turned her head to the baby, her eyes filling with tears.

'I'm sorry. I hope life improves for you.' Alice pulled the nursery door closed behind her and left the manor. She wanted to be alone with her thoughts; in the last twenty-four hours her world had been turned upside down, and she didn't quite know what was going to hit her next.

29

Alice looked at the empty space next to her. The sheets and pillow were uncrumpled: Gerald's side of the bed had not been slept in. Hugging her pillow, she gazed at Baby Alice sleeping in her cot, blissfully unaware of her namesake's worries.

Three months had passed since his return from the front; three months of turmoil, getting to know the new Gerald with his moods and temper tantrums. At first, Alice had put it down to the fact he was still recovering from the horrors of war, but now she was worried. He no longer looked at her in the way he had done that day in the church. She felt he was bored with her already, and all talk of an engagement or wedding had long since been forgotten. She was his nursemaid and easy lover, the one who kept his bed warm when he was not out gambling with his so-called friends or drinking and womanizing. Mrs Dowbiggin and Faulks must have seen how things were, but they said nothing, keeping their heads down and getting on with their jobs as if his behaviour was nothing out of the ordinary. How wrong she had been to think that he loved her. He'd wanted her, but that's all it was. There was no love there. She should have known that; after all, she'd been warned by just about everyone.

A tear trickled down her cheek. To think she'd let Jack walk away from her for this cad. Once again she'd ended up being used, all for the sake of trying to better herself and for trying to keep Baby Alice close to her. Better to have no home at all than be treated like a prostitute. What was it that made men look at her in that way? Did she have 'Tart' written across her forehead, invisible to women but there to be seen by all men? She sniffed and controlled her tears as she heard the front door go and Gerald swearing as he took his riding boots off in the hallway before making his way up the stairs and into bed.

'You still here? God, I thought you'd be long gone.' He slurred his words as he lunged across the bedroom and collapsed on the bed. Mumbling and smelling of drink, still dressed in his clothes, his breeches covered with mud from riding, he pulled the bedcovers over him.

Outside Alice could hear his horse pawing the gravel. The poor creature, he hadn't even unsaddled and stabled it before coming indoors. Jack would have seen to it if he'd still been employed at the manor, but since the onset of war he'd only worked for himself and his father. Alice lay still until she heard him snoring; then she quietly rose and dressed before picking the sleeping baby up in her arms and going downstairs.

Placing the still-slumbering baby on the large sofa in the drawing room, she arranged the cushions to stop her from falling on the floor, and then went outside to unsaddle the distressed horse. The sun was shining, but there was a slight hint of autumn frost in the air with the early morning mists clinging to the river in the valley below.

'Shh, now. What a state you're in. He must have ridden you like the devil.' She approached the sweat-flecked horse, whispering softly as she took hold of the harness and stroked it on its neck. Once it was calm, she began leading it in the direction of the stables.

'I'll take that for you, Miss Alice. It isn't a job for a lady.' Faulks appeared out of the kitchen door and came towards them with his hand outstretched. 'I thought I heard the master return. I can't believe he'd leave his horse in this state. He used to be such a proud horse-man.' The butler shook his head as he took control of the reins. 'Mrs Dowbiggin's got the kettle on, if you want to join us for an early morning cuppa.'

Alice nodded and, leaving him to take the horse into the stables, headed back to the drawing room to check on Baby Alice before joining the housekeeper in the kitchen.

Mrs Dowbiggin was still in her flannelette nightie and dressing gown, her long grey, thinning hair in cotton rags to give it a bit of curl.

'Oh my Lord – Miss Alice, I didn't expect you in the kitchen at this hour. Look at me, I'm not even dressed. What will you think of me?'

'Don't worry, Mrs Dowbiggin. I'm only glad you're up and that the fire's going. It's cold out there. Faulks says there's tea on the go. Is it all right if I join you?'

'Don't be silly, lass, you don't have to ask. Here, sit yourself down and I'll get you a cup. It's been a while since you've sat in here with us. I must say, I've missed your company. I don't get much out of old Faulks nowadays.'

Alice sighed and gazed into the fire, silently clasping the cup in her hands as Mrs Dowbiggin busied herself in the kitchen.

'You look troubled, Alice. What's wrong? Do you want to tell me? If not, just say I'm to mind my own business.'

'I can't tell you ... You all warned me, but I thought he loved me. I thought I was the only one and I was besotted. I've been such a fool!' Alice hid her head in her hands, tears dripping through her closed fingers.

'Now then, pet, you were only trying to better yourself, and I don't blame you for that. But even before Master Gerald went to war, he used to play games with young women. Yours won't be the first heart he's broken.' Mrs Dowbiggin put her arms around her and held her tight. 'Just make the best of it, lass. At least you've got a roof over your head and you're well fed. Baby Alice needs a mother and you are all she's got, because her uncle never looks at her twice. Poor little thing – no mother or father, and an uncle who doesn't have the time of day for her. If I were you,

I'd tell him that you are moving into the spare bedroom with her because she's teething. He won't mind – he's coming home drunk most nights anyway. And it'll give you a bit of peace for a night or two.' Mrs Dowbiggin squeezed Alice, hugging her extra tight. 'There, I'd better get dressed before Faulks comes back in. You sit there and have your tea. I'll pop in and see if Alice is still asleep.' The old housekeeper bustled out of the kitchen shaking her head. She'd known it would all end in tears, but there was no telling a lass when she was head over heels in love.

Alice sniffed and wiped the tears away with the back of her hand as Faulks walked in.

'The horse is seen to, Miss Alice. She's stabled and wiped down and fed. I still can't believe that the master would leave his pride and joy like that. I don't know what the world's coming to.'

'Neither do I, Faulks,' Alice sniffed. Conscious that Faulks was uncomfortable at the sight of her crying into her tea, she made an effort to smile.

'May I say, miss, I can't understand the way he's acting. I've known Master Gerald all his life and he's not the gentleman I thought he was, miss.' He coughed apologetically into his hand.

'He's definitely no gentleman – we've both been fooled. But what to do about it, I don't know.' Alice smiled and got up to return to Baby Alice. At least she was welcome in the kitchen once again and had allies in Faulks and Mrs Dowbiggin.

*

It was a true autumn day: the rain hadn't stopped, and the winds howled around the manor. Alice and the baby were cosy and warm in the nursery with the fire blazing in the hearth. As she watched the little one playing with her teddy and ball, Alice felt more content than she had in a while. Gerald had been gone a few days now and she was thankful for a bit of peace. Since she'd moved into the spare bedroom, he'd been less attentive, virtually ignoring her sometimes.

Suddenly she heard the front door slam and the sound of Gerald's voice laughing and booming as he ran up the stairs. But he was not alone; there was an answering peal of high-pitched laughter, and then the sound of a woman talking in a foreign language that Alice couldn't understand. She froze as she listened to them frolicking on the landing, the shrieks and laughter getting louder as they went into Gerald's bedroom and closed the door behind them.

Alice stared out at the pouring rain. How dare he bring one of his whores into the bed he'd shared with her? Her temper started building as she heard the giggles from the adjoining room and imagined Gerald muttering words of love. She looked at the baby playing contentedly and decided to walk in on the loving couple. Gathering her skirts and jutting out her chin, she marched out onto the landing and threw open the bedroom door.

'What the blazes! How dare you enter my bedroom!' Gerald looked out from the bed, eyes blazing with anger. 'Get out! Get out now!'

'Who is this, Gerald?' The dark-haired woman gave Alice a disdainful look.

'She's nothing, Tatiana, just a servant who doesn't know her place.'

'Surely no maid would be so bold as to enter your room when they know you are busy?'

Gerald leapt up from the bed, pulling his braces up and buttoning his flies, as Alice looked at the Russian beauty who had taken her place. Or rather, whose place she had taken, for this was the woman he'd always been in love with, while Alice had never been more than a plaything to him.

'Get rid of her!' commanded Tatiana, her foreign accent making the words sound even more contemptuous. 'I don't want a maid who's so rude to her mistress. She's obviously not been trained well.'

Alice protested, 'Tell her, Gerald – tell her I'm more than a maid, that we were to be married. Tell her.'

His face as black as thunder, Gerald pushed her out of the door, then slapped her hard across the face. Grabbing her arm, he forced her into the nursery and picked up the innocent Baby Alice under his other arm, making her scream in shock and surprise. The cries of Alice and the baby echoed through the manor as he stormed down the stairs dragging them with him. He released Alice's arm just long enough to open the front door, then threw her down the steps and set the baby on the ground. As Alice crawled, sobbing, to shelter the baby from the rain, her blonde hair lank and wet, he stood in the front doorway looking down on them.

'Get away from here. You're nothing but a common whore. And you can take the brat with you. I don't want to see you or it ever again – you are both mistakes.' His white shirt clung to his chest as he bellowed the words that cut through the air and into Alice's heart. 'Go on, get off my property before I set the dogs on you.'

Alice stood in the pouring rain, holding the crying baby. She could see there was no love in his heart for them, not a scrap of affection. He glared at her, as if waiting for her to plead, but she wasn't going to beg; she'd never begged for anything. Her tears mingling with the cold rain, she turned and walked away, Baby Alice screaming in her arms. She had her dignity, if nothing else. As for Gerald – good riddance; he wasn't worth it. If that was a gentleman, then Old Nick himself had better manners.

The rain fell like stair rods, cold and biting, while Alice clung to the shivering baby, trying to shield her from the rain with her body. Her heart felt heavy and tears stung her eyes as she set off down the road, walking without knowing where she was going. With all the strength in her little arms and legs, Baby Alice fought against her guardian, still screaming at the top of her lungs.

On and on Alice walked, into the village of Dent, past the closed doors of the Moon, past the Battys' yard, with the coffins still propped against the walls, and on past the fountain where she'd flirted with Jack. There was no door where she could find sanctuary, no one she could turn to with the little bundle that now lay quiet in her arms, too exhausted to struggle. She was a stranger in her own village. Remembering all the past hurts, a wave of desperation swept over her.

By the time she got to the church bridge that spanned the beer-coloured waters of the River Dee, the baby's body felt cold and limp in her arms. She stood on the parapet, looking down at the white foam swirling round the willow roots and crashing over boulders as the floodwaters swept down the valley to the sea. Her long blonde hair dripped onto the wet, frozen body of Baby Alice as she bent her head over her.

'Forgive me,' she whispered, kissing the baby tenderly on the forehead. Then she clambered to the top of the bridge, clutching Baby Alice to her chest. Tears filled her eyes and she was trembling as she looked down into the gushing waters.

'Oh, no, you don't. I can't let you do that.' A strong voice came from nowhere and an arm clasped her around the waist, preventing her from leaping into the pounding waters. 'I'll not have your death on my conscience.' The strong arm pulled them both back from the edge and deposited them by the roadside.

Jack stood over Alice and the baby as they huddled together, a picture of despair. Tenderly he bent down and picked up both frozen bodies in his strong arms and carried them to his waiting trap.

As he lifted her in, Alice put her arm around him. It was Jack, the one she had hurt so badly, the one who had every right to turn his back on her. She cried into his soaked jacket and looked desperately into his eyes as he laid her underneath a horse blanket, wrapping Baby Alice up next to her.

'Right, you're coming home to Dale End where you belong, with me.'

For once, Alice did not argue. She wanted so much to belong. Perhaps life was going to be all right, now she finally knew her place.

30

The sky was heavy with snow, and the biting wind made Alice's cheeks glow red as she sat behind the fell wall watching the lights go on down the dale. No lights were visible at the manor; it was in darkness, empty and cold like Gerald's heart. He was long gone. Taking Tatiana with him, he'd fled the dale in the middle of the night, bankrupt and in disgrace, with creditors lining up from Dent to Kendal. Rumour had it that he'd left the country.

The two loyal servants he had abandoned to their fate were now doing very nicely for themselves. Mr Faulks had wasted no time in asking Mrs Dowbiggin for her hand in marriage, and the pair of them were now running a successful tea room in Sedbergh. Alice was glad they would have security in their old age. Although they still argued like cat and dog, they couldn't live without one another.

Wrapping her shawl around her against the cold,

she smiled as she watched Jack and little Alice in the yard down at Dale End. Jack was feeding the dogs and the little girl was helping collect the eggs from the hen house, holding her skirt up to carry them into the house, just the way Alice herself used to do when she was a child. Daintily carrying the eggs across the yard with the help of her dad. Dad – how easily that rolled off the tongue; but that was what Jack had become and young Alice knew no different. She didn't remember the night that they'd been thrown out of the manor in the pouring rain, and Jack had found them and taken them home with him to Dale End. There they had stayed, loved and content, in the cottage that had been Alice's childhood home.

Alice watched as Jack lit the oil lamp in the window; time to wander down and make the evening meal and sit contented next to the fire. Her finger played with the wedding ring that Jack had so lovingly put on her finger last New Year's Day. How she loved him, and he her. Young love was foolish; she knew that now. All the time she'd been searching, he'd been there, under her nose, with everything she ever wanted. What a fool she had been, her head turned by everything false, when she'd had the love of a good man all along. Her hands rested on the bulge of her unborn baby; soon their family would be complete, a little brother or sister for Alice. A new life to nurture and care for in the family home.

Getting to her feet, Alice carefully picked her way down the path, the first snowflake of winter slowly melting on her face. Perhaps they would build a snow-man tomorrow, or perhaps the little family would just keep warm indoors and watch through their window as the dale turned into a winter wonderland. Whatever they did, they would do it with love, the two Alices safe and secure with a good, strong, loving man by their side. A Dales man, one of few words but every one of them true, and with a love so strong that she knew they would take on the world together, for ever.